Roopa Farooki

Bitter Sweets

MACMILLAN

First published 2007 by Macmillan
an imprint of Pan Macmillan Ltd
Pan Macmillan, 20 New Wharf Road, London N1 9RR
Basingstoke and Oxford
Associated companies throughout the world
www.panmacmillan.com

ISBN-13: 978-1-4050-8928-9 HB
ISBN-13: 978-0-230-01687-3 TPB

Typeset by Intype Libra Ltd
Printed and bound in Great Britain by
Mackays of Chatham plc, Chatham, Kent

Visit **www.panmacmillan.com** to read more about all our books and to buy
them. You will also find features, author interviews and news of any author
events, and you can sign up for e-newsletters so that you're always first to hear
about our new releases.

For my mother, my husband and my son,
because they are all funny, kind and beautiful
– although not necessarily in that order.

Bigotry tries to keep truth safe in its hand
With a grip that kills it.

Rabindranath Tagore, *Fireflies*, 1928

The truth is rarely pure, and never simple.

Oscar Wilde, *The Importance of Being Earnest, 1895*

Nadim Rub's Most Magnificent Deception

HENNA WAS THIRTEEN when she was gleefully married off to the eldest son of one of the best families in Calcutta, and her marriage was achieved by an audacious network of lies as elaborate and brazen as the golden embroidery on her scarlet wedding sari. Henna's paternal family were liars by trade, shopkeepers from the Bengal who had made their money by secretly selling powders and pastes of suspect origin, to alleviate the boredom and fatigue of the British expats serving out their purgatory in local government in pre-Independence India. Those glory days had fled with the British some ten years previously, but Henna's father was still never one to miss a business opportunity – when he heard that the wealthy, landed and unusually fair-skinned Karim family from Calcutta would be visiting their farms around Dhaka, he wasted no time in undertaking an effective reconnaissance.

His initial modest plot had been to nurture a business alliance, but he became more ambitious when he discovered that a rather more lucrative and permanent alliance might be up for grabs. He learned that their son

Rashid, who preferred to be called Ricky, was of marriage-able age, but was so bizarre in his preferences that his frustrated family had not yet managed to find him a wife. He had been educated abroad, and insisted that his wife be someone he could 'love', an educated, literate girl with the same interests as him.

Nadim Rub looked at his wilful, precocious daughter, who constantly missed school and cheeked her tutors, who stole her aunts' film magazines to pore over the photographs of the movie stars in thrilled girlish detail. She was athletic enough to avoid him whenever he tried to beat her for these misdeeds, sometimes nimbly running away over the neighbours' rooftops where he couldn't follow. His daughter had inherited his cunning, and her dead mother's looks. She still had an adolescent slimness but had suddenly developed enough of a bosom to pass for a woman, rather than a girl. He formulated his plan.

A shopkeeper is also a salesman, and Nadim knew exactly how to persuade his daughter to go along with him. He caught her hiding at the bottom of their over-grown garden one school day, lying flat on her stomach behind the coconut palms, while she nonchalantly studied magazines instead of her books. When Henna saw her father approach, she leaped up and prepared to run, but he appeased her with an unusually jovial smile, and offered her a paper bag of dusty sweets, which she took warily.

'Henna moni, I know you hate school. And you're too good for this provincial backwater. You should be some-where better, like Calcutta, the honoured daughter of a wealthy family who could buy you all the sweets and magazines you could ever desire. It's what your mother would have wanted for you.'

Henna listened with interest – Calcutta was glamorous, the sort of place where the movie stars came from. And for once, her fat, ignorant Baba was right – she did hate school.

Enlisting the help of his sisters, Nadim made sure that Henna learned to carry herself in a sari with rather more elegance that she had hitherto shown, and with careful application of kohl, rouge and powder, managed to make her look older than her years, and almost as pale as the Karims. He had her tutors teach her to play tennis, Ricky-Rashid's favourite sport, which with her natural athleticism she picked up quickly. He found out through bribing the Karims' servants which books were to be found in Ricky-Rashid's room, and bought cheap copies for his daughter to read. He discovered she was still illiterate, and almost beat her again – all his dedicated preparation ruined because his lazy harami of a daughter had wilfully chosen to waste her expensive schooling. He stormed impotently at her while she pranced elegantly on her aunt's makeshift tennis court during one of her lessons, her precise strokes cruelly making her plump teacher race breathlessly from one side to another.

'Baba, you're being silly. Just get one of these monkeys to read out some bits to me, and I'll memorize them. It's easy,' Henna said calmly, swinging her backhand return dangerously close to his ear; 'monkeys' was the disrespectful term which she used for her long-suffering gaggle of tutors. She was enjoying the charade, the pretty new clothes, the make-up, the dissembling; she even looked forward to the prospect of learning lines from the Shake-spearean sonnets her Baba had brought. It was like she was an actress already.

Nadim pulled strings, and used bribes of his suspect poppy powder to insinuate himself into Mr Karim's presence at a club gathering. He made sure he dressed well enough to look like landowning gentry himself, and in better clothes his generous rolls of fat could be mistaken for prosperity rather than greed. He pretended that the shop was his sister-in-law's family business, and that he oversaw it out of loyalty to his dead spouse. He told them about his sorrowful burden – he had a daughter so lovely and gifted that no suitable boy would dare make an appropriate offer for her; he confessed humbly that he had been guilty of over-educating her. He was worried that she would be an old maid, as she was already seventeen years old. Intrigued, Mr Karim arranged for his own reconnaissance, and saw the beautiful Henna as she visited her aunt's house in a rickshaw, demurely holding her tennis racket and appearing to be engrossed by a volume of English poetry. He was satisfied with her paleness and her beauty, although less so by her slim hips. Deciding that the worst that could happen is that she might die in childbirth giving him a beautifully pale grandson, he arranged for a meeting.

'My friends call me Henrietta,' Henna lied charmingly, offering tea to Ricky-Rashid's parents, discreetly not looking at Ricky-Rashid at all.

'And mine call me Ricky,' Ricky-Rashid answered quickly, directly addressing her delicate, painted profile, hoping he might have fallen in love at first sight with this sonnet-reading, tennis-playing beauty. She was nothing like the moneyed nincompoops he had been introduced to before. Flouting the traditional etiquette of the meeting, he instead displayed the manners of an English gentleman, and got up to relieve Henna of her heavily laden tray. He looked defiantly at his stern parents, and for once saw them beaming back at him with approval.

The Calcutta wedding was a glorious affair, Henna's premature curves barely filling out her gold and scarlet wedding sari; her thin wrists, slender neck and dainty nose weighed down with gold. Due to the generous concession of Nadim Rub in allowing all the celebrations to take place in Calcutta, despite his fervent protested wish that it had been his life's dream to give his daughter a magnificent wedding in Dhaka, the Karims matched his generosity of spirit by offering to pay for all the festivities. Ricky-Rashid had even dismissed the idea of a dowry as barbaric, to Nadim Rub's further joy and Henna's fury – the deal she had previously brokered with her father was that she would get her dowry directly to keep for herself. Sitting graciously by Ricky-Rashid's side, her lovely eyes narrowed imperceptibly as she saw her flabby Baba working the room and accepting congratulations. Casting those eyes down demurely, she vowed to keep all the wedding jewellery that her father had borrowed from his sisters; she wasn't going to let the fat fibber cheat her as well as everyone else.

Following the wedding, Henna lay in Ricky-Rashid's quarters in her new and sprawling home, eating liquorice sweets while she waited for him. Impressed by the four-poster bed, like the ones she had seen in the films, she had dismissed the maid and jumped up and down on it in her bare feet, still wearing her elaborate sari, before stretching out and trying some poses. When Ricky-Rashid finally entered, looking sheepish and nervous, carrying a book and a flower, she tipped her head up and pouted, expecting a movie-star kiss. She naively did not know that anything further might be expected of her.

Ricky-Rashid, taken by surprise by his new bride's apparent forwardness and feeling even more nervous, kissed her quickly and, reassured by the softness of her mouth, kissed her again. Something was wrong – she tasted of liquorice, like a child. Liquorice was not what he expected his first night of married love to taste of. He felt a wave of panic that he was woefully unqualified to initiate his confident bride, who was now looking at him with a mixture of curiosity and sympathy. Deciding that faint heart never won fair maiden, and deciding further that the only way out of this sea of troubles was to take arms against it and confidently stride in, he aggressively pulled Henna to him with what he hoped was a manly, passionate gesture, crushing her breasts against his chest and circling the bare skin of her waist with his hands.

Henna, disappointed by the kiss, was wondering whether to offer some of her sweets to Ricky-Rashid, and was taken utterly by surprise when he suddenly pounced on her. She jumped as though stung when she felt his clammy hands on her bare skin beneath her sari blouse, and despite her heavy sari, nimbly slipped away from him and off the bed. Ricky-Rashid was acting like one of the villains in the movies that she'd watched, and was doubtless planning to beat her – perhaps this was how husbands behaved from their wedding night onwards. No wonder her mother was dead and all her aunts such grouchy miseries.

'I won't let you,' she said warningly. She wouldn't let her big bully of a father beat her, or anyone else who had ever tried, and she certainly wasn't going to allow this milky-faced academic to succeed where so many others had failed. Her eyes flashed scornfully at him.

Ricky-Rashid's heart wilted like the drooping rose he was still holding. His attempt at manly domination had gone horribly wrong, and from being surprisingly enthusiastic, Henna now wouldn't let him near her. And no wonder – he'd acted like a thick-booted oaf. An intelligent, spirited beauty like Henna should be wooed, not tamed. That's what he'd intended when he came in with his rose and poetry – he was going to proffer her the flower on bended knee and read her the romantic verse that he knew she loved. But her tossed-back head and invitation to a kiss had distracted him, and in the ensuing liquorice-induced confusion he had let his baser instincts take over. Intending to apologize, he walked around the bed towards her, but she simply skipped over to the other side, looking at him warily. Her scorn was dreadfully attractive, and his hand still tingled from the brush with the naked skin of her slim waist.

Defeated, and embarrassed, Ricky-Rashid sat heavily on the bed. 'I'm so sorry. I wanted this to be a wonderful, romantic night for us. And I've already ruined it.' He turned to face her and held out the flower to her. 'Look, I brought you a rose.' He sighed and put it down next to him.

Mollified, Henna sat back on the bed, a little way from

Ricky-Rashid, and continued eating her sweets. 'You are silly,' she said. 'How could trying to beat me possibly be wonderful or romantic?' She picked up the rose and sniffed it disinterestedly. 'I think it's dead,' she said, dropping it dismissively on the floor. She nudged the pink flower head experimentally with her prettily painted toes, separating out the soft wilted petals.

Ricky-Rashid looked at her in astonishment. 'Beat you? Why on earth would I try to beat you?' His surprise was so genuine that Henna realized she may have misunderstood his intentions, and perhaps given away her ignorance in some indefinable way.

Distracting him with a truce, she nodded towards the book. 'So what's that? More Shakespeare?'

Ricky-Rashid answered with even more genuine surprise. 'No, it's Byron.' The name was very clearly written on the cover; Henna must be terribly short-sighted. 'I brought it because there's a poem I wanted to read to you. It reminds me of you.' Hoping he might yet be able to salvage the evening, he opened it, and started to read,

> *She walks in beauty, like the night*
> *Of cloudless climes and starry skies;*
> *And all that's best of dark and bright*
> *Meet in her aspect and her eyes.*

He paused and looked at her expectantly.

'Hmm, that's pretty,' Henna answered, hoping he wasn't expecting her to comment any further.

'It loses something in translation,' admitted Ricky-Rashid. 'Perhaps I should read it to you in English?'

'No!' said Henna shortly. In their brief meetings before the wedding, she had only just about been able to keep up the pretence that she had a working knowledge of English, although it had proved much harder than simply pretending to be literate. Despairing of her, her English tutor had eventually given into expediency, and had given her some set phrases to learn, and developed a subtle sign language that indicated to her which phrase to use when. This had worked fine when they were in the large sitting room, with her tutor sitting at a respectful distance, within her sight, and Henna enunciating, 'I Think It's Simply Wonderful' and 'Good Gracious, No' and 'Would You Like Some More?' when prompted. However, alone with Ricky she doubted that she'd last two minutes of English conversation undetected. Aware that her response had been unnecessarily vehement, she added sweetly, 'To be honest, I'm a bit too tired to listen to poetry readings.'

Ricky-Rashid had no more weapons in his amorous armoury – his flower was discharged and in pieces on the floor, and his book of Byron's romantic poetry, which he was sure Henna had said was Simply Wonderful in a previous meeting, was being summarily dismissed. With nothing else coming to mind, he decided to try his luck by pressing on with the book. 'So why don't you read the next two lines yourself? They say everything that I think about you.'

He passed the book to Henna, who took it unwillingly. She looked at the incoherent black jumble of text for a couple of moments and knowledgeably nodded, before saying in her little-used English, 'Ricky, I Think It's Simply Wonderful.'

'I knew you'd like it,' said Ricky-Rashid triumphantly. Perhaps tonight would work out after all; he edged closer to Henna, to take the book out of her hands. But as he saw how she had been holding it, that nagging feeling came back, the feeling that he had felt on their first uncertain kiss.

'But how could you read it upside down?' he asked. Something was very wrong, very wrong indeed. Why was she holding the book the wrong way round? Henna could surely not be as short-sighted as all that.

Aware that instant distraction was necessary, Henna smiled as meltingly as the movie stars she'd learned from and, holding out her slender hand to Ricky-Rashid, she said, 'You can kiss me again if you like.' When Ricky-Rashid didn't move, she moved towards him instead, and he couldn't stop himself kissing her and pulling her nubile body into his arms, while the urgent physical sensation fought with his racing mind. Liquorice again, the taste of liquorice, the supple too-slender too-girlish body, the comment about the beatings, the thickly accented Simply Wonderful, the upside-down book, and again, the unavoidable, intoxicating taste of liquorice sweets . . . childhood sweets.

Controlling himself and pushing her away, Ricky-Rashid held the breathless Henna at arm's length as he looked at her closely, her lipstick and powder rubbed off by their embrace, her enormous eyes ludicrously over-made up by comparison. 'How old are you, Henna?' he asked quietly.

On his wedding night, Ricky-Rashid slept alone, tormented by the discovery, coaxed from Henna with gentle words, bribes, promises and yet more sweets, that his educated seventeen-year-old bride was actually an illiterate shopkeeper's daughter, a thirteen-year-old child who had married him as a way to skip school and fulfil a schoolgirl fantasy of becoming an actress. Disturbed by the memory of her body, Ricky-Rashid was disgusted by himself for having wanted her so much – a child, she was just a child, and he had almost . . . it didn't bear thinking about. He was no English gentleman, he was practically a pervert.

It was the night that every one of Ricky-Rashid's hopes and dreams of a life lived in truth and sincerity, of an idyllic western-style marriage, was ground into a red, muddy sludge like the powder from which Henna took her name. She had stained him and blotted all his future aspirations, and he simply couldn't wash away the marks. He was forced to be complicit in the lie – she would have to remain his wife or everyone would know how he and his family had been tricked and shamed. She would have to be educated privately at his parents' house, and remain out of society until such time when she would no longer give herself away.

Ricky-Rashid had previously hoped to bring his wife with him when he returned to the varsity for his studies, but his vision of living like an English couple in his student halls had also been shattered. He would return alone, and would no longer pretend that he was the Ricky he had tried to fashion himself into, the cosmopolitan intellectual around town; from this time on, he would call himself

Just Rashid. He would not sleep with Henna until she was seventeen and had finished school, but the feelings she had innocently awoken would not go away, and in an attempt to scratch the persistent itch of desire he would spend the next few years having frustrated and unsanitary sex with kind-faced, matronly prostitutes, all the time guiltily thinking about Henna's unripe, forbidden body.

The Alchemic Conception of
Shona Kiran Karim

FROM BEING A willowy prepubescent, by seventeen Henna had developed into a rather buxom adolescent, with teenage spots and child-bearing hips that no longer had any cause to earn disapproval from her expectant father-in-law, who had patiently waited several years for a grandchild. Despite the pocked skin and the puppy fat, Henna was still very good-looking, and remained a convincing actress. From the unpromising start with her in-laws, who had exploded with anger when Rashid had nervously revealed the truth about her background the day after the wedding, she had managed to win them back with her wiles and charm and studied innocence. She was the victim in all this, after all, a child-bride sold into a marriage under the threat of violence by her vile father, treated like just another one of his grubby business deals. During Rashid's long absences at university overseas, she made herself indispensable to the Karims, and they disloyally found that they preferred her lively company to that of their stilted son, or even his spoilt younger brother. She eventually became, as her wily father had predicted, the favourite daughter, and by contrast, returning Rashid was treated as the prodigal when he came back for his vacations, with his academic affectations, funny foreign clothes and, worst of all, his funny foreign ideas.

Henna planned and hoped to get pregnant as quickly as possible once Rashid was willing to start marital relations with her. Her attempt at marriage as a way to avoid education had not succeeded; she had been unwillingly forced to continue with her lessons, and although her only interest was in the dramatic arts, she had eventually learned to read and write in both Bangla and Urdu, to converse inefficiently in English, and been given a reluctant grounding in maths and the sciences. Although privately educated by necessity, like any other schoolgirl she was made to take public examinations. She was anxious about the results, not because she might have done badly, but because she was vain enough to worry that she might have done well – although with her committed laziness such fears were ungrounded. She certainly didn't want sparkling grades, which would doubtless lead to the indefinable horror of further education that Rashid had been undertaking. Henna knew that motherhood would succeed where marriage alone could not. She knew self-interestedly that bearing Rashid's child would keep her in her cosseted position, and that once she was a mother, there would be no more forcing her to stay at the dull books. She would simply hand the child over to the nanny and then start training for her dramatic career in earnest.

Lying back on the same four-poster bed on which, years before, she had unsuccessfully faked the reading of a poem from an upside-down book, Henna surreptitiously glanced at her wristwatch from over Rashid's straining shoulders. She decided to try a different sort of faking altogether to encourage her monotonously pumping husband to climax before she died of boredom or, worse, missed her favourite radio drama. This time, at least, Henna's performance was successful, and she was rewarded with Rashid finishing the job with much greater efficiency than he had hitherto shown, for which she showed a vocal appreciation that although insincere was almost kindly meant. Rashid's pride in accomplishment, that he had finally managed to make his wife enjoy the act of physical love, was dwarfed a few weeks later by his further pride in achievement, that Henna had conceived and was pregnant with their first, and what she was later to ensure would be their only, child.

Once the pregnancy had been thus dishonestly and enthusiastically achieved, Henna was completely indifferent to both Rashid and the new life growing inside her. Only the heartbeat at Henna's occasional check-ups reminded her about the child. All she cared about was that she would now be afforded truly special treatment, and was able to loll lazily in the house or on the veranda, flicking through her film magazines, playing her imported Elvis Presley records and shouting occasional orders to the servants to bring her sweets from town, or to make her tea with condensed milk and fried pastry delicacies. In the spirit of the swinging sixties, she cut her hair daringly short, right up to her shoulders, and wore it loose in a shining bob like one of her favourite film idols. Her in-laws looked on indulgently – Henna had become their little princess and could do no wrong. Of course they didn't mind Henna's below-average grades in her examinations – she had far more important things to worry about now. Thus pampered to her heart's content, in pregnancy Henna became beautiful once more, and her skin lost its teenage imperfections and began to glow. Rashid's vain little brother, Aziz, returned from his English boarding school and developed a thumping crush on her, competing with the servants to fulfil her tiniest requests for the reward of a smile or a patronizing pat.

Rashid, mystified by the shift of power in his family household that had occurred, simply accepted it, in the same way he had always accepted his father's omnipresent disapproval. This paternal censure was magnified when he finally finished his studies, as he started training for accountancy rather than taking over the running of the family properties. He still nursed a secret hope that he and Henna would be able to move abroad one day, to the green and pleasant lands in which he had been educated, and believed that a professional qualification would pave the way. As it happened, with his father's death they were forced to move abroad faster than he thought, to a land much greener and wetter than the England of his idyllic student memories.

Everybody had wondered how Mr Karim, a Muslim in India, had managed to hold on to his grand Calcutta property during the troubles of partition in the late forties. When other Muslim families had been forced to hurriedly abandon their homes and belongings as they made for

West or East Pakistan, the Karim clan had simply re-located over the border to their property in the Bengal for a few years, with the swiftness and relative safety afforded by wealth, and had returned to Calcutta when the worst of it was over. As the new head of the family, forced to look after his father's business affairs whether he wanted to or not, Rashid discovered that the key to their dubious Calcutta comfort was a Mephistophelian pact that his father had made with a well-known local businessman. Mr Karim had signed their Calcutta property over to this Hindu acquaintance, on the understanding that the property would remain safe if already in Hindu hands, and had paid a rent for the privilege of returning. The gentleman businessman, on Mr Karim's death, proved to be more of a businessman than a gentleman – he explained regretfully to Rashid that he had kept the rent low during Mr Karim's life out of deference to their long-standing friendship, but he could no longer afford to be so generous. He raised the rent so steeply that it would barely be covered by the income from the Bengali farms over the border in East Pakistan. Although the family had the trappings of wealth, Rashid saw that they were on the verge of bankruptcy. How would they continue to manage the house, the servants, or Aziz's school fees abroad? He took his first bold decision as the head of the household, and moved the entire family over to their estates near Dhaka.

Henna was furious that she was being packaged back to the Bengali backwater she had been persuaded to marry to escape – who had ever heard of an East Pakistani film star? Everyone knew that only Indians made movies. She started working on a new plan, for when things had settled down, of moving with Ricky to Bombay to one of those modern beach-front apartments she read about in her magazines, where she would socialize with the jet set and meet Bollywood directors who would be overcome by her beauty and cast her as their new romantic heroine.

Their child, tired of being ignored for so long in the womb, fought for recognition by arriving a couple of weeks prematurely, cheating Henna of her last fortnight of idleness. Henna had travelled the short distance to her father's house, not to have the child there as family tradition dictated, but with the sole intention of showing off her pregnant prosperity and sophistication to her blood relatives, most of whom she hadn't seen since her wedding. Caught short when her waters broke on her arrival, Henna found herself obliged to honour tradition despite herself. Even with the aid of child-bearing hips, Henna had a difficult birth as a result of her indolence during her pregnancy, when even the most rudimentary antenatal exercises had been ignored. Squatting on the ill-fated birthing stool on which her mother had died giving birth to a still-born brother, swearing and complaining viciously throughout the whole ordeal, Henna vowed that it was an experience that she wouldn't be repeating. Too bad for Rashid if it wasn't a boy.

When their baby girl eventually emerged, Rashid, however, was far from disappointed. He looked in awe at his tiny daughter, so delicate and perfect in snub-nosed profile, with a wide-open mouth screaming to be listened to, demanding that she finally be heard. She wasn't the milky aristocratic colour of the Karims, but nor did she have the swarthiness she might have inherited from her maternal grandfather. Instead, she was the colour of pale sand, a golden, rosy colour, with an equally golden burnish glowing across her dark-brown downy hair. The names they had discussed before, family names, now seemed prosaic and inappropriate, and insufficient to describe this magical, radiant creature. Rashid tentatively raised this with Henna, knowing that with his collective family behind her even more strongly since his father's death, Henna would be the one to have her way.

'You can call her whatever you want,' said Henna ungraciously, turning over painfully in bed. 'She's yours, isn't she?'

Grateful, despite the bad-tempered tone and Henna's obvious indifference to their daughter, Rashid suggested naming her Shona Kiran, the Golden One, the Ray of Sunshine, in deference to her colouring, and to all the new optimism in his life she now represented.

Golden Shona had been conceived with a lie, and was born in a liar's house, and into an inevitable understanding that it was always better to comfort or conceal with a lie than to hurt or expose with the truth. When older, and finding herself telling meaningless benign fibs about why she was late for work, or falsely admiring someone's new haircut, she would be unable to explain whether this need to lie was something innate, or something taught her from infancy by her mother and maternal grandfather. Whether its origin was in nature or nurture, her childhood was a battleground in which the truth never conquered, and in which she knew it was an ironic fallacy that the truth would out. Shona's lies were small, delicate, gossamer things that were woven inextricably into the fabric of her life, and were made anew each day. She spun a web so intricate and fine that only she really knew what was truth or not, and sometimes she deceived herself, so that even she no longer remembered.

Ignored by her teenage mother, Shona craved her attention and followed her around ceaselessly with tottering steps, in the hope she might be seen. One time Henna unusually conceded, and announced to the servants and to the chauffeur that she was taking Shona to the doctor's, for some imagined childhood ailment. In fact, Henna went to the clinic for herself, for what was euphemistically known as 'womb cleansing', and, leaving Shona to the clinic's nurses, returned with her womb duly cleansed of any further unborn life. Henna had two more womb cleansings, always taking Shona as her excuse, and eventually was persuaded that there might be simpler forms of birth control than abortion. Shona silently witnessed the lies her mother told, and even though she didn't understand them, she knew never to give anything away, and even nodded sweetly when the servants asked her if she was feeling better.

Until she was almost four, Shona was a silent witness to everything, as it took her that long to learn to talk. The ambivalence between what was said and what was meant was too difficult for her to unravel at first, and she knew that there were things that should be said which were not. In addition to learning the language of lying, with its complex grammar and syntax and timing, Shona was spoken to in no less than three languages: her mother's Bengali, the Urdu of the Karim household and the English that Rashid insisted on using with her, in the hope that she would learn to speak English like a native. When Shona finally did speak, so late that everyone was beginning to despair of her as retarded, she was suddenly acclaimed as a genius, a not quite four-year-old who understood three languages! Rashid had a friend who had been on a business trip to the UK, and for her birthday he requested that he order the largest, fluffiest teddy bear that he could buy from the grandest toy store in London.

'He was bought in a magical place called Hamley's, which is in England and very far away, and he flew over the sea and deserts and mountains to reach you,' Rashid explained solemnly to his daughter.

'I love him, Papa!' squealed Shona delightedly, hugging the bear somewhat awkwardly due to its ungainly, disproportionate size. She posed for a touching photo with the bear, Rashid's wise-eyed little girl soberly holding up her magnificent prize with an appropriate sense of awe, and he congratulated himself on his gift. It was some months later, when he was with Shona in the playroom, that he realized that she had almost never touched the bear again, except to carelessly pull its button eye out. She had probably found the teddy too big and cumbersome to play with, and had dragged it to the corner of the playroom, where it sat disconsolately. He realized that she hadn't loved the bear at all, and had said she loved it for his sake only. Touched on one hand, Rashid felt deeply sorrowful that Shona, at so young an age, had already been forced to learn the language of diplomacy. His golden one had lost her childhood innocence from almost before she could speak.

By the time Shona was ten years old, her uncle Aziz had taken over running the family lands from Rashid, allowing her father, now a qualified accountant, to get a job with one of the large multinationals which had opened a Dhaka office. Aziz had run the estate so successfully that he had diversified, and had also bought some lands in West Pakistan, in the Punjab where some of their distant relatives had settled. It was with these relatives that Rashid sent Henna and Shona to stay in 1971 when civil war broke out over Bangladeshi Independence. Henna had hoped that Lahore would prove another Calcutta, and was sorely disappointed at how dry, dull and provincial the town was; like it all needed a good dusting.

Shona, however, loved Lahore, with the dry heat that was so much more pleasant than the crushing, constant humidity of Dhaka. She loved the rambling old stone house in the genteel quarter of Gulberg, with its walled garden and wrought-iron swing. She was admired for her golden skin and her impeccable manners, and made all her father's relatives comfortable with her insincere compliments and admiration of everything from their clothes to their cooking. What Shona loved most about Lahore, though, was that there was a boy called Parvez staying in the Gulberg house, a distant relative of the distant relatives; he was from Karachi, and filled the house with his music, playing an eclectic mix of classical Asian and English pop records on the jumpy old gramophone, often accompanying the melodies with either his sitar or guitar, which he played with an amateur's enthusiasm. He was fourteen, and although Shona was only a few years younger than him, and only three years younger than her mother had been when she married, she felt like an awkward child around him; he was almost a man, and he had the easy grace and manliness of the film actors that her mother so admired. With his half-grown moustache, he reminded her of Omar Sharif, whom she'd seen in her mother's movie magazines. Instead of following around her mother, Shona started shamelessly following Parvez around the whole of Gulberg. He was good-natured and didn't mind her tagging along. Once she followed him up to the roof of the house with some syrupy sweets that she had asked the cook to make, knowing they were his favourite.

'Hi, Parvez,' she said shyly in English, their common language, as Shona had not yet learned Parvez's native Punjabi. She breathlessly came up through the twisting stairwell. 'I've brought you some rasgullas, and some cold pomegranate juice.'

'Thanks, Goldie,' he said affably. 'Too hot for rasgulla, but I'll take the juice.' Shona stayed in the shade of the stairwell and watched Parvez standing out in the beating heat of the full sun, only slightly relieved by a light breeze as he twisted twine around a bamboo cylinder. A gloriously coloured structure sat limply at his feet, like a shot-down bird of paradise.

'What are you doing?' she asked. 'Is that a kite over there?'

'Yes, it's a kite. Do you want to come-see?' His smile

was so magnetic and kind that Shona felt herself melting like the ice in Parvez's juice.

She stepped over willingly, while Parvez explained what he was doing. 'I'm just fixing it together. You need to wind the twine round the cylinder like this so you can release it quickly when you catch some wind; this way it can just unroll, like a yo-yo. And you can also pull it in quickly the same way, to keep the kite taut.' Remembering his juice, he politely picked it up and downed it quickly, wiping away the sweet purple drips from his mouth with the back of his hand. Shona watched this small gesture with close fascination, before forcing herself to look back at the kite.

'How will it fly?' she asked. 'There's not very much wind at the moment.' Normally there would be dozens of kites flying from the rooftops over Lahore, but Shona couldn't see any that day.

'There's enough,' said Parvez. 'Come on, Goldie, I'll show you. Come stand here.' Shona stood between Parvez's arms as he showed her how to unravel the twine, demonstrating by rolling the hollow bamboo cylinder over the rod on which it was threaded. He then took the kite and climbed to the highest point of the roof, cavalierly standing close to the edge, while Shona held on to the twine and prayed he wouldn't fall.

'Run when I say,' he called, 'and when the kite is in the air, stop and let out the twine.' Shona, desperate to impress and not fail in this challenge, gave the kite more attention than any lesson she had had in her life and ran urgently at the signal. Feeling the kite tugging in the air just above her, she released the twine and saw it soar higher. 'That's it, Goldie!' shouted Parvez encouragingly. He ran back to Shona and, standing behind her once more, his arms around her to guide the rod that she was holding, he showed her when to pull the kite in and when to let it out, to keep it swooping above their heads.

'It's working, Parvez, it's flying, it's really flying!' she said excitedly. But she wasn't truly excited about the kite, she was just grateful to the kite for giving her an outlet for her heightened emotion, for her extreme, unlimited happiness at that moment, because Parvez was standing so close to her.

As if by magic, other kites began to fly up from the neighbouring rooftops to join theirs as the boys and girls of the Gulberg district realized that there really was enough wind that day. And then across the sweeping city skyline more and more kites sailed into the bright blue sky. It was as though they had lit a beacon to announce that the skies were friendly once more. Shona saw the brightly coloured creatures shimmer and swing gracefully in the heavy air, and giddy with delight at what they had unleashed, leaned back into pomegranate-scented Parvez for support. Closing her eyes for a moment, she thought to herself, for once with unblinkered honesty and candour, 'This will be the man I marry.'

The Puppy Love of Parvez Khan
and Shona Karim

SHONA AND PARVEZ eloped when she was just twenty-
one, on the day she finished her final exams at Karachi
University. Before they met her, Parvez's family already
disapproved of her – an arriviste from Bangladesh, over-
educated, and most likely dark-skinned. What good would
she be for their son, who despite their relative poverty was
certainly handsome and engaging enough to marry a nice
Pakistani girl with a decent dowry? In turn, Shona knew
that her mother and father disapproved of 'Cousin'
Parvez, as he was loosely described, and that if they knew
her reason for going to university in Karachi was simply
to be near him, they would have forbidden her to go
altogether. He wasn't well off – a sin in Henna's eyes as
she had married brilliantly, despite a whole host of disad-
vantages, and didn't want her daughter to undo all her
good work. He wasn't university-educated, having helped
to expand the family restaurant after he had finished
school – a sin in Rashid's eyes. Rashid himself had gone
to Merton College, Oxford, but had thrown himself away
on an illiterate child; he wasn't going to let his daughter

make the same mistake in marrying a partner who wasn't her intellectual equal.

It was Shona who had instigated their love affair – she had been persistent in keeping in touch with him during her adolescence, making him an unwilling pen pal by her sheer perseverance. When she was eighteen she finally arrived in Karachi to study. He met her at the Karachi Tennis Club for drinks and was charmed to discover that his golden-skinned teenage fan club had become a golden-skinned, curvaceous woman, with her mother's good looks and her father's gentleness. She had a childish sense of mischief and humour that he shared. He was disconcerted by her foreignness at the beginning, but she would soon speak Punjabi so flawlessly she sounded like a native, her skill at putting on the appropriate accent not unrelated to her mother's acting talent. On the occasion of their first handshake, they both felt an electric shock, an instant frisson of attraction, a shiver up their spines, that warned Parvez, and confirmed for Shona, that this would be the one. Over the next few years they became the secret golden couple of the club and campus, both so attractive, and so utterly devoted to each other that they were inappropriately tactile in public, hands unconsciously knotting and intertwining, legs or shoulders brushing for that brief, sweet moment of clandestine contact. It was as though being in love was a talent they shared.

Shona was taking a break during the first week of her final exams, indiscreetly walking in the park with Parvez.

She was far from her usual merry, sweetly smiling self, and was disconsolately plucking dusty flowers from the bushes and pulling them apart. Parvez squeezed her hand comfortingly. 'What's up, Goldie? Are you worried about the French literature paper tomorrow?' he asked gently.

'You know what I'm worried about, Puppy,' she said sadly, pulling away her hand and throwing herself on to a bench.

'Shh! Don't call me that in public, people will talk,' he said in mock horror.

'What will people talk about that they haven't talked about already?' asked Shona curiously, momentarily forgetting her resolve to be dramatically melancholic that day.

'They'll say that Parvez is a puppy – a low-down-dirty-little-dog.'

'Oh, you mean a *kuttar bacha*?' giggled Shona, getting the joke and accidentally saying the swear word out loud.

'Shh!' Parvez said again, in greater mock horror. 'Now people will really talk. Parvez is a son-of-a-bitch, and his girlfriend swears like a sweet-maker.'

'You mean a sailor?' asked Shona.

'I mean a sweet-maker – you remember me telling you about my Bhai Hassan? The one who opened the sweet shop in London. He can swear for the whole Punjab. Whenever he comes back he's all Bloody this, and Bloody that. You'd think he worked in a halal butcher's, not a confectioner's.'

'You are silly, Puppy,' Shona giggled, cheered up despite herself. But then she felt her good cheer dissolve almost immediately, as she said forlornly, 'I don't know what I'm going to do without you. No one else makes me laugh like you.'

Parvez sighed. They had had this conversation many times before in the months coming up to Shona's exams. 'I keep telling you, Goldie. You won't have to do without me. When you finish, we'll go back to Dhaka together and I'll ask your father if we can please get married, and we'll live together for ever, and the gossips will have to find something else to talk about.'

'That sounds nice, but Papa will never say yes, not even for me. He'll ask why you don't have a degree.'

'A degree!' Parvez scoffed. 'Anyone can get a degree!' He saw the look on Shona's face and added quickly, 'Anyone who works hard, like you, I mean. But how many people can say that they've turned their family business around, and increased their turnover and staff by four-fold in as many years?'

'No one,' said Shona staunchly. 'Your family have been lucky to have you.' She added, a touch disloyally, giving away where her new allegiances lay, 'Papa tried hard at the family business, but he almost ran our farms into the ground before Uncle Aziz took over.'

'And I'm going to do more! Your dad is the big Anglophile, isn't he? Well, what would he think about his daughter moving to London! You know Bhai Hassan wants me to go and help him with his business over there.'

'He'd hate it,' said Shona. 'He's always wanted to move to England. For you to take me there would be like admitting he's failed. And besides, Papa isn't even the problem – he wouldn't like it, but he couldn't do anything about it. It's Amma who would never let me marry you.

She warns me against you every time I go back for the vacation, and she doesn't even know we're together. She just hears the gossip.' She sighed, 'And your family don't even know me, and they don't like me already. Puppy, I don't know what to do.'

'Shh! I told you not to say that in public,' Parvez said in a stage whisper, and Shona giggled again and reached for his hand.

A middle-aged lady in a voluminous apricot-coloured shalwar looked disapprovingly at Shona as she walked by, and stopped by the bench to address her in ringing tones.

'Daughter, do your parents know that you hold hands with Strange Boys in parks, hmm?' the lady said, looking loftily down on them.

'Auntie, this is my wife, so unless you're stopping to give us your best wishes for a long and happy life together, I suggest you buzz off,' said Parvez with all the arrogance and confidence that his entrepreneurial youthful success had brought. As the lady teetered off in her high heels in disgust, Parvez made a low buzzing sound in rhythm with her walk. And as she became aware of what he was doing, and walked away faster, he increased the pitch and frequency of his buzz until she practically ran from them. Shona, at first mortified, was soon in fits of laughter.

'Puppy! You are so naughty. Bad, bad Puppy,' she smacked him and laughed out loud again.

'You see, Goldie, we have to get married. No one else thinks I'm funny at all,' said Parvez. He looked at Shona's pretty, unmade-up face, her lips very full and pink against the gold of her skin, and said, 'I wish we were married already, so I could kiss you whenever I wanted to.'

'And if we were married already, we wouldn't have to beg all our families for permission. We could just go to London and tell them all later.'

'Well, I promised to fly over and see Bhai Hassan to discuss the job,' said Parvez flippantly. 'Pack your bags and we can go together.'

'You're teasing me, Puppy. That's not nice,' said Shona reproachfully. 'And besides, I've got my exams this week and next.'

'We can go after your exams,' said Parvez, less flippantly. Why hadn't he thought of this before? He and Shona didn't need to be stuck in the rut of tradition – it was the 1980s, for God's sake, they could get married when and where they wanted; they were grown-ups, and they didn't need their parents' permission. And they didn't need their parents' money – he had already proved himself as breadwinner for his family, he could certainly look after Shona on his own.

'Puppy, are you being serious?' said Shona, noticing the change in Parvez's expression. He had the faraway look that came over him when he was planning something; it made him look like a misty-eyed dreamer but in fact was a sign that his head was ticking and turning over with ideas. Parvez looked into Shona's solemn, chocolate-brown eyes and dropped to one knee in front of her.

'Shundor Shonali Shona, my beautiful Golden Goldie, do you know that you have eyes that a man can look back centuries in, and still see his future? Of course I'm serious! Marry me after your exams. We'll fly to London the same evening. I'll organize everything – I'll get your ticket and arrange the marriage licence.'

'We can't get married just like that,' said Shona, taking refuge in being sensible to avoid being overcome by the superb honeyed sweetness of the moment. 'What about witnesses, and all that sort of thing?'

'I'll drag them off the street if I have to!' said Parvez with romantic gallantry. 'Ho!' he shouted to a couple of students cycling towards them. 'Do you want to be our witnesses? The lady has just agreed to marry me.'

'Drunk,' muttered one of the students to the other as they sailed by.

'You see,' Parvez repeated with faux dejection, getting up from the grimy path to sit beside her on the bench. 'No one thinks I'm funny apart from you.' Dusting the dirt from his knees, he added, 'Fortunately I wasn't wearing my best trousers today – it must be fate. If I'd decided to wear my good trousers this morning I might not have been able to propose at all.'

'You are the funniest puppy in the world,' said Shona, finally giving in to the moment. 'And yes, I will marry you next week, in front of witnesses dragged from the street, in my best travelling sari and with trainers on so we can run away when they come to get us.'

'Goldie, I think I might have to kiss you anyway,' said Parvez as Shona, laughing delightedly, swatted him away, her sombre mood lifted entirely.

'Buzz off, strange boy,' she said cheekily, flapping at him ineffectively.

'Bzzz,' said Parvez, avoiding her swatting hands and moving closer. 'Bzzz,' and he took her in his arms and kissed her like they did in the movies, oblivious to the curious looks and outrage of the rest of conservative Karachi parading through the park in their Sunday best.

Shona went back to her studies, and told the girls on campus that she'd be flying home straight after her last exam to explain why she wouldn't be around for any post-exam celebrations. She told the family she was staying with the same thing. Shona dissembled guiltlessly; she had lied for the past three years in order to keep seeing Parvez, so that the girls thought she spent far too much time holed up at home, and the family thought she spent far too much time socializing on campus. Before picking up her books to do some last-minute revision for her French literature paper, she picked out the sari in which she'd decided to get married. A gorgeous, orangey golden silk – like the sunrise on her new life with Parvez.

The wedding day was deliciously romantic. Ludicrously overdressed in her orange-gold sari, Shona sat her last paper and rushed out of the examination hall to see Parvez waiting, wearing his best suit and a flamboyant buttonhole, his sitar case in his hand, with a motorized rickshaw chugging black smoke over his peacock finery. Before her student friends could see, she disappeared into the rickshaw with him, and they stopped at the campus where she had stowed her bags. At the registrar's, Parvez, good as his word, called two people off the street to be their witnesses – they were workmen trying to fix the street lights, but were all too happy to take a break from the hot job for the fan-cooled registrar's office.

'Are you sure this is legal?' she asked bemusedly.

'Of course, smile for the photographer!' Parvez said. He had hired someone to take a few shots of them as they signed the papers and yet more shots as they came out of the office, with the grinning workmen behind them.

Shona was to look at one of those photos later, her sari blazing in the sun, her face looking bewildered but happy as she looked up adoringly at Parvez. And Parvez looking like he owned the world: handsome, confident, laughing at the camera, an arm protectively around her, as though he had enough strength for them both and would look after them for ever. Perhaps she and Parvez really did have a talent for being in love – in some ways, apart from their silly sense of humour, it was all they had in common. But it was incontrovertible: they were The Couple That Were In Love, and whose foolhardy, romantic elopement only substantiated the fact further. Twenty years later, she was to wonder where it all started going wrong.

The Crushed Rose Petals of a Tooting Confectioner

A FTER THE ROMANTIC high of their elopement, the sticky, crowded wait at the airport and cold, dry plane journey made for a deeply unromantic wedding night, but it didn't even occur to Shona to complain. She just snuggled up to her new husband under the Pakistan International Airlines blanket, and enjoyed the simple intimacy of being able to watch him sleep, his eyelashes fanned against his cheek, his breath deepening but his face remaining poised, and his jaw firm, as though still conscious that he was in public and under scrutiny. In the half light of the sleeping plane, Shona looked at the other husbands and fathers sitting around her, with their fat bellies, bald pates and slack-jawed, half-open mouths, and her pride in her handsome husband soared.

When the stewardesses started serving breakfast, Shona put on her headset and watched *Chariots of Fire* on the airplane TV. Her papa loved the film, and she heard his own cut-glass accent in the accents of the Oxbridge students who ran for England. She considered changing out of her sari, but the airplane loos were unpromisingly busy and there wasn't enough room in the cubicles of the Dubai stopover. Besides, it was probably best if she didn't meet Bhai Hassan in casual western dress. She wasn't sure how traditional he was, and as the first member of Parvez's close family that she'd be meeting, she wanted to make a good first impression.

As they descended towards Heathrow, Shona watched the blue sky around them dull to grey, cold-looking clouds and pulled the blanket, which she had now commandeered for her exclusive use, closer to protect her. She was glad that she had packed a shawl – she would get it out as soon as they got their bags back. As they approached for landing, Shona, who had seen desert, snow-capped mountains and wondrous oceans on their journey over, was unimpressed. So this was England, the place of her father's dreams, the location of all his happy memories and interminable university stories – this grey, patchwork quilt of a country. Even the cheerful chatter of the fellow passengers now seemed muted with the weather, and they lowered their voices to hushed whispers; or perhaps it just felt that way with the air pressure in her ears. She looked down at her sari, which seemed outrageously garish in this new gloomy and solemn world – dressed for a party, she had been taken to a wake.

'Hey, it's not that cold, it's not even raining,' said Parvez, sensing Shona's disappointment as they got off the plane. 'I want my money back – I think they took us to the wrong country.' There was a touch of concern in his bonhomie; Shona's muted reaction to this muted new country was giving him his first niggle of doubt as to whether they had done the right thing. Shona gave him a slight, tremulous smile and squeezed his hand, wondering how she was ever going to feel at home here. Perhaps the trick was not to think about it as a home, but just a long holiday, like the time Papa had taken her to the beach at Cox's Bazaar to learn to swim, or when she and Amma had gone to Lahore together, and first met Parvez. This was her honeymoon, wasn't it? How many of the tittering, giggling girls at college would have Just Died and Gone to Heaven at the idea of a honeymoon in London? Shona had got so good at lying she could even persuade herself that she was happy, which made it much easier to persuade the man standing by her side.

'Happy honeymoon, Puppy,' she said without a trace of telltale discontent, and kissed him on his slightly stubbly cheek. Parvez relaxed and banished the niggle, reassured that she was going to be all right.

Parvez, determined to be the manly, efficient one, went to the American Express office at the airport and changed some of his travellers' cheques, for what seemed a vast amount of money to Shona.

'That'll do us for a couple of days,' he said wisely, fastening the notes with the thick gold clip he had started using, which he thought looked rather natty, and which Shona thought looked rather garish.

'Just a couple of days?' said Shona faintly. London was clearly a lot more expensive than Karachi. She had no idea how much Parvez had in savings, but she knew he wasn't rich, and after paying for both their tickets it couldn't be that much. Shona's family had always been relatively wealthy, so she had never had to worry about money before. Now she wished she had some savings of her own to contribute – otherwise Parvez might have to start working straightaway, and her honeymoon might be very short indeed.

The cab journey to Tooting took up a distressing amount of Parvez's precious pinned notes. Standing at the cab rank with her glamorous sari flapping in the wind, with Parvez in his wedding blazer, with their hotchpotch of luggage littering up their feet, Shona was aware that they looked preposterously out of place. The cabbie, seeing them, was prepared to be jovially patronizing, but was stopped short by Shona reading out their address in her father's cut-glass English accent, which now had additional hints of Harold Abrahams absorbed from *Chariots of Fire*.

'Could you possibly take us to Tooting High Street in SW17, near Tooting Broadway station?' she asked, as Parvez hoisted up their bags.

'Blimey, I wasn't expecting that face to have that voice,' said the cabbie, nodding respectfully at her. 'Are you from London, dear?'

Parvez cheerfully answered for her, 'Not yet, but we soon will be, I hope.' He laughed good-humouredly, but the cabbie didn't laugh with him. Parvez's English was good, but his accent was definitely Pakistani, and the cabbie's respect disintegrated like a puff of smoke on hearing the familiar immigrant Paki accent. He looked at Shona crossly, as though she had tricked him on purpose. Parvez was unsure what he had done to cause the sudden sinking good humour, but didn't say another word in

English until they reached the grimy, litter-strewn streets of Tooting.

Bhai Hassan was delighted to see his young cousin and lovely new wife. He was less happy when he realized that they were runaways, who were intending to stay in London, and who had nowhere to stay except with him. After giving them a welcoming cup of comfortingly sweet tea, served with rasgulla and burfi from the shop, he showed Shona to the spare room, and made an excuse to take Parvez into his 'office', the table at the back of the sweet-shop kitchen.

Kicking off her shoes, Shona was finally able to unwind herself out of her now crushed and rather worse-for-wear sari and pull on a pair of trousers and a long silky shirt. Looking out of the window through the stained yellowing net, she was shocked to find herself wondering where she and Parvez were going to be able to make love, and properly begin their honeymoon. Certainly not in this tatty spare room of Bhai Hassan's flat above the confectioner's. She lay back on the single bed and imagined Parvez's arms around her, in a suite at the Karachi Hilton, lying on Egyptian cotton sheets strewn with rose petals.

In the kitchen, Bhai Hassan was prosaically pounding rose petals to a damp and fragrant sludge with sugar to make the syrup for one of his sweets. 'Bloody hell, son,' he said in English that was pure south London. 'She's a nice girl but you can't keep her. You can't just roll up with a girlfriend in a foreign country and say you're married and you're going to live here. You practically kidnapped her. Our family will be out for your blood. And her family have probably reported her missing to the flipping police by now. She'll have to go back. I'm Bleedin' amazed you got her through immigration in the first place.'

'She's not going back, Bhai. She's my wife, and I love her and she's staying with me.'

'Stop, you're making my Bloody heart bleed,' Bhai Hassan said, giving the tattered remains of the rose petals a final vicious bash. 'How are you going to afford her? You'll barely be able to keep yourself in London, let alone a wife. She don't look like she's used to earning her keep.'

'Well, you asked me here to help with the business. I'll work with you, and rent us a house. If you could just let us stay with you until then. . .'

'A house?' roared Bhai Hassan in outrage that quickly dissolved to laughter. 'Do you really think I can pay you enough to rent a house while I'm living in the Bloody flat above the shop?'

Parvez felt the niggle of doubt that he had dismissed at the airport come creeping back. He couldn't go crawling back to Pakistan with his tail between his legs; he had to make this work. He looked helplessly at his cousin for just a moment before pulling himself together and saying firmly, 'A flat, then. We'll get our own flat. I'll work with you and leave Shona free to manage our home and do whatever else she wants, continue her studies maybe.' He added with a touch of pride, 'My wife is a very intelligent woman, a college girl, you know. Just finished her final exams. She could've gone to university here in England, but she chose Karachi, just to be near me.'

'So she's not that Bloody bright,' said Bhai Hassan crushingly. 'Besides, how do you think a college girl will manage your home? I'll bet she can't even cook. I know the sort, had servants all their lives and can't make a Bloody cup of cha without someone else boiling the water and pouring the milk.'

Parvez received this disquieting insight with a nonchalant shrug; it was probably true that Shona couldn't cook, or sew, or make a cup of tea. So what? He hadn't fallen in love for her domestic skills. Besides, he knew how to cook from his time in the family restaurant; maybe he could teach her.

'So can we stay with you? Just for a bit?' he asked, with a pleading smile and the big, persuasive puppy-dog eyes that had earned him his pet name from Shona.

It was Bhai Hassan's turn to shrug. His good-looking young cousin had a lot of charm, he'd give him that. He'd be a definite front-of-house asset with the moneyed ladies of Tooting, especially with his new plans to expand the sweet shop to a tea house. Sod the bloody family – apart from Parvez, they never wrote to him anyway, except to ask for money.

'It doesn't look like I have much choice,' he said with resignation, pouring his tortured rose-petal sludge into a hot pan to melt, the sweet scent rising mournfully from the steam and hanging in the air like a mistreated spirit. Parvez bounded across the table to hug him, but Bhai Hassan smacked his hands away in an attempt to hold on to his elder cousin authority. 'Arré! Careful, this stove is hot! So when can you start work. Tomorrow?'

'In three days' time, if that's OK,' Parvez said sweetly, with the carefree innocence of someone about to spend well beyond his means. 'First, my wife and I have plans for our honeymoon.'

Shona had almost drifted off to sleep, curled up on the narrow single bed, oblivious to the honking, Tooting traffic on the streets below, when she became fuzzily aware of a naked Greek apparition in the room. Blinking swiftly, she realized that Parvez was getting changed right in front of her, and was wearing only his underwear. His caramel-coloured chest was smooth and hairless, and the muscles in his back moved like poetry as he pulled on a pair of casual trousers.

'Hey, sleepy head,' he said, noticing her stir. Clearly unembarrassed by his state of undress, he sat next to her and kissed her on the forehead. 'Sorry to do this to you, but you'll need to pack a few things for a couple of nights. We've got to head off soon.'

'Where are we heading off to? We've only just arrived,' asked Shona bemusedly, disturbed by the proximity of so much handsome flesh.

Parvez kissed her again. 'Didn't you say that you've always wanted to stay at the Hilton?'

This particular Hilton wasn't quite as plush as Shona imagined the Karachi Hilton to be, but the room had all sorts of exciting conveniences. A kettle with little sachets of tea and coffee and gingerbread. A very white, very shiny bathroom with wrapped-up soap and sachets of shampoo and shower gel. A perplexing-looking trouser press, which Shona couldn't quite work out. A TV which announced 'Welcome, Mr and Mrs Khan' across its screen. It was this last which made Shona squeal with excitement; it was the first time she'd seen her married name in writing and it made it all feel official, substantial. She was a married woman now, and had been for a whole day and a half. When she pulled the curtains open, she jumped up and down with excitement all over again. 'Puppy, look at the view! It's the park! This is Hyde Park, Papa told me about it. There's a boating lake there – can we go boating, can we?'

'If you want,' said Parvez, amused. 'Do you want a cup of tea?'

'I'll make it,' Shona said. 'We had a kettle like this in the common room on campus.' She put the water on to boil, and told Parvez seriously, 'The important thing about making English tea is to put the milk in first, so it doesn't scald. And to warm the pot first. And to wait until the water is just off the boil before you brew, and not let the tea be over-brewed when you pour. And you put in one spoon of tea per person, and one for the pot. Except we only have teabags here, so I'll just put in two.'

'I had no idea it was so complicated a business,' said Parvez, pleased that at least one of Bhai Hassan's dire predictions had been proved wrong. He sat on the bed and pulled off his shoes.

'Papa used to make tea like this at home. He never let the servants make it because they used to stew the tea and put in canned evaporated milk.'

Parvez smiled and pulled Shona on to his lap, kissing the tip of her nose. 'Goldie, can I be honest with you? I'm really not that bothered about tea right now.'

'Neither am I,' answered Shona, feeling the same tingle up her spine that she had felt the day she first learned to fly a kite, and the same electric shock she had felt the first time they had shaken hands at the Karachi Tennis Club after their long separation. She realized with slight trepidation and high anticipation that her anomalous time as a married virgin was about to come to an end. As she lay back on their plump, white pillows, Shona was aware of a gentle fragrant fluttering, raining over her. She opened her eyes to see Parvez scattering pale pink rose petals rescued from Bhai Hassan's kitchen across their bed. She sighed blissfully and pulled Parvez down towards her.

That afternoon, and evening, and night, and morning, Shona and Parvez were to discover that they had something further in common besides a silly sense of humour and a fondness for nicknames. The urgent physical attraction that they had mistaken for love was the forerunner of an intense sexual compatibility that was to keep them together for twenty years. Any arguments, disappointments and frustrations were put aside, resolved, absolved in the bedroom, crushed with the salty-sweetness of their lovemaking, and melted away in the early hours of the morning, evaporating like discharged ghosts with the sticky heat of their bodies. These bodies were instantly, instinctively comfortable with each other, hand fitting hand, mouth fitting mouth, curve fitting hollow. And as they grew older, their bodies, so finely attuned to each other, so used to sharing the same bed, were to dissolve into each other, her contours into his planes, arms and legs that knotted together like tree roots, so that even in their sleep they were in an embrace.

The Relative Cost of Gold

SHONA AND PARVEZ, during their three-day honey-moon in London, were able to act like a real couple for the first time. None of the secretive liaisons in the parks, waiting for a busybody to berate them or prying eyes to report them, none of the accidental encounters at the tennis club or campus library, no more engineering chance meetings with mutual acquaintances, or pretending to be somewhere other than where they really were. Shona could bask in the openness of the new arrangement, putting off the moment when she'd have to call home and explain what she had done. They held hands as they walked down Oxford Street and through Soho and kissed more often than was decorous even in bohemian London, where back-combed punks with metal studs looked with pity at these unwitting new romantics with their floppy silk shirts. They stopped for a cream tea in one of the nicer tea shops on Piccadilly, and Parvez proudly told the highly made-up waitress that it was their honeymoon.

'But where are your rings?' she asked, after congratu-lating them. On hearing that they weren't an essential part of the ceremony in Pakistan, she raised her fashionably plucked eyebrows and told them, a touch condescendingly, 'In this country, we wear rings when we're married.' She waved her hand – 'Like this, see?' – showing a diamond-studded band.

Furious for being treated like an ignorant Paki yokel for the second time in as many days, Parvez marched Shona down to the various jewellers on Old Bond Street.

'I'm not having people think that we're rednecks from the villages, and I'm not having people think that we're not really married,' he stormed, talking more to himself than Shona.

'It doesn't matter, Puppy,' said Shona appeasingly. 'I don't care whether people think we're married or not.' She was secretly thrilled; she had been wondering whether she might get a ring, and looked hopefully at the elegant display in the window at Tiffany's. However, both she and Parvez baulked at the prices they saw; gold didn't cost nearly so much at home, and Parvez was determined that Shona should have no baser metal than her own namesake.

Fortunately, Bhai Hassan, who had built up a network of useful cronies during his time in London, knew 'a-man-who-did'. Parvez resisted showing his ignorance by asking what-he-did, and was repaid by Bhai Hassan giving him the address of Dominic, a Diamond-geezer in both senses of the word, who ran a shadowy but industrious jewellery workshop above a hair salon in Hatton Garden.

'Dominic's a Diamond, I mean a Bloody Nice Bloke,' Bhai Hassan translated kindly for Parvez. 'He'll make you a couple of rings for a song if you get him the gold to work with.' Parvez pulled out his beloved gold money clip and looked thoughtfully at it. The next day he replaced it with an inexpensive wallet, and the following week he was to surprise his wife with a shining copy of the wedding rings at Tiffany's that she had admired, and a gleaming pair of delicate golden earrings that he had had made with the leftover gold.

Shona displayed an excitement for Parvez's benefit which didn't reveal how deeply it saddened her that her gift should have to be his loss, and which consequently could not show how deeply this act of unselfishness had touched her. She had lots of expensive, gem-set jewellery at home, mainly cast-offs inherited from her mother, but nothing that had been given with such love. Sitting in the squalid spare room of her husband's cousin's flat, she told herself she could do without money, without the trappings of privilege and the unthinking ease of life that she had been so used to, as long as she had Parvez.

The Beginning of the Double Life
of Ricky-Rashid

RASHID WAS PRACTICALLY middle-aged when he first fell in love. At forty-three, he had matured and filled out and become better looking than the callow, milky-faced academic of his youth. His figure was no longer skinny, and he now wore a suit rather well; the slight grey in his temples was distinguished rather than ageing, and his profile seemed fine-boned rather than weak. Although outwardly he appeared fit and well and even attractive – he was only forty-three after all – inside he felt defeated, worn and ancient. Like a ruin left abandoned to take its punishment from a brutal sun and the encroaching jungle.

The last twenty-five years of his life had been a study in apathy and disappointment. He had married a pretty child who had become a thick-waisted tyrant, who tolerated him while she took over his home, and with whom he had perplexingly proved infertile after their first child. He had given up his academic and professional dreams to mismanage his family's landed interests until his more adept younger brother was old enough to take over and undo the damage he had well-meaningly caused – his sacrifice both unappreciated and unacknowledged. He had been gifted a wonderful daughter, who until her late teens was the only good thing, the only golden ray of sunshine in his life, but from whom he had been estranged ever since she had ill-advisedly gone to university in Karachi rather than England. He had loyally ignored the gossip he had heard about her behaviour in Karachi with a certain Pakistani boy, believing her when she returned home on her vacations from campus and assured him that there was no truth to the rumours. He had been repaid for his trust by her proceeding to elope with that same boy on the day she finished her final exam.

The only thing that Rashid had managed to be consistent at was his work. After a dozen years with the same multinational he had joined in his youth, following many mergers and acquisitions, he found himself a fairly senior figure in the finance department and had to travel widely in the Middle East and Asia. He spent very little time at home, but home now meant very little to him – Henna didn't care if he was there or not, she didn't even need him as an appropriate escort to the parties she went to, or as host for her evening soirées, as the still unmarried Aziz was more than happy to oblige in his absence and she clearly preferred his company. Rashid suspected that when he was at home, his presence was an annoyance to Henna – she simply put up with him, as his mere existence enabled her a pleasant life as Mrs Karim. In the same way that she was stuck with him, he felt stuck with her. He had made a deal with her when she was thirteen; when he had accepted the marriage, he had become her guardian as much as her husband. He couldn't divorce her now, it was much too late, and besides, where would she go? Frankly, he suspected that if he ever broached the subject, he would be the one to move out, such was Henna's hold on the household, his extended family and all the retainers. They were faithful to her first and then to Aziz, not to him; his constant absenteeism did not help to engender their loyalty. And of course, Shona wasn't there any more. There was nothing of hers left but some of her old childhood toys, like that eyeless old teddy she had never loved. She had asked the servants to pack up and send on her belongings to London, where she and Parvez had moved after their elopement. She had seized for herself the English life that Rashid had wanted to give her. He hadn't seen Shona for months now – he guessed that her concerns were all with her husband and his Pakistani family, not with him or even her mother, who were now too distant to matter.

Rashid had been surprised when an appointment came up at work, and he discovered that he had been recommended for it. It was rather similar to the job he currently did and involved a similar level of travel, except the job was to be based out of the UK, in the company's regional centre in the south-east of England. After all these years, England! The place he had dreamed of living, working, raising and educating his family. Again, it was much too late. And he probably wouldn't get the job anyway; he'd need to fly to the UK for the interview. He mentioned it to Henna when he arrived home one evening at the Dhaka town house, catching her before she disappeared off for the night.

'Hold on, someone's come in . . . no, don't worry, it's

Just Rashid,' he heard Henna say to one of her cronies on the telephone as he walked in. Leisurely finishing her call, she addressed him distractedly as she attempted to fasten her earrings in front of the mirror in the long, dark hallway. 'It's just you and Ammie tonight, Rashid. Aziz is having dinner at the club, and I'm on my way to Farida's for our drama and supper evening.' Fiddling with a stubborn catch at her left ear, she added vaguely, 'I think Cook might make you some koftas or curry, or something.'

'Perhaps I could join Aziz at the club?' suggested Rashid hopefully. Eating alone again with his doleful mother didn't seem too enticing. She had once resented his frequent absences; now she seemed to positively resent his presence. Like everyone, she liked him much less than Henna and Aziz.

'If you do, you'll need to take a rickshaw there and get a lift back with Aziz – I need our driver to go to Farida's.'

Rashid sighed. Getting a rickshaw through the hot and sticky night was the last thing he wanted to do after a hard day's number-crunching.

'Henna, before you go, there's something you should know.'

'Yes, well, quickly then,' said Henna with barely concealed irritation. Her earrings now firmly in place, she was painting her mouth with a plum lipstick that matched her sari and her pretty sandals.

'There's a new opening at work. It's more senior, with more money, but it involves lots of travel in Europe and being based in the UK. They've asked me to an interview, but I'd need to go to England for it.' Rashid hesitated, before bravely admitting, 'I said I'd think about it.'

'Well, what's to think about?' she said impatiently. Rashid was so slow sometimes. 'They'll pay for your flight, yes? And your accommodation there? So you should go for the interview and see Shona and that Pakistani. Take them some presents, so they think we're not cross any more. Tell her to come home occasionally – people are beginning to talk. And you can buy me a raincoat from Burberry – Farida has one and is always showing off about it.'

'But what if I get the job?' asked Rashid, not sure that Henna had been listening.

'Well, you might get lucky, but don't get your hopes up,' said Henna, with a tone that was meant to be kind, before barking 'Cholo!' to the waiting driver. 'I really have to go now.'

Rashid followed her outside, and with natural politeness held the door open for her as she elegantly stepped into the back of the enviably air-conditioned Rover that he had so recently vacated. 'But what about the travel, and being based in the UK?'

'Rashid, you travel three days a week anyway. No one's going to notice if you travel a bit more,' Henna said with unconscious cruelty, shutting the door to signal an end to the conversation.

Rashid watched the car speed off. That had actually gone better than he thought it would – Henna had practically encouraged him to go for the job. Looking back towards the veranda, he saw his mother looking down at him with woeful, accusatory eyes. He decided that braving the sticky night was the better of the two evils. 'Hey, Ammie, I'm going to meet Aziz at the club,' he shouted to her with barely concealed cowardice, and walked swiftly out of the gate to the street before she could object, hailing his own rickshaw and letting the damp dust of the street settle in the creases of his good suit.

It was the same suit that Rashid was wearing as he sat in the BA Business Class lounge at Paris Charles de Gaulle airport. At no little inconvenience to him, his company had booked him a flight to Paris as the cheapest option, requiring him to board a separate plane to London, with a four-hour wait in between. He'd had a shower, read the papers and drunk enough spicy tomato juices to make him feel distinctly queasy, and he still had two hours left to kill. He settled near the TV, where he could watch the news for distraction. He was sorely tempted to get terribly drunk, but didn't want his first return to England for years to be clouded by alcohol – he wanted to return to his spiritual home with dignity. Yes, with dignity. The very thought made him sit up straighter, and his profile stiffen with distinction. That was how Veetie Trueman first saw him, wielding his *FT* like a shield against the grimy masses and looking like a Roman statesman, like someone who belonged.

Veetie was acutely conscious that she, by contrast to the elegant gentleman sitting in the armchair, looked like a scruffy interloper on entering the Business Class lounge, her grey suit crumpled at the back from sitting stiffly in the hot Parisian cab, and the collar of her white shirt wilting at her pale neck. She was obviously ill at ease with the supercilious reception staff, handing over her boarding card timidly as though she expected them to refuse her entry, and was struggling with two ungainly cases and a document bag that she was ill-equipped to manage along with her own substantial handbag. Rashid barely noticed her, glancing up only briefly at the noise made by her untidy, clattering entrance.

'You can't bring all those bags in under your hand-luggage allowance, dear,' said the BA representative patronizingly.

'I know,' replied Veetie tiredly, as though she'd had to give the explanation before. 'They're not all mine. They're my colleagues' – they've taken our client for a drink and asked me to look after their bags. They're joining me here later.'

The receptionist handed back Veetie's boarding card sniffily, saying, 'You can leave excess bags over there,' nodding towards a rack set in the wall, 'but at your own risk.'

Veetie tried to wheel the cases over to the rack, but one fell over, causing her to stumble awkwardly. Rashid, with natural gentility, got up politely. 'Here, let me help with those.' He lifted both cases easily and put them in the rack. 'Shall I put that bag in as well?' he offered, indicating the document bag.

'No, I'd better hold on to this one. Thanks so much,' gushed Veetie, unused to such gallantry, especially from such an attractive, distinguished-looking man. She collapsed in a seat near him, pretending to watch the TV but surreptitiously stealing long glances at him, admiring his patrician nose and creamy exotic colouring. Perhaps he was Spanish, or South American – but his English was perfect and unaccented, unless received pronunciation counted as an accent. Maybe he was Indian? Although so correct and poised, he wasn't very much older than her – maybe in his mid forties, or perhaps even younger. She noticed that he wasn't wearing a wedding ring.

Rashid would later say that it was Fate that had led him to love – Fate (and not frugality caused by squeezed corporate travel budgets) that had forced him to make this inexplicable airline interchange so close to his destination, Fate (and not rudeness on the part of her colleagues) that had Ms Trueman carrying excess hand-baggage to the Business Class lounge long before her plane was due, and Fate (not the location of the TV) that he had been sitting near enough to overhear her plight and help her.

In fact, when spinning this romantic tale, Rashid would conveniently forget that despite all this intervention from Fate, once he had helped Veetie with her bags he had not been interested enough by the timid smile on her flushed face, nor in the thin figure not set to advantage by a creased high street suit, to take any further notice of her beyond a polite nod once she took her seat. Despite all the best intentions of Fate, aided by budget restrictions in his own company, and regrettable chauvinism in Ms Trueman's, Rashid would have sat opposite the future love of his life and simply ignored her. He would have dropped his eyes back to his paper, sinking behind its peach-coloured safety and then left to get his plane. Fortunately for Rashid, Veetie no longer believed in fate and took some action for herself.

Veetie was in her late thirties, and had only recently become the sort of woman who took things into her own hands. She had spent most of her life having decisions made for her by other people, first by her Home Counties parents, and then by her controlling boyfriend, whom she unthinkingly and unwisely replaced with an exact replica when he left her. Her parents had bullishly argued against her going to university, insisting that Lucy Clayton Secretarial College would provide her with impeccable qualifications for a regular income, and invaluable training for her future career as a wife. And so Veetie spent her twenties as a secretary in the City and her early thirties as an administrator, but in fact devoted all her real energy to being a homemaker, for two successive partners who didn't appreciate her devotion enough to want to make the arrangement permanent. It was when she turned thirty-five that it became obvious to her that Pete, her boyfriend of five years, had no intention of asking her to marry him, or even remaining faithful. It became equally obvious to her that the decisions made for her by other people had not been the most helpful, and that nothing was going to happen for her unless she did something about it herself. She left Pete and enrolled in the Open University in French and Business Studies; with her degree eventually achieved, she fought for more recognition at work. It had been a major coup for her to have been taken on the business trip to Paris, even though the senior colleagues had treated her like a bag-carrier throughout the whole day, ending with the final and supreme put-down at the airport bar, when they had decided that their hand luggage was too cumbersome to keep with them and had dispatched Veetie to take their bags to the Business Class lounge, clinking their whisky glasses as she made her embarrassed, over-burdened exit.

Although Veetie was disenchanted with her love life to date, she was far from the motivated career woman she now professed to be to her personnel department during her biannual appraisals. Secretly, she remained a home-loving romantic, still deeply wanting to believe in love at first sight. In the three years that had passed since she left Pete, she had been looking for her White-Knight-Mr-Right, and hoped that the simple act of looking might be enough to help her find him. If she'd had to sum up her first impressions of Rashid in three words, she would have said, Distinguished, Kind, Gallant. Everything that she was expecting of her White-Knight-Mr-Right. She looked at Rashid hopefully, wishing that she might catch his eye and start a conversation, but Rashid was unused to being the object of any sort of attention, least of all female attention, and didn't notice. So Veetie took a deep breath and, leaning forward, asked, 'Will you let me buy you a drink? It's the least I can do, for helping me, I mean.' She'd intended to hold out her hand and introduce herself, but Rashid looked up and looked shocked. Oh God, she thought, spotting the tomato juice at his side, perhaps he didn't drink, perhaps she'd mortally offended him. Or perhaps he didn't think that women should buy drinks for strange men at airports.

After what seemed an eternity, but was really just a moment, Rashid spoke. 'That's very kind, but the drinks in the lounge are free, you know. You don't have to buy them.'

Veetie felt heat rising back to her cheeks. 'I didn't realize,' she said apologetically, before admitting, 'I don't fly Business Class very often. In fact, I don't fly Business Class at all. This is my first time.' Rashid was charmed by Veetie's candour, her refreshing honesty, and looked at her properly, noticing her hesitant smile and her pink and white complexion heated by the delicate flush. With her blonde hair untidily falling out of what had been a neat chignon earlier in the day, she seemed really quite young. Remembering her comment at the front desk, he wondered who her obnoxious colleagues were, who had left this frail, pale English rose to carry their things while they rudely excluded her from their drinks gathering.

'But thank you very much for offering, Ms. . .?'

At the polite prompt for her name, Veetie, who said she no longer believed in fate, made a choice that was to have consequences for the rest of her life. Perhaps, deep down, she knew that this moment was the belated beginning of her grown-up life, and that her long-standing childhood nickname, along with all the disappointments it represented, was no longer good enough for her. Whatever the reason, she made a break with her entire past, and rather than introduce herself as Veetie, chose to tell him her true name, the name with which she'd been christened. 'It's Verity, Miss Verity Trueman.'

On hearing her name, Rashid's head snapped up like someone who'd been slapped awake. His wide-open eyes looked clearly and deeply into Verity's as though scales had fallen from them, and the shining road ahead was suddenly clear. He looked at Verity and saw something more than her fragility, more than her timid smile and delicate complexion – he saw a glimpse of his future, and his fate. He saw the woman with whom he could finally fall in love.

'Ricky,' he said, after some effort. 'My name is Ricky. Ricky Karim, at your service.' The saying of his real name thrilled him, an affirmation of who he really was, and who he could be again. He held out his hand to Verity and she took it, aware that something magical had happened, but not knowing what had caused it.

'Miss Trueman, or Verity, if I may call you that? Would you like to get something to eat? I have a couple of hours until my flight, and I can help you with those bags.'

'That would be lovely,' said Verity breathlessly, feeling like Cinderella. She walked out of the lounge with Ricky in her cheap shoes, with her good, but over-stuffed bag, as though walking on air, as though saved. She even smiled at the stuffy BA staff, who looked at her with poorly concealed distaste, as though to sniff, 'Well, really.'

Ricky-Rashid had an unconscious Dickensian belief that the name unveiled the soul; no man named Uriah Heep would ever be a romantic hero, no boy named Twist could expect a straightforward life. And in Ricky-Rashid's book, that by which we call a rose would certainly not smell as sweet if it were called by a less fragrant name. Which is why he had so often longed to doff 'Rashid', his Indian name, the name that bound him to his duty, and to become Ricky once more. Ricky, the English gentleman and scholar, Ricky the Lionhearted, the powerful, for whom all the limitless opportunities and giddy potential of life was waiting. But he had defaulted, for many years, to being dull, limited Just Rashid – Rashid, meaning he who followed the right and narrow course, just another Indian accountant with a plump wife and pedestrian life. In Ricky-Rashid's experience, names meant something; after all, his child-bride Henna had lived up to her name in being a beautiful flower which had seemed fragrant in fresh youth, but whose touch had left him a marked man. He had named Shona Kiran to be his golden one, his little ray of sunshine, and so she had shone for him obediently in her childhood, creating the only bright spells in his dark, wooden life.

Ricky-Rashid realized that what had defined his life with these two women was their need to lie to him – reassuringly on Shona's part, brutally on Henna's, but always to lie. Lies had penned him in, and wrapped him in tangled webs he couldn't unravel. What he had always longed for was a life lived in truth, and all that was decent and true was what Verity Trueman represented. He felt he knew everything about her just by knowing her name. Ricky-Rashid knew at that moment that Fate had decided to be kind. He saw himself leading a different sort of life with a different sort of woman – a life beautiful in its frankness and openness. He would share everything with Verity, he would tell her everything she asked. But of course, she would never ask about his other wife, or his grown-up daughter, because she would never know that they existed.

Ricky-Rashid's double life began that day – a life that he split by his name. In England, he was Ricky, Verity's husband, a leading light in the local community and keen member of the tennis and cricket clubs, an enthusiastic gentleman and scholar, successful in his work, who lived life to the full, cheerfully tolerated his stuffy in-laws and was exasperatingly happy with his wife. In Bangladesh, he was Just Rashid, Henna's absentee henna-pecked husband, a rarely missed dullard who travelled a lot on business. Ricky would believe that all his time as Rashid, his twenty-five years of married life to Henna, had been illusory, his training ground, his purgatory, lightened only by the birth of his daughter. All that time, he had simply been waiting for his real life to begin. He had been waiting for Verity as long as she had been waiting for him, and she had finally arrived.

The Triumphant Return of Ricky
the Conqueror

T HE DAY AFTER Ricky met Verity Trueman and took her for supper at one of the least indifferent brasseries that Paris CDG had to offer, he went to his interview and performed with an urbane brilliance that he had not realized he still possessed. He was Ricky the Conqueror once more, the College Captain of Cricket and Captain of Men, with fire in his belly and a steely glint in his eye. Ricky realized how high the stakes were – getting the job meant a future in England with his own English rose, if she would have him.

The Global Head of Finance was impressed, and although he did not offer Ricky the job on the spot, made it clear that he thought Ricky was a very serious con-tender. He asked Ricky, off the record, whether his poten-tial relocation might cause any problems, suggesting that he might need to discuss it with his family and would need a certain amount of time to organize the move.

'I can move here as quickly as you need me,' Ricky said without a flicker of doubt. 'My daughter already lives in England, she'd be delighted if I were to move here.'

'And your wife?' asked the Global Head of Finance, a touch indiscreetly.

'My wife and I are separated,' said Ricky firmly. 'I have no ties in Bangladesh.'

Satisfied, the Global Head of Finance suggested that Ricky meet the team of people he'd be working with, should he be successful. The next week, Ricky would receive a call in the Dhaka office; the job was his.

Ricky the Conqueror's next task, which he was to take on the very same day, was that of wooing his English rose, although he didn't think of her as a rose at all; roses were showy, bumptious, over-ripe and blowsy, and like sirens they tempted you with their scents towards a bed of thorns. No, Verity was more like a violet; pale and shy, as delicate as whimsy. You needed to tread around violets at your feet as carefully as you trod around the dreams you had laid out on your narrow path – Ricky knew from experience that the slightest false step could crush them.

Ricky had already started putting his old life aside for his new life, beginning by cutting short his afternoon reunion with his errant daughter in order to be free to take Verity to dinner. He had arranged to meet Shona after his interview, at the tea-shop-cum-sweet-shop in Tooting, where Parvez was still working. Ricky hadn't seen Shona in months, not since her unexpected elopement, but while they had their tea (made on Shona's specific instruction the way she knew her Papa liked it), instead of deploring her ill-advised marriage to a Pakistani pauper, instead of drinking in the sight of her and revelling in her warm and happy glow, instead of passing on all of Henna's instructions, he found himself looking at his watch. It was almost 5 p.m. In an hour, Verity was due to leave her office, but he hadn't yet called her to arrange where to meet. He had intended to call her earlier, but his interview had overrun and he had been coaxed into pressing flesh with his new colleagues.

'Is there something wrong, Papa?' asked Shona, disconcerted that for the last hour, her father hadn't shown even the slightest sign of telling her off or commenting on her betrayal, as though it was already swept under the carpet and forgotten. He had hugged her with an unnatural bonhomie on his arrival, congratulated her on her Finals result (a respectable 2.1), told her enthusiastically about his interview and completely failed to mention either her marriage or her husband, or even comment on Parvez's infuriating absence. Now he just seemed distracted. Perhaps it was all too much for him to take in after his long flight: her new life in England, coupled with her new conspicuous poverty, given away too easily by the downtrodden area in which they lived, and by the confusing subcontinental familiarity and tackiness of the Tooting tea shop in which her husband worked. And this despite her well-pressed English clothes with the trendy shoulder pads and her gleaming golden wedding ring. Perhaps he had arrived intending to tell her off, but now felt too sorry for her to say I Told You So. Was that why he was hiding behind this odd and uncharacteristic bravado? Shona wished she could have met him in town, perhaps at the

Ritz, but she would not have been able to afford the bill. She surreptitiously glanced at the clock on the wall behind the tea-shop counter; Parvez had better come back from that damn Cash & Carry soon – tardiness was no way to give a good impression to a father-in-law. Her father was fidgeting with his watch strap distractedly, and showed no signs of having heard her. She hoped he would relax over dinner, berate her and Parvez, and get it over and done with. Shona sipped her tea, and cleared her throat noisily to ensure her father's attention.

'Of course, you'll stay for dinner, Papa? You must meet Parvez, and you can see our flat, it's just round the corner, we redecorated it ourselves.' She was pleased that they had at least managed to move out of Bhai Hassan's spare room in time for her father's visit.

Ricky, who had been thinking about where he could take Verity for their date, looked up at his daughter's wide eyes and lied with a merciless readiness that surprised even him.

'Jaan, I was just thinking that I should head off soon. I have an early flight in the morning and I'm still jet-lagged from yesterday. And the interview took a lot out of me. I'm sorry, I know it's been a long time.'

Shona nodded. This was the Papa she knew, tired, anxious and apologetic. He probably didn't want to see how she lived; it would upset him to see his daughter in a one-bedroom flat in this grimy part of London, however content and independent she professed herself to be. 'I suppose that I'll see you lots more in the UK if you get this job. Amma says you'll be travelling to and from here all the time. You can see the flat when you're next in town. Parvez will be sorry to have missed you.'

As Ricky went to leave, still looking at his watch, barely looking back at his daughter, Shona again misread his distraction for sorrow. She ran up to him and hugged him tightly at the doorway, protesting furiously, 'I'm very happy, Papa. Please don't think that I'm not. Parvez looks after me, I don't want for anything. I really couldn't be happier.'

Surprised by her vehemence, wondering what had brought it on, Ricky answered, 'I believe you, Jaan. I believe you are.' It made it easier for him to believe his daughter was happy and no longer needed anything from him, as it made it easier for him to ease himself away from her embrace and towards the phone box a safe distance away, knowing that on the other side of London, Verity was sitting listlessly in her office, waiting for his call.

Ricky eventually decided to take Verity for dinner at Rules off the Strand and, on seeing her discomfort, wished he'd chosen somewhere a little less stuffy. But once ensconced in a cosy booth, her boxy navy-blue jacket removed to reveal a pretty dress, the generous helpings and good wine helped her unwind. Verity found Ricky a disarmingly good listener, he seemed to hang on her every word, and she found herself opening like a flower, telling him about her past, about Pete and the one before who was just like Pete.

'I just wish I'd been less naive and stupid about it all. I'm almost thirty-eight, and I've wasted most of my life with people who didn't really care.' She looked at Ricky, who was nodding sympathetically, and apologized, 'Goodness, listen to me. You shouldn't let me go on so much. You haven't told me anything about you yet.'

'There's not much to tell,' said Ricky honestly, refilling her glass courteously. 'I had an arranged marriage when I was very young, which didn't work out. And I've been alone for a very long time. Too long, really. I'm forty-three, and I feel like I've wasted most of my life by not being with someone who cared, or whom I could care for.' Ricky smiled ruefully. 'I guess that's something we have in common.'

Verity's pale blue eyes widened, and she instinctively held her hand out across the table towards Ricky. He took it with great care, as though it was a fragile gift he'd been offered, before laying it back on the table underneath his own warm palm.

'Would you like coffee, Verity?' Ricky asked, seeing their officious waiter approach, and intercepting the request before the haughty tones of the waiter could put Verity back on her guard.

'No, thank you,' she answered, smiling nervously towards the waiter, withdrawing her hand discreetly to dab at her mouth with her napkin. Ricky nodded and asked for the bill, trying not to show his disappointment that Verity didn't want to extend their evening. Once the waiter had left, Verity, showing yet again that she had become the sort of woman who took things into her own hands, asked Ricky with a nervousness that even a gin and tonic and half a bottle of wine could not disguise, whether he might prefer to have that coffee back at her place.

'I know you've got an early flight tomorrow, so it's all right to say no. I was just thinking that we might not see each other for an awfully long time . . . that is, if you want to see me again. I can see how it might be difficult . . . with the distance, I mean.'

Ricky was seduced once more by her candour, by her laying herself on the line, awaiting his verdict, her wide-open eyes so used to being let down. It was like looking in a mirror. 'There is nothing I'd like better than to have a coffee with you at your place,' he said simply. He had only just found Verity, there was no way he was letting her go.

They took a cab to her little flat in Clapham, immaculately kept but with a cheerful splash of clutter in the spare room that reminded him of his own untidy study, and which made him feel instantly at home. He walked around the flat, looking at her books – romantic novels and Jane Austen – and her degree proudly displayed on the wall. He saw the photographs of her with her stern, horsey-looking parents, and of her on her horse, Brontë, that she kept at home. They had coffee and talked until the early hours, and this time Ricky did not need to present a flower, or to quote from a book of poetry, or to pounce manfully, to be able to hold his true love. He merely had to sit and wait, enjoying the rare pleasure of being himself. And when he finally had to leave, it was

Verity who kissed him, shyly turning up her head as she walked him to the door, and she tasted of bitter coffee, sweetened with brown sugar. A grown-up taste that he came to cherish above English tea.

Of Sunflowers and Sunny Side Ups

S HONA AND PARVEZ had been married for some time, and were perplexed as to why all their frequent and enjoyable lovemaking had not yet succeeded in bearing fruit. For the first few months, they had been philosophical, thinking perhaps they simply needed to be patient. The few months after that, while Parvez remained genial and relaxed, Shona became paranoid and tetchy. She had intended to put off continuing her studies for motherhood, and yet motherhood was stubbornly eluding her.

Convinced that it was their fault for being too naive and easy-going about the whole thing, she adopted a more businesslike approach to the matter of conception. She stood on her head after making love, and read voraciously on the best diets for them to follow. Parvez found the loving inedible messes that Shona used to produce in her attempts at home-cooking were replaced with unsalted, barely heated green leafy vegetables and steamed fish. His usual morning tea was switched for unappealing herbal alternatives, and his whisky bottle inexplicably banished. But Shona's enthusiastic efforts out of the bedroom were unfortunately not much more effective than their joint efforts within it. Every time her irregular menstruation began, she locked herself in the bathroom and cried secretly.

On one such occasion, Parvez had returned to the flat unexpectedly in the middle of the day to surprise Shona with some flowers, and heard muffled sobs through the bathroom door. He tried the door, but it was locked. 'Goldie, are you in there?' he asked unnecessarily, before asking the more pertinent question, 'Are you OK?'

He heard Shona blow her nose noisily, and answer in a tremulous voice that was intended to be stern, 'I'm fine. I'm just going to the loo. What are you doing back here?'

'I brought you a present, come out and see.'

'Just leave it somewhere, I'm going to be here a while. It's a woman thing.'

Parvez, nonplussed by this odd behaviour, stayed at the door. 'Are you sure you're OK – you don't sound it.'

'I said I'm fine – can't I get some damn privacy in my own bathroom?'

'I'm not leaving until I see that you're OK for myself. I'll be waiting in the living room.' Parvez tossed his flowers on the well-scrubbed kitchen table, annoyed that his gallant gesture had been circumvented, and, stalking to the sofa in the living room, sat down heavily.

Shona remained stubbornly in the bathroom and Parvez, watching the seconds and minutes tick by, eventually gave up. He went back to the bathroom, which opened off the back of the kitchen and, sighing, leaned his forehead against the door, the palm of his hand touching it. 'Goldie, I need to get back to work. Will you be all right?'

Shona had composed herself, and her voice sounded firm and almost cheerful, in an uncanny imitation of her father's false bonhomie the day he had visited, as she said, 'Of course, darling. There's no need to worry. It's just a stupid girl thing – sorry I'm taking so long.'

On the other side of the door, as she spoke to Parvez, Shona was mirroring him, her forehead leaning against the door, the palm of her hand flat against it, as though she could feel the heat of him through the white painted wood, trying to draw some solace from his closeness without having to let him near. She turned her face and looked at herself in the mirror above the sink, her eyes red, her face puffy and disfigured with tears, all its cheerful definition dissolved by her unhappiness. She was such a pitiful sight that her resolve almost weakened, and her fingers traced the door with yearning, willing herself to tell him the truth. It was too hard. Hearing Parvez finally walk away, she called out with the same firm, cheerful voice, 'I'll see you when you get back, thank you for the present, Puppy.'

When she was sure that Parvez was gone, Shona opened the door carefully and saw the golden sunflowers that he had left on the table. She picked them up and unaccountably held them to her nose even though she knew there would be no scent. She collapsed to the floor clutching them, letting the raw sobs tear wantonly through her body.

That evening Parvez came home to a smiling Stepford wife, wearing her pinny with pride as she cooked up a fish stew with yet more inedible vegetables, the flowers sunnily smiling from a vase at the centre of the table. She ran to the door and kissed him as he came in and Parvez, relieved that the mood was over, kissed her all the way back to the kitchen.

After dinner, Shona mentioned casually that she had picked up some leaflets from the local GP. She suggested they make an appointment. The surprise sunflower day was thus to mark the beginning of months and months of tests, in which Parvez's sperm was analysed and criticized, as were the contents of Shona's barren, non-ovulating womb.

'It's me,' Shona said to Parvez, over breakfast some months later. Having been persuaded by the gynaecologist to relax the restrictive diet she had previously forced Parvez to adopt, she had made his favourite dish the night before, lamb koftas, only slightly burnt this time, and maybe with just a bit too much garlic. Shona's cooking had not greatly improved, although Parvez was always uncomplaining and even complimentary at her efforts in the kitchen. As a result she had begun to think that her cooking was now quite acceptable, and for a special treat she gave him a couple of the less burnt koftas on the side of his fried eggs, with plenty of the juices from the pan to moisten his toast.

'Mmm, smells great, Goldie,' said Parvez insincerely, looking sorrowfully down at his quite acceptable sunny side ups ruined by the addition of burnt meatballs and black charcoal bits swimming in oily juice. 'I really don't think it's you, it's probably me.'

'It's me,' Shona disagreed stoutly, 'Look at my parents – they couldn't have any kids after me. I remember Mamma used to drag me off secretly to a clinic sometimes, but whatever they did, it didn't help. I must have inherited their infertility.'

'Well, if they were infertile, how did they have you?' Parvez asked.

'They were both very young, Mamma was only eighteen. Maybe they just got lucky.'

'Well, I was the one who got lucky, wasn't I,' said Parvez, reaching out to stroke Shona's forearm, so gently that the little hairs shivered under his palm. 'Really, Goldie, it's much more likely to be me. You're doing everything right. You eat like a Saint of Good Nourishment and they think you're responding to the medication. I'm the one with the lazy swimmers.'

'And I'm the one with the lazy ovaries.'

'If we're both that lazy, we should be spending a lot more time in bed. We could start after breakfast . . .' He traced an equally lazy line up Shona's arm to her bare shoulder, and back down again to her fingertips.

'It's not the right day yet – we have to hold off until

the day after tomorrow,' Shona said matter-of-factly, pouring herself another cup of decaffeinated tea.

'Arré, when did you get so businesslike . . .' Parvez said regretfully, returning his attention to breakfast. Realizing that there was no way he could avoid eating the koftas in front of Shona's watchful gaze, he made a manly attempt to spear some with his fried eggs.

'Puppy, if it doesn't work this time, what are we going to do about the next stage?' Shona asked delicately. She didn't need to say any more; if simply stimulating Shona's hitherto unproductive ovaries to ovulate didn't succeed, the next stage of assisted conception had a long waiting list, and after that there were only procedures which would most likely have to be done privately.

Parvez sighed and pushed his eggs away. 'I'll sort out something for us. I might be able to get a loan.' Shona didn't say anything in reply. There was no way he would get a loan; he had already taken one out to buy a share in the restaurant business across the road from the sweet shop, and it was all he could manage to pay the interest and the rent and their meagre housekeeping. Seeing her face, Parvez got up and walked round to her side of the table, kneeling at her side, and stroked the wedding ring on her hand. 'I promise, my Shundor Shona, that I'll work something out. I'd sell my soul to make you happy.'

Shona smiled a small hard smile, unconvinced by his expansive offer. Parvez squeezed her hand and, to lighten the mood, started one of their little in-jokes, delivering a corny chat-up line that usually made her laugh.

'Hey there, gorgeous, how do you like your eggs in the morning? Scrambled or Fried?'

'Unfertilized,' answered Shona automatically, although with little joy. She was already thinking how they might raise the money for private treatment and, not for the first time, she felt some resentment of their impoverished circumstances. She could perhaps sell her jewellery that had safely arrived from Bangladesh, but she didn't know how much it was worth, and it was all she had to pass on to her children, if they ever had any. If she was still at home her father would have been able to pay for all her treatment – but he was no longer responsible for her, and that had been her choice, not his. Perhaps she could remake that choice and ask him to take care of her once more in this one sensitive matter.

Shona thought about alternatives, but all roads and possibilities led back to one incontrovertible truth – her father was the only one who both could and would lend her the money for treatment; he was the only one who could help. She decided to visit her father's London apartment; she would go that very day.

A Glorious Spring Wedding for
Verity Trueman

Ricky and Verity accelerated their relationship in a manner that was viewed as positively unseemly and inappropriate by Verity's parents and friends. They advised her against getting involved too quickly with this foreign divorcé who, apart from being Asian, seemed too good to be true. Secretly they were jealous; Verity's poor life choices and unluckiness in love had always provided a secret, unworthy comfort to her nearest and dearest. Her parents had privately believed that their dowdy daughter would never get married, and although they had outwardly complained about still having her on their hands, they knew that this meant she would always need them. And her friends knew that whatever they did in life, they would never be as badly off as poor little Veetie, what with her horrible, feckless Pete, and the one before who was just like Pete; she made them all seem quite successful by comparison. So it was unthinkable that Verity, when she was quite beyond the age that anyone should reasonably expect to marry, was now in the throes of true love with an almost handsome, moderately successful, jet-setting businessman, who seemed to harbour only honourable intentions towards her.

The question that everyone asked, although no one asked out loud, was why would such a man choose Verity? Why would such a man, who could surely choose from many better-appointed contenders, choose a nervous, ageing administrator with a tremulous smile, whose youthful bloom had so clearly faded, leaving nothing to recommend her excepting a thinness of figure which was currently quite fashionable, and her English rose colouring? Perhaps it was because she was blonde – didn't Asian men always like blondes? They didn't understand the secret of Verity's innocent seduction, because they had never seen Ricky for the man he was before he met her; a man who had been unhappy for almost all his life. The secret was simple; with Verity, he saw the hope of happiness. That was all. That was enough.

Verity's family and friends actively made it their business to try and expose Ricky and find out the ulterior motive he might have for seeing their Veetie, persuading themselves they had only her best interests at heart. Ricky, aware of their suspicion, was acutely aware that they had good reason to be suspicious; he was still a married man, after all. He therefore went on an extraordinary charm offensive, wooing Verity's inner circle with the same enthusiasm with which he had wooed and won Verity's heart.

Invited to dinner back at Rules off the Strand, Gerry and Babs, Verity's horsey parents, found to their disappointment that their barbed comments that Ricky might be seeking a British passport failed to offend him or put him off. Instead he agreed with them that it was the first question he would ask any foreign adventurer intent on such a fair prize as their precious daughter, and reassured them that his corporation provided him with a flexible working visa for the UK and the markets with which he had to work, so that a British passport would prove neither necessary nor convenient. Looking across the table at their embarrassed daughter, whose earnest eyes silently pleaded, please like him, please don't chase him away, they found their stiffness melting, and even more so by the time they had got to the brandies that Ricky generously ordered. The third time Ricky asked them to dinner, it was to ask the permission of Gerry for his daughter's hand, and Gerry, touched despite himself at such old-fashioned good form, found he had neither the reason nor will to refuse. Shaking Ricky's hand, he surprised himself by hoping that Veetie didn't make a balls-up of this relationship like she had all the others.

Ricky's proposal to Verity, just a few months after they met, took her by surprise, as she had first taken him by surprise. Despite now having his own company flat in London, near the commuter station for his office in Slough, he often stayed at Verity's Clapham flat, sharing the bitter coffee that she brewed first thing in the morning before he left for his office or the airport, and last thing at night when he returned, taking her face between his hands to kiss her gently, as though she might break at his touch. One such evening he returned from a week's absence in Bangladesh and found Verity more nervous than usual, with no welcoming coffee brewed. She turned her face when he went to kiss her, and so he brushed his lips against her cheek and sat in the armchair opposite her, removing his tie. Ricky already understood Verity too well to be annoyed with her, or to suspect that this odd behaviour had anything to do with him.

'Is something wrong, Verity? Has something happened at work?' he asked gently, leaning forward. He often listened sympathetically to Verity's stories of mistreatment at the hands of her colleagues, and guessed that something had upset her. The sooner she found another job, the better. He had even started looking for openings in his own company that might interest her.

'Something's happened, Ricky. I've been dying to tell you for days, but I just couldn't tell you on the phone. To be honest, I've no idea how you'll take it. I hope you'll be OK with it.'

Ricky felt his heart sink; it was like his wedding night all over again, a sudden revelation that was about to break his happy idyll. Was his Verity ill? Or had she found someone else? He said nothing, and just looked at Verity, waiting dumbly for her to pronounce the sentence that would dash all his dreams. Verity took a deep breath, trying to control the quiver in her voice.

'I'm pregnant. I know you thought that you couldn't have children, and I thought it was too late for me. But there it is, I'm pregnant.' Looking at Ricky, whose mouth was wide open in shock, Verity lost the battle to stay calm and firm, and quickly pleaded, 'Ricky, please say something. Please tell me you're pleased.'

Ricky closed and opened his mouth, struggling to master himself, before managing to say, 'Verity, are you sure, are you absolutely sure?' Verity nodded dumbly, waiting for him to pronounce the sentence that would dash all her dreams. What if he didn't want the baby, what if he thought they were too old for children, what if he just wasn't ready to make this sort of commitment so early in their relationship? Five years ago, Pete had made her abort their child, saying he wasn't ready for children. She couldn't lose this one, she just couldn't. This was her last chance to have a child with someone she loved, maybe her last chance to have a child at all.

Ricky stood up, walked heavily over to the armchair where Verity was sitting and, kneeling down, put his arms around her waist and buried his head in her lap. Realizing he was crying, Verity started crying too, for herself, for him, for the baby. Imagine letting herself get knocked up at her age, like some stupid teenager. Everything had been going so well, and somehow she had managed to ruin things for them all. 'Oh, Ricky,' she said helplessly. Ricky looked up at her, his face wet with his tears.

'How can you ask me if I'm pleased? Verity, my darling Verity, we're going to have a baby, we're going to be a family.'

Having started to cry when she had feared the worst, now the worst was over, Verity found she simply couldn't stop. Ricky lifted himself onto one knee before her and, taking her hand, surprised them both by saying, 'Verity Felicity Trueman, I think you'd better marry me as soon as possible, and make me the happiest man on earth.'

Fighting to smile through her tears, Verity just sobbed and nodded, holding tightly on to Ricky's hand.

The engagement thus confirmed, Ricky truly was the happiest man on earth. Barely six months before, his daughter had eloped with a Pakistani, leaving him bereft and abandoned in his dark Dhaka house, with no one to love him and nothing to reflect upon except how his life had passed him by and how it was too late, much too late, to do anything about it. Now he had a job and a home in England, and a woman who both loved and needed him, who had agreed to marry him, and was about to bear his child. His real life had begun, and taken over the old life that he had doffed as quickly as he had doffed his old name. He was looking forward to his first English Christmas with Verity, and the only dark clouds on the horizon were the fortnightly trips back to Bangladesh, to keep up appearances with Henna.

Given the circumstances, Ricky did not think Verity would want a big wedding; it was his second marriage, there was an obvious reason to marry in haste and they were hardly of an age for meringue lace and orange blossom to be appropriate. He was thinking of a simple civil service at the Chelsea Registry Office, with confetti thrown on the steps outside, and then a champagne lunch for ten at the Ritz, just with Verity's immediate family, their witnesses, bridesmaids and best man, whoever that might be. He would wear his best suit, or perhaps hire a morning suit, and Verity would look charming in a pill-box hat and Chanel suit, beautifully tailored to hide the signs of a telltale bulge.

However, on meeting some of Verity's female friends, whom she had kept away from Ricky until the engagement in the sure knowledge that they would flirt with him and show him what he was missing by tying himself down to her, Ricky realized how much this wedding meant to Verity. Her friends, with their shiny lipsticked mouths, fashionably sprayed hair and talon nails, had all been married already, and said how pleased they were that it was finally little Veetie's turn. She had been a bridesmaid several times, and they had all but given up hope of her becoming a bride. As Verity smiled and nodded to her friends' questions, comments and suggestions for their wedding, Ricky saw that his quiet Verity had always dreamed of the day when she could walk up the aisle in a gleaming white dress and have her moment in the sun, for once the centre of attention. The day where she could prove to all her friends and family that she was quite as good as the rest of them, as she too had finally found someone to love her.

Ricky regretfully abandoned all thoughts of the pleasant little lunch for ten, and enthusiastically helped Verity plan their glorious spring wedding at her parents' village, with a cream satin dress embroidered with false pearls on the bodice, an organist to accompany her up the aisle of the pretty local church and a wedding breakfast for a hundred in a marquee on her parents' land. The hardest part for him was finding enough guests to fill his side of the church; he invited a good deal of his work colleagues, and his local cricket club and tennis partners. He surprised his boss by asking him to be his best man. He explained the lack of immediate family apologetically to Verity – his mother was too unwell to make the journey from Bangladesh, his brother Aziz was needed to look after her, and besides, they had never approved of him moving to England, so much so that they were all but estranged. 'So you see, Verity, you are my family; you're really all the family I have. And you're all the family I need,' he told her sincerely, and Verity was touched that she was enough to replace his mother and brother for him.

The wedding itself passed in a vivid blur for Ricky. Satisfied by how truly happy Verity looked and acted, his only regret was that his daughter wasn't there to participate. She was only thirty miles away in a poky flat in Tooting while he was sipping champagne in a flower-filled tent, with his new in-laws laughing at his jokes. He wished he could have invited her and then cast a magic spell so that she would forget all about it; in a funny way, he thought Shona would have been happy for him, on this day of all days. In a funny way, he thought she would have understood.

The Importance of Not Forgetting to Check Under the Bed

R ICKY WAS BARELY back from his honeymoon in Florence when Shona called, quite out of the blue, to say that she needed to see him.

'Papa? Good, I'm glad you're in. I need to see you about something urgent, I'll be over in an hour.'

Ricky, who had only popped to the company flat to pick up some of his books, looked nervously around. It seemed to him to have every telltale sign of his double life on its neutral, uninhabited walls. 'No need to rush all the way here, Jaan. I'll come over to you. Did you want me to take something to Bangladesh for you? I can pick it up from your place.'

Shona didn't want to see her father in Tooting in case word got back to Parvez. She didn't want him to know anything about the meeting. 'No,' she said firmly, 'it's really best if I come over to you. I know where it is, I've looked it up in the A–Z. I'll see you soon, Papa. I'll bring you some food from here, some samosas and things . . .'

Ricky, reverting back to Just Rashid, lost the will to argue and let Shona have her way. Looking round the flat more closely, he decided he really didn't have too much to worry about. It was fortunate that he and Verity stayed here so little, he mainly used it as storage for his non-essential items, as Verity's flat was so tiny it could only just about fit his clothes, toiletries and work things. He then remembered with a cold shudder that Verity had offered to come over with him that morning to keep him company, not wishing to lose the easy intimacy of their honeymoon. Thank goodness he had urged her to stay in bed and relax. Imagine how it would have been to answer the phone to Shona with his pregnant wife in the room, his two worlds colliding down the wire. He would have had no idea how to have dealt with it; perhaps if it were to happen, he could simply speak to Shona in Bangla, so Verity wouldn't understand or suspect anything. But he never spoke Bangla to anyone, so that would seem suspicious in itself.

Shaking his head at the narrow escape, Ricky began methodically tidying away anything in the flat that he thought looked suspicious. The framed picture of Verity was taken down, wrapped lovingly in a tea towel and hidden in the bedroom drawer which held the spare bed linen. He replaced it with a shot of Henna and Shona which he had kept for just such an occasion. He inspected the bathroom for any feminine pots and potions and put them away; Verity kept a towelling robe hanging on the back of the bathroom door, which he removed and hung up in the wardrobe. The bedroom looked tidy and sterile, like a hotel room. The kitchen had very little in it, just some tea and coffee. It all seemed quite harmless. Satisfied, he popped out to buy some milk to make tea with.

He might take his daughter out for lunch somewhere, if she had the time. That would give her less time to inspect the flat. He wondered what the urgent matter was that she had to discuss, and why she wanted to come halfway across London to discuss it. Of course! She was doubtless having trouble with the Pakistani; that's why she didn't want to see him in Tooting. Well, he'd be as supportive as possible, and not tell her I Told You So; he knew from experience that life was too short to spend it tied to the wrong person.

Shortly after Shona was due to arrive, the phone rang again. She must have got lost and needed directions. Ricky picked up the phone. 'Hello, Jaan,' he said automatically.

'Darling it's me. Who's Jaan?' asked Verity with surprise.

'I knew it was you,' said Ricky, cursing himself for his stupid assumption. What was it he'd told his junior colleagues during a training seminar the other day? 'Never assume, ladies and gentlemen. A lesson as vital in business as it is in life. Remember what assume spells – "ass-u-me" – when you assume, you're making an ass out of both you and me.' They had all laughed respectfully at his little witticism – he was their boss after all. 'It just sort of means "Darling" in Urdu, I thought I'd surprise you.'

'Well, Caro Ricky, you certainly did,' laughed Verity with relief, pleased to have a chance to use the smattering of Italian she had picked up from the honeymoon. 'Are you going to be long? I thought I might make us some lunch.'

'I'm sorry, I am. My books are in a mess and I need to

sort them out to find the ones I'm looking for. I'll be back in a few hours.'

'Well, I can come to you and cook over there, if you like,' Verity offered sweetly. 'I said I didn't mind keeping you company.'

'No, I want you to stay home and rest,' said Ricky firmly, before adding jokily, 'We can't have you gadding about town in your condition.' Verity giggled and was about to say something, when the doorbell rang, followed by a sharp rap on the door. Shona had arrived.

Ricky stood stock-still, aware that his nightmare had occurred. His two spinning worlds on a collision course in this apartment, Verity on the phone, listening and wondering who was visiting, and Shona's knuckles descending to rap once more on the door, signalling the fatal impact. She had only to open her mouth, and call out, 'Papa,' and that would be the end of everything.

'Well, aren't you going to get that?' asked Verity.

'It's just a delivery for the man in the flat next door. He had to pop out, so I said I didn't mind getting it for him,' said Ricky with extraordinary presence of mind, skipping speedily as far out of the room as the phone cord would allow, so Shona wouldn't be able to hear him through the door. 'I'd better go and sign for it. I'll see you later, Verity darling.' Just as he hung up the phone, Shona's voice called out, ringing clearly through the whole flat, 'Papa? Papa! Are you there?'

Ricky took a deep breath, composing himself before opening the door. 'Sorry Jaan, I was on the phone,' he apologized.

'Was it Amma?' asked Shona, kissing him on his cheek and walking in to survey the apartment with daughterly interest. 'This is a nice place. Lots of space just for you, though. You must rattle around in here.' Oh God, thought Ricky. She's left the Pakistani and wants to move in with me. Attempting to change the subject from that of his apartment's spaciousness, he just said, 'No, it wasn't your Amma. She never calls me when I'm away on business.'

'Well, London isn't exactly away on business, is it?' pointed out Shona. 'Amma says you practically live here five days a week.' Ricky shrugged in acknowledgement; in fact, he only went back to Bangladesh every fortnight, and then just for a couple of days. However, it didn't surprise him that Henna had not remarked upon his lengthy absences; she probably hadn't even noticed, as she was just concerned with the keeping up of appearances, too. He had become vaguely aware, on his last visit, that Henna and his little brother appeared to have widened the personal interests that they were pursuing beyond Henna's amateur dramatics, and were now spending an unseemly amount of time with each other. The revelation had filled him with nothing so much as relief – if they were busy flirting they would have less time to suspect him of any untoward behaviour.

Shona inspected the untidy boxes of books in the middle of the living room. She recognized some of her father's favourite volumes and cherished first editions. 'Goodness, Papa! What are all these doing here? Won't you miss having them at home?' When she lived at home, she remembered how her father would shut himself away in the cheerful untidiness of his office, his little haven to which her mother, Nanu, uncle and the servants never sought entry; and away from the disconcerting hubbub of the household, he would sit with just his books for company. His books were his comfort in Dhaka – they were his best friends, his companions.

Ricky wished his daughter was as unobservant as her mother. He shrugged his shoulders casually. 'Well, you know what your Nanu is like. I asked for a few books, and she had Musharaf bundle up the whole lot of them and send them over. I was just sorting them out.'

'Are you going to send them back, then?' asked Shona, nodding with understanding. Her grandmother had no interest in her son's books, and would be very likely to ask her old retainer to send them all, rather than go to the trouble of picking out a selected few.

'Well, I thought about it, but it's such a needless expense. I may as well keep them here and take them back as I need them. And besides, it's nice to have them here in the evenings. And I read a lot on the plane,' Ricky added uncomfortably, before again attempting to distract Shona from his discomfort. 'Would you like some tea, Jaan?'

'I'd love some, thank you,' replied Shona, wondering why her father seemed so ill at ease. Seating herself on the sofa, she picked up his favourite leather-bound collection of Shakespeare's tragedies, and looked searchingly towards Ricky who was busying himself in the kitchen, with dawning comprehension. If her father had decided to keep his books here, he must really have started to think of London as home. But if this was where he was living, where did that leave his relationship with her mother? She wondered if her father had heard what some gossips were saying about her mother and uncle, and had decided to stay away on purpose. Her poor father. Chased away from his own family home by the unkind, unfounded words of busybodies; no wonder he had sought refuge in England, the place of his happy bachelor days. But this flat was no refuge, it was certainly no home from home; grand though it was in dimensions, it was severely lacking in character and comforts – the only personal feature was the photo of her and Amma on the mantelpiece, and even this had a somewhat wistful air, as though harking back to a past life.

She followed Ricky into the kitchen, marvelling at its gleaming state of disuse – the enamel hob looked like it had never been cooked on. Opening the fridge to deposit her gift of samosas and bhajis, she noticed that it was empty, apart from a pint of milk. Of course, her father couldn't cook for himself. She guessed he ate out most nights, or perhaps ate at work.

'This place needs a woman's touch, Papa. It's like a hotel room, it's so impersonal. Do you want me to come round and decorate it for you?'

Ricky smiled at the genuine concern in his daughter's voice. 'It's company property, so I can't do too much to it. It's fine, I like it.'

'Still, it's no way to live. I could make it cosier for you. Bring some flowers, some nice cushions and candles. Help you put out your books. I could even come round and cook for you the odd night. I've become quite a good cook now – Parvez loves my koftas.'

Ricky remembered why his daughter was here in the

first place and sighed. She clearly wanted to stay with him. 'That's very kind of you, Jaan, but really, there's no need.' Picking up the tea tray on which he had carefully laid a pot of tea, the sugar bowl and the milk jug, he walked through to the sitting room. There seemed little point in putting off the inevitable, so as he sat down, he raised the subject of the Pakistani with fatherly concern. 'So how is young Parvez? I'm glad you're feeding him well.'

Instead of responding with the anticipated barrage of complaints about her husband, Shona surprised her father with her warm and effusive reply. 'Parvez is wonderful. He's got a great business head; he's already bought part of a restaurant across the street. He's managing that as well as the tea shop now – he works so hard he hardly has a spare minute. He barely plays his music any more – you remember how he used to love his music? All he does is think about us and our future.'

Ricky was confused. This didn't seem to add up at all. If Shona was happy with the Pakistani, then why was she here? Had she heard rumours about her mother's insensitive flirtation with hapless Aziz? Pouring the tea with a delicate splash of milk, he passed a teacup to his daughter. 'Thanks, Papa,' she said and, reaching for the sugar, noticed something odd. 'Papa, the sugar's brown.'

'Sorry, Jaan, I know. It's all I have.'

'But why brown?' Shona asked. Her father had never had brown sugar in his life, as far as she was aware.

'I have it with coffee, in the mornings sometimes.' Coffee? Shona raised her eyebrows, and Ricky felt obliged to explain himself. 'I've discovered that coffee is better at keeping me awake if I've had a long flight, or have a long day ahead. They drink a lot of coffee at work here in England. Sometimes you can't even get tea. I guess I've just got used to it now. Coffee, I mean.'

At this uncharacteristic gabble Shona realized that her father was lying to her, but she had no idea why he would lie about something as inconsequential as coffee and brown sugar. Deciding not to let herself get distracted by her papa's strange behaviour, she bravely plunged into the reason for her visit. 'Papa, I need to ask you for something. Parvez would be furious if he knew that I was asking this, that's why I had to come here.' Ricky waited, on tenterhooks, saying nothing. 'I'm going to need you to lend me some money. In fact, give me some money. It's very important.'

Ricky tried to stop himself sighing with relief. How obvious it was, and how dense he'd been. His daughter, living in poverty in south London after her ill-advised love marriage, had something urgent to ask him – of course, it was just to ask for some cash. It was so simple, and so easily resolved. He could wave his pen like a magic wand over his cheque book, and make all his and her troubles go away with one magnanimous gesture.

'Of course, Jaan. How much do you need, say about £500?' Doubtless she needed the money for some unexpected repair, or to replace one of the old appliances in her kitchen.

Shona took a deep breath. 'No, Papa, I think more like £15,000. Maybe even more.'

Ricky almost dropped his teacup. 'Shona, are you in trouble? Is Parvez in trouble with his loan?' He'd heard stories about these south London loan sharks, getting people into debt and charging outrageous interest. But how could they be so much in debt so soon? They'd not even been in England for a year. Shona realized instantly what her father was thinking, and reassured him quickly.

'No, Papa, no. It's nothing like that. It's for something private, something medical.'

'But are you ill, Jaan?' asked Ricky with concern, looking at Shona critically. She had never looked healthier, but these women's things sometimes didn't show.

'No, Papa, I'm not ill. Neither is Parvez. But I do need the money. Please don't ask me to explain why.'

'Jaan, that's a lot of money, I'll have to talk to your mother about it.' Ricky was thinking about the wedding and honeymoon that he had already paid for, and the plans that he had to buy a house with Verity. He had done a great deal of creative accounting so that Henna would not suspect the enormous sums he was siphoning off his salary each month; fortunately, an increase in his salary had ensured he could continue sending an acceptable sum back to Bangladesh.

'Papa, please. I don't want Amma to know. I don't want anyone to know. It's cost me a lot to even come and ask you, but I have no one else to go to.' Shona put down her teacup, looking almost tearful. 'Please think about it, Papa. You're my last hope.' Dabbing at her eyes, she got up and asked where the bathroom was.

'The bathroom's ensuite, through the bedroom,' said Ricky distractedly.

Shona walked swiftly through to the bathroom where, after locking the door, she put down the toilet seat and sat on top of it. If she gave her father a little time by himself, thinking that she was crying in the bathroom, he would hopefully be more likely to capitulate to her outrageous request.

Looking around, she saw that there was toothpaste in the bathroom, but no toothbrush. Doubtless her father was keeping it in his toiletry bag, as though he was living in a hotel and was expected to pack up at a moment's notice. All his clothes were probably still neatly folded in his suitcase. Wandering back through the very neat, bare bedroom, she wondered where his suitcase was; it wasn't on top of the wardrobe or anywhere obvious. Opening the wardrobe, she saw no luggage there, either, just a solitary cream towelling robe hanging up, looking rather lonely. Something was wrong, very wrong indeed. If her father was no longer living in Bangladesh, he must be living here. But where were all his clothes? Feeling a touch guilty, she gently pulled open one of the drawers. It was empty apart from bed linen. The rest of the drawers were empty altogether. There must be some explanation. Of course, the suitcase was under the bed! Dropping to her knees, she looked underneath and saw no suitcase at all. Instead, she saw a pair of cream bedroom slippers, with pretty stitching on them. She realized that they matched the towelling robe in the wardrobe. Shona's mind ticked over rapidly. Coffee and brown sugar. The bare, uninhabited flat. The unexplained absence of both toothbrush and suitcase. The inexplicable presence of both towelling robe and pretty cream slippers. Ladies' slippers. Her father wasn't living here, after all. He was, very possibly, living with a lady who wore size 6 shoes, who liked coffee and brown sugar.

Going back to the living room, after rubbing at her eyes to make them red and tender-looking, Shona sat down silently opposite her father. Ricky asked gently, 'Shona, Jaan. This is clearly very important to you. But how do you think I'm going to be able to hide spending £15,000 from your mother?'

Shona looked straight at him. 'Papa, you're an accountant. And you're a very good accountant. I know you can hide spending £15,000 from Amma.' She glanced downwards, before giving an almost imperceptible nod towards the bedroom. 'You can hide all sorts of things, if you want to.' She added significantly, reassuringly, 'We both can.'

Ricky realized instantly that Shona knew. He didn't know how she knew, but she did. He also knew that she wouldn't tell. Her eyes made a promise to him, Keep My Secret, and I'll Keep Yours. The fatal impact he feared would never happen and their family would remain safe in ignorance, held together by the close-knit embrace of their lies. Shona reached for his hand and squeezed it. 'Papa?' she said questioningly. Ricky nodded slowly, and squeezed her hand back. They had made a deal, and shaken on it.

'Can I take you out for lunch, Jaan?' Ricky said, with a rueful smile. His clever, observant daughter. She was wasted on her mother, wasted on that Pakistani. Wasted on him, even.

'That would be lovely, Papa. But just a quick one. I need to get back before Parvez misses me.'

Ricky picked up Shona's coat and helped her into it

with instinctive courtesy, the natural gentleman. The phone started ringing as they left the flat, and they glanced at each other only for a moment before tacitly agreeing to ignore it.

The Middle-Naming of the Sons of Parvez and Shona Khan

AFTER THE INVASIVENESS and discomfort of the fertility treatment, when Shona's pregnancy was finally confirmed, she was too overjoyed to believe it. Although constantly sick right from the beginning, and gaining weight at an alarming rate, she superstitiously insisted that she and Parvez not celebrate, or even tell anyone, until she had her first scan. The scan showed the pregnancy was well established, and revealed the reason for Shona's unseemly size and unusual level of sickness – there were two heartbeats instead of one. They were having twins.

After they left the hospital, Parvez picked Shona up and gleefully swung her around. 'Goldie – we've hit the jackpot! It's like these bloody London buses. You wait years for a baby and then two come along at once! Instant families!'

'Parvez, put me down!' protested Shona firmly. 'Think about the babies.'

Surprised by the unexpected solemnness in her tone that replaced her usual flirtatious banter, and even more so by the alien sound of his real name from her lips, Parvez put her down immediately. 'What are you first-naming me for?' he asked reproachfully. 'You only call me Parvez when you're upset with me. Aren't you excited, Goldie?'

'I'm sorry, Puppy,' Shona said appeasingly. 'Of course I'm excited. They're my children, too. It's just that we have to be careful now – we're so lucky that we conceived, I don't want anything to harm them.' Parvez was pouting, and she added, to mollify him, 'Besides, I'll need to get used to calling you Parvez when the babies come along. We can't have them thinking that your name is Puppy. They should learn to call you Baba.'

'Why Baba?' complained Parvez peevishly. 'It sounds like a cartoon elephant. Baba indeed! You don't even call your own father Baba. And it's not as if I'm even Bangla-deshi,' Parvez said.

'Well, Abbu then,' said Shona. 'They can call you Abbu like good little Pakistani boys.'

'I don't want good little boys,' retorted Parvez, his voice softening as he added, 'I want good little golden girls who'll look just like their Amma.' He traced Shona's jawline. 'The prettiest Amma in the world,' he whispered, kissing her.

'I'm pretty sure that they'll look more like you,' Shona said after their kiss. 'You have stronger genes.'

However, when the boys were born, tiny and perfect, in a south London hospital, Parvez couldn't see himself in them at all. Sitting quietly with Shona some hours after the terror and excitement of the birth, he found himself inspecting them critically. They were so pale, paler even than Shona, with the milky whiteness that the Karim clan had. They looked like milky-faced Karims through and through. Shona, holding the little aliens, looked up at Parvez's handsome, confused face, willing him to keep hold of the thrilled reaction he had when the first bloody baby had emerged, willing him to feel the paternal pride in their shared achievement. 'This one has your eyes, I think,' she said, passing their first-born to him.

'But his eyes are blue, Goldie,' replied Parvez, holding his child gingerly. He instantly regretted his prosaic comment; out loud it sounded almost petulant.

'All babies' eyes are blue, Puppy. But he will have your eyes, I can tell,' Shona said firmly. 'And this one has your nose,' she added, brushing her lips against the tiny forehead of the child that lay in her arms.

Parvez saw this tiny, delicate gesture and realized what was wrong, and why his reaction to these tiny longed-for miracles was now so muted. Since Shona had first come to Pakistan for her studies, he had suffered no other competition for her affections; no one else had ever come close. Her father seemed to love her, but despite living near her in London, had kept a distance that was so respectful of their privacy that it bordered on the disinterested. And as for her mother – Parvez had no time for Shona's self-seeking, self-interested mother. She had deigned to visit them just once during the whole of Shona's difficult, uncomfortable pregnancy, during which she had sniffed at their surroundings, criticized their home and put the fear of God in Shona about the actual birth by telling her how her maternal grandmother had bled to death. Henna had proceeded to spend the rest of her trip shopping in town, buying the Burberry raincoat that absent-minded Just Rashid had so far forgotten to get her, despite her repeated requests. No, Shona had no one apart from Parvez, and Parvez had no one apart from Shona, his Bhai Hassan notwithstanding. It was just the two of them, Shona and Parvez, Goldie and Puppy, against the world.

But suddenly, in the last six hours, the children had stopped being part of Shona and had become their own independent, crying, breathing persons; two little people that Shona would love just as much as him – in fact, more than him, as they were two, and he was only one. And they were her creation – she had made them with almost no help from him; he had simply accompanied her to the fertility clinic a few times, and masturbated into a tube. Every other visit and painful medical procedure, Shona had handled alone, while he went to work and continued building up the business. He was no longer the only man in Shona's life – now he had competition. He was already jealous of Shona's children.

Grateful that Shona hadn't realized the unworthy thoughts muddling his head, Parvez squeezed himself a bit closer to Shona on her hospital bed. The baby in his arms squirmed a little, and then settled with a yawn. 'What shall we call them?' he asked Shona. She smiled benignly; they had discussed lots of names, some family ones, some silly ones, but had agreed to make no decisions until they were born.

'I think we should name them both after you.'

'Parvez 1 and Parvez 2? Like Thing 1 and Thing 2 in Dr Seuss? I like that.'

'No, I think we should call them Omar and Sharif. After their daddy with the movie-star looks,' she said sweetly, without any hint of sarcasm.

'They'll never forgive us, Goldie,' laughed Parvez, pleased despite himself. 'Ouf!' he said, as, disturbed from his brief slumber, Sharif grabbed his finger with a healthy grip. 'This one's strong, let's call him Samson instead.'

'I think that's Jewish,' Shona said vaguely. 'Let's stick with Omar Sharif.'

'Those can be their middle names,' suggested Parvez. 'Why don't we call one after your Baba, and the other after my Abbu?'

'I think Papa would like that,' Shona agreed. 'Rashid Omar Khan and Khalid Sharif Khan,' she tried musingly. 'Those seem such big names for such little boys.'

'They'll grow into them,' Parvez said.

But they never did grow into them. They were called by their middle names throughout infancy by unthinking habit, one of Parvez and Shona's silly, long-running jokes, like their own pseudonyms of Puppy and Goldie. Once they got older, whenever their father or mother called them by their formal first names, on rare occasions when propriety or sternness demanded, the boys replied reproachfully, with the woeful puppy-dog look copied from their father, 'What are you first-naming me for?' As though they were being unfairly told off for something they hadn't done.

The Married Life of Ricky Karim and Verity Trueman

RICKY AND VERITY had their first argument shortly after their wedding and, predictably enough, it was about names. Ricky came back late one evening from the airport and, on drowsily entering the tiny Clapham flat, was surprised to see that Verity was not only still awake, but sitting at the table, surrounded by forms and paperwork.

'Hello, darling,' she said brightly, on seeing him hesitating at the door. 'Would you like some coffee? I've just put on a new pot. It's decaffeinated.'

'Verity, darling,' said Ricky, crossing the room to kiss her. 'You must make sure you get enough rest, it's not good for the baby. What on earth are you doing up at this ungodly hour? It must be close to midnight.' He checked his watch, 'In fact it's one in the morning; that cab must have taken me round the houses.'

'I couldn't sleep. I was lying awake waiting for you to come back, when I realized that I've been married for over four weeks, and no one would even guess it. I went into a shop yesterday and I paid for some groceries with a cheque, and they called me "Miss", not "Madam". Here I am, practically forty, married and pregnant, and I'm still getting called Miss! And you want to know why?'

Ricky sat down and took off his tie and jacket. 'Well, you're not forty yet, and you certainly look nothing near it. And they might not have seen your wedding ring. And you're not really showing very much yet. You're so slim normally that the extra weight looks like nothing. You could hardly see a thing even in your wedding dress; all the guests who didn't know you were pregnant kept saying how lovely you looked now that you'd gained a few curves.'

Verity acknowledged the compliment and patted Ricky's hand, but said almost sternly, 'It's not because of any of those things, darling. It's because my cheque book said Miss Verity Trueman. What else are people going to think?' So I've decided to write to everyone: the passport office, the driving licence people, the banks, everyone, and get them to change my name to Mrs Verity Karim. I really should have done it weeks ago, but we were so busy with the wedding, and the honeymoon and . . .'

Ricky surprised them both by interrupting Verity vehemently. 'No! Verity, I'm putting my foot down. I absolutely forbid it!'

'But forbid what, darling?' asked Verity, confused.

'You changing your name. You have a perfect name. You should absolutely never change it. Your name is beautiful and wonderful, and it's staying the same.'

'But Ricky, darling. Everyone I know changes their name when they get married, it's practically odd not to.'

'Well, then, let's be odd. Your name is important to me – it stands for everything I love about you.'

'But Ricky, I want to change it. Don't you understand? I want to be Mrs Verity Karim. I want the world to know. Don't you?'

'Verity,' Ricky said heatedly, 'I don't want you changing your name. I wouldn't have married you if I thought that you'd be changing it.'

'Ricky, that's just cruel!' said Verity, her lip trembling. 'How can you say you wouldn't have married me . . . It's only my name I want to change, it's not me . . .' Blinking back tears, she ran to the kitchen.

Ricky realized he had gone too far, and went after her. 'Verity, I'm sorry, I'm tired. I didn't mean to upset you. You just took me by surprise. We'd never even discussed you changing your name.'

Verity had been dabbing her eyes ineffectively with coarse kitchen towel, which she put down quickly when Ricky came in, busying herself instead with the coffee percolator. 'I'm not upset,' she said bravely, her eyes still wet with the tears she hadn't managed to wipe away. 'I just came in to get the coffee.'

'Here, let me do that,' said Ricky appeasingly, and taking the steaming pot of coffee off the plate, poured out two cups, stirring in the brown sugar; he brought them through to the sitting room.

Verity sat down heavily beside him on the sofa, her face messy with sudden unhappiness. She nursed her hot coffee for a moment, and then said quietly, with a gentle hiccup, 'Don't you want people to know I'm your wife?'

'Darling, of course I do!' said Ricky. 'We haven't done anything in secret – we had an enormous wedding in your parents' village and announced it to the world.' Lightening the mood had never been his strong point, but he joked feebly, 'We'll get the wedding shots back from the photographer soon, in case you don't remember.'

Verity hiccupped sadly again, 'I don't mean the people at the wedding. I mean your people. Your family. Why haven't I met your brother, or your sister-in-law, or your mum? Or any of the people from Bangladesh that you see when you're here? Don't you want them to know that you married an English girl?'

Ricky paused for a moment, wondering what sister-in-law she could be talking about. Then he remembered that he had once let slip to Verity about Henna's presence in the house back in Bangladesh, and had passed her off as Aziz's wife, which didn't seem quite like lying. Buying a bit of time, he reached over to his jacket and pulled out some of the dark bitter mints that Verity liked; he had bought them at the airport while waiting for his plane home. Setting them on the table between their coffee cups, he took Verity's hand firmly. 'Darling, I meant what I said before. You're my family. Those other people mean very little to me, and I mean very little to them. Even my own Ammie makes it very clear that she prefers not to have me around, she would rather have Aziz and her daughter-in-law, and so that's what she's got.' So far, so true. He took a surreptitious breath and, looking frankly into Verity's eyes, prepared to lie to reassure her. 'And of course they all know about you. It's me they disapprove of, not you. They didn't like me before, for not managing the farms and being a dutiful son and heir. And now I've gone and married an English girl in an English church, hardly the act of a good Muslim.'

Verity sniffed, not quite appeased, and said, 'I just don't want to be excluded from your world. I've been left out enough in my life as it is.'

Ricky answered, sincerely, 'I don't want you to feel that you're excluded from my world. You can't be, you and the baby are my world.' Seeing Verity's eyes lift towards him, shining with hope and happiness, he made a decision, and committed to it so quickly that he surprised himself with his resolve. 'If it'll make you happier, I'll only go back to Bangladesh every month, or less if I can manage it, and only for an overnight stay at most, just to check on the lands and that Ammie's still kicking and complaining. And I'll stop seeing the people who turn up from Bangladesh – I only meet up with them out of politeness anyway.' He thought with a fleeting, genuine sorrow about Shona – the imaginary visitors from Bangladesh were almost always an excuse which would allow him to see her occasionally; he would have to try and see her during working hours now. Besides, Shona didn't need him; she had his money for whatever secret she had planned; she had her husband and her life in Tooting. She was more of an exile from the family than even he was.

Verity nodded, her tears almost dried up, and was even able to give Ricky a tremulous smile. 'That would make me happier. But I still don't understand. You'll share your life with me, but not your name.'

Ricky had an idea. 'Why don't we share our names, Verity? If it means so much to you to take my name, I'll take yours, too. What do you think? Mr and Mrs True-man-Karim?'

Verity was astounded. 'You'll take my name, too? I mean, you don't mind? On your passport and everything?'

'What?' said Ricky, this time his attempt at humour judged a bit more accurately. 'Don't you like the idea? You mean you'll share your life with me, but not your name?'

'Oh, Ricky,' said Verity, hugging him with sudden delight. 'You do love me! You do want the world to know about us.'

In the congenial coffee-scented embrace that followed, in those early hours of the morning, while Ricky fed Verity her favourite bitter-mint chocolates, he reflected that spinning a lie was like spinning smooth threads of chocolate; it melted in the mouth sweetly, and made everything so much more palatable. He had no intention of changing all his paperwork – he would keep a separate set for his different lives; his Bangladeshi passport would remain the same, but the British passport which he could apply for now that he and Verity were married would carry his new, married name.

The second disagreement that Ricky and Verity had was also about names. This time it was about the name of their child – a wonderful long-limbed little girl with pale, creamy skin and lustrous chestnut hair. Ricky, predictably, wanted to name her Verity, but this time Verity put her foot down with a new confidence that motherhood had imposed, and quashed the argument before it could begin. 'Really, darling. Nothing could be sillier. Neither of us will know who you're talking to when you call us. And Verity doesn't have a nice short version. Everyone called me Veetie for years; they're still doing it now. You don't want to wish that on our child, do you?'

Ricky thought of Verity's unprepossessing parents bellowing 'Veetie' at his little girl, as though her fate would already be sealed to emulate the unhappy early adulthood of her mother and, shuddering at the idea, capitulated. 'No, I wouldn't, darling. You're right, as always.' He paused a moment. He had another suggestion that had come from seeing Verity's French books while they were being unpacked in their new home counties house near his Slough office. A slim volume by Voltaire had caught his attention and given him an idea. 'Had you ever thought about Candida? Like Candide, only for a girl. I think it's a lovely name – it means truthful, honest, sincere, forthright. Lots of good things, a bit like Verity, only different.'

'Candida . . .' mused Verity, trying it out. 'Candida, Candy, Dida, Didi . . .' Holding their little daughter in her arms, she spoke softly to her, 'Candida? Are you a Candida, little one?' She looked up at Ricky. 'I think it's a lovely name, darling. And it shortens so nicely, doesn't it? Who could ever be cruel to a little girl called Candy or Didi?'

Ricky took Verity's face between his hands, looking at her wide-open blue eyes and the faint blush on her cheek. He kissed her carefully on her forehead, on the bridge of her nose and on her thin, soft lips. 'I don't think we'll need to abbreviate. No one will ever be cruel to our little girl,' he promised Verity.

He wasn't to know that, in twenty years or so, their little girl would meet a notorious heartbreaker, the lead singer of a band with a cult following, who paid his rent by occasionally waiting tables in his father's restaurant.

The Musical Memories of Sharif Khan

MUSIC IS MY memory. If I were to tell you when my life began, when our story began, I wouldn't start with our birth in a south London hospital, or my mother's birth on a Bengali birthing stool at her maternal grandfather's house. I would tell you when I first had the sensation of being alive; the first time I heard the cha-cha-cha, the ay-yi-yi, the wails, grunts, groans and mournful sighs of discharged love – the first time I heard song.

And if I were to tell you when I first started living, it would be when we started to control that cha-cha-cha for ourselves – with the beat-beat-beats and the explosion of words and melodies in our mouths. It was when we started the band, in the flat above my dad's restaurant.

Our parents were a local success story. My father had gambled on getting a loan to buy a share in a restaurant, and eventually took it over, moving us to the two-bed flat above it when we were toddlers. By the time we were teenagers he had opened a second restaurant, further up the Northern Line at Balham, cunningly buying it with a long lease before the first signs of gentrification appeared in the area. We abandoned the honking, tooting traffic of the flat on the Broadway, as my dad did well enough to buy Amma and us a nice family house on the Heaver Estate in Tooting Bec, one of the most respectable addresses in Tooting. Again, he bought it before the prices rocketed.

While my father was the business success of his family, my mother was the academic success of hers. Once we were at school, she followed us, returning to school herself. She took an MA in modern languages, and then a teaching qualification. She didn't teach in our school, but in a private girls' school in Wandsworth. She spoke to us in English as pure as that of the chilled angels frozen on any dreaming spire; she chose not to speak to us in any other language as we were growing up, and insisted sweetly that our father didn't either. Her intention was to avoid us having foreign accents that might set us below our fellow pupils – she wanted us to have accents that would set us apart, English accents as crisp and stiff as architecture, that would carve the way for us in our future endeavours. When we eventually learned our father's native language, we spoke it like the firangis we had become. We were never taught our mother's Bangladeshi; we only heard her speak it on the phone to her own mother. On the occasional family trips to Dhaka, never more frequent than every other year, we were like deaf and dumb aliens, trapped in our bubble of well-spoken English.

But everyone believed that our parents were successful for another reason, a deeper reason than their business and academic prowess, than their fight from an unprepossessing start as penniless immigrants back into the middle classes from which they had originally hailed in their native lands. They were successful, because they were The Couple That Were In Love. Everyone saw it, everyone knew it. From the moment of their romantic elopement to London, to their walking down the Tooting streets with our double buggy, hands instinctively intertwined, only letting go when Omar or I started to cry.

We don't know when it started to go wrong. Maybe, just as our early toddler tears forced their hands apart, as we grew up, we forced their hearts apart, too. Perhaps we drained the love from them, taking it for ourselves so they no longer had enough for each other. Drawing love out of them, as poison from a wound, taking away the dizzy giddiness of love, and leaving them clear-headed, empty and cold.

They used to sit together in companionable silence, in a loose embrace on the sofa, her legs sprawled across his lap while Abbu listened to his music or fiddled with his sitar, and Amma marked her papers or read her French novels. Sometimes they would delight us with their silliness, a childish silliness that could have been put on for us as a show, but more likely was simply for themselves alone and we just the fortunate spectators. A new Indian pop song would come on the radio, and Abbu, who had never lost his Punjabi accent, would leap up and swing Amma around, oblivious to the customers eating below our flock-carpeted feet, dancing and singing along. '*Ilu,*

Ilu!' he'd bellow tunefully, and with a comic waggle of his head, and pressing his heart, would finish the chorus, '*Ilu, Ilu!* means I love you, I lah-uv yo-ou!' As we clapped along, Amma would only mock protest and giggle with pleasure, her papers and books forgotten. They were just in their early thirties and, despite being parents, could at times still look like the young lovers they had been when they first met.

But as the years went by, those incidents became more and more rare and the loose embrace on the couch less and less common. They still held hands when they walked, but it was now a gesture of habit rather than affection. They only seemed to hold each other in their sleep, and for this reason more than any other, Omar and I used to get up out of our beds in the mornings and join them in theirs, clinging to either side of them while they clung to each other, to share that moment of instinctive intimacy before it dissolved with the consciousness that came with the morning light. 'My men,' Amma would say, as she woke sleepily and looked at us; but somehow we already knew that Abbu was being excluded from that seemingly inclusive term. Abbu spent more and more time with his business colleagues, with his music; Amma came back later and later from work, and spent more time with her books. They stopped spending so much time in the same room – Abbu would continue to listen to his records in the living room, but Amma would often disappear to the kitchen or her bedroom and listen to French stations on the radio, saying she needed to keep abreast of things for school.

Alone, Abbu would cover the cracks by sharing his

music collection with us – his vinyl and tapes and CDs, like sympathetic comrades, providing wise words and comfort, and sometimes a searing insight so sharp that it hurt him like a physical pain. At those moments, his sorrow was tangible, palpable.

Our parents' new unhappiness polluted the very air we breathed. We began to look nostalgically at old photos, with smiling faces and turned-up eyes, and wondered how we had managed to live through and yet simply miss the time they had been happy. Before the cold war that followed with our adolescence, we had been embarrassed by their outrageous, demonstrative affection. Had someone told us what would happen, wouldn't we have savoured every moment, every loving word, every unthinking embrace in between?

If an unhappy marriage was my father's lasting failing, his last failure, and the one that offered another type of poignancy, a new kind of pain, was demonstrated by his increasing dependence on music. My father had always appreciated music, but now he began to cherish it, pouring his emotion and energy into it and using it to fill the vacuum left by love. When he listened to 'O Mio Babbino Caro' in our living room, his handsome face became equal to the most beautifully crafted cinematographic shot of weeping Mafiosi in La Scala. But he didn't simply weep – he was transported. He became more democratic in his tastes, now treating jazz and opera, pop and soul, and classical Indian melodies as equal in his own United

Nations of Music. It was a bittersweet gift as, despite all his efforts, his gift was simply that of knowing and appreciating great music – he played a little, but he was acceptable rather than good. He could strum a sitar, a guitar, and he even learned to play something recognizable on keyboards, but he could never play a tune as he would want it heard. He could never write a melody that would transport him. His displaced yearning for the love he had lost made him a musical dilettante – a jack of all instruments but a master of none.

My father didn't lose his love for music, but his resentment about his mediocrity added to the unhappiness he already felt. His wife was withdrawing, remaining close to him only in her sleep, and his musical mistress had only held up another mirror to his shortcomings. He played up a very slight deafness in one ear, hoping this might suffice as the excuse for this lack of talent, and listened to Beethoven like a martyr. But the bitter truth was, he could not pretend to have any cultured skill or aesthetic gift that might win our mother back; he could not claim to be an unfulfilled artist who had just played at business for her sake, to give her back the material comfort she had given up when she chose him. The unfortunate truth was that he was a businessman who played at art.

When we began the band, he was at first irritated and then appalled to hear the type of music we were playing – Indie punk rock was not yet invited across the iron curtain of his living room to join his private United Nations. Perhaps he was even a little bit afraid – afraid that his children would succeed where he had failed, that they would not only become accentless English gentlemen, with pale faces that barely hinted at their ethnicity, but that they would become musicians too. When I became more serious about music, at the expense of my schooling, he urged me into the restaurant business instead, and to give up my musical ambitions. Sometimes, I think he might have unconsciously done this so I might have the opportunity to fail where he had proved he could succeed.

The Balti Ballads of Tooting Broadway

S HARIF WAS FIFTEEN when he decided to start the band. He was already quite handsome, although not in the same way his father was, less swarthy and finer boned. He had puppy-dog eyes that were chocolate-brown and appealing – Shona still insisted that they were his father's eyes. By his teens he had become conscious of the fact that you couldn't tell his ethnicity immediately by looking at him, which slightly embarrassed him – he didn't want people to think he was a wannabe white; he thought 'coconut Bounty Bar' was one of the worst insults bandied around his school, worse than Paddy or Paki. To counter any such accusations, he grew his black hair long and straight, defiantly let his teenage bum fluff grow on his chin and adopted an Asian sarf London accent, which he used comfortably to win the respect of his cronies, and which he dropped effortlessly when he loped back home to the gentrified Heaver Estate, his school tie hanging so loosely that it looked like a noose. Sharif was not only handsome, but with his new, vaguely rebellious look and his air of studied insouciance, he was now quite cool.

Better than cool, he was street. Girls began to pay attention to him, and he began to notice them back.

He started the band for four reasons, in this order:

1) It would be cool to be the lead singer in a band
2) Girls liked people in bands, especially the lead singers
3) Being in a band would irritate his dad
4) Oh, and he truly believed that Music was to be his Great, All-Fulfilling Destiny

He held the auditions in the flat above the restaurant in Tooting Broadway, where he had once lived as a child. His dad rented the flat to one of the cooks and two of the waiters. Sharif was a charmer, and often cadged fags off them in the alley behind the kitchen door, making them feel at home with his modified, expedient accent. They were fond enough of him to let him use the flat – it was Monday night, anyway; they would all be downstairs at work, and there wouldn't be anyone eating in, at least not until the pubs closed.

Sharif, armed with Pringles and a mixed nut collection stolen from his mum's larder, and Kingfisher beers filched from the restaurant fridge, set up the living room with his guitar artlessly draped across the ancient sofa, and some sheet music for decorative effect. After a couple of unpromising turns from a couple of lads in his class, one of whom inexpertly played the fiddle, and the other who had uselessly demonstrated his proficiency with the clarinet, Sharif broke into one of the beers himself. He was surprised that the third person who turned up was Micky

O'Shea, a stocky Irish lad from the year below him, who was known for being a bit of a scrapper and had the broken nose to prove it.

'It's a fourth-year band, Micky. Sorry, mate,' Sharif said with the unquestionable superiority that the automatic hierarchy of school bestowed.

'Fock off, man,' said Micky respectfully. 'Y've not even heard me play yet.'

Sharif considered this and nodded magnanimously. No one further had turned up. He might as well get some entertainment from the carrot-topped runt.

Micky pulled his guitar strap over his head and played a stunning riff. Sharif was annoyed and impressed; he was no mean guitarist himself, and could recognize talent in others. He maintained a stoical face and, giving nothing away, passed a sheet of paper to Micky. 'Can you read music, too?' he asked.

Micky nodded. He squinted at the hand-written squiggles for a few moments, humming in his head, and began to play. After a few bars he stopped and, shaking his head at the shaky writing, began again. Sharif listened, enraptured, trying hard not to let his pleasure show at the fluid harmony of the chords. 'This is good,' said Micky, when he reached the end of the page, 'but your notation's crap – did you just copy it down by ear? Y'know y'can buy sheet music for lots of bands – I've got Oasis and The Smiths.'

'I didn't copy it down, Micky, I wrote it,' Sharif said haughtily, secretly thrilled at the company in which Micky had unconsciously placed him – Oasis, The Smiths and Sharif Khan. 'We're not going to be some shite tribute band, we have to write our own stuff. It's about credibility.' He got up to take back his sheet, when his own credibility was marred unavoidably by his geeky little brother bursting into the flat.

'Sharif, what are you doing here? Abbu's going to kill you!' said Omar, breathless from racing up the stairs, blood dripping from his nose. He paused, seeing Micky, and although surprised, nodded politely towards him. 'All right, Micky,' he said, looking questioningly towards Sharif.

'All right, Omar. What the fock's happened to y'face, man? Were you in a fight?' Micky asked with interest. Sharif held his breath – please, he pleaded wordlessly towards Omar, please say you were in a fight, please say someone hit you. Say anything that might preserve an iota of our dignity, just please don't embarrass me in front of a carrot-topped third year, by saying . . .

'No, I just get nosebleeds sometimes. The doctor thinks they're stress-induced, although sometimes I get them when I run too fast or something,' said Omar apologetic- ally, taking a seat next to Sharif on the couch and wiping his nose. Sharif exhaled heavily and shifted himself imper- ceptibly away from Omar, disassociating himself without even realizing what he was doing.

'Oh,' said Micky with disappointment, while every- thing else in his demeanour said, 'Wimp.'

'I'll speak to you later, Micky,' said Sharif, masterfully taking control of the situation. 'I'll let you know. I've got lots of other people to see. Fourth years, you know. It's meant to be a fourth-year band. But I'll keep an open mind about you.'

'Thanks a million, Sharif,' Micky grinned, revealing his

train-track brace and crooked incisors. 'I'll see youse both later.'

Sharif looked at Omar, still pitifully sniffing and dripping blood, and, sighing with resignation, went to get some Kleenex and held them to his brother's nose, applying the pressure with a practised hand. 'Hold your head back a bit,' he commanded. Omar obeyed, and the bleeding began to abate almost immediately. 'So why is Dad going to kill me?'

'It's Monday, remember? Nana's come over for dinner, and you're half an hour late. Amma's fretting because she's made some massive effort to cook an English meal for him, but now the roast is drying out, the veg are getting soggy and the crisps and nuts she bought for pre-dinner nibbles have mysteriously disappeared. Abbu's furious with you. I said I'd come and get you.'

'Shit,' said Sharif. 'Of course, Grandad! I completely forgot that the old man was coming round. Where did you say I was?'

Omar gave him a small conspiratorial smile. 'I said you had to stay back for extra after-school maths, after your lousy results in that last test.'

Sharif grinned. 'You excellent little liar!' he said with admiration, 'Utterly believable and blameless. I owe you one, kid.' He nudged Omar gratefully with his shoulder, lifting off the blood-soaked tissues experimentally. 'So how did you know where I really was?'

Omar pulled out Sharif's flyer, announcing the auditions,

from his trouser pocket. He put it on the table, gently smoothing it out. 'I saw it on the notice board outside the music room,' he explained, before adding a touch reproachfully, 'Why didn't you tell me? I can play. I can play keyboards *and* guitar. And I'm a grade above everyone in our year, apart from you on the guitar.'

Sharif felt caught out, and said a touch shiftily, 'Well, I didn't think you'd be interested, and Indie rock bands don't really need pianists, and we've already got two guitar players . . .' he trailed off, as Omar was looking at him frankly and unconvinced, with dried blood sticking like rust to his nose and upper lip. 'And the thing is, it's not just about playing, you've got to be, well, a bit cool to be in a band.'

'Like you and Micky?' asked Omar.

'Like me and Micky,' agreed Sharif. 'Micky might be a third year, but he's almost the same age as us, and he's bloody hard. When he gets a bloody nose, it's not from a friggin' stress-induced nosebleed.'

'I can be hard,' said Omar crossly. 'I hit Tariq back when he punched me at football practice. I punched him so hard I broke my thumb and had to go to Casualty.' He pounded his fist lightly into his palm at the memory.

Sharif looked at this innocent gesture and said pityingly, almost kindly, 'You didn't go to Casualty because you hit him hard, kid. You broke your thumb because you don't even know how to make a bloody fist.' He took hold of Omar's still clenched right hand, and said, 'For a bright boy sometimes you bloody baffle me. Look, kid. Look at what you're doing. Your thumb is meant to go on the outside, Omar. Put it on the outside!'

Omar splayed his hand and looked thoughtful as he flexed his fingers and put them back into a fist, this time with the thumb on the outside, instead of neatly tucked in as he had it before. 'It doesn't feel right,' he confessed humbly. 'God, I'm rubbish. Why didn't you tell me before?'

'I didn't want to hurt your feelings,' Sharif shrugged. 'Sorry, I should have told you.' Seeing how bereft Omar looked, Sharif got up and pulled him to his feet, and said jokily, 'Well, kid. At least you got the brains in the family. All I got was the looks.' Omar shrugged. Too upset to play along or attempt a smile, he hung his head, looking down at his stupid weak hands. Sharif softened, and found himself saying something that he was sure he'd regret. 'Well, I said I owe you something for covering for me tonight. Why don't you come to our first practice session and see how it goes?'

Omar looked up, and when he finally smiled, it was like a soft white cloud drifting across a pale sky. 'You mean that, man? That would be so cool.'

''Course I do,' said Sharif insincerely, already cursing himself. He had wanted an über-cool Indie band, and now he was stuck with his geeky brother, a ginger third year, and he had already agreed that spotty Stevo Morgan would be on drums, as he was the only boy in his class who had access to a full drum kit.

While they walked down the narrow stairs past the takeaway, Sharif flicked some gum out of his pocket to cover up the beer smell and companionably passed one to Omar. As Omar took it, he asked Sharif, a touch nervously, 'Sharif, when we start rehearsing and that, could you please not call me "kid", not in front of the others. You're only fifteen minutes older than me.'

'Even if it was the other way round, I still think I'd call you "kid". But don't worry, man, I won't embarrass you,' Sharif said reassuringly. You do that to yourself, he sighed silently to himself. And such was the inauspicious birth of the Balti Ballads of Tooting Broadway, in the flat above the restaurant–takeaway.

Deciding the band's name was no easy process. Sharif, as founder member (after all, he had held the auditions, he had the flyer to prove it), thought that he had the right to name the band, and had already decided upon Balti Boys. He made the announcement at the inaugural meeting of the fledgling band, which found them once again in the flat above the restaurant. Sharif was confident of Omar's support, and was surprised when, on this occasion, Omar chose to differ. Nibbling on the peanuts that they had once again filched from Shona's larder, Omar asked, 'I get the Boys bit, but why Balti? We've got nothing to do with Balti. Abbu doesn't even have Balti dishes on the menu. Where's the logic in that?'

'What, so you think we should have a name that matches something on Dad's menu?' said Sharif scornfully, annoyed that Omar was questioning his authority in front of Micky and Stevo. 'The Prawn Dhansak Boys of Tooting Bloody Broadway?'

'I agree with Omar,' piped up Stevo. 'What the fuck's Balti got to do with me and Micky? How about Broadway Boys?'

'Yes, why don't we call ourselves the Broadway Boys?' agreed Sharif sarcastically. 'And while we're at it, why don't we wear bloody stockings and heels and audition for Forty-Fucking-Second Street.'

'Why don't we just call ourselves "Tooting"?' offered Micky. 'Or SW17? Stevo's right, we've got fock all to do with Balti, and everyone can see we're bloody boys.'

'But I don't mind the Boys bit,' Stevo objected. 'How about Tooting Boys, we're all boys from Tooting, apart from Micky here.'

'I am focking so from Tooting,' Micky countered furiously.

'Well, you don't *fucking* sound like it, Paddy,' said Stevo with the infuriating superiority of a fourth year talking down to a third year. Stevo could get away with saying things like Paddy, as his dad was Irish.

Micky turned white with fury and stormed to the other side of the room, sitting down heavily on an over-padded armchair. 'Zitface,' he muttered under his breath.

'Listen, I want Balti Boys,' insisted Sharif stubbornly. 'We need people to know there's some bloody Asian influence in the band.'

'There's only you and Omar,' pointed out Stevo, scratching his spotty chin and sprawling his long, lanky legs out in front of the sofa. 'You're only half the band.'

'Well, we'll be playing my bloody songs until one of you gets off your arse and writes some of your own stuff, so I'd say my influence was quite bloody significant,' retorted Sharif heatedly. Bloody insubordinates. He'd half a mind to go it alone.

'So if you and Omar are the Balti part of the band, what are Stevo and I?' asked Micky, having calmed down a bit.

'You're the Boys,' said Sharif patiently.

'But we're all Boys,' Omar added. He was a touch embarrassed by the storm his first comment had unleashed, but again his intellectual pride would not allow him to ignore the flaw in Sharif's argument.

'Well, what else do Micky and Stevo have in common?' Sharif muttered. 'He's ginger, he's not, he's a third year, he's not, he moved here five years ago, he's lived in Tooting all his bloody life, his dad runs the Crown, his dad works in a garage . . .'

'Well, we're both Irish,' suggested Micky.

Sharif snorted, 'And what have the Irish given to music? Bloody Eurovision winners, The Corrs and Daniel O'Donnell. Bloody soppy balladeers. We may as well call the band Bloody Balti Ballads . . .'

Sharif took a breath to continue his scornful rant, when Micky and Stevo surprised him by looking at each other, and roaring 'Yeah!' in unison.

'Bloody Balti Ballads, that's a rocking name!' said Stevo, 'That's got to be the one.'

'It's wicked, man, that's focking inspirational,' agreed Micky, stepping across the room to shake Sharif's hand.

Flattered by the sudden effusiveness that had suddenly materialized out of so much bad humour, Sharif decided that the name he had unintentionally come up with wasn't half bad – it was definitely more subversive and rock than Balti Boys.

'Omar?' he asked, unnecessarily, as he already had a majority vote, but didn't want his brother to feel left out.

Omar shrugged. 'I don't mind it. I still don't think we've got a lot to do with Balti, but whatever, man, I'm easy. D'you think they'll let us put "Bloody" on the posters, though?'

Sharif smiled indulgently. Sometimes his brother didn't have a clue. 'Don't worry about the bloody posters, man. We've got to become a bloody band first.' He stood up authoritatively. 'Now that we've got our name, let's work out when we're going to rehearse. We've already got our first gig – Mr Crowe is giving us a slot at the end of term concert if we can get our act together.'

Of course, Omar was right. Mr Crowe, their music teacher, was fond of both Sharif and Omar for their musical ability, but he wasn't having 'Bloody Balti Ballads' emblazoned on his posters across the school hall or on his concert programme. He curtailed the name to 'Balti Ballads' and, just to prove a point to the local governors about his ability to nurture local talent in the community, added 'of Tooting Broadway' in brackets.

After the first concert, everyone was talking about Sharif's band, and his unembarrassed, bravura performance during which he lurched across the school stage and abused his guitar like a latter-day Hendrix. The girls, who had been curious about Sharif before, now looked longingly at him as he passed by them in the school corridors, with his floppy, straight hair and his noose of a tie.

Overnight he became the sort of boy who literally had heads turning. And somehow, the band's new name stuck.

'Tell me about it,' Omar asked urgently, sitting on Sharif's bed in his checked M&S pyjamas. Now seventeen, going on eighteen, he had grown a lot taller, but had barely filled out. Despite taking up some martial arts classes, he was still scrawny and lanky, and his emerging fluff only accentuated his weak chin.

He had been waiting for Sharif ever since he sneaked out of the back window at 11 p.m., keeping himself awake by reading his revision notes for the end of term exams. It was the early hours of the morning before Sharif had climbed back up the drainpipe. He was now stripping off his clothes, his body much more developed and photogenic than Omar's, and wearing only his boxers, climbed into bed, nudging Omar off to the end.

'I'm fucking knackered, kid. What are you still doing up?'

'Come on, Sharif, tell me about it!' pleaded Omar. 'Who was it?'

'A gentleman doesn't tell,' Sharif said smugly, readjusting his balls in his boxers at the memory.

'You're not a gentleman. Come on, man. Who was she?'

Sharif sighed with mock annoyance. 'Well, man, if you insist. You know Cassie Rantell?'

Omar frowned. He knew Cassie; she was from the neighbouring girls' school. Short, sporty and busty, with a wild mane of golden curls and a reputation for shagging the more athletic boys from school on the Common. Although a nice enough girl, and good-natured enough not to bear any grudges when her conquests failed to call her again, she herself was hardly a conquest for Sharif to boast about. She'd even shagged Stevo Morgan last term (who'd become admittedly better-looking since antibiotic treatment had dealt with his teenage acne).

'I didn't think she'd be your type,' Omar said. 'A bit young, and a bit, well, she gets about a bit, doesn't she?'

'Of course she's not my type, shitwit,' said Sharif derisively. 'But she has a very hot big sister, almost nineteen.'

'Omigod,' said Omar. 'Ali Rantell? Hasn't she left school already? She's really fit – how did you get to meet her?'

'I met her last week – she came up to me after that gig we did in that crummy pub in King's Cross. She's a bit of a gig groupie – she was really drunk, and put her hand on my crotch while we were talking, so I took her number and asked her out.'

'Where did you go?' asked Omar, trying to keep the slight jealousy from his voice. He had been at the same gig, and while he and the others had been diligently packing up their gear, it seemed Sharif had been chatted up by a gorgeous older girl. He'd been in the band for two years and had never received the sort of attention that Sharif got. Sharif had been getting lucky with the 'gig groupies', as he called them, from the very beginning; but the only girls who ever talked to Omar just looked over his shoulder to where Sharif was standing and waited for him to disengage himself from whoever he was with, waiting for him to notice them.

'I didn't think she'd be a cheap date, so I took her out to the Ministry, out over at Elephant. Took a couple of tabs, saw some of the guys out there. Took her home and that was it.'

'Oh, right then,' said Omar, disappointed. Normally when Sharif went out like this, he had wild tales of sexual prowess to report, everything from blow jobs in club toilets to knee-tremblers in back alleyways, always clandestine, and always outside. Omar felt that listening to the stories, participating vicariously, somehow took the edge off his own virginity.

'She had a fantastic arse, though . . .' continued Sharif wistfully. 'Even you'd have got the horn for her, man. She had a butt like a ten-year-old boy.'

'What's that meant to mean?' asked Omar, sitting up, offended.

'It's an American expression,' Sharif explained patiently. 'It just means she had a great, tight, little butt. I heard it once in an Arnie movie, a real classic one.' Omar sat back down again. A classic Arnie movie was a virile enough reference for him not to take further offence. Sharif continued dreamily, 'You know, man, when you've got a girl like that bending over in front of you, you feel like a bloody king. I felt like shouting "I'm King of the World."'

'You watch too many movies, man,' Omar said critically. 'No wonder you plough all your exams. Besides, I thought you just took her home.'

'I did,' said Sharif smugly. 'I took her back to her front

door, halfway up a block of flats. And I knew she was well up for it because when we were making out, she rubbed herself against me, and didn't say a word when I got hold of her butt under her skirt . . .'

'You didn't do it outside her front door!' said Omar, gasping at the audacity. Her parents could have come outside at any moment.

'Don't be daft. She told me we could get up to the roof of the building on the fire exit. She's a bit more experienced and sophisticated than the girls from around here; she wanted me to do her from behind while she held on to the railing, which I thought might be weird 'coz I couldn't see her face. But I had a great view of her tight little ass, and the rooftops across Tooting, and she was bloody loving it. I'm telling you, man, when I was coming I felt like a king.' Sharif was silent, in reverence at the act, at the memory, already anticipating the next time.

'Are you going to see her again?' asked Omar quietly.

'Yeah, I think so, if she calls me I'll see her. I might even call her myself. For a good-looking girl she was really dirty. She was a bit too keen, though – afterwards, she kept asking me if I liked her. She kept saying, "You like me, don't you?" and kept kissing me needily when I didn't answer.'

'Why didn't you answer?' asked Omar.

'Well, it's a stupid question, isn't it? I say yes, she'll think she's my fucking girlfriend. If I say no, I'm a bastard. She must have known that I liked her a bit – I paid a mint to take her out and get her loaded. I don't have to do all that just to get laid. Girls only ask that because they want reassurance.'

Omar was silent at this. It was a question he asked in his head all the time, to his parents, to his schoolmates, to the girls who looked past him at the gigs, to his brother even. 'You like me, don't you? Please say you like me.' Sharif was so lucky never to need reassurance – to be so confident that he would be loved and desired just for being himself.

'I'll get off to bed, man. I've got a test tomorrow,' Omar said, heading back to his room. Lying alone in his bed, staring at the moonlight reflected on his ceiling, he tried to imagine making love to a faceless body; someone who took pleasure in him touching them in the most intimate way possible, and who made him feel like a king, and wanted nothing more from him for all of this than the simple reassurance of being liked.

Parvez Khan Mourns the Loss of Love

FAILURE SHOULDN'T BE surprising – it's just a part of life, like breathing and eating and singing. We fail at something at every stage in our development, every small success preceded by failure after failure. And sometimes followed by it, too. Each first faltering infant step preceded by flump after flumpy fall chest-first on the floor or, if you're lucky, into someone's arms. We fail at exams at school, which seems terrible, until we leave school and then we fail in all sorts of new ways that we hadn't even known about before. At our driving tests, at having children, at understanding those children, in our financial decisions, in our workplaces . . . and then we fail to keep our tempers about our failures, and let our bad humour affect those unfortunate enough to be close to us.

So we shouldn't be surprised when we fail at love. But we are. Of course, everyone expects the odd hiccup at the start – kiss a few frogs until you find your true love, and all that. That's different – that's the search, the thrill of the hunt, the seeking of the One to make your life complete. But when you've found the woman of your dreams, when you look at her longingly and find out to your absolute surprise and delight that she's looking right back at you and seems to think that you are the man of her dreams too; and you make a relationship, a home, a life of shared love and shared ideals and infinite happiness – how could that possibly fail?

Of course, you are astounded when it starts to go wrong. You absolutely deny it. How could that small errand she refused to run for you mark the beginning of the end? Don't be stupid, she just didn't want to go out of her way to the post office, there's not really one on her school run, and you could pop it in on the way to work anyway. Of course she wasn't being difficult, of course you're not cross about it. It's nothing, just a letter you had to post to the bank.

But then, how could you suddenly feel such intense, dramatic anger with her for simply scraping her fork on her plate at dinner? The dinner is still as abysmal as it used to be when she first attempted to cook, but after all this time you no longer compliment or reassure her, and she no longer expects you to. There's no school run any more; there's just the two of you at home, sitting across the yawning chasm of the dining table into which all conversation sinks. She used to follow your progress in doing little jobs around the house with loving, appreciative eyes – so why does she now follow you around the house with resentful eyes simply because you came back from the garden twenty minutes later than you said you would? And why does she complain about your muddy boots? You were weeding the back borders, the very borders she had insisted on having and you had fondly agreed to, even though you'd have preferred lawn to the end, so you and the boys could have had a bigger space for a kickabout or cricket, or maybe even a vegetable patch. You were weeding around the buddleia, the rosemary bushes, the pink roses that you'd bought together – you'd bought them when you first moved into the house, your first home together with the luxury of a garden. She used to love you coming into the house after looking after her plants, with the scent of rosemary on your fingers. You used to bring in a sprig of rosemary for her, too.

You'd forgotten to bring one in for her this time; in fact you'd forgotten that you used to do it at all, but surely that's no crime. You've had other things on your mind – the worrying dip in profits at the second restaurant in the summer, the competition of the new Italian, and the latest hire who hasn't been pulling his weight. Sitting alone in the kitchen with your muddy boots, your empty wine glass still on the table, your muddy footprints jigging cheerfully on the tiled floor, you can smell the scent of rosemary on your fingers yourself. Didn't someone say that rosemary was for remembrance?

And why does she clunk everything about so much when wiping up the mud, and why do you clunk everything about so when you are cleaning yourself up? And why do you take your drink to one room to listen to music, whilst she goes to the other to watch the TV? When did talking become so difficult, so alien? You've been together for ten, fifteen, twenty years. You've had children who have grown up in a loving home. Everyone says you're so lucky, everyone thinks you're the perfect couple – The Couple That Are In Love. You don't know when you started losing love. You can't explain when the window of your heart opened up to show that you were falling apart, day by day, hour by hour, minute by thudding minute, just waiting for the relief of the night, when you can escape into your happy dreams and wind yourselves around each other like you used to do, and at least be at peace in your sleep. You wish you knew when you started failing at the one thing that was the shining success of your life.

You don't believe it, and so you ignore it and hope that the disappointment and dread that comes with every waking morning will go away. And yet every waking morning it remains – you know it when your sleeping embrace loosens, and your legs and arms unwind and stiffen, and the curves and hollows that fit each other so well move callously apart to the cold, uninhabited far reaches of the bed. Let it leave, let the disappointment and dread leave – haven't we suffered enough? Isn't the losing of love bad enough, without watching the sorry corpse of it decay in our lives, in our lips? Let our unhappiness expiate our bad temper, our shortcomings, our failures and failings, and let us love again.

You think you'll never love again. You just want her to stop being a nagging shrew, and you want to stop being the interminable old bore who makes inappropriate gags and tells pointless long-winded stories about your blessed business, stories that she needs to cut across in company with her own truncated versions, so she can get on and serve the pudding. You show more regard for the dog than you do for her; and now so does she.

And all the time, in those moments when you remember your romantic youth, and the blush of the first and only real love you ever had, whom you miss even though she is lying thin-lipped and silent, just a foot away from you in your bed, all you want to say is, For God's Sake Please Stop This And Let Us Love.

Shona Khan Discovers Photos
from the Past

SHONA WAS IN her early forties when, much like her father before her, she found herself having something of a mid-life crisis. She looked around at her comfortable three-bedroom house in the gentrified Heaver Estate, at her pretty garden with rosemary and sweet-scented pink rose bushes planted at the end, at her days spent teaching in a convivial, middle-class school. She looked at her own middle-class, middle-of-the-road life that was punctuated by stilted, suburban dinner parties in which she attempted to make up for her mediocre cooking with expensive raw ingredients and lavish puddings; that was made bearable by her occasional art courses, her newly acquired Labrador puppy, and . . . what else, exactly? Her children had left home, and it was just her and Parvez again; only this time they had all the material comforts that they had done without before. They should have been happy – they had it all: time, space and companionship. And yet Shona felt bereft, perhaps unreasonably bereft. She felt that she had somehow grown into the wrong person, and was living the wrong life, and had only just begun to notice it.

It was a sad truth that as the children grew up, Shona and Parvez began to grow apart, as though the very fact of their growing was driving a wedge between the couple who had been such hopeless, dreaming romantics. They had been united in the struggle against their disapproving families, united in their struggle against their new-found poverty in the UK, united in their struggle to have the children they so desperately wanted and united in their front towards their children, to bring them up the best way they knew. But the more their children grew, the less they needed them, until eventually they had nothing against which to unite.

Omar was his family's pride and joy – his entire extended family participated in the credit for his fantastic success in his Oxford entrance exams, earning him a practically guaranteed place in illustrious, ancient New College with a two 'E' offer. When he got straight Bs in his A levels, everyone excused the quite average results for nerves and his rambunctious brother keeping him up with their band at all hours throughout the summer of the exams. His grandad, Nana Rashid, practically wept when he heard that his English grandson was going to his alma mater, as though his own life was being relived the way it should have been.

Sharif, meanwhile, had failed in all his exams, apart from music, quite spectacularly. He was uninterested in going to college, and took up his father's offer of working in the restaurant. Again, his family found something to be proud about – their eldest son taking up the reins of the family business. What could be more fitting than that? True, his childhood musical hobby seemed to continue to distract him, but it was something he'd grow out of as he began his real working life. Now he had responsibilities beyond messing around in sound-proofed basements with his old schoolfriends.

Both boys left home the same week, not very long after their eighteenth birthdays, Omar to go to college, and Sharif to move in with friends in Collier's Wood. Parvez, seeing how much this affected Shona, surprised her with one of his romantic gestures, which had become so rare that she had practically forgotten he ever did them. She came back from school, and in a tall, brown box on her doorstep, tied with a pink ribbon, was an adorable Labrador puppy, with melting brown eyes and a dark chocolate coat, like an Andrex puppy in negative. Still in her sensible teacher's coat and court shoes, standing on the doorstep, she pulled him out, and giggled delightedly as he scrabbled affectionately at her and licked her face.

'Do you like him?' asked Parvez, opening their front door.

'Oh, Puppy, I love him!' exclaimed Shona, stepping forward to put her arm around Parvez in an embrace that was awkward as it was unusual. Parvez, surprised and pleased by their sudden renewed intimacy, put his own arm around her and kissed her on the top of her neatly bobbed hair. She hadn't called him Puppy for years; once the children were old enough to speak, she had stopped calling him Puppy in front of them and had switched to Abbu or Dad. And whenever they were in company, she had made sure to call him Parvez, until eventually it had seemed that they were always in company, whether with the boys or someone else, so it had been a natural transition to call him Parvez on the rare occasions when it was just the two of them. And he himself had stopped calling her Goldie, although sometimes he satisfied himself with 'Shonali', the affectionate form of her name, which was quite appropriate enough for company.

'I thought about getting two of them, to keep each other company,' said Parvez, 'but then I thought we had enough trouble with the last two, so perhaps it was time to give us a break, and just look after single figures.'

Shona smiled, but this time, the smile didn't reach her eyes. She had mistaken the gift as a romantic gesture, but now saw it for what it was – an attempt to replace the boys and paper over the cracks with another shared endeavour. Still, the puppy was undeniably gorgeous. She stepped back from Parvez and, closing the front door behind her, asked, 'What shall we call him?'

'You name him, Shona. Your names are the ones that stick,' said Parvez, without rancour. 'Maybe I'll give him his middle name.'

'Well, he's Irish,' said Shona, inspecting his collar. 'Perhaps we should give him an Irish name, like Patrick.'

'Pat the puppy?' laughed Parvez. 'Are you sure that's wise? The poor thing will get enough attention without his name being an instruction.' He took the puppy and patted him lightly and enthusiastically. 'Pat the puppy, Pat the puppy.' Watching the puppy squirm with pleasure at the attention, Shona started laughing and Parvez, grinning that his joke had worked, added, 'Why don't we call him Bob for his middle name?' He bobbed up and down with the scrabbling, excited puppy in his arms. 'Bob the dog, Bob the dog.'

'OK, Patrick-Bob. That's his name. Is that all right with you, sweetie?' she cooed, but she was talking to the puppy, not to Parvez, and chucked the puppy under his chin. As she walked through to the kitchen, Parvez put down the puppy and joined her. 'Are you checking that we've got enough chitlins and vittles for when the rest of the Waltons come to visit Patrick-Bob for supper?'

The fun of the moment had already passed, and Shona took a deep breath, fighting the urge to snap at Parvez for his silliness. 'Yes, Parvez,' she said patiently, 'That's exactly what I'm doing. I'm also making a cup of tea if you want one.'

A month later, Shona was sitting at home during the mercilessly damp autumn half-term break. She had too much time on her hands, which she had begun to find was a Bad Thing. Too much time meant that she started thinking, and when she started thinking, she found she wasn't thinking particularly happy thoughts. Thoughts like – This isn't the real me; maybe once it was, but it's not any more. This isn't my real life; maybe once it was, but it's not any more. Maybe I'm just waiting for my real life to begin . . . Consequently, Shona started to find herself chasing away time as urgently as most people chase away boredom. She cleaned her already clean house, making their Ugandan cleaning lady's job deeply unfulfilling. She baked chocolate-chip cookies from a packet recipe, and, realizing she had no one to share them with, ate half of them miserably herself in front of daytime TV until she remembered that cookies were the sort of food you could send by post and packed up the remainder to go to Omar and Sharif. She listened distractedly to French radio, and flipped listlessly through the Ikea catalogue. She considered visiting her father, whom she hadn't seen in months, but didn't know how she would answer his first and most obvious question: 'So, how are you, Jaan?'

She remembered that she had a chore to do, something that she had been saving for just such a rainy, listless day. She went up to the attic, pulled out a large cardboard box of photos, collected in their little packets from the developers, and the smart grey albums that she had recently bought to arrange them into, and brought them down with her to the sitting room. It wouldn't take too long to stick the photos in – what would take the time was organizing them into some kind of order.

The photos went back years, from when she had first married Parvez; they were all the pictures they had taken together before they had become a family. Once the children had come, all the family photos had been pasted proudly into a set of golden lacquer albums that Parvez had bought her as a present, ready to show to guests, and for the children to fumble through when they were bored. She also kept a few photos on display in the living room in sturdy wooden frames, which she would occasionally update as new shots took her fancy. Rather than going to the trouble of putting the replaced photos back with their original set, she simply popped them in a manila envelope that lived at the top of the box, telling herself she would sort them out later. It was this envelope that Shona came across first, and she spread the photos across the carpet.

These were the most poignant photos, as they were the ones which had once had pride of place in her living room, and which had eventually become so familiar that they had lost the power to move or delight, becoming mere wallpaper before being decisively rejected for new, more recent developments.

The first picture that caught her attention was the photo she always thought of as her wedding picture. Her orange silk sari blazed in the sun as she looked up with bewildered adoration at her laughing, handsome husband, as though she couldn't quite believe what they had just done, and that he would now be hers for ever. They were so happy, so foolish in their happiness; they both had the myopic look of people who couldn't see further than each other, as though they were all that existed in the world, The Couple That Were In Love. The photo reminded her of secret assignations in the Karachi Tennis Club, of pink rose petals in a Hilton bedroom, of making love surreptitiously in the syrup-sweet-smelling flat above the confectioner's when Bhai Hassan went out; it was like facing a ghost of her past. Handsome Parvez, looking straight through the camera lens and into her eyes seemed to be saying, 'See, you can't deny it. We've changed. Look at what we once were, Goldie. And look at what we've become.'

When did it go wrong? Shona asked herself. Perhaps it went wrong the moment she took this photo off their mantelpiece and replaced it with . . . with what? She couldn't imagine what she could have possibly replaced this picture with. Then she remembered; it had been the first picture of Parvez and herself holding their scrunch-faced newborn boys, taken in the hospital after they had given them their names. She looked for the photo and, finding it, was surprised to see that this time she was looking adoringly at her children instead of at Parvez, her myopic blind adulation reassigned instantly, whilst Parvez looked directly at the camera again, a studied beam on his face instead of a spontaneous laugh. 'See what happened, Goldie? I didn't change, you did. You cared more for them than you did for us.'

So what? she argued back to him. So what if I cared more for them? I went through hell for them. I black-mailed my own father for the money to have them, I went through the most painful, invasive treatments you can imagine again and again until it worked, I carried them with fear every day until they were born, afraid that we'd lose them and have to start again, I spun them from my flesh and knitted them from my own blood and bones. They were my blood, my boys. I poured everything I was into them. You just masturbated into a tube, and were too busy with the business to come to the clinic with me all those times; you thought it happened like magic, with the effortlessness of the gods. Of course I changed! And you should have changed too, but you didn't. You stayed the happy-go-lucky twenty-something I married; you left all the changing, all the coping and the managing to me, while you kept cracking your silly jokes and doing your silly work to keep us in not quite the manner we'd been accustomed to back home.

'So that's it!' said another photo of Parvez triumphantly, standing with his hand on Shona's shoulder, while
she posed with her mortar board and her MA diploma.
'You resent me. You've resented me for not suffering like
you did, for not being as rich and successful as the family
I took you from. Don't you think I'd have taken every
little bit of pain from you, if I could have, every bitter
disappointment month after month when you cried and
mourned every time you bled? I loved you, Shona. It
wouldn't have mattered to me if we'd never had kids, as
long as we had each other. Everything I did here – starting
the restaurant business, expanding it, buying the house – I
did for you.'

Don't be stupid, replied Shona. I don't resent you. Why
would you say that? How could you feel how I felt? And
I know everything you've done for us; we have a good
life, a beautiful house, a nice car that I still haven't learned
to drive. I don't resent you for not suffering like me; but
why couldn't you have changed with me, Parvez? Why
couldn't you have grown up, too? I can't explain what
happened to us; all I know is that slowly, gradually, every
single little thing you said or did just felt wrong, as though
you could never do anything right again. And so I snap
and criticize and nag, until you throw accusations at me,
saying things like, 'You resent me,' and then you begin to
resent me yourself, for being what I've become. So maybe
it is all my fault; I didn't just make the boys, you know.
I made us, too. I sought you out in Pakistan, I looked for
you and made you mine. I was responsible for our beginning; maybe it only makes sense that I should be responsible for our end.

Sitting on the floor, surrounded by photos of her past, betrayed and exposed by the images of her legion former selves, Shona hugged her knees and began to cry quietly to herself. Patrick-Bob, who had turned out to be a she rather than a he on closer inspection, scuffled into the living room and nuzzled against her. Pulling herself together, Shona gathered all the photos before the dog could put muddy paw prints on them, and put them back in the envelope, back in the box, and put the box back in the attic.

As she walked into the kitchen to get Patrick-Bob's water, she saw that she had left the french windows to the garden open, and that tiny paw prints had made a merry, muddy dance all over the kitchen tiles. Sighing, but at once relieved for this new diversion, Shona cleaned the kitchen floor until it sparkled, and made dinner for Parvez. When he came back, she was unreasonably cross with him for the accurate charges that his photographically captured self had made in her imagination, and answered all his attempts at conversation with monosyllables, scraping her plate clean because she knew the sound annoyed him.

'I picked up that book you said you needed, Shona,' Parvez said, when he had finished eating.

'Right, thanks,' said Shona disinterestedly, continuing to scrape her plate, even though she didn't know which book he was talking about.

Parvez sighed, and battled on, '*The Iliad*. Don't you remember? You said you needed a copy of *The Iliad*, you said you needed it for school.'

'Yes, I did. Thanks,' Shona repeated, finally putting down her jarring cutlery.

Parvez got up from the table and pulled the book out from his briefcase. 'They didn't have the Penguin Classic version you wanted, so I got this one instead. It cost quite a bit more, but it's beautifully illustrated; I thought you might prefer it.' He put it in front of her, and waited expectantly for her approval.

Shona looked at it cursorily and, instantly appalled, flicked from the inside front cover to the back pages in disbelief. A glossy coffee table version of *The Iliad* was the last thing she needed. What on earth had Parvez been thinking? Did he really think that pretty pictures were all that mattered in a book? She resisted the urge to snap, and said matter-of-factly, 'It's a bit too heavy for me to take into school; and I really wanted the foreword and notes in the other version. Just leave me the receipt and I'll return it when I go into town tomorrow.' She got up and took their plates to the sink to rinse.

Parvez looked at her stiff back and said quietly, unable to keep the reproach from his voice, 'You could at least say thank you, Shona. I was trying to do something nice for you.'

Shona didn't turn around, and carefully put the plates in the dishwasher. She knew she should apologize for being so offhand, but she couldn't stop herself saying instead, in the same matter-of-fact tone, 'But I did say thanks, Parvez; I said it twice.'

Chased outside by the icy climate within, Parvez disappeared to the garden to do some useless task out there, and the rice pudding Shona had put on for dessert burnt dry as he stayed out twenty minutes longer than he said he would. Shona binned it without telling him, and when he came back in, his muddy boots messing up her newly cleaned kitchen floor, she said nothing in criticism, and clanked the mop and bucket round with an eloquent noisiness that said it all. It was funny, she thought, that she hadn't minded cleaning up after the puppy, but cleaning up after Parvez filled her with an anger that she couldn't even express. Parvez courteously poured her another glass of wine, and himself a whisky, and disappeared to lose himself in his music in the lounge. She took the wine without comment, and went upstairs to their bedroom to watch a comedy on the television.

Much later, when Parvez came up for bed, she pretended to be asleep, but he knew that she was awake as she didn't automatically turn into him, resting her head in the hollow between his head and shoulder, as she did in her sleep. He whispered to her, 'I just want you to be happy, Shona. You want me to be happy too, don't you?'

It was the simplest question, and she suddenly realized it was the most profound. It was far easier to answer than the hackneyed, 'Do you still love me?' Because how, Shona thought, could you talk about love after twenty years, when the relentless tank of habit is all it's become, from the wedding bands you still wear, to the golden earrings you put on every morning that were his first present to you, to the united front you present to both your families and to your friends? It would be stupid, infantile, to still talk of love. But did she still care if he was happy? That would answer it all. Did she still care if he was happy? Because she knew that if the answer was no, she could start to withdraw, to disengage, to break apart and mourn the loss.

The saddest thing for Shona, on that still, chill night, were the silent tears that she began to shed on realizing the brutal answer to his question; not the tears themselves, but her realization that her tears weren't even for him, but for the coldness of her own unhappy heart.

The Octopus in the Garage

S HONA WAS UNDERSTANDABLY annoyed when she wasn't considered the automatic replacement for the post of head of languages at her school when old Monsieur Matthieu retired. She had already given thirteen years of service to the school, and was certain she merited to be first in line. She wasn't sure if the perplexing decision against her had been made because she was a woman, or because she was Asian, or because she didn't have any overseas working experience, or simply because she wasn't considered good enough. When the newly appointed head of languages turned up, male, Caucasian, barely older than her and scrubbed up well enough to charm the head teacher, she was even more annoyed. And his language experience was in Spanish, of all things. Spanish! Who learned Spanish in England? Everyone learned French, and maybe a bit of German or Italian if they were arty or romantically inclined. No one learned the language of the Costas here; Shona privately believed that the sort of Brits who went to Spain were the sort of people who thought that speaking English louder and more slowly would miraculously make them understood to the pesky foreigners. She and Parvez had taken most of their family holidays in different parts of France, when they weren't dutifully visiting Pakistan or Bangladesh.

Jane, the head teacher, organized a little drinks gathering on Friday after school to welcome the new arrival and to say goodbye to Monsieur Matthieu, who had already turned sixty-five and had been kindly caretaking the post until his replacement was able to begin. Shona had already decided to dislike Mr O'Connor on sight and was irritated when Monsieur Matthieu introduced them to find the arriviste Irishman attempting to charm her in the same way as he had charmed the head. 'Well, Mrs Khan, or Shona, if I can call you that, you've certainly received a glowing press from your old boss. I hope I live up to your exacting standards.'

'I think you may have been misled, Mr O'Connor,' Shona said frostily, with just the barest veneer of politeness. She was holding her glass of white wine stiffly, and not sipping from it at all. 'I've heard my standards are nowhere near as exacting as yours.'

Monsieur Matthieu, who knew that Shona was still smarting about being passed over, thought about saying something to defuse the situation before remembering that he was now retired and didn't have to care any more. 'Oh look, nibbles!' he said. 'How marvellous. I'll see you in a minute, my dears. Must get to them before Jonty wolfs the lot.'

Left to themselves, with Shona looking mutinous and determined not to break the embarrassing silence, Mr O'Connor sipped his soft drink calmly and eventually said, 'Shona, first of all, please call me Dermot. We'll be working together, and there's really no excuse for not being on first-name terms. Secondly, I know it's no secret that my appointment was something of a . . . disappointment for you. But there it is, and we both have to get on with it. In my experience it's the only thing you can do.' He attempted a slight laugh, which he cut short when he saw that Shona showed no sign of defrosting.

Shona thought such frankness was verging on the ill-bred. Why did he have to say out loud what they both already knew? It hardly helped her save face for him to brag openly that he had got the job instead of her. Some things, most things, in fact, were better left unsaid.

'So what is your experience, exactly?' Shona said. 'Jane was rather vague when I asked.' Seeing as she was stuck with him and couldn't politely get away until someone joined them, she might as well find out what had made him such a good find and worth waiting over half a term for.

'Well, I'm from Ireland, originally. I went to university in Dublin, and then went back to teach near my home town. Do you know County Kerry?'

'No,' said Shona, and then deciding that her curtness could be mistaken for out and out rudeness, which she was well mannered enough to avoid, added, 'I'm afraid I don't. Is it nice?'

'Not so nice that I wanted to stay. I spent four years in Spain teaching in international schools, in Madrid and Barcelona. And then I went to the States and taught in New York, and then I came to London. I'll have been teaching nineteen years come January. I'll bet that makes me sound ancient to a young lady like yourself.'

Shona wasn't sure whether to bristle with annoyance at the 'young lady', or to take it as a compliment. She grudgingly accepted that Dermot was both more qualified and experienced for the job than she was, with her thirteen years trudging the beat in the same school, and found her resentment abating. Perhaps it was just as well. It was enough to have cold war at home, without having confrontations at work to boot. 'That's kind, but I'm hardly a young lady. I've got two grown-up boys, one is at college already.' She said college, rather than university, deliberately, as she always did, as she hoped that those in the know would automatically infer that Omar was at Oxbridge without her having to boast.

'I'd never have believed it. You look far too young to have grown-up boys!' Dermot said with what sounded like genuine astonishment. He's trying to charm me again, thought Shona. 'You must have married terribly young.'

'Are you married?' asked Shona, changing the subject.

'No, not any more. I was, sort of, but not now,' answered Dermot, looking uncomfortable for the first time, ironically as now Shona was actually trying to make an effort.

'So, any children?' Shona asked automatically, wondering what 'sort of' married meant.

'No,' Dermot said curtly. It could almost have been described as rude, but he added no softening sentence as Shona had done.

Shona regarded Dermot with a mixture of curiosity

and sympathy. She remembered, before she had the boys, how she too had snapped curtly at anyone who asked whether she had any children, or enquired when she and Parvez were going to start trying. She still recalled her silent fury at Parvez's father, who had droned on and on about how they were wasting their lives by not allowing themselves to bring the pleasure of children into them. 'You can't imagine the joy that children bring,' he had said smugly, as he sat fatly and fatuously on their sofa during what felt like an interminable visit from Pakistan. Shona had honestly wanted to kill him.

Jane bustled up to them with a tray of her precious nibbles. 'So how are we getting on? Grilling the new boss, Shona? Have you found out that Dermot here speaks five languages! What are they now, Dermot? Let me try to remember. English, Castilian, Catalan, German . . . and what was the other one, Dermot dear?' She fluttered her pale blonde eyelashes at him.

'Italian, but really not as fluently as the others,' Dermot replied with a smile, his composure regained.

'I speak five languages, too,' Shona said, but in a gentle tone and with a smile, so it didn't sound like an assertion or a challenge, but an expression of kinship. She made her excuses and went over to the buffet table to join Jonty, the corpulent English master, who was eagerly hoovering up the prawn thingies without any concern for niceties or mingling.

A couple of weeks after Mr O'Connor's arrival, Shona would have hoped that everything might settle back into the normal, comforting routine. However, it still wasn't quite normal. Although you couldn't exactly call Dermot good-looking, his natural charm and the ease with which he talked to the women in the staffroom had many of them, regardless of age or marital status, almost fighting for his attention, offering to make him cups of tea and asking solicitously after his classes. Young Ms Adams in particular, an attractive singleton in her early thirties, had developed a thumping crush on him, which she was convinced he reciprocated. 'He always asks how I am, every time he comes into the staffroom. What do you think that means?' she confided in Shona, with a mixture of triumph and uncertainty, reapplying her lipstick before Mr O'Connor came back after his class.

Shona replied reassuringly, 'I think it means he wants to know how you are.' She didn't add that he was the friendly type who made sure to ask everyone how they were, sometimes to the point of silliness.

'Exactly!' said Pam Adams, 'That's exactly what I think.' She looked expectantly at the clock, as she had memorized Dermot's schedule and knew exactly when he would walk back through the heavy oak door.

The other thing that wasn't yet quite normal, and this was not specific to Mr O'Connor but seemed to happen any time a new teacher joined, was that everyone appeared to have pulled up their socks, and be working much harder. Instead of the usual banal chatter and flicking through Ceefax that used to accompany tea breaks in the staffroom, now everyone began to stride purposely about with their papers, or bury themselves in their books and marking as soon as Mr O'Connor walked in. It was a natural group instinct of self-preservation, no one wanted to get shown up by fresher, keener new blood, and so everyone pretended to have an über-enthusiasm that tended to wear off as soon as the new teacher had been broken in and broken down by the relentless turn of the clock. Even Jonty, for whom Chaucer could hold no more secrets after a decade of ploughing through Canterbury Tale after Tale with his A level classes, was seen marking up his battered copies and muttering to himself audibly in Middle Englyshe any time anyone was close enough to hear.

Right on cue, Dermot walked in after taking lunch duty and greeted the teachers in the room collectively and individually – a lunch duty in itself, as it took him almost five minutes out of his precious remaining break. Shona, reading Voltaire's *Candide* on the small window seat, stifled a smile as a flurry of feminine activity broke out concurrently with heightened energized working. 'Pam, there's really no need, I'll make it myself this time . . . Well, if you insist, that's really very kind of you, again.' Dermot looked around the staffroom and made a beeline for the only person who wasn't really looking at him.

'Could I join you, Shona?' he asked politely. Shona looked around wistfully at the many empty chairs that he could have picked, instead of squeezing himself next to her on the narrow window seat. Parvez had a customer in the Balham restaurant who did something similar – always taking the same seat at the small corner table and, even if the rest of the restaurant was empty, and the large table next to the corner table was full and blocking his way, making the other customers stand up so he could get to his usual seat.

'Sure, Dermot, if you don't mind holding your breath. It's a bit narrow, I'm not sure it's even made for two.'

'Ah, but you're just a scrap of a girl,' said Dermot. 'There's plenty of room for my skinny Irish backside.' Shona giggled, despite herself. She couldn't help noticing that Dermot was a lot less formal with her than with the others; perhaps that little confrontation at their first meeting had broken the ice.

Dermot coughed, and then asked, 'Is it my imagination, Shona, or does everyone seem to work harder when I'm around? It might sound odd, but it seems as though everyone seems to leap into action when I walk in.'

'It's not your imagination,' Shona said. She added wryly, 'You must have great motivational skills.'

Pam approached the window seat, fluttering prettily, 'Here you are, Dermot. Just the way you like it, strong with two sugars.' She handed it to him, and as Dermot thanked her again, she looked for somewhere to sit down and join them. The window seat, however, was unavoidably contained, and there were no other seats next to it. She hovered for a moment, saying coyly, 'You really should look after yourself and cut down on all that sugar. You can get great substitutes now. I don't have any sugar any more, haven't done for years. Neither does Shona,' she added, generously including Shona in her conversation.

'Ah, but unlike yourself and Shona, I'm certainly not sweet enough already,' said Dermot charmingly.

'Would you like my seat, Pam?' offered Shona, keen not to be gooseberrying in on a flirtatious encounter.

'Shona, if you don't mind, I wanted to ask you something about one of your classes. Could you stay a moment?' Dermot interjected hurriedly, before Pam could accept.

'Well, I'll leave you to it, if you're talking shop,' said Pam, bravely hiding her disappointment. 'I have the most horrendous stack of assignments to sort out myself. Better get on with it, eh?' She walked off quickly and sat down with her papers, her back to the window seat so they wouldn't see her pouting.

'Well?' asked Shona, looking at Pam's too straight back, and feeling a little sorry for her. It wasn't nice of Dermot to flirt and then pass her over immediately afterwards.

'Could I sit in on a couple of your A level French lit classes next week? I have some free periods, and I've not yet had a chance to acquaint myself with your teaching methods. Just to see how you do things here.'

'Of course,' said Shona. 'You don't have to ask. I'm surprised you haven't sat in on my classes as yet. You've been to Mrs Cellotti's Italian class, and Miss Taggart's German class. I was beginning to feel rather left out that the evil eye of the new broom had managed to evade me.'

'Evil eye?' laughed Dermot. 'Very good, I like that.' He lowered his voice, and said a touch conspiratorially, 'The truth is, Shona, I've been a little embarrassed to attend . . .'

'Oh,' Shona said, nodding with understanding. It was because she had gone for his job. It might feel a bit awkward for him to throw his weight around where she was concerned.

'Yes,' nodded Dermot in reply. 'I thought you'd have worked it out. It's just that French is the only language we teach here that I don't really have a working knowledge of, and I was worried I wouldn't be able to follow the class without interrupting you and being a bit of an octopus in a garage.'

'An octopus in a garage?' asked Shona, looking at him for clarification. She was a bit annoyed that the only one who still seemed sensitive to the awkward situation of being passed over for the job was her; at least his odd choice of phrase gave her an easy way to hide her discomfiture.

'Yes, it's a Spanish phrase, como un pulpo en un garaje. It means, like a fish out of water,' explained Dermot.

Shona frowned just for a second. What a silly language Spanish seemed to be. Whoever heard of a phrase like 'an octopus in a garage'? She looked at Dermot, who had broken into a laugh. She breathed with comprehension. 'Oh, I get it, you're taking the mickey. I should have known.'

'No, I swear, it's a real phrase!' said Dermot, still laughing. 'It's just your look of utter disdain, it was priceless.'

Shona pursed her lips and said sweetly, 'Well, you'll get on fine in the French lit class. We read the work in French, but mainly discuss it in English. We're doing *Andromaque*, by Racine. Do you know it?'

'Vaguely, do you have a copy?' asked Dermot.

'Sure, it's in French, though,' Shona said, enjoying the look of exasperation on Dermot's face, before adding, 'But there's a very useful foreword and critique in English. I'll pop it in your pigeonhole before I head out today.' The five-minute warning bell signalling the end of lunch rang, and Shona shifted herself off the window seat. 'I'll see you later, then,' she said affably. She popped her bookmark into her slim volume of *Candide* and, dusting her skirt, started to walk off.

'So, Voltaire's not on the syllabus?' Dermot called after her.

'No, Voltaire is just for fun,' Shona replied, over her shoulder.

'Because this is the best of all possible worlds, and couldn't possibly be better?' he asked her retreating back. Shona turned round quickly, smiling with surprise, but saw that Pam had taken her place on the seat and already engaged Dermot in some cheerful banter. She surreptitiously checked whether the quote was printed obviously on the back of her volume. It wasn't. He didn't speak French, but he knew Voltaire. She was oddly touched that he had read the book that she was re-reading; it was an unexpected, not unpleasant, expression of empathy. It had not occurred to her before how much Dermot and she might have in common. Perhaps it wasn't such a bad thing that Dermot had joined the school. Perhaps they might even become friends.

'Dans ce meilleur des mondes possibles . . . tout est au mieux,' she said to herself. In this, the best of all possible worlds, all is for the best.

The Academic Pursuits of Omar Khan

WHEN OMAR STARTED university, he was swept into
his turret room in the Holywell Quad of New
College on the crest of a wave of familial happiness that
was so powerful it practically carried him up the winding
stairs. His manly, capable father brought up the heavy
cases that Omar would never have been able to manage
himself, and his mother plugged in the kettle and looked
tearfully out of his window at the grey-green quad, the
elegant chapel at odds with the substantial stones of the
thirteenth-century walls. While Omar unpacked and his
parents sat on the bed and drank tea, a couple of second
year students wandered up to his room to give him the
invitation to PPE drinks that evening.

'Well, that's nice, darling, isn't it?' said Shona. 'You'll
meet everyone on your course tonight. You make new
friends so quickly at college,' she added wistfully. Omar
nodded cheerfully, giving away nothing but enthusiasm
for this new adventure.

It was only afterwards, once his parents had gone, that
he locked the door to his turret room and lay face down

on his bed, ignoring the knocks of further enthusiastic students from his staircase, calling to introduce themselves. He had arrived at New College, Oxford University; he had arrived in this venerable centre of learning under the pretext of being academically gifted, and he was terrified that he would be found out for what he really was. A mediocrity. A run-of-the-mill, middling Mr Average, as his three Bs at A level testified. Whenever he had been asked about his disappointing grades, he had asserted with much bravado that after he had got his unconditional offer from Oxford, he had let his studies slip, and been too busy with the band over the summer to concentrate on his exams. He lied so fluently that he could almost believe it himself; almost, but not quite. The truth was that he had worked like a demon towards his exams. It was true that the monotony of constant revision had been relieved by playing a few gigs, but they were nothing terribly strenuous. In fact, after he had spent fourteen hours studying with nothing but strong brewed tea to sustain him, a forty-minute set in a local pub or club was a walk in the park. The terrifying truth was, he had worked as hard as he possibly could, and still got three Bs; the terrifying truth was that they were the grades he deserved.

If he had to explain how, despite his obvious mediocrity, he had managed to get an unconditional offer in the first place, he would have described it as a combination of dumb luck and plagiarism. During the Oxford entrance exams, he was lucky enough to get papers with questions that matched those he had already prepared over the previous summer as part of his revision. For the actual interview, he had crammed a year's worth of *Economist* and *FT* articles, and found that he was able to expound other peoples' words and opinions with much more confidence than his own when it came to meeting the politics and economics tutors. He had not done so well in his philosophy interview, as he was expected to think for himself rather than quote knowledgeably. But he had the good luck that this particular philosophy tutor was also involved in a scheme which supported black and Asian candidates, and so he suspected that he had probably benefited from positive discrimination.

Omar wished, not for the first time, that he was someone else. Someone like Sharif, who was confident enough to be himself, and was loved and liked for being who he was. Omar felt he, by comparison, was a faker, a dissembler. He had carved out a niche for himself, created an identity for himself in reaction to Sharif. If Sharif cared nothing for books or academia, then Omar could care for nothing else. If Sharif was to be the rebel, then Omar could be the model student. Omar found it relatively easy to be a model student, in that he found it easy to be quiet, clean, attentive, punctual and rigorous in handing in well-prepared work. He discovered that being a model student meant that everybody, including his teachers, mistook him for a bright student. And yet Omar sincerely believed that he was blessed with neither superior intelligence nor original thought; he had only two abilities, the ability to read quickly, and an excellent memory that allowed him to memorize and repeat all he read.

Omar sat up on his bed, scratching his stomach disconsolately. He splashed some water on his face at the sink in the corner of his room and looked at this face reflected back at him, blank, expressionless, pale. Even his colour was indistinct; he was neither brown nor white. It could be anyone's face, he thought to himself. It was a blank canvas. He looked at the family photos on his shelf, and imitated his mother's articulate, thoughtful expression, and then his father's handsome laugh, and then his brother's sexy smoulder. He blinked and looked at himself again. If it could be anyone's face, that meant he could become anyone, he could mould it into the face he wanted. The face of a someone, rather than an anyone; someone who was intelligent and academic. He had played the part of a model school student, so why couldn't he play the part of a model Oxford student? It was just a question of theatre – he had to say the right lines, wear the right clothes, attend the right classes and lectures, so that no one would be able to tell him apart from the real students here, the clever ones who got their places on merit. As long as he read everything he was told to, as long as he learned it and repeated it in an appropriate order, who would notice the difference between assiduous research and straightforward plagiarism? No one had so far. 'And no one will now,' said Omar to himself, leaning his forehead against the glass. He had to make a choice – to hide in his room forever, or to let himself out and play his part.

At that moment there was another knock on the door. This time Omar opened it, hanging his towel over his shoulder. There were three students in the hall, a handsome boy in a checked shirt, with a flush of high colour across his cheeks, accompanied by a pretty red-headed girl, and a bespectacled boy who looked even more skinny

than he did. 'Hello Rashid!' said the handsome boy cheerfully. 'I'm Jim Oakley, I've got the room at the bottom of
the staircase. I thought you'd died in there. We hadn't
heard a peep from you since your parents left.'

'Yeah, sorry,' answered Omar sleepily, stifling a fake
yawn, and dabbing at his face with his towel. 'I must have
fallen asleep. Had a late one last night, you know what
it's like.' He shrugged sheepishly as Jim and his companions nodded sympathetically, and perhaps even with
approval. 'It's Omar, by the way,' he said, stretching out
his hand. 'Pleased to meet you all.'

'Omar? You know it says "Rashid Khan" on the
staircase list downstairs,' said Jim.

'Oh, that's my middle name. Well, Omar's my middle
name really. But it's what everyone calls me. I'll ask them
to change it when I get a chance,' Omar explained with a
smile.

'Yeah, tell me about it,' said the other boy. 'I'm Ted,
and they've put Edward on my sign. Edward, I ask you!'

'We thought you might want to come to the JCR with
us,' said the pretty girl. 'There's a tea for all the new
students.'

'Sure,' said Omar and, putting his key in his pocket,
shut the door behind him on his old life, and his old
mediocre self, and walked down the winding spiral staircase to his new one. 'So, what are you reading?' he asked
companionably as they made their way downstairs. 'I'm
reading PPE.'

After the flurry of the Freshers week, with the drinks parties and the long evenings in the bar, Omar found his natural place in the college community. Unlike school, where he was without doubt at the bottom of the pecking order, at college he found he was accepted quickly. Part of this was to do with Jim, who was clearly the most popular boy in his college year. After the first day, when Jim had taken it on himself to knock on every door in the staircase and take command of the introductions, Jim never had to knock on a door again. He was lucky enough to have an enormous room at the bottom of the staircase, with a view to the street rather than the college. Despite the size, his room was always full of visitors, and the notepad that hung on his door was constantly covered in scribbled messages.

Against the odds, given the competition, Omar found that he and Jim became friends quite early on, from the first time he had helped Jim back to their staircase after too many drinks at one of the welcome parties. He was glad he didn't have to drag him up too many stairs, as Jim was quite a bit bigger than he was. He put him on his bed and as he turned to go, he heard Jim lurch. He raced over with the waste-paper bin, into which Jim threw up messily and copiously. 'Thanks, Omar, you're a bloody good mate,' mumbled Jim. 'Come round for tea tomorrow.'

Omar remembered the invitation, although he doubted that Jim did. Returning up the street to college at teatime, he heard music from Jim's room and thought he may as well pop in. He hovered nervously outside the door for a moment and, hearing voices inside, debated whether to knock; when he finally did, it was so lightly that he thought it might not be noticed. However, Jim opened the door immediately. 'Omar, you're late, come on in. I've started cutting cake already.' Omar wandered in, and felt he'd walked into a tardis. Jim's room seemed to have expanded with the volume of people that filled it; some he didn't even recognize. He sat next to pretty red-headed Karen, from the staircase, and chatted about the hangover he didn't have. Jim, the perfect host, brandished an enormous purple-spotted teapot and poured Omar a cup of tea, before popping over to have a few words with him. 'Are you going to the Union thing next Thursday?' Jim asked, slurping ostentatiously from his own cup of tea.

'I can't, I have to nip back down to London for the night,' Omar said regretfully, as everyone else seemed to be going.

'Parents giving you grief already? Or is it your girl-friend?' asked Jim.

'Neither, I've just got a gig,' Omar said modestly. 'I'm in a band.'

'That's fantastic!' said Jim. 'Listen, everyone, did you know that Omar here is in a band in London!' He turned back to Omar. 'So what do you play?'

'Oh, just guitar, and I do some backing vocals. I don't really sing.'

After that, Jim insisted that Omar fetch his guitar and play for them and, sheepishly, Omar agreed. At Jim's tea party, he was suddenly the star turn, while the students listened and whooped. His reputation as one of Jim's crowd in college was thus established, and in the following weeks he was surprised to find that so many likeable people seemed to like him. Even more surprising, no one thought that he was particularly unusual or geeky for spending eight hours a day in the Bodleian or college library, when not attending lectures or tutorials, emerging only for social events, meals and evening drinks. He really wasn't that odd at all, he realized; he was like almost everyone else.

One evening, after Hall, Omar was cramming on the Cold War and détente for a politics tutorial, when there was an urgent knock on his door. 'Omar, mate, you've got to let me in NOW,' Jim whispered. Omar opened the door.

'What's up, Oakley?' he asked, honoured that Jim had come up to his room. Jim hardly ever had to visit other people's rooms for company, people came to him.

'Bloody Boring Benjy saw I was in from the street, and he's coming round to visit with that appalling girlfriend of his from Christchurch. I had to escape or I'd be stuck with them for hours.'

'Won't they think it a bit odd that you've suddenly disappeared?' asked Omar, a bit disappointed that Jim hadn't come for a chat.

'Nope, I didn't let them see that I'd seen them, I had my head over my desk. They'll just think I nipped out, and hopefully get bored and go away,' said Jim cheerfully, sitting on Omar's armchair and reaching for one of his biscuits without waiting to be asked. 'Cool, I love Hob-Nobs,' he said, his mouth full.

'Your table manners are appalling,' chided Omar. 'Would you like a tea, or coffee, or hot chocolate?'

'I know, my mother keeps telling me,' Jim said, before adding dramatically, 'Tea, please. I'm positively *dying* for a cup of tea.' Looking critically at Omar's drinks selection, he asked, 'Why do you have so much hot chocolate? You don't even drink the stuff, do you?'

'I keep it for the girls, it's all they ever ask for,' admitted Omar.

'God, I know. Bloody girls are costing me a fortune in Baileys, hot chocolate and biscuits; maybe if I go cold turkey and stop supplying refreshments, people will stop coming,' Jim said, with only half a smile. He looked out of Omar's window. 'God, you've got the best view. I wish I had a room like this. You've got the sunset and the spires. You're out of the way, so no one can see if you're in, and it's small enough to have no one crowding you like you're the bloody JCR. It's an utter curse having a big room . . .'

'Do you really think people come to you just because you've got Baileys and a big room?' asked Omar, interested.

'No, they come for my sparkling wit and repartee,' said Jim, this time with a proper smile, as he accepted his tea graciously. 'You know what? I'm glad Bloody Boring Benj turned up. I've been working for hours, and I didn't realize how much I needed a tea break.'

'Having an essay crisis?' asked Omar sympathetically, trying out this new snippet of college lingo that he had learned.

'Yeah, but I've had enough. I think I'll go to the bar after this and scrounge the papers off the second years to copy out.'

'Won't the tutors notice?' asked Omar, perturbed by the openness of Jim's subversive intentions.

'I've thought about it – the trick is to borrow lots of papers, not just one. After all, it's only plagiarism if you borrow from one person. Borrow from lots, and it's research,' Jim said innocently. He saw a brief flash of frozen horror on Omar's face, and stopped mid-munch. 'Are you all right, mate? You look like you've seen a ghost.'

'No, I'm fine,' said Omar, realizing that he hadn't been found out, and that Jim hadn't come upstairs to expose him. He was just making conversation. 'You just reminded me of my own essay crisis. It's hard keeping up and playing with the band. I'm down in town again tomorrow.'

'Another gig? You guys must be doing well,' said Jim. 'Do you have lots of groupies following you around?'

'My brother has a few,' said Omar. 'He's the lead singer, and . . . well . . . girls seem to like him.' He nodded towards a family photo sitting on top of the cupboard, in one of Shona's chunky wood frames. It was a half-posed picture from that summer, with all of them at the sunny garden table. Shona and Parvez were standing behind the boys with poised smiles to the camera, waiting for the timer to go off, while Sharif and Omar were sitting at the table with part-finished beers in front of them, looking at each other and laughing at some private joke. Omar liked the picture, as there weren't many photos of him laughing and he thought it made him look less like himself. Although there was the telltale give-away of the beer, whichever way Omar looked at the photo, whether with eyes wide or with a squint, it always seemed to him that Sharif's beer glass was half-full, and his own was half-empty. He wondered if that's what other people thought, too. He looked expectantly at Jim, waiting for the inevitable comment, the one that tended to follow in just a few seconds. One . . . two . . . three . . .

'Christ, your brother's good-looking!' said Jim, right on cue. Omar gave a disappointed smile at being proved right again; even his brother's two-dimensional image in a four-by-six-inch frame was more influential than him, when he was sitting here, real, living and breathing and offering tea and biscuits and sanctuary. Jim saw what he had done instantly, and added diplomatically, 'I mean, your whole family's bloody good-looking. Your dad looks like James Bond. And is that really your mum? She looks about thirty.'

'Yeah, well, add ten and you'd get it about right,' said Omar, unoffended. 'So, like I said, Sharif gets all the girls.'

'And what about you? No little band bitch waiting for you back in London?' Jim said affably.

Omar shrugged, and smiled despite himself. 'Nope, no band bitch. No bitch at all. Unless you count the new puppy that's at home. What about you? Have you got a girlfriend back in Cornwall?'

'Nope, no girlfriend, and no boyfriend either; just a pitifully large circle of close acquaintants to make up for the gaping hole in my sex life.' Jim sighed comically, and took another slurp of his tea. When he saw Omar's jaw drop, Jim asked, 'You knew I was bi, didn't you? It's hardly a secret; one look at my record collection gives it away.'

'Well, I like Abba and Erasure too,' argued Omar. 'Sorry, I didn't realize. I'm a bit dense about noticing things.' They sat in silence for a moment, Omar worried that he'd embarrassed Jim. He opened his mouth to say something, but had barely muttered, 'Um, I guess . . .' when Jim sprang up and put his hand over Omar's mouth, indicating towards the door in mime. Omar was too shocked by the physical contact to do anything. Jim's hand was very warm from holding his cup of tea, and smelled of soap and cookies – it smelled like his mother's hand. Then Omar understood, and crept towards the door, where voices could be clearly heard coming up the staircase, the unmistakable braying of Bloody Boring Benj and his horsey girlfriend. Omar gently clicked the lock on the door and scribbled quickly on the back of his notes, 'Benj in same Philosophy class as me; he's probably come up 2 wait here until U get back.' Jim nodded, rolling his eyes as the voices got closer and louder and, mouthing, 'Sorry about this,' he flicked off the light. They sat con-spiratorially in the shadows, lit only by the flickering gas fire, until Benj and his girlfriend got to the door, the girlfriend complaining shrewishly about the number of stairs she'd had to climb in her new high-heeled boots.

Benj rapped sharply on the door, and then waited a moment and rapped again. 'Omar, you there?' he called.

'He's not there, Benjy. You can see his light's not on,' the girl said. 'Anyway, I only wanted to see Jimmy, he's so sweet. Not his hangers-on.'

'I just thought his light was on outside. Maybe it was the next window along,' mused Benj. 'Let's go and see Abigail, she's just a couple of staircases down.'

'Just as long as she's on the ground floor,' grumbled the girl, tip-tapping down the stairs.

Omar waited a moment, and flicked the light back on. Jim let out a great sigh of relief. 'Sorry about that, you can see why I had to escape. They're such tossers. "Jimmy's so sweet." Makes you want to puke.'

'Maybe you're too nice to them. My mum's a bit like that. Nice to everyone, sometimes insincerely. If you're always nice to them, how would they know you don't like them?'

'How could they honestly think that anyone *would* like them?' said Jim bitchily, but with such apparent wide-eyed sincerity that Omar had to laugh.

'I was going to say, before they came up, that I guess it must be hard, being bisexual. Like you don't quite belong to one thing or another, or that you can't quite be yourself,' Omar asked, hoping it didn't sound too personal.

'Well, maybe back in Cornwall it was hard. I wasn't terribly open about it there; I was the head boy at my school. I kissed girls in public and boys in private. But here, in Oxford, it's different,' Jim said thoughtfully. 'Haven't you noticed, Omar? Here, no one quite belongs, and no one is quite themselves. They're all big fish from little ponds and they don't know what to do now they're not special any more. They're all playing a part – pretending to be clever, pretending to be best friends with people they met a few weeks ago, pretending to care about all the twee Oxfordy stuff like the Union and rowing and stripy scarves and crap like that, just to fit in.'

Omar felt chastened, and relieved at the same time;

he'd been wallowing in his complexes and melancholy, and yet here was Jim blithely saying that everyone shared the same disease as him. 'I guess we're all guilty of doing that a bit,' agreed Omar. He felt a great weight lifted from him.

Although the threat of Benj had also been lifted, Jim stayed for another cup of tea and finished the rest of Omar's HobNobs, inspecting his record collection with a mixture of glee and groans. 'Are you sure you won't come down to the bar?' he asked when he finally made to leave.

'No, I'll try and finish this essay off the old-fashioned way,' said Omar, 'but good luck with sharking the second years.'

As Jim got up, Omar couldn't resist asking him, out of pure self-interest, 'So what do you think you do, if you don't want to play a part, if you just want to be yourself?'

Jim smiled naughtily. 'You do the only honest, sincere thing that an Oxford student can do,' he said, gesturing towards the moonlit buildings beyond Omar's turret window. 'You admire the bloody architecture.'

Between Greek Tragedy and Courtly Romance

THE DAY THAT Dermot was due to sit in on her lesson, Shona walked into her classroom a good five minutes early, to see that he had already installed himself at the far end of the long, oval table at which she took her class. He was being accosted by the anally keen Imogen, a bespectacled, frazzle-haired student who must have raced straight up to the room after her lunch to get a head start on her classmates.

'Of course, Racine's not a patch on Euripides,' Imogen was saying pompously. She was taking Greek and Latin A levels, and planned to read Classics at university. She was turned towards Dermot, away from the door, and wasn't aware of Shona's entrance. 'He tries to write ancient Greek tragedy, but what he actually writes is seventeenth-century French courtly romance. I mean, look at this from the second act – "Je l'ai trop aimé pour ne le point haïr" – it's just pure romantic cliché, isn't it, sir?' Dermot looked confused, and seemed visibly relieved at Shona's entrance, his eyes eloquently asking for help.

Shona coughed to alert Imogen to her presence, before

translating kindly for Dermot. 'I have loved him too much not to hate him now,' she said. 'It may also be considered a universal truth.'

'Miss, you should have said you were there,' Imogen said reproachfully, putting down her book.

Shona was going to ask Dermot if he wouldn't mind taking a seat by the window, away from the table, so that he would be more of an observer than part of the class, but at that moment, two of the other girls rushed in. 'I told you we were late, Harriet,' said a worried-looking, pretty girl, with thick, dark hair cut squarely at shoulder-length.

'We're not, we're two minutes early, aren't we, Miss?' said a confident, crop-haired blonde, with a pointy nose and a too-short skirt.

'You are indeed,' said Shona, checking her watch. 'As you can see, we've got Mr O'Connor joining us for this class. He's not here to check up on you, he's just observing how we do things here, so do just be yourselves.' The other girls joined the class, the last one still in her lacrosse kit and apologizing for being late, and they all squashed themselves up at the centre of the oval table, rather than take a seat next to either Shona at the head of the table, or Dermot at the other end.

'Très bien. Bonjour tout le monde, on va commencer,' said Shona. 'Imogen here was just telling us how she felt that Racine was romantic rather than tragic. There are certainly complex relationships in *Andromaque*, and if you're not already familiar with the characters from Greek texts, mapping them out can be useful. Who wants to start us off?' Predictably, Imogen raised her hand quickly and keenly. 'Thank you, Imogen, let's start with Oreste . . .'

Later in the class, Shona had Becky, the pretty, dark-haired girl, reading Oreste and Charlie, the lacrosse player, reading the part of his friend, Pylade.

'Vous me trompiez, Seigneur,' Charlie said, attempting to sound righteous and to roll her r's at the same time.

'Je me trompais moi-même,' Becky said mournfully.

'Thank you,' Shona said. 'So what exactly does this exchange mean, in the dynamic of the play? Harriet?'

'It's where Oreste is forced to come clean about his feelings for Hermione,' said Harriet casually, as though she were talking about a daytime soap. 'Oreste admits why he's really come to see Pyrrhus; it's not because of ambassadorial duty, but because he's still in love with Hermione and wants her back. He wasn't just fooling his best friend, he was fooling himself. And now they both know the truth, their mission has to change.'

'Very good,' Shona said, pleased that Harriet could give such a simple explanation of a complex moment. 'But let's dig a little deeper. Is this really just about fooling oneself? What does Pylade mean when he says "Vous me trompiez"? Is he just saying, "You tricked me, sir," as though it was a gag between friends? Pylade is indignant, he's upset, this is something more than a joke gone wrong. What do you think "Vous me trompiez" could mean in this context?'

'You misled me?' asked Charlie.

'You disappointed me?' suggested Becky.

'You deceived me,' stated Dermot.

'Exactly!' said Shona triumphantly, before she registered who had said it. 'Umm, thank you, Mr O'Connor.' A touch flustered, she continued, 'It's about deception, and self-deception, a very powerful crime against a friend, and against oneself. Their honour and integrity is bound in the truth. For Oreste to self-deceive, he has been lying to himself, and so he's been divided.'

After the double lesson had finished, Dermot helped Shona rearrange the chairs neatly around the table. 'That was fascinating, Shona,' he said sincerely. 'Your enthusiasm for the text is really infectious. I think even our little cynic Imogen might have re-appraised her views about it just being a love story.'

'She's entitled to her opinions,' shrugged Shona. 'I'm not against love stories, but they're rarely as simple as she might think.' She began wiping the board clean with deep, efficient strokes.

'But you think it's a universal truth that deep hate follows deep love? Isn't that a simplification? It sort of implies that you never really loved someone unless you hate them afterwards, that can't be right.'

'I don't think I really believe that. I was probably just putting Imogen in her place. I don't think true love turns to hate, when it goes away, I mean. I think it just . . .' Shona paused in mid wipe and shook her head. 'What am I saying? You didn't come to my class to hear my opinions on true love . . .'

'I'm sorry,' said Dermot, his chair-arranging complete. He went to the door, and held it open for her.

'What for?' Shona asked sharply, turning to face him, wishing she hadn't said so much.

'For interrupting in the class. I got carried away, I couldn't resist.'

'Oh, that,' Shona said, smiling. 'You're quite forgiven. I'm glad you felt able to participate.'

As they walked down the corridor, Dermot said, 'You know, I might get *The Iliad* out of the library and read it again. I want to know more about Hector; he's the missing hero in *Andromaque*, isn't he? He's already dead at the start of the play, but his heroic presence infiltrates everything – the unseen husband. Pyrrhus is nothing by comparison, he just can't compete for Andromaque's affections. She'd rather be unhappy with the memory of true love, than happy with a real, breathing love.'

'The library copy's missing. I ended up buying my own. I'll lend it to you if you want,' offered Shona generously, trying not to think of her own unseen husband, and the memory of true love. 'It's the Penguin Classic version,' she added.

The Balti Ballads Play Brick Lane

WHEN OMAR REACHED the gig venue in Brick Lane, he was suitably impressed. 'This place is fantastic!' he said in awe to Sharif and Stevo, looking at the high ceilings and the raised stage of the warehouse. 'How did we get a gig like this?'

'Through contacts,' said Sharif wisely. 'I've been busy while you've been pissing about at uni with pretty buildings and plain girls.'

'Through fucking stupidity,' contradicted Stevo, who was noisily setting up his drum kit. 'We're doing this gig for free again, thanks to your brother's negotiation skills; they're taking five quid on the door, of which we get fuck all. Business brain of the century, our Sharif.'

'Have I told you what a wanker of a banker you've become since you've started that business degree at South Bank?' replied Sharif cheerfully, unoffended. 'Besides, we're not doing it for free – we get free drinks and we get five per cent of the bar.'

Slightly mollified, Stevo said, 'Well, you better give it all to me. I'm owed for the set-up costs of our website.'

'We've got a website?' Omar asked.

'It'll go live next month,' Sharif explained. 'You were away, so Stevo, Micky and I sorted out all the content. Just gig dates and photos and shit.'

Micky, who was in his final year of school, slouched in looking shattered. 'Football practice,' he said grimly. 'Focking Tariq almost broke my foot with a dodgy tackle from behind. He'll be a focking liability in the inter-school play-offs next week.'

Balti Ballads were the first band on when the bar opened at nine p.m., and there were just a few dozen people for their first set. Omar was relieved, as despite the rehearsal session they'd had beforehand, he hadn't really got the hang of Sharif's new songs which were so aggressive and high energy that he could hardly hear the words as he shouted them, or keep up with the relentless rhythms. He'd practised them in college, but with nothing like this pace. He hid behind Micky's virtuoso playing and Stevo's now more than competent drumming, and noticed how they were drawing in more and more people from the neighbouring bars, until the place was packed with leaping, sweaty bodies thrusting their fists in the air in unison with Sharif. Omar was relieved and embarrassed when they finally had a break between the sets – he was expecting the rest of the band to bollock him, but they were so pleased with the response that they just downed their pints. Sharif lit a fag and wandered over to Omar.

'I've got a favour to ask you, kid.'

'Sure,' said Omar, feeling that he owed Sharif something for doing so little justice to his new material.

'You remember Ali Rantell? Well, I'm still seeing her,

on and off. And tonight she's brought her little sister along with her – she's just been dumped, or something. Do you mind taking her for a drink or something afterwards so Ali and I can get off on our own?'

'You don't mean Cassie?' Omar said, appalled. 'Why can't Stevo take her out, or Micky?'

'Micky's seeing someone, and Stevo dumped her once already, so she's not going to go anywhere with him. Go on, mate. She's always liked you – she told me she thinks you're sweet. You might even get lucky. Cassie gets off with everyone.'

'Yeah, well that's the point,' muttered Omar. Although he privately thought Cassie was rather nice, she had an appalling reputation. He looked out into the audience and saw the beautiful Ali sitting gracefully at the bar, radiating huge confidence in a tiny skirt. He could just about see her short, curly-haired sister – she had cropped her hair and looked small and vulnerable. He suddenly felt a bit sorry for her; it wouldn't be much fun for her to be stuck alone at the bar while Sharif and Ali shagged backstage. 'OK, I'll have a drink with her or something,' he said grudgingly.

After their set, Omar wandered over to the bar with what he hoped was a nonchalant air, and raised a hand in greeting to Ali and Cassie. Ali, whom Omar didn't really know, exchanged a few words with Cassie and slid her long legs off the bar stool. 'Good set, kid,' she said, patting Omar's cheek in an annoying imitation of his brother, and strutted over to where Sharif was waiting by the stage.

'Hi, Omar. That was a great set,' Cassie said apologetically, looking reproachfully after her sister.

'Hi, Cassie. Nice to see you. Long time, no . . . see,' Omar said hesitantly, realizing halfway through the sentence that there was no way of avoiding repeating the word 'see', but deciding the bar was loud enough for it not to matter. He kissed her on the cheek, and took Ali's seat at the bar. He had never kissed Cassie on the cheek before, but it had become second nature to do it with the girls in college, and so it was almost automatic. It immediately made him feel better, as though Cassie was a friend, rather than a vague acquaintance whom he knew mainly by reputation.

'Would you like a drink?' Cassie asked. 'You must be parched after all that.'

'Yeah, um, a pint of Stella, please, if that's all right.' Watching Cassie struggle in her purse for change, Omar remembered his manners. 'In fact, let me. What would you like?'

'Diet Coke, please,' said Cassie gratefully.

While they sipped their drinks, Omar looked properly at Cassie, who looked much more appealing than he remembered. Her cropped hair suited her, and she had either lost weight or discovered more flattering clothes, as she looked less busty, and rather svelte in her dark jeans and black, shiny vest. After Omar had run through asking after all the mutual friends he could rack his brains for, wisely omitting Stevo, he had to resort to asking how she was herself.

'Oh, I'm OK,' said Cassie, with a studied nonchalance that Omar recognized from his own experience to be put on.

'Well, how's college, and life and stuff? Are you seeing anyone nice?' Omar asked this before he remembered that she had just been dumped. Shit, shit, shit.

'No college, yet. I'm retaking my A levels. I kind of screwed up,' Cassie said, dropping the nonchalant air as she looked deep into the dregs of her Diet Coke and pulled out the lemon slice. She starting chewing on the sour skin. 'No someone nice in my life, I got kind of screwed over. Screwed Up, and Screwed Over.' She gave a feeble laugh at herself. 'Hey, I should give that to you guys for a song, it sounds like one of yours.'

Omar looked back out to the stage, wondering how long Ali was going to be. 'Would you like a proper drink?' he asked kindly. He didn't mind listening to Cassie's problems, he was quite good at listening.

Cassie turned to him with a sigh. 'You're sweet, Omar, but all I really want is to go home and eat something. I didn't want to get dragged out by Ali, and she made me drink all these vodka shots to cheer me up, and I don't think it helped.'

'Do you want me to help you get a cab, then?' Omar offered.

Cassie shook her head. 'No, I promised I'd wait for Ali. I can't just leave her in Brick Lane, she'd be furious.'

'Well, would you like to pop out and get some food then? Some dinner? No point you starving while you're waiting.'

Cassie looked up gratefully again and nodded, with a

slight smile. He went with her to get her coat, before they walked out into the chilly bright lights of Brick Lane, and realized, as someone tried to sell him a rose out of a plastic bucket at the exit, that he had asked someone to dinner, and they had said yes. To all intents and purposes, he was on a date, with a girl.

In the curry house, Cassie politely ordered a veggie biryani, which was one of the cheapest things on the menu, and fell on the poppadums with indecent haste. Omar felt comfortable enough with Cassie to order a Coke for himself, something he would never have dared to do with Sharif and the boys, and listened sympathetically while she told him about the demise of her last relationship. It seemed that the boy, not a local one, had also been seeing a friend of hers; and when she had found out and confronted him, he had pointed out that she was just too much of a slut to go out with properly; he had just been using her for sex. And to make it worse, her hardly virginal friend had continued to see him, without any apologies, and had in fact cut Cassie out of her life instead. It was an unpalatable story that she seemed to find a lot easier to tell on a full stomach.

'Thanks, for this,' Cassie said. 'I feel so much better now. I think all that vodka was just making me maudlin.' She mopped up her remaining curry with a bit of the naan bread that Omar had insisted on ordering. 'The thing that hurts is that I really thought that Nico liked me. I didn't think he loved me or anything like that, but I really thought he liked me. It's all I wanted. It didn't seem so much to ask for.'

'It's not so much, it's all you deserve,' Omar said,

covering her hand with his in a comradely gesture. Cassie was a nice girl. He had always thought that she seemed sweet, and could never understand why she slept with so many people. Didn't she realize what people would think of her, what it did for her reputation? 'Did you like him?' Omar asked.

Cassie looked at him thoughtfully. 'I did like him; but then, I think I started to like him just because I thought he liked me. I'm always doing that.' She dipped her head and ran her hand over the back of her bare neck in an unconscious gesture, smoothing back her boyish crop. 'What about you, Omar? Are you seeing anyone at college?'

Taken aback at the perfectly normal question, Omar stuttered, 'No, not really.' Bizarrely, he thought about Jim and his legions of fans, not so unlike Sharif really. 'Not at all, in fact. I've made some really good friends, with other guys and girls. It's been really good so far.'

'I'm sure you're a really good friend,' Cassie said, looking straight at him.

After Omar paid the bill, with Cassie insisting on taking his address to post him what she owed, they stumbled out into the night and back towards the club, high on curry and spices. In a dark part of the street, Cassie stumbled against Omar on purpose, pushing him a little way down a shallow alleyway.

She stood in front of him for a moment, and then started kissing him. Omar was too shocked at first to react, and then thought, She really is a sweet girl, she's quite pretty . . . what would it matter if I kissed her back?

It's just a kiss. And so he started kissing her back, hesitantly, and as he did so, found himself drawn closer and closer to Cassie's body, his hands slipping down over her bottom, which was really quite nicely firm and tight under her jeans. Cassie put her hands over his, unembarrassed, making his grip on her bottom tighter. With this gesture, something snapped in Omar, and he started kissing her fiercely, almost aggressively. In a cruel, dark moment on the dark street, while Cassie pressed her body against his and reached down for the buttons below his waist, Omar was appalled to find himself wanting to shag her, then and there, to turn her round and push her roughly against the wall, to prove himself with her, to use her. He didn't feel passion or excitement towards her, he simply felt cold and in control. The emotion he felt was like violence. 'You like me, don't you, Omar?' she said, with innocent appeal. And Omar began to understand why she had ended up being mistreated quite so often.

'I do, Cassie, I do really like you. You're a nice girl,' Omar said firmly, pushing her away gently. He removed her hands, and held them kindly. 'You're a nice girl, and you don't need to do this just because I bought you dinner, or because I listened to you.'

'Don't you think I'm attractive?' asked Cassie, in a small voice, turning away.

Omar squeezed her hands reassuringly. 'I do. I think your new hair really suits you, and you have a fantastic arse. A butt like a ten-year-old boy, as Sharif would say.' He was rewarded with a slight puff of a giggle from Cassie, as she turned back towards him, eyes shining hopefully. 'I'm sorry I kissed you back and misled you – you are pretty and you are very nice. But I just don't feel that way for you.'

Still holding her hands, Omar pulled her out of the alleyway and started walking her back towards the club. 'Well, this is new. I normally get rejected afterwards, not before,' Cassie said, but not quite disconsolately.

'Maybe you should wait a little while, then you might not get rejected at all.' Omar knew he had no experience in these matters, but continued regardless. 'I think that blokes, especially blokes our age, are basically selfish. If you offer them something, they take it, and ask themselves whether they want it afterwards.'

Cassie walked on for a bit in silence, and said, 'You know, the first time I did it, I was only fifteen. It was on the green outside school. It was dark, and I thought he really liked me, and I didn't enjoy it at all but I thought he would like me even more afterwards. But he only said he liked me to my face, and told everyone else that I was a bloody good ride. And the next person I went out with expected it, and said I couldn't really like him if I wouldn't, after I'd already done it with someone else. And I did it, just to wipe away the last time. And it was better, but not much. I'd had sex with four people before I was sixteen.' She scuffed her toe against the curb. 'Maybe I am just a slapper.'

'You're really not,' said Omar fiercely. 'Men are just bastards,' he added without thinking. He had to stop and laugh. 'God, that made me sound like a girl, didn't it . . .?'

Cassie squeezed his hand, and stopped to kiss him on the cheek. 'I think you really are a sweet man, Omar.'

When they got back to the bar, Ali and Sharif were waiting for them. Ali looked thunderous, and Sharif was casually leaning against the wall, with a fag dripping out of his mouth. 'About bloody time. I've been waiting fucking forever for you,' Ali said crossly to Cassie. 'Come on, we're going.' She didn't say goodbye to Sharif, and made off down the street with Cassie in tow towards the minicabs, with strides as long as her miniskirt would allow.

Omar looked at Sharif, waiting for an explanation. 'So, nice date with Cassie?' was all Sharif said, after a long pause. 'Snog her, did you? Or just shag her against the wall?'

Omar pursed his lips, and thrust his hands deep into his pockets to stop himself shaking Sharif. 'That's bang out of order, mate. She's a sweet girl, you've no right to talk about her like that. And yes, we had a nice dinner, thank you.'

'Oh, put your handbag away before I get scared . . .' retorted Sharif in a bored voice. 'Is it your time of the month or something?'

Omar ignored the jibe, and nodded towards Ali and Cassie, who were getting in a cab. 'Did you and the lovely Ali have a fight, then?'

'Not exactly. I just said that I thought we might stop seeing each other so much, start seeing other people,' Sharif said casually.

Men really are bastards, thought Omar. He'd bet that Sharif waited until after they'd had sex before he said it. 'What brought that on?' he asked diplomatically.

Sharif shrugged. 'She was just getting a bit territorial.

Complaining that we never meet at our flats, that we're always outside somewhere when we, you know . . . But that's how I like it. What does she want me to do – stay over and have breakfast with her bloody family?' Sharif stubbed out his cigarette. 'I'll miss her a bit – for a pretty girl she was pure filth.' He looked at Omar. 'Are you coming back to mine tonight, or staying at home?'

Omar felt his stomach churn with loathing for his brother, and looked at his watch. 'I'll do what I did last time, I'll get the coach back to college. They run through the night, and I've got lectures in the morning.' Sharif's behaviour had helped him find the little bit of indignation and bravery to say what he'd been thinking about for a while. He swallowed nervously and said, 'Sharif, I need to talk to you. You know how hard it's been coming down for gigs with me being at college. I just don't think I can do it any more.'

'Don't be soft. What are you saying? You're going to leave our band? Just because you're fannying about in college somewhere hardly an hour from here – give me a break,' Sharif scoffed.

'Yes, I am. I can't be part of the band any more,' Omar said. 'I'm sorry.'

Sharif heard the seriousness in Omar's voice, and looked at him with a sudden cold fury, as though he'd been betrayed. 'You know what, kid. You can't stop being a part of the band, as that would mean that you actually belonged in the first place,' he said cruelly. 'I'm not sorry you're buggering off. I only let you in because I was sorry for you. You were always the weakest link.' Nodding at the doorman, he walked back into the club.

Omar walked down towards Liverpool Street. He would get a bus to Marble Arch to get the Oxford Tube back to college. He realized how much he was looking forward to seeing Jim over tea and biscuits, and telling him about his last gig.

The Trouble with December Evenings

JONTY AND SHONA were sitting in the staffroom, long after the end of school, and were both avoiding going home for similar reasons. Jonty had argued with his wife, and was flicking through the Ceefax pages, going through a packet of bourbons all by himself. Shona was doing some marking, which she could just as well do at home, but didn't really want to. Things would be better at home when Omar came back for the Christmas holidays; she hoped he hadn't made any plans with his new friends from college. She wondered what he'd think of Patrick-Bob. And Sharif would come back for Christmas Day, maybe she could persuade him to stay until New Year. It would all be back to normal then; they could go back to being a happy family for a few days.

Jonty and Shona were both surprised by Dermot walking into the staffroom. Jonty had stopped trying to look busy around Dermot, and raised his hand in a silent greeting. 'Hello, both,' Dermot said affably. 'Still burning the midnight oil?'

'It feels like midnight,' Jonty said despondently,

looking at the pitch-black gloom outside. 'Where've you been?'

'I was setting some stuff up in the language lab,' Dermot said vaguely. 'It's hard to get some time in that room without someone else hogging it.' He looked at his watch. 'Well, it's six-thirty, so I think that it would be permissible to have a drink. Anyone care to join me?' He looked expectantly at both of them. 'Jonty, are you game?'

A text beeped on Jonty's mobile. He looked at it and sighed. 'From the Trouble and Strife. Sorry, Dermot. I think I had really better get home. Maybe Shona will go with you?' He finished off his last bourbon biscuit wearily.

Dermot looked at Shona. 'Well, Shona, how about it? Will you join me for a drink? A very quick one, I promise.'

'No thanks,' said Shona. 'I'd better be getting home, too. My husband will be wondering who's going to burn his dinner tonight . . .' Privately, she would have rather liked a drink, but didn't like being the second choice. Dermot had clearly wanted a laddish drink with Jonty and was only asking her to be polite.

Shona was waiting at the damp bus stop, and opened her umbrella as she felt the first spots of rain. Bloody miserable December evenings, she thought to herself, as though it was all December's fault that her evenings had become so miserable. A dark blue car pulled up next to the bus stop. Hope he gets a fine, parking in the bloody bus lane, she continued to gripe. She was surprised when Dermot wound down the window and said, 'Do you want a lift home, Shona? It's a grim evening. You're just in Tooting, aren't you?'

'Hi, Dermot. No thanks, really, I'm fine,' Shona demurred, but looking down the icy road, she saw no cheerful red bus in sight. 'Well, OK then, if it doesn't take you too far out of your way. It's just near Tooting Bec tube.' She hopped in, and pulled the seat belt on. 'So, I guess you didn't get your drink?' she said politely.

'Well, I didn't really want to sit in the pub by myself on a Friday night. I'd probably bump into half the students littering up the local, anyway.'

Shona laughed. 'Did Pam ever tell you about the time we bumped into some of our girls in the Admiral's Arms one afternoon? We both had a double free period as it was GCSE exam week, so we skived off to the pub, and saw a group of our girls from the lower sixth on the other side of the bar.'

'What did you do? Report them?' asked Dermot, amused.

'Oh God, no. They shouldn't have been there, and neither should we. So we all did the decent thing, we pretended we hadn't seen each other, drank up quickly, left, and didn't mention it once we got back to class.'

'Outrageous!' laughed Dermot. 'Jane would not be pleased!'

'You're not to tell tales about Pam and me to the head,' Shona said firmly. 'We'll flatly deny it,' she added with a twinkle.

'So, any plans for the evening?' asked Dermot. 'What are you going to burn for your poor husband tonight?'

'Oh, the usual,' Shona answered airily. 'What about you?'

'I've got a hot date with Tamarind, my local Indian. I can never bear to cook for one on a Friday. I always get a takeaway.'

'Is that Tamarind Khan, in Balham?' Shona asked with interest.

'Might be. It's up on Balham High Street, near the Boots.'

'That's one of my husband's restaurants,' Shona said delightedly. 'You might have seen my son in there from time to time, he's started working there. Answers to the name of Sharif. Very handsome lad, always has the girls after him.'

'Must take after his mum,' Dermot said, 'but I can't say I've seen him. Maybe he doesn't work on Friday nights.'

'Oh, maybe not,' said Shona, although she was sure that Sharif was meant to work five days a week. 'Well, I'm glad I'm not taking you out of your way. Balham's just a few minutes from me.'

'We're almost at Tooting Bec now,' Dermot commented. 'Have you never thought about driving to work? It's only a few minutes in a car, but that bus must take forever.'

'Haven't learned to drive yet,' Shona said lightly. 'I started some lessons after I had the boys, but it didn't quite agree with me. And the lessons were so expensive, it seemed a bit wasteful. Parvez took me out a few times but I never felt comfortable with him as my teacher. It was the only thing we ever argued about, back then.' She looked out. 'Could you just drop me off here, near the station? I need to get something from the corner shop,' she lied. She didn't want Dermot driving her all the way home. She didn't want him to meet Parvez, who would probably offer him a drink for his gallantry. She wanted to keep her school and home life separate.

'I could teach you, if you want,' suggested Dermot, pulling over and parking. 'I taught my ex-wife to drive, and she'd failed four times before she met me. I'm a good teacher – it's what I do, after all.'

'I'm sure you are,' said Shona as she stepped out onto the pavement, noticing that it was the first time he had mentioned his 'sort' of marriage since their first stilted meeting. 'Thanks for the offer, but I think my driving days are over. And thanks very much for the ride.' She waved enthusiastically as he drove off, and then turned down the street to walk home.

The school play that Christmas was Noël Coward's *Private Lives*, directed by the sixth-formers under Jonty's watchful, jaundiced eye. Two performances took place on Tuesday and Wednesday of the last week of term, and most of the teachers turned out for the closing party, some with their partners. Parvez had begged off; he normally turned up just to show a united front with Shona, but he really didn't like plays, or theatre, and it clashed with a concert that he wanted to listen to on the radio. After some deeply diluted mulled wine, with so much orange juice added that it was verging on the pink rather than red, most of the teachers headed off to the Admiral's Arms, led by a triumphant Jonty with his embarrassed, sober wife. Shona and Dermot were hemmed into a banquette by the merrymakers, and sat squashed together.

'I knew you'd come out for that drink with me eventually,' Dermot said, clinking his pint glass with Shona's white wine.

'I didn't know you drank Guinness,' Shona said a little stupidly, feeling a bit tired and drunk after the long day.

'I'm Irish, of course I do. I also play the fiddle and dance with my arms glued to my sides,' he answered seriously.

'Do you?' Shona asked, before seeing the twitch in Dermot's mouth. 'Oh, you are taking the mickey. This time, I mean.'

'Am I? I admit I don't play the fiddle, but you've not seen me dance,' laughed Dermot. Shona noticed what white, straight teeth he had. Very un-English teeth. But of course, he wasn't English. Dermot cleared his throat. 'I meant to ask you something, Shona, something about Racine.'

'Sure, what is it?' Shona said amicably. She knew she was on very safe ground with Racine.

'What were you going to say, that day, when you said true hate doesn't follow true love, but something else does? What were you going to say takes the place of true love, once it's gone?'

'I'm not sure that's a question about Racine,' Shona said quietly.

'Maybe it's just a question, then,' Dermot answered.

'Fairytale of New York' struck up on the pub jukebox. Pam, looking very pretty and flushed, with a lot of make-up and a slinky black top, staggered over to join them. 'Where's your handsome husband tonight?' she asked Shona.

'Oh, just busy,' Shona said lightly.

'Shame. Tell him that I missed him,' Pam hiccupped, adding to Dermot, 'Have you met Shona's handsome hubby?'

Dermot shook his head. 'I've not had the pleasure, but I take it that he's quite a catch.'

'Ding and double-dong,' confirmed Pam, 'and he's sooo funny. And he can really dance, too. Tell him, Shona.'

'Oh, I don't like to brag,' said Shona, unable to keep a straight face. She'd not seen Pam this tipsy in ages. Pam downed her drink and pulled Dermot by the hand. 'Come on, Dermot. Dance with me to this one. It's Irish, you know.'

'That I know, Pam,' said Dermot, rising to the occasion with a smile. He let Pam pull him off his seat, and went to dance with her. 'You'll see if I was lying about those arms, now,' he said in an aside to Shona as he got up.

Much later, Shona left the pub, swaying just a tiny bit. As she tip-tapped up the street in her smart heels, she heard someone shouting her name behind her. 'Shona!' Dermot called. 'Hold up!' He ran up to her. 'Isn't your husband picking you up?'

'No, there's a concert he wanted to listen to this evening, and I didn't want to bother him. I thought I'd just get the bus. I don't think you or anyone else is in a fit state to give me a lift tonight,' Shona said. 'Are you heading back to the pub?'

'No, I think I'll call it a night, too. I'll walk you to the bus stop. It's on my way to the station.'

'Sure,' said Shona, although she had already kissed him goodbye that night, on the cheek. She had kissed everyone on the cheek before she left the pub. It was unusually affectionate for her, and proof that she was a little tipsy, but then it was Christmas.

They walked together wordlessly, until Dermot broke the silence by saying, 'I should apologize to you, Shona. I lied to you when we first met.'

'Oh, don't worry about it. I'm sure I've lied to you thousands of times. Everytime I've said Nice day, Nice haircut, Nice assembly, Nice class. Thousands of times,' she said lightly, wondering why she was suddenly being so frank.

'No, really, this is important. I never lie, and I really don't want to have lied to you.'

'What was it?' Shona said, amused at the passion in his tone.

'When I said I didn't really have any children. That was a lie. I did have a child once. She was premature. She died the same day she was born. That was eight years ago.' He said it matter-of-factly. 'I know I was only a father for a day, but I was a father once, and I shouldn't have lied.'

'Oh my God, Dermot, I'm so sorry,' Shona said, woken out of her pleasantly woozy stupor with shock. The fear of losing her children had been her worst nightmare, and one that haunted her throughout her pregnancy. She went to touch his arm with sympathy, but he kept walking, and so she hurried to keep up with him. They were silent until they reached Shona's bus stop.

'Well, here we are,' said Dermot, but he didn't make to go. He just stood there.

Shona had made a decision while they were walking, and said to him bravely, 'You wanted to know what follows when true love goes away? It isn't hate. It's just a nothing, like a void or a vacuum. It's nothing but emptiness.' She looked up at him to kiss him goodbye again; she wished she was brave enough to kiss him on the lips, she could excuse it on the drink, on Christmas; she could deceive herself and him that she hadn't really meant to; she could apologize and say that she was aiming for his cheek but had just missed.

But she didn't have a chance to see how brave or foolish she was, as Dermot said, 'Goodbye, Shona,' and took her by surprise by kissing her quickly, but deliberately, on the lips. There was no mistake, and no apology.

As he walked off, Shona leaned back on the bus stop for support, her knees suddenly weak. She didn't look after him, but stared fixedly ahead at the lights of her approaching bus. When the bus arrived, she sat on it in such a daze that she went two stops past her house and had to get another bus back.

Châteauneuf du Pape in a Clapham Common Flat

THE NEXT DAY, Dermot was conspicuous in his absence from the staffroom. 'Maybe he's in the language lab?' said Jane.

'No, I saw him in the library,' said Jonty.

'I think he's avoiding me,' whispered Pam conspiratorially to Shona, joining her on the window seat. 'I'm sure he wanted to kiss me when we were dancing last night, I could tell. And when he left, he didn't say goodbye to everyone like you did, he just got up and belted off.'

'You might be right,' answered Shona neutrally.

Pam noticed the lack of enthusiasm in Shona's voice, and asked, 'Are you a bit hungover or something? You look dreadful.'

'I'm fine, just a bit tired. And this is how I look without make-up,' Shona said flatly. She had not put any make-up on deliberately, and had worn a dreadful sack of a dress that her mother had sent her, which she normally wore to clean the house in. It was her equivalent of a hair shirt. She thought she was making amends.

Looking at herself in the mirror in the ladies' loo,

Shona saw herself clearly, and realized how ridiculous she was being. It was just a drunken kiss that she hadn't even instigated, and it was probably Pam who had got Dermot all wound up, not her. She combed her hair and applied a bit of lipstick. She looked vastly improved, and felt immediately better. However, as she went to her pigeonhole, her spirits sank. Along with the prep that her students had left for her was a small folded-up note, in Dermot's tiny, precise hand. 'Shona, if you are available, please meet me at Clapham Common tube station tonight at 6 p.m. I have some questions on Racine I'd like to clear up with you before next term. No need to RSVP. Yours, D.'

So what now? Shona thought to herself. She owed him a meeting, didn't she? Just to clear the air before the next term, as he said. Otherwise it could be very awkward working together. And if she didn't go, what did that mean? He had told her not to RSVP, so would he just wait for her, and get the message when she didn't turn up? What message would that be exactly? That she didn't want to be friends, that she didn't forgive him for kissing her when she was tipsy? Well, that wasn't true. She did want to be friends with Dermot; she valued his friendship, even. She could talk to him about books, and language, and literature, and art exhibitions. He had gone with her when she had taken her class to see the performance of *Andromaque* at the Riverside Studios, and talked with enthusiasm about the staging. Sometimes he made her laugh, but most often he made her think. She thought he was probably the most intelligent person she knew. She didn't want to lose him as a friend and colleague over a silly misunderstanding, caused by too much unnecessary truth-telling after too much unnecessary drinking.

She folded up the note, and put it in the pocket of her grey sack dress. Then she called Parvez and told him she'd be late home as she had an off-site meeting with her department head.

Shona was at the tube station fifteen minutes early. She stood nervously by the gates, checking her reflection in the Photo-Me machine. She reapplied her lipstick and then wiped it off, thinking it looked too obvious. She reapplied it, and then wiped it off again, definitely. She was meeting a colleague, she told herself. She really didn't need to look or feel pretty. She pulled out her copy of *Andromaque*, and looked at the pages, not really reading them. When Dermot arrived, she would give him a bright smile and a firm kiss on the cheek. Then he would know that they were friends again, and everything would be back to normal. He'd know that she wasn't cross, and that she knew that he hadn't meant anything by what had happened last night.

At ten minutes before six, Dermot arrived at the station. He didn't come up the escalator from the tube, as Shona had expected. He came down the stairs from the street. When he saw her, he broke into a smile so genuine, of such unadulterated relief and hope, that her firm intentions withered – he practically shone with happiness. He walked quickly towards her, and she reached her arms around his neck and kissed him passionately, breathlessly. Her knees felt weak again. When he pulled away, it was to hold the length of her slight frame against him, and kiss her reverently on her forehead.

Shona pressed her face against his chest, and said disconsolately into his jacket, 'Vous me trompiez, Seigneur.'

'Je me trompais moi-même,' he answered. Shona looked up at him. He was still smiling, but she was practically tearful.

'I'm so glad you came,' he said, unnecessarily, as Shona could read it on his face with more eloquence than his clumsy words could express.

'I think I had to,' Shona answered. He held her close to him as they walked upstairs and out of the tube station, on to the wet, icy street.

'You look beautiful today,' he said sincerely, smoothing a strand of her hair back in place, and brushing his thumb against her full, un-made up, lower lip.

As Shona and Dermot walked along the muddy paths of the Common, his arm protectively around her in the security of the darkness, Shona asked, 'Why here? Why Clapham Common tube?'

'It's where I live,' answered Dermot.

'But I thought you said you lived in Balham?' Shona asked with a frown.

Dermot stopped walking, and kissed her where her brow had furrowed. 'You said I lived in Balham, and I let you assume it because I didn't want you to think I was going out of my way when I drove you home. I thought you might not let me take you any more.'

They walked a little further and sat on a bench, hidden

from the road by the trees, and started kissing again, Shona's small hands reaching inside his jacket to feel his warmth. As they clung to each other like teenagers, Sharif and his new girlfriend approached the bench from across the Common.

'Shit, someone's already there,' he said with disappointment, stopping short a hundred feet from the bench. It was one of his many preferred venues for making love, if you could call it that. He peered through the dark and distance, trying to make out the shadowy forms that were holding each other. 'I think they'll be there for a while. Look at them, they're practically shagging.'

The pretty girl he was with squeezed his waist, and turning to face him, slipped her hand inside his back pocket. 'Don't worry, babe. I know somewhere else we can go.'

As they walked on, Sharif turned and looked back at the embracing couple, sure that there was something disconcertingly familiar about the shape of the woman's hair, but the girl's insistent pull on his hand distracted him, and he didn't think anything more about it.

Oblivious to her passing son, Shona was aware of nothing but Dermot and the cold air separating them. 'Where do you want to go, Shona?' Dermot asked between kisses. 'There's a little bar near here, or we could go to a quiet pub or café, somewhere we can talk.'

Shona didn't answer. Only passion, she felt, would take her through this; if she stopped and talked, she would realize what she was doing and stop altogether. 'Let's go to your place,' she said finally.

'Shona, are you sure?' Dermot said with concern. 'I don't want to rush you into anything.'

'I'm sure,' she said.

As they entered Dermot's bijou bachelor pad, they were still kissing, even as they tumbled through the door. 'Would you like some wine?' asked Dermot.

'No, thank you,' Shona answered. Whatever she was going to say or do, she wanted to say or do it with a clear head so she would have nothing to blame it on apart from herself. She didn't even look at the apartment, she simply pulled off her coat and started undoing Dermot's jacket.

'Shona, we need to talk, about all of this, about us,' Dermot said gently.

'Afterwards. Let's talk afterwards,' she said, not realizing until she said it what she had just proposed. Dermot understood; instead of embarrassing her by asking, 'After what?' he simply took her hand and led her through to his bedroom.

'Only because I have to get you out of this God-awful dress,' Dermot said, pulling the long zip down the length of her back.

'It's my hair-shirt dress. I was doing penance for having impure thoughts,' Shona explained, pulling it down her shoulders.

'And I thought it was just us Catholics who felt guilty for impure thoughts,' Dermot said.

Shona had said that they would talk afterwards, but was surprised at how much Dermot talked to her as they made love. With Parvez, their lovemaking was animal, instinctive and silent, there was no need for words. With Dermot, he admired her, reassured her, asked if she liked this, or liked that, and asked how this or that felt; he was exploring her, learning about her, and in a strange way this vocal, intellectualized lovemaking felt much more intimate, almost uncomfortably so, as he asked her to admit all her likes and feelings and thoughts, so nothing was left hidden or secret. As they moved together, he asked her to look at him, and she opened her eyes to find herself looking straight into his, and their eyes remained locked, connected until the end; she had never noticed the colour of his eyes before – they were grey-blue. Afterwards, Shona lay back, her arms behind her head, and reflected that it was either the best or worst sex she'd had in her life; she was unable to decide which.

Despite the cold of the evening outside, the flat was warm, and Dermot, naked above the duvet, stroked the insides of her arms. 'Would you like that wine, now?' he asked.

'Yes, please,' Shona answered politely, as though nothing at all had happened, and he had offered her a cup of tea in the staffroom. He got up unselfconsciously and still naked, walked through to the kitchen. Parvez would have put his shorts on before he left the bedroom. Shona noticed how pale his skin was compared to Parvez's. It glowed in the low light of the flat. She looked around at his room for the first time. It was filled with books. Huge numbers of books. There were books on literature, books of literary criticism, books on language and grammar, huge coffee table tomes on Dalí and Catalonia, books on Spanish regions, books on philosophy. She saw Voltaire, Rimbaud, Molière, Hugo, and a new copy of Racine, all in translation. She felt instantly comforted. It was the sort of bedroom she would have liked, if only she had the shelf space. It was like her father's study in Dhaka before he repatriated all his books to London.

Dermot walked in with two glasses of dusky red liquid. 'Oh, I'm sorry,' said Shona, 'I thought you knew, I never drink red wine.'

'You said you never drink red wine unless it's a really, really good one,' answered Dermot. 'This is a Châteauneuf du Pape.' He passed her a glass. 'Cheers,' he said, clinking lightly.

'Gosh,' said Shona, sipping it appreciatively. 'This is wonderful. Do you normally keep fine red wines at home to drink by yourself?'

'No,' said Dermot, with a touch of embarrassment. 'I bought this one after you said you only liked really good red wines, with the vague hope that you'd share it with me one day.'

Sitting up, pulling the covers up over her breasts, Shona put down her glass and said reproachfully, 'You never told me. All this time, this last term. You never told me, you never even gave me a hint.'

'You never gave me the slightest impression that you'd be interested if I did tell you,' Dermot replied frankly. 'I asked you for a drink once, and you said no, you had to go back to your husband. I went out of my way to find time with you. I waited for you so I could offer you rides home, but you never waited for me, you never asked me to give you a lift.'

'When?' asked Shona. 'When did you start to . . .' She didn't know how to finish the sentence, it felt juvenile to say 'like me', as though they were in the school yard themselves, but nothing else seemed appropriate. '. . . like me?' she finished feebly.

Dermot sighed. 'I liked you almost from the moment we met – not the day we met, when you were a frosty witch, but almost straight away afterwards. You're funny, and you're so kind to everyone, and I think . . . you might be the most intelligent woman I know.' He kissed her on the forehead again, holding her temples gently on either side. 'This is what I like about you, right here, in your head. You have a wonderful mind, Shona. It's like the British Museum, with hidden gifts in hidden rooms. I want to wander in it with you and roam around.'

Shona was speechless. He thought she was funny; everyone knew that Parvez was the funny one, not her. He saw her well-meaning dissembling for kindness. And unlike Parvez, he liked her for her intelligence, not despite it. It all brought her back to the chivalrous ghost in the room, the unseen husband of the happy, dead memories. 'Don't you want to ask me about Parvez?' she asked.

Dermot exhaled deeply. 'To be honest, Shona, I don't. I know that he's a nice guy, Pam's told me all about him. I know he's good-looking and successful, and that you've been with him for twenty years and raised a family with him. I also know there's something wrong with you and him, or you wouldn't be here with me. I don't want to know any more.'

'You don't think it's your concern?' asked Shona.

'No, you're my concern. I told myself that I could be happy just being your friend, but I was fooling myself; when you kissed everyone in the pub yesterday and left, I couldn't stand it. I've waited a long time to meet someone like you, and I'm not going to give up on you just because you're tied to someone who you don't love any more. I turned forty-one in October, Shona, I'm forty-one years old, and I have nothing to show for my life, absolutely nothing, apart from a moderately successful career.'

He's younger than me, she thought, but she felt the young, foolish one. She had no idea what she was doing here, in this flat, in this bed. It had come from nowhere.

Dermot stroked her hair. 'When did you know that . . . you felt something for me?' he asked.

Shona hugged her knees. 'I didn't know, I didn't even let myself know until I saw you tonight. I wasn't jealous when I saw you flirting with Pam, I didn't mind that you didn't flirt with me, I didn't notice that you were waiting for me to give me a lift home, I didn't even think you had wanted to ask me out for a drink that time, I thought you were just being polite. All the time I was telling myself that I just wanted us to be friends. I just like your company so much, I just like you so much . . .' she trailed off. 'I deceived myself,' she said humbly. 'It's something I've got good at doing, in one way or another.' She finished her glass of wine. 'I'm sorry, Dermot. I really think I had better go now.'

'Shona, please stay. Let me take you out, or cook for you. I promise that I never burn dinner,' Dermot said appealingly.

'I'm sorry, Parvez will be waiting for me. I said I had a meeting with you.'

'Oh, Shona,' he breathed with disappointment, closing his eyes. 'Let me drive you home, at least.'

'No, I don't think that's a good idea. But could you walk me to the tube? I don't think I'd know how to get there. I wasn't really paying attention on the way over.'

Dermot watched Shona dress for a moment before pulling on his jeans, and stepping behind her to help her with the zip. 'You must burn this dress,' he said. 'On the other hand, maybe you should wear it every day. Then no one apart from me will be able to see how heavenly you are.' He pushed aside her hair from the back of her neck as he pulled the zip up to the top, and kissed the skin there, between her hairline and her collar. Shona felt her knees go weak again and she turned round, leaning on his chest of drawers, and kissed him again, as though she really couldn't stop.

They walked back to the station slowly, with a sense of finality. As they approached the steps down to the underground, Dermot pulled her round gently to face him. 'Shona, this wasn't just tonight, was it? I don't want to embarrass you by getting all dramatic, but please don't tell me that this is all it'll be.'

Shona felt seen clearly, and seen through, all at once. She felt like a character in one of the novels she taught, like Anne in *Moderato Cantabile*, letting her almost-affair of a few days last her for her lifetime of monotonous marriage. She stepped back from his arms, and asked, 'You tell me, Dermot. How it can be anything more? All we can have is more nights like this, stolen time when I'll be watching the clock, wondering what excuse to come up with next. And you'll get tired of it, and who can blame you, and you'll go find some lovely unmarried girl, like Pam, whom you can have a proper relationship with, and have children, and have something to show for your life.'

'I don't want a girl like Pam. I don't want children with someone I don't care for. I want you. Don't worry about me getting hurt; I'm a big boy, and I can look out for myself.'

'Well, maybe I'm the one who'll get hurt,' Shona said quietly, her face turned away from him even while he pulled her into his arms.

'Look at me, Shona,' Dermot commanded. And she looked into his grey-blue eyes and felt that connection, that overbearing complicated intimacy she had felt while they were making love. She and Dermot shared neither a silly sense of humour, nor a natural physical compatibility. She realized they shared something quite different, something less accessible and more insidious, something innate; it wasn't a feeling she'd had before, and she didn't know how to put a name to it. Dermot continued, 'You said you liked me before. How do you say that in French?'

'I like you is just "Tu me plais", you please me,' Shona explained, taken aback by the question. 'You don't really translate "I like you" directly, as that's "Je t'aime", which means something . . . quite different.'

'Which "I like you" did you mean?' asked Dermot. At Shona's silence, he said, 'You don't have to answer that, it wasn't a fair question. But I need you to know something. I like you; I mean, I think I'm falling in like with you. And I meant what I said, about not giving up on you.'

Shona blinked back silent tears. She didn't think she was funny, kind or intelligent; she thought she was dull, deceitful, and downright stupid to have got herself into this situation. And yet, despite all her faults, she had somehow become loved once more; somehow, in the course of her deceit and dissembling, she had become lovable.

Burnt Cookies and Driving Lessons

O N THE LAST day of winter term Dermot arrived in school earlier than usual, hoping that Shona would have had the same idea and that they might have some time to spend together before the rest of the staff blundered in with Christmas goodwill. In fact, she arrived late, like all the others, barely before the nine a.m. bell, and distributed a batch of home-baked cookies before rushing off to her middle-fourth class. There were no more lessons after the mid-morning break, as the grand hall was turned into a Christmas fête, with stalls manned by parent, teacher and student volunteers. During the noisy and bustling set-up, accompanied by the school Barber Shop Quartet rehearsing Christmas standards, Dermot sought refuge in the staffroom, and for once got his own tea as his usual fan club were engrossed in comparing the presents they had been given by their various classes. He munched on one of Shona's chocolate-chunk cookies, which really weren't that bad as they had probably twice the number of chocolate chunks that were required, which disguised the rather thin and burnt biscuit they nestled in.

He was slightly perturbed by the realization that Shona's first act on having gone home, after they had confessed their feelings and made love, must have been to bake a batch of cookies.

On cue, Shona walked into the staffroom, struggling with the heavy door as she balanced some little presents in her arms. On seeing Dermot eating her cookies, she gave him a bright, artificial smile, before joining Pam at her spot on the window seat. Shona didn't give him a second glance, and let Pam chat animatedly to her while she smiled and laughed occasionally. She was wearing make-up and her hair was perfect; she had neither dressed up nor dressed down. When Pam left the seat, Dermot swallowed his tea anxiously and approached. Shona smiled brightly again and asked casually, 'So, Dermot, are you going to the fête later?' She had none of Dermot's nervous dryness, and she cast him no meaningful glance. She was acting perfectly normally – it was as though he had imagined the night before.

'I thought I might,' he almost stammered. 'Just to give, you know, a show of support.' When Shona looked like she was going to turn her attention back to her tea, he asked, 'And you?'

'Oh, I'll stick around until they call the raffle. You never know, I might get lucky and win the stash of home-made wine that Jonty's donated,' Shona said cheerfully.

'Well, I was after that little stash myself,' Dermot said, his nervousness abating with annoyance at Shona's insouciance. How could she not feel a little bit of what he was feeling? 'You can't have Châteauneuf du Pape every day, after all.' After dropping that hint, he looked deeply in her eyes for longer than was discreet, and saw that she was giving absolutely nothing away. She was the picture of serene normality. So this is how she thinks it's going to be, he thought. She's going to pretend that nothing happened, and wipe it away like a third-year pupil's bad conjugation on the whiteboard. He turned his attention to Pam, who was furiously pretending not to be interested. 'Pam, are you doing anything for the fête?' he asked with a charming smile that crinkled the edges of his eyes.

When Shona left the staffroom, Dermot made an excuse and followed her swiftly; she went into the little cubby where the staff pigeonholes were, which led through to their cloakroom.

'Shona,' he said urgently, shutting the door firmly behind him.

'Oh, hi Dermot, you surprised me,' said Shona pleasantly, taking out the little Christmas cards and tardy prep that littered her pigeonhole, shuffling through them. Even alone, she didn't show a sign of dropping the act. He had no idea how she could dissemble so fluently after what had happened between them. He remembered something she had said to him, about lying to him thousands of times about little things.

'It's not going to be like this,' he said calmly, taking a step towards her.

'Like what?' she replied innocently, still looking at her papers. 'Did you have some questions about next term's syllabus?'

Dermot walked up to Shona, took her in his arms and kissed her fiercely, pinning her against the wall. She just stood there for a moment, not reacting at all, her arms hanging limply by her sides and still holding her papers; but then Dermot felt her almost lose her footing as her knees went weak, and he held her more tightly, almost picking up her slight frame as her lips softened against his.

'Dermot, please,' Shona said quietly. 'Someone might walk in any moment.'

Dermot let her go, and reached forward and smoothed a strand of her hair back. 'I know you feel something for me,' he said. 'I can't go through the holidays not seeing you.'

'Maybe it's better just to leave it,' Shona said, leaning back against the wall, as though her treacherous legs still couldn't quite support her, looking down at the scuffed wooden floorboards. 'I don't know how we'd manage it.'

'I do,' said Dermot. 'I've been thinking about it.' He put his palm to Shona's cheek, and was gratified to see that she turned her face towards it. 'Shona, please look at me,' he asked. Shona looked into his eyes, and he looked back into hers, chocolate-brown with flecks of gold, dark liquid eyes sparkling with depth. 'I could give you driving lessons over the holidays, and you could repay me by giving me some French instruction. No one would think anything of it – it would just be two colleagues helping each other out.'

'Let me think about it,' Shona said after a long pause. Dermot looked into her eyes again, and unthinkingly leaned in towards her. 'You're getting too close,' she said, half holding her breath.

'You've got too close already,' Dermot answered, his lips almost brushing hers. The turn of the squeaky brass knob made them both jump, and Shona dashed sideways into the cloakroom, leaving Dermot leaning awkwardly against the wall.

'Dermot, are you all right, dear?' Jane asked with concern, wondering what her head of languages was doing.

'Not quite,' Dermot answered truthfully. 'I think I've got a bit of a funny head. I'll be fine in a bit.'

Dermot went back to the staffroom, and was persuaded to join Jonty roving around the fête, chatting to the parents and students he knew from the stalls. He saw Shona doing the same, and when he accidentally caught her eye, her face again gave nothing away. Watching her slim figure in the crowd, Dermot felt a knot in his stomach. Shona was offering him nothing more than the cheap, shining hope of a tawdry affair – to be with him in secret. He almost wished that was all he wanted; it would make things so much less complicated. But he knew that he would never have started anything with Shona if he didn't secretly hope and believe that she could eventually leave her husband and be with him properly, honestly, out in the daylight where everyone could see.

He realized bitterly that he was no different from any mistress of a married man. He didn't just want to sleep with Shona, he wanted to wake up with her and read the Sunday papers with her, and listen to her quiet, clever comments and funny asides. He didn't just want to sleep with Shona; he wanted to do everything with her.

But driving lessons might just be a start.

Becoming Accustomed to a Face

OMAR WAS WORKING in the elegant arched library of the Radcliffe Camera. He didn't need to refer to anything at the Rad Cam itself; he'd brought his own notes and his own books borrowed from the faculty libraries. He'd just fancied a change of scene from the Bod and the college library; the Rad Cam was one of the few buildings as pretty on the inside as it was on the outside. He put down his biro and looked dreamily at the delicate stonework on the pillars. Suddenly, he felt warm, dry hands over his eyes, a familiar smell of soap and biscuits. 'Penny for them,' whispered an amused voice in hushed tones.

'They're not that cheap,' he whispered back.

Jim removed his hands, and crouched grinning by the side of Omar's desk. 'I know how cheap mine are, but then I'm an old tart,' he said with deliberate campness. Looking at his watch, he said in his normal voice, at an inappropriate volume, 'Sod this for a lark. Let's go for a drink.'

The students on the desks around Omar looked at Jim

with distaste, and one of them even shushed him. Jim looked at her rudely and shushed her back, rolling his eyes with unjustified indignation. Stifling a laugh, Omar got up, leaving his books and papers, and ushered Jim out. As they left the building, both Omar and Jim burst out laughing with the easy familiarity of friends who found everything funny as long as they were together. 'That was rude,' he chided Jim, when they calmed down.

'Well, silly old bitch, if she's that concerned about her work she should go somewhere less picturesque,' Jim said unrepentantly. 'What were you doing there? I thought the Bod was your usual poison.'

'Oh, you know me. I was just admiring the architecture,' replied Omar with a shrug. 'And you?'

'Ditto. King's Arms or the Turf?' asked Jim.

'I guess the King's Arms, it's nearer,' said Omar.

'Turf it is,' said Jim, putting his hands deep in his pockets and striding off.

'I really don't know why you bother even asking me,' muttered Omar, without any real annoyance, walking quickly to catch up with him.

The Turf Tavern was filled with a heady scent of mulled wine and was quieter than Omar had seen it, but it was quite early in the afternoon. If he hadn't been working on his last essay of the term, he wouldn't have let Jim persuade him to stay for a second pint. Jim insisted on ordering a new brew on the blackboard, Fuggles Chocolate Ale. 'Come on, with a name like that it's criminal not to try it,' he burped. Despite dedicated practice, the nice Cornish lad still wasn't very good at holding his drink.

'It doesn't taste like chocolate,' said Omar, who was still extremely sober as his time with the band had hardened him up. He started humming a tune he had recently begun working on.

'Is that one of your brother's?' asked Jim, his handsome face flushed with the heat of the pub and the drink.

'Nope, one of mine,' said Omar, a little proudly. 'It's called "Screwed Up and Over". A friend of mine from Tooting gave me the idea.'

'Are you going to give it to the band? Belated parting gift?' asked Jim.

'Well, I thought about it. But I know Sharif wouldn't think it was right for the band. A bit too bluesy, and the lyric is really for a girl. I guess I just wrote it for me.'

'You should go solo. You're the one with the bloody talent. Sod the rest of them,' said Jim a little drunkenly.

'Thanks, Oakley, you're a mate,' grinned Omar.

After the third pint, Omar thought he really had better get back to the library, if only to pick up his papers. He walked Jim back the short distance to his room out of habit. 'How come I'm always the one who has to look out for the college drunks?' he said as he opened Jim's door for him with the key that Jim kept strung round his neck on a slim leather string, trying not to choke him in the process.

'I don't think you really drink,' said Jim, staggering into the room and collapsing in his chair. 'I think you've got a little tube that collects all the beer in a plastic bag hidden under your jumper.' By the time Omar had made him a coffee, still humming 'Screwed Up and Over', Jim had sobered up a bit. 'Fuggles Chocolate Ale? What a bloody rip-off. I think they just gave it a Christmassy name to sell the stuff off. I bet you at Easter it's called Fuggles Eggnog Bunny Ale.' He rifled through his CDs and, bizarrely, put on the soundtrack of *My Fair Lady*. 'I've grown accustomed to the tune that she whistles night and noon . . . accustomed to her face . . .,' he sang along with a tuneless bellow.

'Mate, you're the one who should be going solo,' Omar said dryly. 'Are you heading back to Cornwall at the weekend, then?' Michaelmas term officially ended on the Friday, and most people were heading home, as the college ground to a halt.

'Yep, lucky old me,' said Jim. 'My parents are picking me up on Saturday morning.'

'Mine are coming Saturday afternoon,' nodded Omar. 'It'll be weird being back home for Christmas; I haven't made any plans for New Year's yet. Sharif and I normally go to the same place, but he's not really forgiven me for leaving the band yet. He's got bloody righteous about it all.'

'I meant to ask you,' Jim said suddenly. 'Do you want to spend New Year in Scotland with me? My cousin has a flat up in Edinburgh and he's throwing a bash for Hogmanay or whatever the heck they do up there. It should be great.'

'Wow, that would be fantastic!' said Omar, deeply flattered, although he and Jim were clearly best friends now, and no one described him as a hanger-on any more.

'I'd love to, but I'll need to see how my folks are.' Seeing Jim raise his eyebrow, Omar quickly qualified, 'Not to ask permission or anything, but I just think that things have been a bit funny at home. My mum called me last night and said she really missed me, and she sounded sort of upset. I don't think they've been getting on.'

'Sure. Well, why don't you see?' said Jim reasonably. 'It would be nice to see you in Scotland – I think I might miss your ugly mug over the hols.' He let out a slight, embarrassed laugh. 'I guess I've got accustomed to your face.'

'Aw, thanks mate,' said Omar, a bit embarrassed, too. He downed his mug of coffee quickly. 'I'm going back to the library. Do you want me to pick up your stuff from the Rad Cam for you?'

'Cheers, that would be great,' Jim said. 'See you in Hall?'

'Yeah, see you later,' Omar said. As he left he saw Karen from his staircase, who looked like she had been waiting for him to leave, nip out of her room and walk up to Jim's door with a box of his favourite biscuits.

'Hey, Jimmy,' she said cheerfully, opening the door. 'Knock, knock!'

'Darling, how did you know I had the most hideous munchies!' he heard Jim cry with delight. Omar shook his head ruefully. All the girls had a crush on Jim.

Back in the Radcliffe Camera, Omar decided not to bother to try and finish his essay on international politics. His head was too fuggled by the chocolate ale. He started on some reading for the following term for philosophy of mind, on self-deception. One of the books compared it to Orwellian doublespeak – the ability to hold two contradictory beliefs in one's mind at the same time. He read about the divided self – one person with two parts, one of which must be necessarily lying to the other in order to deceive himself; whilst at the same time, the part that is deceived knows that he is being deceived, as he is the same self. The trouble with philosophy, Omar thought, was that he found himself thinking about what he was reading, rather than simply committing it to memory; it took up a lot more mental energy. He found the idea of self-deception hard to get his head round, as he was sure that it was practised so often as to lose all its cachet. 'I didn't drink very much just now,' he thought to himself, testing the idea. He didn't believe it. 'My parents are happy,' he tried, but again he didn't believe it, he wasn't even slightly deceived. 'My brother loves me,' he thought. Aah, that was interesting. He felt a conflict, a tug in his head; he wanted to believe it, but he didn't quite; but he didn't quite not believe it, either. 'I'm still a virgin because I haven't met the right girl yet and because I'm not a git like Sharif, who would take advantage of girls just because they're willing.' Well, that gave him a satisfying moral high ground. Did he really believe that was why he was a virgin? It was true that he hadn't had much opportunity, but then he thought of the dark thoughts he had briefly entertained towards Cassie – a violent, cold-blooded itch that needed scratching. Perhaps he was no better than Sharif, just less honest.

He looked at Jim's papers that he had collected up, along with the pair of glasses that Jim vainly almost never wore as he didn't think they suited him. 'He's just a friend,' he tried, daringly, 'that's all he is.' Yes, thought Omar, that was right, he believed that. There was no deception in that at all. And yet why, insisted an annoying little voice in his head, when he formulated this belief statement, did he refer to his friend just as a 'He'? Why did he dare not speak his name? Hadn't he got accustomed to his best friend's face, too?

'I'm fuggled,' thought Omar, finally, to himself. 'I'm fuggled and I'm thinking a load of crap.' He was glad when the bell signalled that the library was shutting. He gathered all of his and Jim's papers, and left.

Ricky-Rashid Makes a Damning Discovery

IT WAS JUST a few days before Easter, and Ricky was still jet-lagged after a duty trip back to Bangladesh, where his mother was cussedly clinging on to ill-health and ill-humour, and Henna and Aziz barely attempted to share a single meal with him. He'd just chaired an all-day meeting at the company offices in London Bridge, and was shattered to the point of illness. Verity and Candida were right, he should have taken early retirement at sixty. He had only stayed on to improve his share options, because he was worried about the sort of income they'd have once he retired. They'd need to rent out the Clapham flat, or let it go. Despite his tiredness, he asked the cab to drop him off at Clapham, rather than going straight home; he knew that he had better check on the flat while he was in town. At the flat, he had trouble opening the door due to the small mountain of junk mail that had gathered there. All else was well, although the place was a little dusty – he'd call Ana, the local cleaning lady, to give it a once over. He decided to walk to the main road to hail a cab, rather than call his corporate cab company – it was a bright, crisp day, and the air might do him some good. He passed the local florist on the corner of his street, and on a whim, bought some flowers for Verity. The only decent blooms were the roses, and even those were a bit blowsy, but he picked some pale pink ones and had them tied in brown paper with a pink ribbon.

As he walked down a little terraced street towards the main road, the sort where the houses had all been converted into flats, he was distracted by a car with conspicuous L-plates turning too quickly into the road and screeching to a halt a touch too wide of the kerb. The couple in the car, a slim woman and a tall man, got out swiftly and banged the doors, and Ricky, sure that they had been arguing, hung back under a plane tree, not wanting to be the unwilling witness to a scene. Instead, he was embarrassed to find a very different kind of scene taking place, with the couple colliding into a passionate embrace on the pavement, kissing ardently and unreservedly on the apparently empty street. The woman's back was to him, but there was something disconcertingly familiar about the cut of her hair. 'I'm so late, I've really got to go,' said the woman regretfully.

'Not right now, just stay a little bit. We've only just got back,' said the man, looking at her adoringly, smoothing her hair back from her face.

'Yes, right now,' said the woman firmly, unhappily. 'I'm sorry, I'll be missed.'

'You're right, you will be. Tu me manques déjà,' said the man. 'See, my French really is improving.' He still hadn't let her go.

'More than could be said for my driving,' said the

woman. She turned and walked swiftly away, and then turned and walked back just as decisively to kiss him again. The man held her face between his hands, and brushed his lips tenderly to her forehead.

'Go on with you,' he said gently. 'You're right, you'll be missed.' He watched her retreating back, and then shaking his head with a rueful smile, took the L-plates off the car and let himself into his flat.

Ricky stood paralysed with pain as he watched Shona take leave of her lover. His daughter was having an affair with a man who lived in Clapham. His daughter was in her forties now, with quite grown-up children, and she was having an affair, with a man who lived in a flat in Clapham. The last time he had seen Parvez and Shona together, they hadn't seemed that cheerful, but that was twenty years of marriage to a Pakistani for you. But this, this was different – he recognized tenderness, he recognized a look of love. Shona loved this man, and yet she was forcing herself to continue living with the Pakistani, the uneducated man she had ill-advisedly eloped with when she was barely older than Candida was now. How long had it been going on? Oh God – Ricky thought of Shona's pale, pale children, who he was convinced took after his side of the family. Were they even Parvez's? Gossips had joked that the twins looked practically half-caste, but that was just a joke in bad taste, wasn't it?

It was a nightmare he could never have dreamed of

having: his daughter reliving his life, his lies, his long-running deceit. He thought he had escaped blame and censure for living his double life – apart from some minor administrative inconveniences and more long-haul travel than he would have liked, he had been guiltlessly and wholeheartedly happy. But now, here was his punishment. He had let his daughter down – he was responsible for this. Ricky felt an icy hand close around his heart – it was too much, it felt like his heart was breaking. A dull heavy ache in his chest and shooting pains up his arm made him clench his fist, and the blowsy roses fell to the ground, scattering their petals like pale confetti. The light and shadow of the plane tree swam into nothingness ahead of him, and he walked a few faltering steps, before passing out cold, hitting the pavement with a heavy thud.

Dermot, looking out of his window after Shona, saw an elderly man tottering by the trees. Another neighbour-hood drunk, he thought prosaically; Clapham hadn't become half as gentrified as most people thought. He saw the man sway down the street briefly, before falling over. He'll get up in a moment, thought Dermot, but the man didn't get up. Sighing, he went to get his phone, but a sudden burst of rowdy noise got him running back to the window. Some kids came cycling with irresponsible speed round the bend of the pavement, and almost hit the prone body. They were white, black and Asian, a politically correct union of criminal adolescence. One of them stopped his bike and ran back to the old man. Well, that's shown me, thought Dermot, feeling slightly ashamed for his cynical judgement of the kids. However, the apparent good Samaritan simply took out the old man's wallet and disappeared back on his bike up the street. 'I think it's dead,' he called to his mates.

'Oi! You little bastards, get back here,' shouted Dermot, heaving open his window. He ran down his stairs, his phone still in his hand, to where the old man – who was really dressed well enough to be an old gentleman, with smartly cut hair and highly polished shoes – was still definitely alive. And had not a whiff of drink about him. Loosening the man's collar, Dermot called 999 and put him tentatively in the recovery position.

Dermot was in the ambulance when Ricky came round. 'It looks like you've had a heart attack, sir,' a young, fresh-faced paramedic said, efficiently ministering to Ricky.

Ricky ignored him, and looked with confusion towards the concerned face of Dermot. 'What are you doing here?' he asked.

'I found you, sir. You collapsed outside my building. I thought I'd better come with you until we could get hold of your family. Some kids stole your wallet before I could get to you, I'm afraid.'

Ricky nodded, struggling with the tightness in his chest. What a nice fellow he seemed. He sounded educated. 'What do you do, young man?' he asked recklessly.

'I'm a teacher, sir,' Dermot answered, surprised by the question.

Ricky closed his eyes and lay his head back down,

capitulating to the paramedic, who was urging him to keep still and relax. 'My daughter's a teacher,' he said, more to himself than anyone else.

When Verity and Candida arrived at the hospital, Dermot was surprised to see that the daughter looked little more than nineteen or twenty. Much too young to be a teacher. The old gentleman must have been thinking about a different daughter. 'I can't thank you enough for finding my husband,' his wife said tearfully, wringing his hand with gratitude. 'When I think of what might have happened . . .'

'Mummy, it's OK,' said the daughter. She had a confident accent of pure Home Counties privilege. 'They think Daddy's going to be fine.' She shook Dermot's hand. 'You've been very kind, but we mustn't keep you.'

'Well, if you're sure. You've got my number if you need me to make a statement about the stolen wallet,' Dermot said. The young girl was refreshingly capable and there was something about her he couldn't place, something familiar. As he left the hospital by the side exit, he narrowly missed Shona racing in from the hospital car park.

Shona Khan Makes a Damning Discovery

WHEN SHONA HAD returned home to Tooting, there had been two messages blinking on the answering machine. One was from Parvez, saying that he was extending his golf afternoon with dinner in Wimbledon – he was being taken out by a supplier. Shona cursed herself for not checking her messages at Dermot's – she hadn't needed to rush home at all. The second message was almost indecipherable with background noise and bleeping, but it sounded like Mr Crackle-Beep-Buzz Karim was at St George's Hospital following a heart attack, and was she a relative? Numbed with shock, Shona sat down on the chair, with Pat-Bob delightedly jumping on her, and played the message again. She called Parvez on his mobile, and heard the handset merrily ring in the kitchen. Parvez was always forgetting his phone. She called Sharif, who was meant to be at work. He answered his mobile. 'I'll be there in ten minutes, Ma. I'm just up the road in Collier's Wood.' He drove them to the hospital in Parvez's car, which he was no longer insured on.

Ricky-Rashid had been moved to a private room by the time Shona arrived. She almost didn't find him, as they had managed to get his name completely muddled up with someone else and he had been registered under Trueman-Karim. She was advised that his condition was stable and, too relieved to argue over administrative failings in the NHS, Shona left Sharif to park the car and went up to the waiting room. There were just a few other people there. A thin, blonde woman in an oyster-coloured twinset that didn't suit her pale colouring was dabbing at her red, puffy eyes. Sitting opposite her was a young, dark-haired woman, talking to her in a muted, soothing voice and holding her hand. In the corner, a tearful young couple were embracing fulsomely. Shona looked at them grimly – they looked as though they were enjoying their grief a bit too much. Go get a bloody room and leave the rest of us in peace, she thought uncharitably.

The young, dark woman got up. 'I'll get you a coffee, Mummy, and then we should go. Daddy just needs some rest. We'll come back tomorrow.' The girl was maybe nineteen, or perhaps twenty, given her self-assured manner. She was wearing a flowing skirt in silver silk that was so light it billowed about her ankles when she walked, with tennis shoes and a fitted white T-shirt. Shona thought ruefully that only youth could carry off an outfit like that. The girl walked so lightly herself that she could have been a dancer. Shona looked after her as she left the room, reminded of what it was like to have been young and graceful, an age when you still believed that you could control your own destiny. 'She walks in beauty, like the night . . . Of cloudless climes and starry skies . . .' she thought, remembering the dusty volume of Byron's poetry that used to live in her father's Dhaka study.

A pitiful sniff reminded Shona of the wretched-looking mother, whose face was a red splodge of unhappiness. Her handkerchief looked crushed and sodden. Shona felt a surge of sympathy – here was real grief, not like that irritating couple who were using it as an excuse to neck inappropriately in public. She went over to the woman and offered her a clean tissue from her pocket pack. 'Excuse me, would you like one?'

Verity looked up in shock. The kindness of strangers was a phrase which had meant very little to her until she had met Ricky, and she was surprised to encounter it twice in one day, once with that nice teacher, and now with this pleasant-looking woman. 'So very kind,' she choked out. And accepting the tissue, she blew her nose hard and felt a little better. Aware that she was making something of an exhibition of herself, she explained to the nice young lady. 'It's my husband, you see. He's everything to me. I couldn't bear to think of something happening to him, and then it just did.' She blew her nose again, and carried on, 'The silly thing is that he's fine now. But I still feel awful just thinking about what might have happened . . .' She trailed off as her face collapsed into another messy heap of tears. Despite the fact that the woman was several years Shona's senior, Shona calmly took the used tissue from her and passed her another, as though she was a student crying in the playground.

'Of course you're upset,' she said gently, 'and it's best to let it out.'

Verity attempted a quivering smile. 'Are you visiting, too?' she asked.

Shona nodded. 'My father. I've just heard that he'd had a heart attack, but they think he'll be fine.'

'My Ricky had a heart attack,' Verity replied, composing herself a little. 'I kept telling him to slow down, but he keeps working so hard, and travelling all over the place. He's only just back from Bangladesh – it's no good for someone his age.'

'My family's from Bangladesh,' said Shona slowly, finding herself looking at the poor woman assessingly instead of sympathetically. Her father had just been in Dhaka visiting her Nanu; until the phone call she hadn't even known that he had come back. The woman looked up and, seeing Shona's suddenly hard expression, misinterpreted it as criticism.

'I'm sorry, I shouldn't blather on so . . .' she said miserably, looking down at her feet. Shona, ashamed at herself for her suspicions, looked down too. Her own guilty affair had made her paranoid. But then she couldn't help noticing the woman's feet, which were just a few inches away from her own. They were a couple of sizes bigger than Shona's feet – probably size 6. Shona reminded herself that size 6 feet were perfectly ordinary and in themselves indicated nothing of significance; but then the woman's pretty, dark-haired daughter returned, without the promised coffee.

'Sorry, Mummy, the machine coffee doesn't look up to much. The black coffee button isn't working, and there wasn't any sugar at all, much less brown. Let's go down to the hospital café.'

'If you think so, dear,' replied Verity, gathering herself together. She hesitated shyly before turning to Shona. 'Thank you so much for the hankies.'

'Really, don't think anything of it,' said Shona, who could no longer deny the significance of size 6 shoes, especially combined with coffee and brown sugar. But that had been years ago, before the boys had even been born. She was distracted from drawing any disturbing conclusions by Sharif swanning in, looking very pleased with himself and even more handsome than usual, so much so that one part of the kissing couple stopped in mid-embrace to admire him.

'I have just met the most gorgeously amazing girl,' he said, sitting down on the seat that Verity had vacated. 'Here you go,' he added, giving her a cup of machine tea.

'I didn't ask you to get me tea, I asked you to park and come straight up,' Shona said pointedly, looking at him crossly.

'Ah, but the Amazing Girl was by the drinks machine. She had a walk like pure poetry, and the most amazing name, like something from a song: Candida Trueman-Karim.' Sharif pronounced the name reverently, giving attention to every syllable. 'Can-dee-da,' he sighed blissfully.

Shona's tea-holding hand shook so much that the tea spilled and squelched wetly over her. Fortunately it was only lukewarm. She looked at her son, who showed no signs of noticing her reaction to the name. He probably didn't even remember that Karim was her maiden name; it was such a common name, after all.

When the nurse came over and said that they could see the patient, Shona asked Sharif if she could see him alone.

Ricky-Rashid was lying wired to a heart monitor, and with a drip standing to attention by his side. Now he knew that he was unlikely to die he was slightly embarrassed to have Shona called to his bedside. What did he think he would do – confess his sins and ask her for absolution? Expect her to confess her own? Tell her to look after her mother? To look out for Verity and Candida? It all seemed stupidly melodramatic now that he was placid and rather bored and simply waiting to get better. Still, when she walked in, he couldn't help feeling cheered to see her, especially without the Pakistani. She was wearing the same clothes from earlier that afternoon.

'Papa, you had us all so worried,' she said, going to him and kissing him on the cheek. She sat down beside him and held his hand. 'I was so relieved when they said you were stable. There was a name mix-up, so it took a little while to find you.'

'I'm so pleased you could come, Jaan,' Ricky-Rashid said, a little insincerely, squeezing her hand with the modest amount of energy he could muster. 'I'm sorry about the mix-up – there's someone else here with a similar name, and I think they've put me under that instead. Trueman-Karim or some such.'

Shona nodded, and cleared her throat before saying, 'Yes, I met Mrs Trueman-Karim outside, and her daughter.' Ricky-Rashid looked up quickly, and Shona held his gaze for a little too long to be discreet. 'She seemed very upset about her husband; he's Bengali, too.'

Ricky breathed deeply, and looked down at their loosely intertwined hands – his own hand seemed so feeble next to Shona's golden, glowing skin, with her long fingers and unvarnished, oval nails. He had little doubt that Shona knew; perhaps she was expecting him to confess, after all. For a moment it was tempting. It would be so easy, it would just take a few seconds of weakness, of unblinkered honesty. Naked under his gown, he would become as clean and fresh as a newborn baby, reborn in his new life. Ricky let go of his daughter's hand and smoothed down the sheet; yes, the confession would be easy, but it was the aftermath that would be unthinkable. He would lose everything he had built – his false life in Bangladesh that kept Henna in such respectable comfort, that kept his mother at such disapproving distance; his new life with his wonderful wife and daughter. He could imagine the hurt in Verity's eyes, even more painful than the tears she had bravely tried to hide as she had visited him that day; betrayed yet again, by the one man who had promised he never would. To be told that their marriage was an illegal sham. She would never understand. Ricky made a decision: she would never need to.

'Jaan,' he said gently to Shona. 'There's something I need to tell you.'

'Yes, Papa,' Shona said encouragingly, leaning forward, reaching for his hand once more.

'I'm afraid I've misled you about something. I know that you thought I would still be in Dhaka today, but as you can see I decided to return a little bit earlier. I had something to do.' Shona nodded, wondering where this was going. Ricky put his hand on Shona's cheek, picking his words carefully. 'You remember the flat in Clapham, the one that I used to stay in when I was in town . . . ?' Shona's eyes widened as she realized what he was going to say. Ricky confirmed, 'I went there this afternoon, I thought I had better check on it, I hadn't been there in a long time, as you know.'

Shona swallowed uncomfortably, before asking, 'And was everything OK, Papa?'

Ricky replied, as gently as he could, 'Jaan, everything wasn't OK. I saw something that I wasn't meant to see, and it almost broke my heart.'

Shona looked at the bleeping heart monitor, and back to her pale father, and understood. 'Is that what gave you the heart attack, Papa?'

Ricky avoided her direct question deliberately. He was aware that his heart rate was rising incrementally, and breathed slowly, so that they wouldn't be interrupted by the nursing staff. 'Shona, there's something I've learned, and which I think you know, too. There are some things that we're not meant to see, that we're better off not seeing. We might look at each other, but we don't always need to see each other, if you know what I mean. All I want, and all I've ever wanted, is for you to be happy.'

Shona said nothing. She wasn't sure whether this was blackmail on the part of her father, or pure kindness. She remembered the first tacit deal they had made in his Paddington apartment all that time ago: you keep my secret, and I'll keep yours. Before, her silence had been easily bought – what was the harm in his having an inconsequential dalliance when away from home, while her mother had been flirting outrageously in Dhaka? But there had been consequences, dire consequences of her silence, because this was no affair to be hushed up. There seemed to be a marriage, a wife, a daughter who was presumably his. A sister that she had never even known. Could he really expect her to pretend that she had seen nothing? But then, the consequences of her own adultery were unwittingly as bad, if not worse. She had almost killed her own father. She owed her father something; she had seen how unhappy he had always been in Dhaka, and how the years in England had transformed his life. She knew that her father was watching her now, awaiting her verdict. She opened her mouth to speak, but was interrupted by Sharif barging in.

'Sorry, Ma. Visiting hours are almost over, so I thought I better pop in and see how you're both doing. Nana, do you feel as bad as you look?'

Ricky smiled weakly. Sharif wasn't his favourite grandson; so brash and handsome, he reminded him too much of the Pakistani. He had only the paleness of his Karim genes to recommend him.

'Quite as bad, son, thank you for asking. They say I shouldn't be in here too long though . . .' Firm steps at the door heralded the appearance of a nurse, who told them that visiting hours were over. Shona drew herself up resignedly.

'Well, considering how long it took them to get us up here, they seem pretty efficient about kicking us out.' She got out of her chair by Ricky's bedside and kissed him. 'I'll come back tomorrow. Is there anything you want?'

'No, thank you, Jaan. I'm sure I'll be well looked after. Company health plan and all that,' Ricky replied. He paused, before asking hopefully, 'It would be better if you came in the afternoon though, rather than the morning, if that would be OK.'

Shona understood. He would have other visitors in the morning, visitors who would probably provide for him better than she could. He had been well looked after for the past twenty years, but she just hadn't seen it. Or rather, she had looked, but she hadn't seen, just as her father had said. As she went to leave, she turned and said to him in Bangla, so Sharif wouldn't understand, 'Papa, I think we both deserve to be happy. I just want you to be happy too.'

Ricky felt the tightening around his chest that had begun in the last few moments start to subside. 'Thank you, Shona,' he said gently. There would be nothing else to say.

At home, Shona sat in the dark of the kitchen and watched the moon in the french windows. She had poured a glass of wine, which she sipped too quickly. She had never felt so alone, and so tortured by secrets and silence. She was half waiting for Parvez to come home, and half hoping that he would call and say he wasn't. At another time, she would have clung to him for support and told him everything that her suddenly tender heart had to say – told him about her father's betrayal and secret life, and her complicity so that she would never know the man her father had become, never know the woman who had made him happy, or the sister that she never knew she had. But that time was gone – she could no longer tell Parvez everything. In fact, she could no longer tell him anything. The only person she could tell the truth to was sitting alone, like her, in a flat a few miles away. She glanced at the phone, and shook her head. She couldn't call Dermot now; it was far too risky. Parvez was due home any minute. She checked her watch; it was almost midnight – still too early to call her mother in Dhaka and tell her about the heart attack. Draining her wine, she decided to call anyway.

The phone rang at the other end with a distant echo and crackle, and gave way to Uncle Aziz's crisp accent announcing that she had reached the Karim residence, and to leave a short message after the tone. 'Amma,' Shona said softly, 'I guess you're not up yet. I thought someone might be up. I just need to tell you something . . . it's Papa, he's had a heart attack. He's stable, and they think he won't be in too long. I don't think you need to worry or fly over or anything, we're taking care of him here. I'm going to bed now, but I'll call again when I'm up.' Putting the phone down, she felt emptier than she had before. She had just lied to her mother by everything she hadn't said.

It was almost one in the morning when Parvez came home, smelling of brandy and contrition. He entered the bedroom quietly, undressing in silence. He knew Shona was still awake, as she was lying on the far side of the bed, very straight and still. 'Shona, I didn't mean to be so late,' he whispered as he got into bed. 'Jay wanted to make a night of it, and I didn't think you'd mind. I stopped by the restaurant on the way home. Sharif told me what happened. I'm so sorry about your father, I'm sorry I wasn't here for you. I know how much he means to you.'

At his words, Shona turned away from him and curled up into herself. He saw she had begun to shiver and shudder, and suddenly she let out great, choking sobs that welled up from deep inside and shook her whole body. Parvez tentatively touched her shoulder, and as she kept sobbing, oblivious to him, he put his arms around her and held her while she sobbed, burying his face between her neck and shoulder. 'Shona,' he whispered, 'Goldie, don't upset yourself so. He's going to be fine.' He kissed her hair reassuringly, but Shona couldn't stop her tears.

'You don't understand, it's never going to be fine,' Shona choked out, 'I can't do this any more. I can't keep pretending it's fine.'

Parvez misunderstood what she said, and didn't let her finish. 'Shh,' he said soothingly, 'I'll look after us. It will be fine, I promise. We'll see him tomorrow, we'll go together.' He stroked Shona's hair and bare arms, and curled himself against her, comforting her with his warmth and physical intimacy, the only way he knew how to comfort her after their long years of marriage. As her sobbing calmed down to deep, ragged breathing, without being quite aware of what he was doing, he began making love to her, and she, half asleep and tearful, found herself responding to him as she always had before, as though simply being next to his skin would replace the closeness they had lost.

Afterwards, Shona went to the kitchen to get a glass of water, and looked back at the silver light of the moon streaking into the kitchen. She had managed to make things worse, if that were possible. She still had the burden of her father's great secret to carry, unabsolved, in addition to her own clandestine affair. And now she had not only been unfaithful to Parvez, but she had compounded her sin by being unfaithful to Dermot, too. If she had to keep any more secrets, tell any more lies, she felt as if she would break.

Shona resolved to see Dermot the next day, and tell him everything. She realized how much she needed Dermot now, as she needed someone to whom she could tell the truth, someone who could hold every secret about her. She needed to know that if she was struck down like her father had been, or knocked over by a bus in the morning, the truth wouldn't die with her – she needed to know that at least one person in the world knew who she really was.

Sharif Khan Meets an Angel in Tennis Shoes

SHARIF FIRST SAW her across a crowded, scruffy hospital corridor, walking so lightly it was as though the bottoms of her feet didn't quite touch the sticky, laminate floor. She was dressed like no other girl he knew, in a flowing silver skirt that swept voluminously in glistening ripples around her legs, with white tennis shoes and a snug, shining white T-shirt that moulded to her slim waist. She looked like an angel, so clean and fresh that she glowed in the unflattering hospital lighting. The other girls he knew seemed like grubby, painted hussies by comparison, with their tight skirts and tight jeans and low-cut tops.

She stopped at the drinks machine, and Sharif stopped and stared. She was soon stabbing buttons in annoyance, rejecting each murky cup of liquid as it appeared. Sharif watched her, fascinated, until she became aware of his gaze, and turned to look at him. She had a heart-shaped face, with creamy pale skin that didn't have a trace of pink, and thick, dark hair. It was the sort of fresh, sweet face that he might have imagined his mother having when she was young. A song started in Sharif's heart instinctively, and he almost said the words out loud, as they were beating so strongly in his head:

And you saw the girl who'd make your dreams come true
She looked like no other, she looked straight back at you.

'I'm sorry, can I help you?' asked the Amazing Girl. Her voice was pure Home Counties, Sharif realized. She certainly wasn't from Tooting. He dropped his usual working-class hero accent and spoke with the voice he used at home.

'It's just that I needed to use the drinks machine, but I'll wait. My mum wants a cup of tea,' he said charmingly.

'Funny,' she said, 'I'm trying to get a drink for my mummy, too. She only drinks black coffee, and this bloody stupid machine is putting out white coffee no matter which button I press.' She tried again, and the machine produced yet another cup of milky sludge. 'See what I mean? Maybe you should go ahead of me, I might try to find another machine.'

Sharif replied quickly, 'No, really, it's OK. I'll wait. I can't stand queue-jumpers.' The last thing he wanted was to have her wander off while he got an unwanted cup of tea. 'I guess you're visiting, you don't look sick,' he hazarded, realizing too late how ungracious that sounded. It wasn't like him to make daft comments when faced with a pretty girl. Normally he was the coolest customer around.

'Thank you, I think,' laughed the Amazing Girl. 'Yes, we're here for Daddy. He had a heart attack from nowhere, but he's all right, thank God.'

'My grandad has just had a heart attack. He's stable, too. Mum literally just found out. We got here in a blind panic,' Sharif answered. He realized how close he was leaning in towards the Girl, as though her sheer magnetism was drawing him closer; he had to force himself back.

'Well, I'm giving up,' she said, after yet another attempt at getting a black coffee. 'I'll see if Mummy wants to go to the cafeteria instead. We should be leaving Daddy to rest, anyway. Good luck with your grandad, and the tea,' she said kindly.

'Do you like music?' Sharif asked, just as she was walking away.

The Girl turned back, looking adorably perplexed by the question. 'Yes, I do. Well, it depends on the music, I guess. Why?'

'It's just that I'm giving a concert this week, not too far from here, in Clapham.' He dug into his pocket and handed her a professional-looking flyer that had been knocked out on Micky's home PC. 'If you're in the area, it would be great to see you there. You might like it.'

'Oh, well, thanks,' said the Girl, looking surprised, but not displeased.

'If you tell me your name, I could put you and a guest on the list at the door, so you won't have to pay,' Sharif persisted, turning to press the button for tea in an attempt to appear rather more nonchalant than he sounded.

'That's very kind of you . . .' She hesitated as she realized she didn't know his name.

'It's Sharif, Sharif Khan. It's sort of my band,' Sharif said modestly, pointing to his name on the flyer.

'That's very kind of you, Sharif,' the Girl said. 'I'm

Candida, Candida Trueman-Karim.' She turned to leave, but then turned back. 'It was nice to have met you,' she said politely, as though she had just remembered a childhood lesson in manners.

Sharif stood by the drinks machine, watching her move away in time to the music in his head. 'Candida,' breathed Sharif, 'Can-dee-da'. He tried it out, and felt the melodic syllables dance across his palate, tongue and teeth. It was a name that was almost impossible to say without a smile; it was a name that left you open-mouthed with longing as you finished it. Can-dee-da.

Candida didn't come to the concert, but called the venue to apologize. Undeterred, Sharif pursued her, hanging around the hospital at visiting hours until he saw her and bumped into her accidentally on purpose. This time, they went for a coffee, and started to go on dates. Sharif was so careful with Candida that he didn't even try to kiss her, until the miraculous day when she leaned in towards him while they were waiting for her train home. He even introduced her to his mother, who must have known that this one was special, as she took an unprecedented interest in Candida above all his other girlfriends, asking her to supper, and asking after her mum, and asking what she did at her art college.

'Your mummy's lovely,' Candida said one evening on the way to one of Sharif's gigs. 'I feel like I've known her forever.'

'Well, she shouldn't monopolize you so much,' Sharif

answered, kissing the top of her head. 'I hardly got to say a word to you during dinner. Sorry about the burnt chicken, by the way.'

'I'm not much of a cook, so I'd never criticize someone else's food,' Candida shrugged. 'Speaking of food, why did you tell your mum that you were working at the restaurant tonight? Doesn't she approve of you playing?'

Sharif shrugged. 'I find it better not to tell Mum when I've got a gig, or she might tell Dad, and as he's my boss he wouldn't be too pleased about me playing hooky from the restaurant. I'm meant to have given up music and be doing real work now.'

'But why play hooky?' persisted Candida. 'Why not just tell them you're taking a night off?'

'Babe, it's much easier not to tell them, and for them to think that I'm working. Otherwise Dad might stop paying me for the nights I'm not there,' Sharif answered guilelessly.

'You're appalling,' chided Candida, not without a grin. 'I think you're one of those bad boys that my daddy keeps warning me against.'

'Do you like bad boys?' Sharif asked, squeezing her waist.

'I do now,' Candida answered coquettishly, and stopped to kiss him full on the lips.

After the gig, Sharif was walking Candida back through Clapham Common when she surprised him by stopping by his usual make-out bench. Pulling him down, she began to kiss him urgently, and against his nobler instincts they were soon passionately making out. 'I'm feeling very bad myself, Sharif,' Candida said breathily. 'I think you're a bad influence.'

Some moments later, Sharif realized with a start that Candida, as she slid his hands underneath her thighs, was giving him an unprecedented licence, and that she was intent on going much further than they had before. As her own hands reached for his shirt buttons, Sharif stopped her. 'Candida, no, I don't want to do this.'

'What?' she said, in genuine surprise, and seeming more than a little hurt. She saw the concern in his eyes in the poor light and relaxed. 'Sharif, really, I want to. Don't worry about me.'

'I mean, I don't want you here. I don't want you outside, on a bench in a park. I want to take you home. I like you. I really, really like you. I want to take you home, and wake up with you.' He gestured hopelessly towards the bench. 'I don't want to do this sort of thing any more.'

'Sharif,' Candida answered gently, 'I've never done this sort of thing before – out in the open, I mean. I just thought it might be fun. And you know I can't go home with you tonight. I've got my own home to get back to, before Mummy gets worried.'

'Maybe you could stay over at the weekend?' Sharif asked hopefully. 'There's a market near me in Merton Abbey Mills. It's got lots of girly, arty-farty stuff that you'd love – scented candles, old mirrors, sequined cushion covers, carved bits of tat . . .'

'Sounds lovely,' said Candida, sitting back upright and

smoothing down her skirt, another pale floaty number, this time with bonbon-coloured stripes. 'It would be nice to spend a proper amount of time together.' She hesitated a moment, and then said, 'The thing is, I'd be happy to stay over, but I really wouldn't feel comfortable about, well, you know, with your flatmates around. The walls in your place are really thin, and . . . well, it's hardly romantic with Beavis and Butthead banging around next door with their PlayStations and girly mags.'

'Point taken,' Sharif said. 'I'm sure I can get rid of them.' He looked around the damp, musty park. 'Did you think that this was romantic, then?' he asked. 'I've never thought this was a particularly romantic location. Convenient, maybe, but definitely not romantic.'

'Of course it's romantic,' Candida said. 'You've got the trees, the stars, the moonlight, and the chance of being arrested for an indecent act in public.'

'You're a funny girl,' said Sharif.

'Funny ha ha or funny peculiar?' asked Candida pertly.

'Funny peculiar,' answered Sharif. 'Utterly perfect in every way, of course, but undeniably, just a little bit . . . mad.'

'Come on,' said Candida, getting up and pulling up Sharif by the arm. 'Your mad girlfriend has a train to catch, and given that you're disinclined to shag me senseless on a park bench, I've got no reason to miss it.'

'When you put it that way, I'm the one who sounds mad,' said Sharif.

Sharif had never planned a romantic weekend before, and was looking forward to it. It seemed so much more clean and natural than what he had done before, furtive fumbling in the shadows of the parks and the streets and the rooftops. He imagined bringing Candida breakfast in bed, and scenting his room with fresh flowers for her.

He was crushed when she called and tearfully told him that she wouldn't be able to come. She said that her mum had been fine about her spending the weekend with her new boyfriend, but that her dad had gone absolutely uncharacteristically ballistic when he found out who she was seeing, and had forbidden her to see him again.

'It was scary, I've never seen Daddy like that. He's the most tolerant, easy-going person I know. He never gets cross or upset about anything,' Candida told him. 'I mean, maybe I should have mentioned to him sooner that I was seeing someone, but I normally don't bother him about who I'm dating until it gets serious. Mummy knew about you, and she was shocked at how Daddy reacted too. He was perfectly cheerful about it until I mentioned your name, then he just blew up.'

'Is he racist or something?' Sharif asked, completely confused as to why a stranger would take such exception to him on mere mention of his name.

'Well, he can't be. He's Bangladeshi himself, and you're half-Bangladeshi, just like me. But he was going on about how he knew all about boys like you, and that you were no good, and that I shouldn't date you, and all sorts of rubbish.'

'He must be racist,' said Sharif. 'There are lots of Asians around who want to forget where they came from.

He doesn't want his perfect little girl dating an Asian boy; he wants you to go out with white boys and breed out all his brown genes and have nice white grandchildren . . .'

'Oh, shut up, you're as bad as him. You don't know him at all, so there's no need to generalize,' said Candida crossly. Sharif stopped in mid-tirade, realizing that Candida would brook no criticism of her father. 'I mean, I went out with Greg last year, and he was black, and Daddy didn't have a word to say against him.'

'Well, I don't see how he could say all those things about me if he doesn't even know me,' said Sharif stubbornly.

'Babe, I know. I asked him exactly that – I asked him to give me one solid reason why I shouldn't go out with you,' said Candida.

'And what did he say?' asked Sharif, holding his breath.

'This is the scariest part. He burst into tears and collapsed into his chair, clutching his chest. Mummy and I were terrified that he might be having another heart attack. He said that if I loved him, I would just trust him and promise not to see you any more.'

'Great – he can't give you a reason, so he resorts to emotional blackmail by asking you to make a ridiculous promise,' Sharif said unsympathetically. 'What did he say when you said you weren't falling for it?' He waited for her response, but Candida didn't say a word. 'Candida, you did tell him that you weren't falling for it, didn't you?' He was aware of his voice rising with slight panic. 'You didn't actually promise, did you? You couldn't have done.'

Candida paused for far too long, and said, 'Sharif, I'm

so sorry. I felt I had to. You know how ill Daddy's been; I couldn't be responsible for his heart giving out again. He needs to stay unstressed, and I know it was totally unreasonable of him, but maybe he's not quite himself at the moment.'

Sharif felt his whole body go cold. 'I see,' he said curtly. It had finally happened; he had fallen for someone, only to find that he felt more for her than she did for him. Perhaps she had only wanted him for arm candy, for street cred, for the sex they hadn't quite had. The irony was awful; he could imagine his cohorts of ex-conquests and his faggy twin cheering Candida in the wings.

'No, you don't see,' Candida said, 'so don't go all cold and distant on me. It's only for a little while, and I've made a decision. I've never lied to my parents before, but when my daddy's health is at stake it seems as good a time as any to start.'

'So you didn't mean it,' said Sharif, feeling waves of relief wash over him. 'You'll find a way to come this weekend?'

'No, not this weekend, and not to London. I don't think that would be very wise,' said Candida. 'But you know, next weekend I might visit a friend who lives down on the Kent coast, in a little seaside town called Broadstairs.'

'I don't think I know it,' said Sharif.

'You'd like it, I think. It's between Margate and Ramsgate, and prettier than both, with lovely beaches perfect for painting. Wouldn't it be a funny coincidence if I bumped into you down there next Saturday, say at the station at midday?'

'That would be a funny coincidence,' agreed Sharif.

Candida laughed. 'Oh, and before I forget, better let your mum think we've broken up, too. Daddy still has to go back to St George's for his follow-up appointment, so Mummy might bump into your mum there, like they did before.' She paused, and said huskily down the line, 'This is quite sexy, isn't it? Forbidden lovers meeting in secret.'

'You have a funny idea of sexy,' Sharif said. 'And this is the funniest break-up I've ever had.'

'Funny ha ha or funny peculiar?' asked Candida.

'Funny peculiar,' said Sharif.

The Romantic Memories of Sharif Khan

I HAVE ALWAYS believed that I wasn't really alive until I first heard music. What I didn't know before, and I only realize now, was that I had never really heard music until the day I met Candida. She put a song in my heart from the moment I saw her, a relentless, haunting melody that wouldn't go away, with an underlying beat that would drum heavily in my chest whenever she wasn't there, just waiting for her to return.

We arranged to meet one weekend by the seaside, and I waited for her at the station, sitting on a bench, lighting cigarette after cigarette. I watched as trains came in and carriages emptied, and I realized that I wasn't angry with her for being late. Much worse than that, I was frightened. I was frightened that she might not have been able to get away, and that I might not see her at all. When she finally arrived, having decided to drive down rather than take the train, she kissed me warmly and complained about the traffic. But I didn't care about the traffic; all I could say was that I had missed her, because it was true.

She drove us to a curving beach lined with enormous

chalk cliffs. There were a couple of families at the entrance to the beach, but once we strolled around the cliffs, it was utterly deserted, nothing but the waves, the flint scattered on the sand, and us. Candida collected chalk that had fallen from the cliffs. She took a piece and asked me to pose for her, while she drew my portrait on the side of a flat, grey rock that rested under the tide line. Then she drew her own portrait next to mine. We sat back on our blanket and watched the sea come in, and the foaming waves dissolve our chalked images as the salt water licked over the rock. 'We're mer-people now,' said Candida. 'We've turned into sea foam and become immortal.'

We held hands and walked down the empty beach. For the first time, I really understood what my parents must have felt to have lost love, as to have found it was so precious that I could not bear to ever let it go. My heart had been collected like chalk from the beach.

'Where are you staying tonight?' I asked. 'Are you staying with your friend in town?'

'No,' replied Candida. 'I'm staying with you.'

In the morning, I left her sleeping in the hotel, and returned with croissants and coffee in paper cups, and pink roses from the newsagents. I'd dreamed of waking her with breakfast in bed and the scent of roses, but in fact she woke when the clumsy door banged behind me. When I climbed back into bed, Candida lay resting against me, her head on my shoulder, her light frame still heavy with the remains of sleep.

'What did you think of me, when you first saw me?' I asked her.

'I thought you were one of the prettiest men I'd ever seen,' said Candida. 'Look, you've got longer eyelashes than me.' She reached forward and gently brushed the tips of my eyelashes with her fingertips. 'Now I have to ask you, don't I? What did you think of me?'

'I thought of music when I first saw you. I saw your back, that swishing silver skirt, and I thought you were a dancer. Your head was held so straight. I followed you to the drinks machine, and willed you to turn around.'

Candida got up and, wrapping a towel around her, went to the window, looking out over the bay. 'I used to come here as a child, on day trips. We'd go to the amusement park in Margate, and then come here for the beach. Daddy and I played a sort of tennis on the beach, with big plastic rackets and enormous spongy balls.' She turned back to face me. 'We had such a perfect day yesterday; it seems crazy that Daddy thinks you wouldn't be good for me.'

I went up to her and put my arms around her, watching the waves roll in over the beach. 'If you ever give me the chance to meet your dad, I'll tell him, I'll promise him, that I would never hurt you, and never leave you, and never let you go. I'd rather hurt myself first.' Candida's face was suddenly very solemn in the morning light, so solemn that I felt forced to ask, 'You do believe me, don't you?'

'Yes, I do believe you,' Candida said. 'That's the scary thing.'

Omar Khan Celebrates May Day in Oxford

OMAR WAS QUITE excited about the approach of mythical May Day in Oxford; the night of all night parties, of dancing until dawn, when everyone would crowd to Magdalen Bridge to hear the choir sing in the sunrise, and then leap off into the water in their black tie and ballgowns.

'I read two people had permanent spinal injuries doing that last year,' said Karen disapprovingly. She was sitting on one of Omar's chairs with a massive cup of hot chocolate. Omar had noticed with some irritation that she now limited her visits to when 'Jimmy' was in residence. He wished she wouldn't come; she was getting more and more territorial about Jim, so much so that Omar felt a bit like a gooseberry in his own college room.

'Bollocks – how would you get a spinal injury by jumping into water?' scoffed Jim, who had spread out a map of Oxford on Omar's coffee table, and was scribbling over it with thick, coloured marker pens.

'The water's not very deep at some points under the bridge,' explained Omar, wondering why he was bothering to back up Karen. 'I think you have to jump from the middle, or not at all.'

'Well, if you say so, mate,' said Jim non-commitally.

'Typical, you always listen to Omar over me,' pouted Karen flirtatiously. Jim grinned cheekily at her, before pouting back at her, causing her to giggle delightedly. Omar almost had to hide a sigh; Karen's single-minded pursuit of Jim was beginning to pay off. They were edging closer and closer to becoming a couple, and there was nothing he could do about it; Jim was far too lazy to avoid being pursued for too long, and far too vain not to enjoy the attention. Omar knew that it shouldn't really bother him – they were both his friends. It was just that Jim was his best friend, and he didn't really want to share him, that was all. To distract himself from the disturbing niggles of jealousy, Omar asked Jim how he was getting on with his party-planning.

'It's all worked out, mate. These flag pins are us three,' Jim started poking them into the map where the college was.

'You're poking holes in my coffee table,' muttered Omar in exasperation.

'Mate, I poke where, when and whom I want,' retorted Jim. 'So, we're here in the college at the start of the night, and we go to the bar for the first party of the night and get tanked up.' He picked up the flag pins and began dancing them along the thick red line he had marked up earlier. 'We then head over to Balliol, to pick up Giles and Lydia from their bar, have a few drinks there just to be polite, and then Giles drives us all over to the big bash in the Parks.'

'Isn't Giles drinking, then?' Karen asked

'God, you and your bloody health and safety obsessions. No, he's not drinking,' Jim said tersely.

'Antibiotics,' Omar clarified kindly for Karen. 'So we're going to stay out in the Parks all night? What if it rains?'

'Good question. If it rains, and all the bars are shut, I reckon we just head over to NCL. They're having a house-party,' Jim said, bouncing the flag pins along to the undergraduate house that sprawled across two buildings at New College Lane. 'Look, did you see? I've marked up wet weather plans with the blue broken line,' he added, with a touch too much pride.

'So you have,' Omar said. 'I think we've finally found a practical use for your new-found interest in military history.'

'Don't mock what you can never understand,' said Jim, who had amassed an impressive collection of children's books on the subject.

'So are we going to the bridge for dawn, then?' asked Karen, looking casually over at the map.

'Duh, it's marked right here – we get to the bridge for dawn, five a.m. or whenever it is, listen to the angelic voices, jump off the bridge, run back and get dried off, and then it's off to the King's Arms for the champagne and croissant breakfast.'

'I think you need to book that,' Karen said.

'I think that the Pantry might be giving champagne and croissants for free to all first years who've signed up for it,' Omar added.

Jim rolled his eyes at the insubordination in his ranks.

'Fine, I'll book the King's Arms for all of us, including Giles and Lydia. And we'll go to the Pantry first to get our free froggy pastry and champers; no point in letting our share go to waste.' He uncapped his red marker and added a line with a little arrow that stopped at the Pantry.

'And that, men, is our plan of attack. Any questions that do not involve wussy health and safety considerations?' Jim asked, in a pastiche of a WWII general.

'You might want to ask Giles if he actually wants you to book the King's Arms breakfast – he probably won't want to pay a tenner for champagne and croissant if he's not drinking . . .' Omar started to say, but was interrupted by his mobile, which played one of his favourite Balti Ballads songs as the ringtone. He went to flick it off, but seeing it was from Sharif, answered it immediately. 'All right, mate?' he asked. Sharif never rang him. He had to want something. He opened his door and stood outside in the echoing stairwell so he wouldn't have to speak in front of Karen and Jim; God, he hoped they didn't start snogging in his room, that would be horrible.

'Kid, I need a favour,' Sharif said urgently, and depressingly predictably.

'I'm not lending you any more, you're the one with the job,' Omar said.

'Not that kind of favour. It's just that me and my girlfriend want to get away for the May Day bank holiday. She's going to tell her parents she's meeting a friend in Oxford; could we take over your gaff?'

'Why the cloak and dagger?' Omar asked.

'Stupid story – her dad's got the impression I'm no good, and has forbidden her to see me,' Sharif said.

Omar choked back a laugh. 'Forbidden her to see you? God, how funny. So does he lock her up at night with a chastity belt?'

'Not funny, mate. I really like this girl. She's . . . well, she's special. You'll know what I mean when you meet her. Even Mum loved her. And we hardly ever get to see each other.'

'You introduced her to Amma?' Omar asked in bemusement; Sharif seemed to have changed overnight. 'Who are you and what have you done with my obnoxious slut of a brother?'

'Very funny. Funny ha ha, I mean,' said Sharif. 'So is that OK? We'll just stay a night.'

'Luckily for you, I'm actually planning to be out all night, so I guess it is OK. Make sure you arrive before formal Hall so I can let you in, about seven-ish.'

'Cheers, kid, I owe you. See you then.' Sharif was about to ring off, when Omar stopped him.

'What's her name? This special girl who's made such a changed man of you?'

'Candida,' said Sharif, surprised by the question.

'Candida? Is she Candy for short?' asked Omar. Candy seemed a more suitable name for one of Sharif's girl-friends.

'Nope, Candida doesn't abbreviate,' Sharif said proudly, before hanging up.

On the big day, Omar was fretting as Sharif was late, and he was in danger of missing his much needed dinner before the long night ahead. Karen and Jim had already gone to Hall, and Omar was sure that Karen was secretly pleased that he'd had to stay behind. Fiddling with his scruffy black gown, Omar tried Sharif's phone again. It went straight through to voicemail. Bastard, he was sure that his brother's Romeo and Juliet sob story was some elaborate ploy to humiliate him in some undecipherable way, or at the very least to ruin his first Oxford May Day. Sod him. Omar decided to go to Hall anyway; he left a scrawled message on his door, and was racing down the stairs when he heard a familiar voice on the landing. 'Where's the fire, kid?'

'Where the hell were you?' said Omar crossly, doubling back and seeing Sharif standing outside the bathroom on the second floor. 'Look, here's my key, you know where the room is. Top floor, turret. See you tomorrow.'

'Hold on, Candida's just in the loo. Don't be so bloody rude. Wait to say hello at least,' Sharif said.

'Well, God forbid I embarrass you with my bad manners . . .' Omar stopped in his tracks as a vision stepped out of the bathroom, smoothing down her hair.

'Oh, you must be Omar. I'm sorry we're late, traffic was murder. I'm delighted to meet you, Sharif's told me so much about you.' She smiled sincerely, and held out her hand.

'No, I'm the one who's sorry,' said Omar regretfully, taking her hand. 'I'm afraid I have to dash off. Make yourself at home upstairs. Hopefully we can meet properly in the morning. Come and have breakfast with us, in the King's Arms.'

Walking down, he paused and looked back up the

winding staircase, where Sharif was talking in a low voice to Candida, his arm placed protectively around her shoulders as they climbed the steps together. Surely Sharif must have seen how much like their Amma she looked? A younger, arguably slimmer version, with skin that was creamy-ivory rather than rose-gold, but the resemblance was incontrovertible. They might have been sisters. Omar shook his head in shock; it was a Freudian minefield. He would have loved to talk to Jim about it, but there'd be too many people about tonight, and Jim would get drunk too fast. Remembering himself, he jumped down the last few stairs and raced across the quad to Hall; he hoped that the lovebirds had saved him a seat.

When Omar arrived at the Hall, they had already started serving up. He looked vainly for Jim and Karen at the front of Hall, where they'd promised they'd be, and couldn't see them anywhere. He felt bereft; I've already become a spare wheel, he thought miserably to himself. Jim and Karen had each other now, and Sharif had just hooked up with an angel; no one needed him. Perhaps they never did. Perhaps he was just a way of treading water, buying time.

He was ludicrously relieved when a voice shouted, 'Hey, Omar, spare seat here!' He recognized the voice. It was Dieter, his occasional tutorial partner in philosophy, an unashamed geek who wore jumpers knitted by his mum, unnecessarily thick glasses, and who frequently forgot to remove his cycle clips. He was sitting with his own usual group, a couple of other PPE-ists, and a mixed bag of mathematicians, biologists and chemists. Like Dieter, they were all deeply uncool. Jim would have refused to sit within a foot of them, and usually only tolerated Dieter because Omar was obliged to share lessons and notes with him.

Omar had no such reservation about associating with the uncool, and sat down gratefully next to Dieter. He liked Dieter. When they did the long and winding walk down to their rotund tutor's house, they had lots of interesting conversations about everything from the Middle East crisis to Chomskian linguistics. Dieter was about a hundred times cleverer than Omar, but he never made him feel small or stupid. In the beginning of the Michaelmas term, before Omar had become firm friends with Jim and been pulled into his starry circle of the college great and good, he had socialized quite a lot with Dieter and the less pretty, less fashionable people that Dieter had been drawn towards. He had found them warm, friendly and always inclusive. It had been with some regret that he had drifted gently away from their comforting circle towards Jim's people, with whom he secretly felt that he was a mere pretender just waiting to be found out and discarded, to be chewed up and spat out like so much gum when he stopped being flavour of the month. His natural place was probably with the geeks, and he always suspected that he would return to their welcoming fold one day, the prodigal son blinded by the light of popularity. Perhaps his time had come.

Omar smiled broadly at Dieter and his group. 'Cheers, guys. Why's formal Hall so packed tonight?' he asked. 'I only waited for late Hall because I thought it would be quieter.'

'Dear, did you not hear the rumours?' said Dieter.

'Did you just call me "Dear"?' Omar asked with confusion. It wasn't like Dieter to be camp.

'No, I said "Deer". Cute dappled things with antlers. Apparently there was a cull at Magdalen, and some of the surplus has gone to us. The rumours are that deer might be on the menu tonight. Change from curry, eh,' said Dieter cheerfully.

'I've never had deer,' Omar said. 'Do you have to watch out for shot or something?'

'No,' said Ledley, a horsey biologist, 'that's more of a problem with birds. I broke a tooth on some shot in a partridge once.'

After the wet vegetable soup, there were groans of disappointment up and down the hall as the familiar platters of rice and poppadums and chutney were laid out on the table, and the ghostly smell of curry invaded the Hall.

'Well, so much for the rumours,' said Dieter. He asked one of the serving ladies politely, 'So, when are we due to have the deer? Is it still hanging?'

'No, dear,' said the lady, 'it's on your plate. Chef didn't know how to cook deer, so he curried it.'

'Bloody hell,' said Ledley, looking despondently at the steaming platters of venison curry. 'What a bloody awful waste of good game. I don't think I can bring myself to eat this.'

'What's it like?' Omar asked Dieter, who was tucking cheerfully in.

'Oh, the usual really. Tastes just like a regular curry,' he said.

Reassured, Omar tried it and agreed. 'It does, doesn't it? Like a chicken curry mixed with a beef one.'

After a while, Ledley shrugged, and, pulling only a slight face, started eating.

After dinner, Omar still couldn't see Jim and Karen any-where. He was dragged slightly unwillingly by Dieter's little group to the bar, where they cheerfully warmed up with beers, and moved on to tequila shots. After the third round of lick, down and bite, Ledley fell into Dieter, who fell into the table, which caused everyone else to fall onto the floor in a hiccuping hysterical heap, with Omar in the midst of them. This is where I really belong, he thought fuzzily, laughing hysterically with the rest of them; life with the geeks didn't seem so bad. Here he would be accepted for what he was, not who he was friends with; here he could be a king, rather than a pretender.

The sound of the crash was heard throughout the bar, and welcomed with an enormous cheer by those standing around. Jim saw Omar and went up to him. 'Where've you been, mate? Been looking all over for you. Didn't you go to Hall?'

'Yeah, I couldn't see you guys anywhere,' Omar said to one of the three Jims that stood above him, trying not to sound reproachful. 'Thought you might want some privacy.'

'You can't have looked very hard,' said Jim. 'We were at the front, like we said, near the High Table.' Omar realized through the fug of tequila what had happened. Of course, to Jim, the front of the Hall meant the end of the Hall where the High Table was set up. To Omar, the front of the Hall was naturally the entrance. Jim, looking impatiently at Omar, and for once less drunk than him, said, 'Anyway, get up. We're heading off to Balliol now to pick up Giles and Lydia.'

'I think I might be stuck,' Omar said apologetically, as Finola, a not too slim mathematician, was lying across his legs.

Jim did his trademark eyeroll, before pushing up his shirtsleeves, 'Up you come, sweetie,' he said, pulling Finola roughly to her feet in a businesslike way. He called her sweetie as he didn't know her name, or the names of any of Dieter's group, nor did he ever have any intention to waste his time learning them; he filed them all under 'R' in his head, for 'Random People I never need to know'. He yanked up Omar too, only slightly less roughly.

As Omar left he waved to Dieter's group cheerfully, and shouted back to them the running joke that they'd started with their first tequila shot. 'Bye, guys, see you later. Why did the Mexican throw his wife out of the window?'

'Tequila!' Dieter's group shouted back, waving their empty shot glasses.

'Thanks for coming to find me,' Omar said later, leaning on Jim a little drunkenly.

'Well, I couldn't leave you slumming with that lot for May morning,' said Jim. 'They might have brainwashed you to join their Geek Gang by the end of the evening and you'd have been stuck with them forever, like some moonie in a cult.'

'I like them,' protested Omar. 'I like Dieter, Ledley and Finola, and the rest of them.'

'You see,' said Jim. 'They'd started already. I came just in time.'

'They're sweet,' insisted Omar.

'Nope, dogs are sweet. They're just wallpaper,' Jim said meanly, waving to Karen who was waiting for them at the porter's lodge.

By the time they got to Balliol, the stroll in the cool, damp air had begun to sober Omar up. In the bar, Jim insisted that he and Karen do some shots together: 'We've got some catching up to do, Omar's well ahead of us.' Omar tried not to feel left out as they licked salt from each other's hands, and bit the same piece of lemon. He was relieved when Giles and Lydia turned up.

'Hey, Giles,' said Jim, thumping him on his broad back. 'And hello, Chlamydia. You look deliciously dirty tonight. Will I catch something if I snog you?' He caught Lydia in his arms in a sweeping gesture.

Instead of being offended, Lydia giggled with so much delight that Karen looked almost cross. 'Oh Jimmy, you're so naughty.'

'Oi, keep your faggot hands off my bitch,' said Giles good-humouredly, heading to the bar; he often used appalling language in an attempt to cover up his old Etonian roots. 'It's going to be a long, long night,' he said to Omar as he passed him, 'and I've got to get through it on sodding alcohol-free lager.'

As they made for the Parks, the light, damp mist became a light but persistent shower, which didn't get much heavier but showed no signs of abating. Normality had returned, as Jim was now the most drunk one in the group by far, and insisted on getting a stinking kebab, which he danced with while bellowing 'Singin' in the Rain' tunelessly along Broad Street. The rest of them decided to follow Jim's military planning, and dragged him along to New College Lane, where the party was still going strong. At some point in the early hours, fuelled by vodka and orange squash as the wine and beer had run out, bottles started spinning, in combination with Truth or Dare.

Omar, who'd been listening sympathetically to a girl crying about her love life in the chill-out room upstairs, walked in just as the bottle landed on Jim.

'Dare,' Jim said.

Omar felt reckless. He had no idea why he instinctively said what he said next, except that he was drunk, and suddenly wanted to get all the doubt out in the open, to let that sword of Damocles finally fall. If it was going to happen, why not make it happen now?

'Kiss Karen,' he said loudly, collapsing onto a cushion at the edge of the circle.

Karen, who was flushed prettily with the heat and the drink, looked at Omar with a combination of outright surprise and gratitude.

'Easy,' Jim said, and bounding up to her, took her in his arms and kissed her chastely on the lips. Karen tried to smile and giggle, but only Omar could see that she was disappointed that he hadn't done anything more daring.

'That was rubbish,' said Giles, who had smoked enough dope to get over the fact that he wasn't allowed to drink. 'You're not eight years old. Open your mouths.'

'OK, but no tongues,' said Jim, and kissed her more fulsomely, a soap opera kiss.

The bottle span again, and landed on Jim once more. 'This is bloody rigged,' Jim said, picking up the bottle and inspecting it, before draining the dregs of warm liquid still clinging to the bottom. 'Dare,' he said again.

'Kiss Omar – with tongues,' said Lydia, getting into the spirit of it, and was gratified to hear squeaks of excitement from the others.

Jim looked at Omar and raised a quizzical eyebrow towards him. Omar, who had been staring at his feet since the Karen kiss that he had stupidly been responsible for, looked up. 'What? No way, man. That would be gross! It would be like incest, or something,' he protested vigorously.

Lydia shrugged. 'You know the rules – if either party backs out on a truth or dare, they have to run round the cloisters naked three times.'

'Cool, we win either way,' burped Jim.

'When did those rules come into play?' said Omar. 'I don't remember agreeing to that.'

'We must have made them while you were upstairs,' said Lydia.

'Come on, mate,' said Jim. 'I'm not running round without pants in this weather. Stick your tongue down my throat and we're done.'

'Why tongues?' protested Omar again. 'Karen didn't have to do tongues.'

'That's because Karen's a lady, and it's bad enough that you made her snog Jimmy in the first place with his kebab breath,' said Giles, blowing out smoke in a deeply mellow manner.

'Oh, let them off, you guys,' said Karen. 'It's not fair if Omar wasn't here when we did the rules.'

While Omar opened his mouth to protest again, Jim strode over to him and, pinning him down by the shoulders, kissed him even more fulsomely than he had Karen, with lots of tongue, to the cheers of the room.

Omar managed to push him off, blurting out, 'Jim!' in shock and outrage. He looked at Jim, and Karen, and Giles, and Lydia, and the whole room staring at him. 'Man, I've got to gargle. That extra chilli on the 'bab was too much,' he said, racing out.

'You idiots,' he heard Karen shout out to the room after he left. 'He's Muslim, you know. I think you've really upset him.'

The bathroom was miraculously free, and Omar locked the door and sank on the edge of the bath. He felt like he was the only still point in the spinning world; he'd been exposed, he knew it. He didn't gargle, even though he felt nauseous. And now his nose was starting to bleed; he hadn't had a stress-induced nose bleed for months; he held a tissue to it with mechanical despondency. After a few minutes, there was a gentle knocking on the door. 'Mate, are you in there?' Jim said quietly. Omar sighed, and wetting his hands, ran his fingers through his hair to cool him down. 'Omar?' Jim called out, a bit louder. Omar opened the door and let him in. Jim shut the door, and joined him on the side of the bath. 'Sorry if I embarrassed you, mate. I just thought a quick kiss would be easier than a naked run round the cloisters, is all. I might have got a bit carried away with the snog. You know me – utter drama queen. Love an audience.'

'You don't need to apologize; I probably embarrassed myself more than you did by running off like that.'

'What happened to your face?' asked Jim, just noticing the bloody stain on Omar's upper lip.

Omar checked his reflection in the mirror and washed away the blood at the sink. 'Nothing, just a nosebleed,' he said.

Jim nodded and got up to go, but then sat back down again. 'We're friends, right? We'll always be friends. Nothing's going to change that.'

'Of course not,' said Omar, surprised.

'So I can tell you anything, and you won't get weird. Because we're friends,' persisted Jim. Omar nodded, realizing with a sinking heart that perhaps Jim was going to tell him that he and Karen were finally an item.

'The thing is, the real reason I kissed you wasn't to avoid a naked run around the cloisters. It was because I thought that the opportunity would never present itself again. That's all.' For a moment, Jim sounded totally sincere, and looked almost sheepish, before adding with his usual bravado, 'Mate, I am so wasted. Do me a favour and ignore everything I say and do tonight. Look, I'm heading back to the party. Are you still up for the bridge at five a.m.?'

Omar looked at Jim, the numb shock he felt replaced

by another, undefinable feeling. A little like the reckless-
ness he had felt when he dared Jim to kiss Karen, again
he suddenly wanted to get all his doubt out in the open,
to let that sword of Damocles finally fall. But this feeling
was an affirmative one, one of near hope rather than
dread. 'Wait,' he said to Jim, and standing up, stood
opposite him and kissed him quickly and softly on the
cheek. 'I thought that might have been my only opportunity, too,' he explained. Jim looked at him in amaze-
ment, and hesitated just briefly before smoothing back
Omar's wet hair from his forehead, taking Omar's face in
both hands, and kissing him back.

Mrs Henna Karim Extends a Cordial Invitation

S HONA HAD MANAGED to avoid thinking about her mother for several weeks following her father's heart attack, until Henna inconsiderately barged back into her life. 'Shona moni,' Henna brayed loudly, into the answering machine at an ungodly hour, 'Shona moni, it's Amma, pick up!' Pausing for a moment, Henna started a sing-song chant that would test the patience of the most charitably disposed acquaintance, 'Pick up, pick up, pick up . . . Pick up! Pick up!'

Shona, bleary-eyed, wrapped a dressing gown around her and obediently picked up the bedroom phone, taking it on to the landing to avoid waking Parvez, who was sleeping heavily with slow and deliberate breaths. Just as she reverted to her cut-glass patrician accent when speaking to her papa or to her colleagues at school, with her Amma, she automatically fell into Bangladeshi vernacular, perhaps to make her feel closer to her, she wasn't sure.

'Ouf, why are you shouting so much? Don't you know what time it is here, Amma?'

'Tch! Why did you take so long to answer?' said Henna

unrepentantly. 'This is long distance, you know. Does the fat Pakistani keep you chained up so that you can't answer your old mother when she calls?'

'Amma, Parvez isn't fat,' said Shona, getting drawn in despite herself.

'Of course not. Parvez is perfect in every way, Rashid is perfect in every way. Everyone is perfect apart from your stupid old mother whom you never call, and who you ignore when she calls you for help.'

'Amma, what's wrong? What do you need help with?' Shona asked, suddenly concerned; she had been thinking that it was unlike her mother to use the endearment 'moni' when calling, and it was also not very like her to become belligerent so quickly; insulting Shona's loved ones and life choices was one of her favourite themes, but normally she warmed up to these with much greater calculation and finesse.

'I can't tell you over the phone. You have to come over here. I need your help, Shona moni. I need you here,' Henna entreated, now sounding almost distressed. 'Please come next week, as soon as you can.'

'Amma, summer term doesn't break up until the middle of next month. I can't just up and leave,' Shona started to explain.

'The middle of next month?' Henna mused, considering the proposal. 'Say on the fifteenth? Yes, that will just about do. Well, come in the middle of next month, then,' she said, suddenly not sounding distressed at all, but businesslike. 'So it's all settled.' Shona pursed her lips, realizing how her mother had just manipulated her, using her lifetime experience of amateur dramatics for that very purpose.

'Amma,' Shona protested, 'you have to tell me why you want me to come. Are you quite well? Is it Nanu? You can't just expect me to pay for a ticket to Dhaka with no reason.'

'Well, get the money from your prosperous father,' Henna snapped at her, 'if your great Pakistani husband is so poor that he can't afford to send his wife to visit her poor old mother.' Realizing from the silence at Shona's end that this tactic was proving less than persuasive, she added, 'Shona, I'm sorry for being cross. But this is important, I wouldn't ask you if it wasn't. Why are you making me give you reasons, when I've told you I can't? Do you want me to beg you to come? My own, my only daughter, my own flesh and blood, wants me to beg? All right then, I'll beg, I am begging you now. Come to Dhaka, Shona moni. I need you here.' By the end of her little speech, Henna's tones had shifted from bridling in cross words to wheedling in honeyed, humble tones.

Feeling instantly ashamed, even while she knew she was being played like putty by a seasoned expert at getting her own way, Shona said, 'Amma, don't speak like that. All right, I'll come.'

Having achieved what she wanted, Henna ended the call instantly, with barely a veneer of civility. 'Good, well I have to go now, Shona. Let me know which flight you'll be on.'

Shona looked at the clock in the passageway; it was four in the morning, and she felt too tired to be angry at her mother. She put the phone down, and went back to bed.

Parvez was in the same position, but his breathing was

lighter and shallow – he had, not surprisingly, woken up. Shona lay down at her end of the bed, and wished she had the comfort of someone's arms around her. She went back to sleep with difficulty, counting the hours and minutes until she would see Dermot again.

'So why exactly are you going to Dhaka?' asked Dermot, as Shona drove them to his flat during her after-school driving lesson.

'I wish I knew. Amma was very persuasive, but managed to avoid giving me a reason altogether. And she went on so much that it just seemed easier to say yes.' She turned briefly to look at Dermot's set profile. 'Go on, tell me I'm a sucker. That's what you're thinking.'

'I wouldn't presume to tell you that you're a sucker; besides, it would be pointless, seeing as you've already worked it out for yourself,' Dermot said with a smile. 'But seriously, you're over forty years old. You really don't need to do everything your mother says, especially without question. Don't go if you don't want to.' He hesitated before adding, 'Besides, I'd miss you.'

Shona looked at Dermot gratefully for much too long, before his warning look reminded her that she was still driving, and she turned her attention back to the mercifully quiet road in a flustered panic. 'Darling, the car's struggling a bit up the hill,' Dermot said quietly. Shona, who hadn't even noticed the fraught engine, pushed the car back into third gear.

'Sorry,' she muttered. She'd never stop her mother

from controlling her, and she was never going to pass her bloody driving test either.

In the haven of Dermot's flat, away from prying eyes and accidental encounters, Shona lay on the sofa with her feet raised onto Dermot's lap. 'Tell me about your mother,' Dermot said. 'You never talk about her.'

Shona hesitated. Ever since she had told Dermot about her father's secret life, she had avoided speaking about her family altogether. She had felt comforted telling him at the time, in the same perverse way that she had felt comforted when she had made love to Parvez; it was the comfort of laying oneself bare, of giving someone else her disquiet and her troubles, expelling her demons from her flesh. But in both cases, she had felt guilty afterwards; in the first instance, she had betrayed her father for her own comfort, in the second, she had betrayed her lover.

She had confessed to Dermot about that night with Parvez, and Dermot had said he understood; he even made excuses for her, saying that she had been confused and upset after finding out about her father's heart attack and then discovering his bigamy. Although he claimed to have appreciated her honesty, she could tell that the truth had upset him, as she had known it would. She had selfishly put her own conscience above his feelings, and she now felt little pride in this deed, which had seemed so noble at the time; how could you say someone deserved to hear the bitter truth, unless they also deserved to be hurt? She had decided to put an end to this new and damaging instinct to confess. The truth was overrated; it was rarely pure and never simple, that was the real truth that she had known since she was a child.

Given this, she wasn't sure if she should, or even if she could, expose her other demon; her ambivalence and resentment towards her mother. Besides, why did she dislike her mother so much? She barely knew her. Of course, she had worshipped her as a little girl, this fragrant, beautiful creature who was constantly flitting out dressed in sparkling, butterfly brightness. While other mothers wore their hair in long, undistinguished plaits, or pulled back into chaste buns, Shona's mother wore her glossy hair cut fashionably at her shoulders like a movie star, where it swung provocatively. But Henna had never paid her daughter the slightest bit of attention, passing her over indiscriminately to servants and nannies when her father wasn't available, except on a few precious outings, when it had just been her mother and her. She couldn't remember why her mother had relented, and taken her out on those visits to the clinic. She had only vague memories of kind-faced nurses, of lollipops and white coats. And after she had left with Parvez, her mother needed nothing else to do with her; it was as though the idea of her daughter was enough and she didn't need a flesh and blood one littering up her pleasant, indulgent life. Shona imagined that she was just a character in her mother's stories, something she used to boast to her friends: My Daughter, she lives in London, you know; My Daughter is an MA; My Daughter's son goes to Oxford. So where does your daughter live, Roshan, the one with the BA in English? Connecticut? Where's that? Oh-well-never-mind, I'm sure it must be nice. And Mina, where does your grandson attend college? Oh, really? Right here at Dhaka University. Well, it must be a comfort to have him so close . . .

Shona had visited her mother once every other year, when the boys were old enough, just so they would be able to say they knew their grandmother. She spoke to her about once a month, during which times her mother was always unfailingly critical. Of her parents, perhaps her father was the one who had misbehaved most profoundly, but despite this her father was the one she understood, and the one who had her love, because he had loved her first.

Aware of Dermot's eyes on her, and the overbearing silence in the room, Shona finally replied. 'There's not a lot to tell. I don't have much of a mother, really,' she said, sidestepping the question with obvious intent. She withdrew her legs from his lap, indicating unconsciously that she would not be receptive to any further questions on the matter.

'Do you not think that's something to tell, in itself?' said Dermot, pulling her legs back, running his hand over her instep. 'I didn't have much of a wife, but the one thing she did provide was conversational subject matter forever and a day.'

'Ah, but you're Irish, you love the chance to talk,' said Shona, seizing the chance to change the subject. 'What did you say your ex was doing these days?'

Back at home, Shona was surprised to find that the deadlock on the front door was already open. Turning the top key, she called out, 'Parvez, did you come back early?' while she considered several plausible reasons why she wouldn't have been back home at her normal time.

'Amma!' shouted a delighted voice. It was Omar. He ran in from the living room, closely followed by Pat-Bob, and hugged her.

'Darling, it's so lovely to see you!' exclaimed Shona, in genuine delight tinged with just the slightest bit of relief. 'I thought you were coming back tomorrow. Abbu and I were going to pick you up.'

'A friend of mine gave me a lift down, I thought I'd surprise you,' said Omar, cheerfully not mentioning that he and Jim had spent the last two days clubbing in London after their Prelims, and had stayed with a friend in Mile End. 'My friend Jim, I think I mentioned him? He hung around for a bit to say hello to you, but had to leave about an hour ago.'

'Yes, sorry darling, I had to ... stay a bit later than usual. Staff meeting thing,' Shona said artlessly. 'What a shame I missed him.'

As they sat down to tea, Omar spoke brightly about the latest family gossip. 'What's the scoop on that angelic new girlfriend of Sharif's?' he asked carelessly, less good at keeping other people's secrets than his own.

Shona's brow furrowed. 'They broke up ages ago,

darling, not long after Easter, unless he has a new girl-friend he's not mentioned to me.'

Omar shrugged, covering up his careless mistake. 'Oh, right then. You know me, always behind on the news.'

'Well, here's some up-to-the-minute news for you,' Shona said. 'I'm going to see your Nanu in Bangladesh after we break up for the summer, around the fifteenth.' She asked entreatingly, although without much hope, 'I don't suppose you might like to come with me? Just for a couple of weeks? I'll get your ticket, it wouldn't cost you anything.'

Omar paused for a moment. He had a few weeks to kill before August, when Jim would be back from his family holiday. He had thought he would just lounge about in Tooting and catch up with friends, but he had lots of time to do that before the fifteenth. And once his mum was away it would be pretty dull at home, what with his dad working, and Sharif doubtless spending every spare moment with Candida, when he wasn't gigging or pretending to work. 'Sure,' he said eventually. 'Why not? I've not seen Nanu and old Ammie for ages.'

Shona hugged Omar from across the table. 'That's wonderful, darling. We'll have so much fun.' She breathed with relief that she wouldn't have to face her mother on her own. She would have her clever son as her protection; her mother was much more likely to behave herself if her Oxonian undergraduate grandson was there. Perhaps then she might choose to play the role of gracious matriarch rather than wicked, scheming witch.

The Dhaka Tea Party

Typically, when Shona and Omar arrived at the Dhaka townhouse, sweaty and tired after the long flight and the hectic drive, there was no one there to greet them. 'Your Amma must be out visiting,' said the young chauffeur, far more louche and familiar than the respectable, elderly driver of past years. They settled themselves in their usual guest quarters, and while Omar fell asleep, Shona sat in the dining room and waited for her mother. A sweet-faced village girl, whom Henna must have taken on since her last visit, brought Shona a glass of cold lemon sherbet with just a bit too much sugar. 'Has school finished already today?' Shona asked kindly, just to make conversation. The girl looked very young, barely older than ten, and giggled, delighted at such a funny question.

'School is finished. Now I am twelve, I work instead,' she said proudly, adding unnecessarily, 'I work here.' She went back into the kitchen with a light, cheerful step.

Shona frowned. Of course her mother would not have seen the value in sending the girl back to school; her own claims to have almost avoided school by a prepubescent marriage were well documented.

Henna eventually bustled in, looking very glamorous despite her age, in a cool-blue silk sari and enormous Gucci sunglasses. 'Oh, there you are, Shona,' she said a touch reproachfully, for all the world as though Shona was the one who had been late.

'Hello, Amma,' Shona said, getting up dutifully and pecking her on the cheek. 'Omar's asleep, he was shattered after the flight. Where is everyone? Where's Uncle Aziz and Ammie? Are they over at the farms?'

Henna had seemed momentarily nonplussed by this perfectly normal question, but then seized on Shona's suggestion too quickly for her answer to seem completely credible. 'Yes, yes, they are at the farms. Let's wake Omar; why must he sleep the moment he gets here? He must get that from the lazy Pakistani. We'll have tea on the veranda now it's a little cooler.' She shouted out for the village girl in the kitchen, '*É*, Banu-Bibi!' but this time, not one, but two, appeared, with similar gentle demeanour but not quite similar enough to be sisters. 'Banu and Bibi, this is my daughter. We'll have some more lemonade, and tea, with pooris and sweets.' She said in an aside to Shona, 'Omar likes sweets, I remember.'

'I think it's you that likes sweets, Amma,' Shona said matter-of-factly, but lightly enough not to cause offence. 'Why do you have two new girls? Where's Osama, the cook?'

Henna deliberately pretended to misunderstand the question. 'Well, you must always have two girls rather than just one, otherwise they get lonely and want to go

back to their village, and you have to start all over again.'
She looked over Shona critically. 'You had better get
changed. You look like a crushed piece of old linen, and
Shameela from my am dram group is coming for tea soon.
We're doing a Gilbert and Sullivan season. We all laughed
when she suggested *Trial by Jury* – she's married to a rich
attorney, and is bringing her elderly, ugly daughter.' She
winked cheekily at Shona, as though to say, They're not
as good as us. We'll have some fun with them.

Shona sighed as she capitulated and went to leave the
room. As usual with her mother, so many things were left
unanswered, unaddressed and hung in a thick, conspiratorial fog in the room. She was deeply unsatisfied with
this first encounter; there had been no explanation for the
sudden rush to come to Bangladesh, or the puzzling
absence of Uncle Aziz and her grandmother, and no
reason given for the ancient cook's replacement. Osama
had often let her sit in the kitchen as a child, while he
gave her tasty tit-bits of the sweet halwa and toasted
almonds that he sometimes prepared for special occasions,
like Eid or birthdays. There was probably a very simple
explanation behind Osama's departure. This, at least, her
mother could tell her. She deserved to know if he had
passed away, or retired. Pausing at the door, Shona turned
back and asked again, 'But Osama? Where is he?'

Henna shrugged. 'He's not Osama any more, you
know. He changed his name in protest against that
bearded Saudi cave-dweller who was hiding in Afghani-
stan; he's Osman now. I told him it was a stupid name. It
doesn't sound Bangladeshi at all, it sounds like the name
of a Turkish carpet-seller. Imagine, an old man like that

doing such silly things, as though he has anything to do with world politics.'

'But where is he?' Shona persisted.

Henna looked at her as though she was a touch retarded. 'I told you, Shona. At the farms with the rest of them.'

Shona looked mutinously between two outfits. One was a gleaming shalwar kameez that she had bought in Tooting. It was in a shade of sophisticated green that she loved, and looked unmistakably Pakistani in design; it would certainly irritate her mother. Or, after having been compared to crushed linen, it was very tempting to dress in it; she picked up a linen trouser suit and shook it out. Why not? She deserved to have a little fun at her mother, after the way she'd behaved this afternoon.

Omar was already on the veranda, still dressed in his jeans and Sex Pistols T-shirt. He was speaking earnestly to Henna about his course, and Shona was pleased to see that Henna was looking both bored and lost, while nodding sagely, and pretending to know what he was talking about. 'Hey Ma,' he said as she seated herself in the wicker chair facing her mother, 'did you know that Nanu is doing a rep performance of *Trial by Jury* and *The Mikado* this week? They're performing at the college. Lucky we got here, or we'd have missed it; and Nanu wouldn't have had any other fans in the audience with everyone else being away.'

Shona looked at her mother in surprise. So was that all

it had been? She had wanted her family to support her from the audience for her latest event, as Aziz and Ammie wouldn't be available. Why hadn't she just said? Shona realized quickly that of course her mother wouldn't have told her over the phone; she had played it just right by making it sound like it was something urgent with dire consequences. With the price of the airfare, the play was the most expensive evening out Shona had ever bought. Henna had the grace to look a little sheepish, and said brightly, 'I think that's Shameela coming through with her daughter,' as she bustled to the door.

Shameela was an elegant woman who was about Henna's age, but looked much older – her greyhound thinness did not complement her, and her face looked especially haggard, with the skin pulled tautly across her high cheekbones and jutting forehead. Her daughter, Parvine, was neither elderly nor ugly; she was only a few years older than Shona, and simply a little bit plain. Her worthy, nun-like looks were not helped by the frazzled grey hair scraped back and held with a plastic clasp, nor by her thick, heavily framed glasses. Despite the unprepossessing appearances, both mother and daughter seemed very friendly, and had thoughtfully brought a gift, a large box of multicoloured burfis from one of the city's most celebrated sweet-makers.

During the gossipy conversation that followed between Henna and Shameela, mainly in English for Omar's benefit, Shona found herself staring a little too much at Parvine – she was thinking that this was what she could look like in a few years, if she decided to wear glasses rather than contact lenses, and let her hair go grey and long rather than colouring and styling it. She wondered what Dermot would think of her then, if she lost her looks before he did.

'These are great sweets,' said Omar politely, biting into a peach-coloured burfi. 'As good as Uncle Hassan's.'

'My husband's cousin,' Shona explained to Shameela and Parvine. 'He owns a confectionery shop in Tooting.' Seeing the warning look from her mother, that clearly told her not to make further reference to her husband's Pakistani, plebeian, shopkeeping relatives, she recklessly added, 'We used to live above his shop when we first moved to London.'

Henna looked thunderous, but regained composure instantly. 'Yes, my daughter was such a free spirit. We always supported her in her whims: going to London, living above a sweet shop. A kid in a candy shop, like the Americans say; I think she inherited my sweet tooth!' She laughed at her own joke, pleased at having turned Shona's embarrassing early poverty into a sugary anecdote.

'I love London,' sighed Shameela. 'I would love my granddaughter to live there so I had an excuse to visit. I would go to the theatre every night.'

Shona asked after Shameela's role in Henna's amateur theatre production, and was surprised to hear the older lady giggle in delight. 'Me? An actress? At my age? We are not all blessed with your mother's looks. I think she keeps a picture in an attic that does her ageing for her. No, I used to be a dancer, many years ago, and I am the choreographer of the dance routines. Your mother puts the others to shame. She should have been a dancer.'

'You dance, Nanu?' Omar said, impressed. 'Wow, that's amazing.'

'And I'm very good,' said Henna proudly. 'You'll see me tomorrow, during the production. You can come to the dress rehearsal too, if you want. It's in the morning.' She threw a significant look at Shameela and Parvine.

Up until this point, Parvine had been rather quiet, sitting very straight in her chair during tea, making polite comments about the pooris and lemonade, but otherwise contenting herself with following the others' conversations. Despite her glasses, she had been myopically observing Omar quite a bit, perhaps trying to make out the slogan on his T-shirt. However, at the mention of the dress rehearsal, as though jabbed into action on cue, she leaned forward earnestly, and in the breathy, quick voice of someone who might expect rejection, said to Omar, 'Yes, my daughter will be at the dress rehearsal. She has been helping me with the costumes. She said she could show you around town later, she knows Dhaka very well, and she's about the same age as you.'

'Sure,' said Omar distractedly, trying to prevent his burfi crumbling into his tea, 'that's really nice of her to offer. If Amma doesn't mind.' He turned towards Shona with an obvious lack of suspicion. 'Amma, did we have plans for tomorrow?'

Before Shona could prevent the obvious set-up and claim they did already have plans, Henna smiled and said, 'How nice, that's all settled then.' Shameela and Parvine smiled just as broadly, and Parvine visibly relaxed back into her wicker seat. Despite her nervousness, her mission had been accomplished, and she glanced to her mother for approval.

After all the tea and refreshments had been exhausted, Shameela and Parvine made their excuses to leave. Omar remained on the veranda, while Henna and Shona led them out. 'Such a wonderful afternoon,' Shameela said in Bangla to Henna. 'And such a pretty daughter, Shundor Shona,' she added, moistening her finger delicately with the inside of her lower lip, before touching Shona's cheek for good luck, 'and clever grandson. A philosopher, no less! You must be very proud.' Henna smiled graciously, and inclined her head like the lady of the manor she had become. Shameela continued as she reached the door, 'And please pass my best wishes to Bhai Aziz and his mother. I'm sorry to have missed them again, but they must have so much to plan for with his wedding coming up so soon.' She smiled conspiratorially at Shona. 'Imagine, a confirmed bachelor like your uncle finally getting wed. If someone like him can change his ways, there's hope for all the unmarried girls out there.'

Shona took this revelation with outward calm, while she finally made the connection between her mother's uncharacteristic cry for help last month, and the inexplicable absences from the household. Gilbert and Sullivan had less to do with this visit than she had thought; she realized now that there were more serious changes afoot. Her mind was ticking over so rapidly with this new information and the possible consequences, that she didn't notice Shameela asking her a question, and had to ask her to repeat it.

'I just asked if your father will have recovered from his

heart attack sufficiently to fly back for the wedding,' Shameela asked. 'We see him so rarely in Dhaka these days.'

'I really don't know,' Shona said honestly. 'Perhaps he won't be well enough . . .'

Henna interrupted impatiently, 'Of course Rashid will be back for his younger brother's wedding.' She added guilelessly, 'And as I've already told you all, you will be seeing much more of him in Dhaka before too long. With his retirement coming up, he won't need to spend so much time in England. I'll soon have my dear Rashid home.' Shona looked at her mother in barely concealed astonishment; what things had she been telling the cream of Dhaka society? For all intents and purposes, her parents had separated years ago; she couldn't possibly expect him to return for good.

'Such a hard worker, putting his family's comfort before his own for so long,' Shameela said with approval, while Parvine nodded. 'He must be looking forward to his retirement immensely.' They finally took their leave.

At the door, in the long dark hallway, Shona and Henna faced each other silently. Shona looked pleadingly at her mother: Please speak to me, please explain it all, please don't make me have to drag it all out of you, don't let it all be unsaid again and again. Henna took a deep breath, and then smiled brightly as she skitted off girlishly to her quarters. 'I've got a visit to make before dinner,' she said cheerfully, over her shoulder.

Shona caught up with her, keeping ruthlessly in step with her. 'Amma, we need to talk, now.' Henna kept walking, trying to shake her off by looking straight ahead and ignoring her, as she had so often when Shona was a tottering infant trailing persistently after her pretty mamma.

'Besides, you must be very tired, Shona,' added Henna, as she reached her door. 'I'll be back for dinner.' She went to shut the door smilingly in Shona's face, but Shona wedged her foot in the heavy door. She was fortunately still wearing her heavy airport loafers rather than sandals better suited to the climate. I can't believe she's making me do this, Shona thought to herself, as she found herself forced to fight with the door in a manner that was hardly dignified. She managed to push the door back open, and stood purposefully with her back against it.

'Mamma,' she said pleadingly. 'We must talk. We really must.'

Henna, having lost the battle of the door, was already at her dressing table smoothing out her glossy hair with an expensive bristle brush. 'What about, dear?' she said artlessly. 'Are you and the Pakistani having problems? Is that why he didn't come with you?'

Shona wasn't going to be thrown so easily this time. 'Amma, you know that Parvez is working. Why aren't Uncle Aziz and Ammie here? Why have the old chauffeur and Osama left? You've fallen out over this wedding, haven't you?'

Henna's back was to Shona, and her shoulders started shaking as though she had a deep laugh rumbling upwards from her stomach. 'You stupid, stupid child,' choked out

Henna through the laugh when it finally erupted. For a moment Shona thought that all was well, and that she had simply misunderstood everything. But then she saw that Henna's laugh was so strong it was bringing her to tears. 'You've fallen out? You've fallen out?' she mocked Shona, imitating her voice cruelly. 'As though we were children squabbling over a ten-taka note in the gutter. Don't you realize what this bloody marriage means?' Shona remained silent, having no idea what had upset her mother so deeply, and not wanting to risk displaying any further ignorance. Her mother had the ability to make her feel very small and simple indeed. Henna took a deep breath. 'No, of course you don't. You only think of yourself and your fat Pakistani and your darling father.' She turned fully to face Shona, who was still standing at the door. 'Sit down, dear,' she said, indicating the divan seat. When Shona remained standing, preferring the support of the door, Henna shrugged and explained in a more composed voice, just slightly trembling with anger, 'It means that I have given that man and his mother the last twenty years of my life, and he repays me by replacing me with another model, and barely a younger model at that!' Shona held her breath, thinking that Henna must have found out about Verity, but then Henna continued, 'An ugly spinster, a doctor who thinks she is so special just because she has worked for a living. Hah! She calls that work? That woman has spent her life looking down people's throats and down her thin nose at real wives and mothers like me.' She looked earnestly at Shona. 'You see? He is bringing another woman to this house, usurping my place in our household, and in our society.'

Shona did not understand why her mother was talking like a jealous wife. Uncle Aziz was free to marry whoever he wanted, although now that he was in his late fifties, most of Dhaka society would have no longer expected it. People joked that he was married to his farms, and to his family. She was about to say something calming to her mother, when she noticed the photo of her mother on the dresser. It was taken maybe ten years ago at a charity event in Dhaka, and her mother looked radiant and beautiful, and very happy. She had seen the photo many times before, but had never registered who her mother was dancing with, as his back was to the camera and the face couldn't quite be seen. Of course, it was Uncle Aziz; her father never danced, and would certainly not have gone willingly to one of those events during his flying visits back, even if Henna had deigned to ask him. Realization finally dawned on her, as she remembered the unkind, unfounded words of gossips all those years ago, and she sat down heavily on the divan.

'Uncle Aziz?' she asked. 'All this time, you and Uncle Aziz? Here in this house?'

Henna looked pitifully at Shona. 'Oh, for God's sake, don't be so naive, child,' she spat impatiently. 'Did you think I would sit here like a grieving widow while your father played with his Air Miles? Playing the English gentleman over in the UK, playing house with some insipid, weak-chinned, crooked-toothed Lady Limey?'

Shona had to admit that she was indeed, a stupid, stupid girl. 'You knew? About Papa and Verity? You know?' Everyone, it seemed, knew about the family skeletons, secrets and hidden liaisons apart from her. She struggled to find a firm place for her confused thoughts to settle. 'So Papa knew about you, too? He must have.'

Henna looked impatiently at Shona. 'Arré, what did I do to have such a slow daughter!' she muttered, practically rolling her eyes. 'If your darling father knew, do you think he would be flying back here with such guilty regularity, do you think he would be keeping up appearances over here with such efficiency, do you think he would be sending back such a big chunk of his salary to us every month? Of course your father does not know; he suspects, as he has suspected us for years because of the bloody gossiping servants, like your precious Osama, but he was too guilty himself to ever confront us. If your father found out, I would have had to divorce him and marry Aziz; and I would have lost my position in society here with the scandal.'

'Would that have been so bad?' Shona asked quietly, almost afraid to speak up amid this whirlwind of revelation, in case it whipped round her and pulled her away with it. 'Then Uncle Aziz wouldn't be marrying someone else now, and Papa wouldn't be riddled with guilt and making himself ill with long-distance travel.'

Henna shook her head. 'Well, your papa won't be weakening himself any more with travel or guilt. He can make up for this sorry mess by coming home and taking up his place as head of the house, so Aziz and his ugly old doctor-didi can be put back in their place, or move out if they don't like it.' She moved swiftly over to Shona, who flinched as though half expecting a blow or more sharp words, but Henna simply knelt by her entreatingly, her hands on either side of her face. 'This is why I needed you to come. I need you, Shona moni. I need you to persuade your father to come back to Dhaka and take up his place here, or my position will be lost forever. Everyone will realize what has happened, and I'll be a laughing stock. Everything I've built here will be gone; I'll just be another pathetic old woman abandoned by her husband.' Getting up, to sit companionably by Shona on the divan, taking her daughter's hand, Henna continued, in a soft, reasonable voice, 'Besides, I've let your father play long enough in England; it's time to come home. He's had twenty years with that wife, which is long enough for any love match to last, and his English daughter is grown up now, so he can't say she needs him. His real family needs him now; his real wife, his old Ammie, his daughter and grandchildren . . .' She looked wide-eyed at Shona, teary with emotion.

Shona wrenched her hand away. 'Ammie prefers Uncle Aziz, and always did. And you clearly did, too. And my family aren't in Dhaka, they're in England, where Papa is now. You'll be taking him away from us, and from everything he loves.' Her voice was getting higher but, unable to stop it, she practically shrieked, 'How long have you known about Papa? About his other family? How long?'

Henna looked calmly at the hand that Shona had rejected, polishing a brilliant sapphire and diamond ring with the edge of her silk sari. 'Well, from the beginning, Shona. I am not as slow as you and your father; I did some snooping and read his correspondence when he came over. At the time I was pleased that he had something to distract him.' Looking up at Shona, she asked, 'Why are you so upset? Didn't you know? If I knew all the way here in Dhaka, how could you not have known right there in London? Didn't you wonder why your father spent so little time in that London flat, and why he got a new place in the country? Didn't you ever visit and work it out for yourself?'

Shona looked down, not wanting to meet her mother's pitying look. Perhaps her mother was right. Perhaps she was just small and simple, hiding her ignorance behind her degrees and her book-learning. 'The boys were born after Papa bought his new house; it was too difficult to visit with the twins, so he used to come to us. I think we went a few times, but he always took us out for lunch or dinner, we never stayed . . .' She added, quietly, as though to justify herself, 'I did think he might have met someone in England. I suspected a long time ago when I went to his first flat, the company one he had in Paddington, but I never thought he was married, with another daughter, another life. I only found out when he had his heart attack at Easter. I saw Verity at the hospital.' She said bitterly to her mother, 'How could you have known, all these years, and not told me? You knew that Papa had a wife, and that I had a sister, all these years, and you kept it hidden. You made Papa keep this stupid lie going on and on, while you must have been bleeding him and Uncle Aziz dry.'

Henna was already getting impatient with Shona. She went back to the dresser, pulled out a lipstick in a golden case and started painting her lips. 'Tch!' she tutted in disgust. 'Your father marries some wilting English flower, raises another daughter and you still manage to make *me* the criminal? Always taking your precious father's side.'

Shona felt like crying, but didn't dare to in front of Henna. It would just confirm her mother's poor opinion of her. 'Mamma, why does it have to be like this? We all know the truth now, so who would you be protecting? We shouldn't have to keep up this pretence.'

Henna, satisfied with her reflection, picked up her handbag and went to the door. 'We won't have to soon. Just make sure your father comes back; he'll listen to you. The sooner he leaves his silly fairy-tale idyll in England and comes back to Dhaka, the sooner everything will be back to normal.' She walked out of the door, saying crossly, 'You've made me late for my appointment now. I'll be back for dinner.' She marched off purposefully, leaving Shona in a crumpled heap of linen on the divan.

I can't do this, Shona thought, exhausted. I was telling myself that the truth was overrated, but the real truth is this: I can't pretend any more, for someone else's sake, that things are the way they should have been rather than the way they are. She stood up unsteadily, and went to pick up the photo of her mother and Uncle Aziz on the dresser. Her unanswered question echoed insistently through her mind: who would they be protecting by bringing Papa back to play-act at happy families twenty years too late? Not herself or Amma, who both knew the truth about Papa's double life already. Not Uncle Aziz or Ammie, who couldn't care less about Papa and would prefer, as Amma knew well, that Papa remain where he was and the status quo remain unchanged. Not Verity or

Candida, who would lose their husband and father, just so that Henna could gain back her trophy husband for appearance's sake, and so Shona could maintain the cheap, flimsy pretence that her parents were happy. And this was worthless now that she could no longer deceive herself that they had a satisfactory, if unusual, arrangement.

Omar knocked softly on the door. 'Hey, Amma, are you OK in there?' he asked.

'I'm fine, darling,' replied Shona, replacing the photo and smoothing her hands over her face before opening the door.

'You don't look fine,' commented Omar. 'Have you and Nanu been arguing again?'

Shona shrugged, and nodded.

'Something of a record, I guess. You managed to hold off for four hours,' Omar teased gently. 'Do you want to go for a walk before dinner? Head out to the bazaar or something.'

Shona nodded again, and managed a weak smile. She remembered something from the teatime, and said apologetically to her son, 'I'm sorry about the set-up, I had no idea they had that planned. You don't have to go, just to be polite.' Shona paused, and then picked her words carefully. 'What I mean is, I don't want you to have to pretend to go along with things that Nanu might have planned, just for appearance's sake.'

Omar looked surprised. 'What set-up?' he asked, before he realized, 'Oh, you mean Parvine's daughter? I didn't think that was a set-up.' He added, 'Really, Amma, there was no need to argue with Nanu about that. I honestly don't mind hanging around Dhaka with someone my own age for a day. If she's anything like her mum and Shameela, I'm sure she'll be very nice. Besides, I'm sure I can protect myself from her; I'm sort of off the market, anyway.'

Shona felt her sober mood lightening. Here at least was some good news. 'I thought you looked particularly happy since you've come back from college. Who is she?'

Omar held his finger to his lips. 'Shh, it's a secret,' he said conspiratorially. He took her arm as they left the house. 'You know, I'm luckier than you, I think.'

Shona looked at him suspiciously. 'Why's that?' She wondered if he was going to compare his new relationship with the state of her own less than happy partnership with his father.

'Because I've got a much nicer mum than you have,' he explained, kissing her on the cheek.

Shona felt much, much better, and squeezed her son's arm.

A Performance, a Bookmark and a Drastic Decision

SHONA AND OMAR dutifully went to the performances of *Trial by Jury* and *The Mikado* that Henna performed on consecutive nights with her drama group. Although the audience numbered at least a hundred, they were without exception family and friends of the cast and backstage crew. They used the hall in Dhaka University, and Shona was reminded of her school production at Christmas, which had been slightly better attended. When they sang, 'She may very well pass for forty-three, in the dusk with a light behind her,' Omar nudged his mum. 'When was your birthday again, Amma?' he asked.

'Shut up,' she said good-naturedly, feeling a little bit old and worn-down compared to her glowing, all-singing, all-dancing mother, who with heavy make-up and under the stage lights, could have easily passed for her sister.

The next night, at *The Mikado*, Shona was amused to notice that her Amma, who despite her age must have had a secret yen to play the starring role of Yum-Yum, had to make do with Katisha. She had deliberately resisted making herself plain enough to carry off the role, apparently allowing the make-up team to do no more than put a high, dramatic flush on her cheeks, and to make her brows heavier. Nor did she deliver the line about not having a beautiful face with much sincerity, although she made up for it with her comic timing and wide-eyed candour when she added, 'But I have a left shoulder blade that is a miracle of loveliness. People come miles to see it.'

'Now that, you can see she really meant,' commented Omar, and Shona choked back a snigger in response. However, when she saw her mother sing back to her bandy-legged suitor, 'Willow, titwillow, titwillow,' so gently and softly, and when she saw her dance with the chorus in bare feet, her toenails gleaming like polished pearls, her face transported, Shona wasn't sniggering any more. This was what her mother had lived for, to perform; perhaps if she'd been able to become an actress or a dancer in her youth, she would have been less of an actress at home with her family. She felt a little sad that this was what Henna was trying so hard to protect – her place in Dhaka society, her place in a well-regarded little amateur dramatic group, which performed to friends and family, coerced spectators who made jokes at her expense while they watched the performance. It seemed so little to show for her mother's life.

In one of the lazy afternoons that followed, Shona was guiltily awaiting a call from Dermot that she planned to take in her father's old, abandoned study. She checked her watch; almost ten minutes. She thought she might seem a bit suspicious hovering so closely to the phone, so she wandered out to the dining room, where Omar had books and papers out, writing notes for his next year's work. 'I didn't realize you were studying linguistics,' Shona said in surprise, seeing a tome by Chomsky open at his elbow.

'I'm not,' said Omar, drinking some pomegranate juice that Bibi had sweetly whizzed for him in the blender. 'It's for a philosophy paper that I'm taking on innatism. You know, nature versus nurture, what's naturally in us, like natural morality, versus what we're taught.'

'Oh right,' said Shona nodding. 'So I guess language is an example of something we're taught.'

Omar shook his head. 'You know, that's what I would have thought too. In fact, according to this, language is an example of something that's innate. I think the idea is that you can't really teach someone their first language, as they'd have to understand the language in the first place to be taught it. So children must already have this innate structure that's ready to accept any language they're first exposed to, and they sort of discover it, or invent it for themselves.' Omar frowned with frustration. 'Well, at least that's what I've copied out. I'm writing it all down, but I don't quite understand it. That's the trouble with me and philosophy – you can't just learn it, you have to . . . get it, too.' He smiled disingenuously. 'I guess I'm just a bear of little brain.'

Shona ruffled his hair affectionately. 'It's enough to be clever, darling. You don't have to be modest, too.' The phone rang, and they both jumped. 'I'll get it,' said Shona quickly; Dermot was uncharacteristically early. But Omar was too quick for her. 'Hello, Karim residence,' he said.

'Oh, all right, mate!' he answered in delight on recognizing the voice. 'Thought it might be you. Hold on, I'm taking it in the other room.'

'Is it Sharif?' asked Shona, as he put the phone down and headed to Rashid's office.

'Nope, Jim from college. Calling from Portugal,' Omar answered briefly over his shoulder.

Shona sighed. While they were gossiping about girls and suchlike, Dermot would call and not get through. Oh well, she'd text him and arrange another time. Glancing at Omar's notes, she thought about what he'd said. Perhaps she had never learned to dissemble, to pretend, to play-act, as she knew she did so effectively; perhaps it had always been with her, part of her heritage from her duplicitous mother and bigamous father, and she had just needed to be exposed to the right stimuli to discover it for herself. She couldn't claim to have been taught to behave this way; it was the way she had always been. Or was deception just another language she'd been taught, along with Urdu, Bangla and English? Was it something that could be unlearned, or was it part of her? Maybe I could learn something new, to replace it, thought Shona; I'm a language teacher, so why can't I teach Amma, and Papa, and me to learn a new language, a new way of speaking, of behaving. She sighed again; how vain she was, as though she believed she really could intellectualize away adultery; it was one of the oldest sins, and one that they were all three guilty of, and it was what had caused this convoluted turn of events. And yet, she was still trying to keep her secret hidden. Because it would be better for the boys, she told herself. Her throat suddenly felt very dry.

Shona reached for Omar's pomegranate juice and, taking a sip, an underlined phrase in his notes caught her eye. 'Shklovskij: People living at the seashore grow so accustomed to the murmur of the waves that they never hear them.' Intrigued, Shona sat down and read on, the lines copied out by Omar's neat, precise hand. 'By the same token, we scarcely ever hear the words which we utter . . .' That was all, it was the last thing he had written; she must have interrupted him before he finished writing out the rest. She picked up the book Omar had been reading to see if there was any more, and his bookmark fell out. A slim copper bookmark, engraved with an etching of New College and 'Omar R Khan'. On the back, also engraved, was 'Yours, JO'. So that was the name of Omar's new girlfriend. Jo. She replaced the bookmark, and found the rest of the phrase in the book: '. . . we scarcely ever hear the words which we utter . . . we look at each other, but we do not see each other any more'. Her father's words in the hospital echoed back to her; she had agreed not to see his double life, if he had not seen hers.

When Omar came back, he was flushed with excitement. 'Jim's been having a miserable time in Portugal, he's already planning his next holiday. He's organizing some trip to go clubbing in Ibiza. I thought I might go, too.'

'Sure, if you can afford it,' Shona said. 'You don't have to ask. Will your girlfriend be going, too?'

'I wasn't asking, Ma,' Omar said with slight reproach. 'I'm a grown-up, and I'll find some work when I get back to pay for it all. And don't worry about girls, Oakley's insisting that this is a lads-only trip.'

'I'm not sure that sounds like any less to worry about,' said Shona dryly. 'And who's Oakley?'

'Oakley is Jim's surname, I call him Oakley some-times,' said Omar, sitting back at the desk and getting out his mobile. 'I'm going to text Sharif and tell him, he'll be sooo jealous; he always wanted to go clubbing in Ibiza, but can't, what with all his . . . um,' Omar hesitated for no apparent reason, before saying, '*work* commitments.' He got back up again. 'In fact, I'm going to email him so I can gloat properly . . .'

'Well, it's about time he started to take his work seriously,' Shona said. 'I don't know what else he's doing with his time. Your Abbu says his constant absenteeism is getting beyond a joke. And send him my love.'

She looked again at the line in Omar's book: '. . . we look at each other, but we do not see each other any more'. She sighed. How true it was; how often had she missed what was right before her eyes, waiting to be remarked upon, to be noticed, to be discovered. With Amma, with Papa, with Dermot. She looked at the book-mark again; it was very elegant, with a slight ripple to the metal above the etching of the college. It was a thoughtful present; what a nice girl this Jo must be. Shona looked again. Of course, it wasn't Jo, it was JO. Jim Oakley; it was from Omar's friend, his best friend at college. He didn't talk about him much at all. In fact, he hardly mentioned him, but he always seemed so happy to hear from him. His face was an utter picture of joy just now, she couldn't remember when she had last seen someone so happy. But then she suddenly did; an image flashed back to her, of Dermot walking swiftly down the stairs at

Clapham Common tube station, and on seeing her, his face breaking into an expression of pure happiness and relief, as he walked straight into her arms.

Oh my God, thought Shona. Putting the book down, she walked swiftly into the garden for some fresh air, taking deep gulps on the humid terrace. She sat down on the swing, moving herself gently to and fro with her feet. I've been deceiving myself, she thought: 'Je me trompais moi-même.'

This revelation made everything suddenly very clear to Shona. She saw that the intricate web her family had designed to keep them together, had actually entangled them, and pulled them further and further apart. Her Amma and Papa's pretence had benefited neither of their children, neither Shona nor Candida, in the end; they should have divorced twenty years ago, when Papa must have met Verity, and Amma had started her affair with Aziz. She thought about what she was doing with Parvez and Dermot, and suddenly felt very cold and very guilty. She'd been judging her parents and, yet again, she was following their lead, their unhealthy pattern of lies and subterfuge. She could no longer argue that it was better for the boys if she and Parvez remained together, unhappily, for appearance's sake, and she could no longer pretend that it was better for either Parvez or Dermot.

I didn't hear the waves; I've looked but I haven't seen, thought Shona. I thought that I was lying to protect the children, and all I've done is push them down the same path as me, the same path as my parents. So Omar feels he has to hide the truth, to protect us, and I'm losing my own son to his secret. And I might have already lost Sharif; he may never forgive me for holding back the truth about Candida during those few weeks when he was seeing her. I made him live with a guilty secret that he didn't even know.

Shona made a decision. This is where it would end. She would tear through that intricate web, and damn the consequences. With a sinking heart, she realized she would have to start with herself; Parvez deserved to be the first to know.

Sharif Khan and the Terrifying Truth

'YOU KNOW, I still can't believe it,' Sharif said to Candida, pulling off another slice of the take-out pizza they were having for lunch. 'Mum is barely home from Bangladesh, and then she and Dad tell us that they're separating.'

'It's such a shame. Your mummy's lovely,' said Candida. 'Your dad's mad to let her go.'

'It's not his choice, poor sod. Mum didn't say in so many words, but she's basically met someone.' He chewed on his pizza. 'And then a week later, Omar finally tells us about his new college squeeze, and it's not a she, it's a he! I mean, I know I always called him a bloody big poofter, but I didn't expect him to go and prove me right. And Mum was right there sticking up for him, like she knew all along. Dad was furious with them both – I think that's the only reason he's let Mum go with so little fight. He's become insanely parochial, and started talking about sending Omar to Pakistan to get fixed up with some poor chick.' He glanced towards the fridge. 'Is my beer cold yet?'

In Sharif's tiny Collier's Wood kitchen, Candida could reach out and open the freezer compartment on top of the fridge without even getting up from her place at the table. As she inspected the contents of the freezer, she said, 'I'm glad Omar's happy, that's all that's important, isn't it? He was clever to run off to Spain so quickly, to leave the fallout behind . . . OK, your beer is sort of cold, my wine still isn't.'

'You can share some of my beer, if you want,' Sharif offered gallantly.

'My hero,' said Candida wryly. 'It starts off with breakfast in bed and roses, and ends up like this. You know, when you said you'd be making lunch for us today, this isn't quite what I expected.'

'I have so little time with you, I just didn't want to waste it cooking,' Sharif said, using a cheeky grin to mask his sincerity.

Candida looked at him coyly. 'Well, we're alone in the flat for once. Aren't we wasting time right now?' Sharif raised a quizzical eyebrow, and then leaped out of his chair and picked her up, carrying her screaming with delight to his bedroom.

Afterwards, with wine so cold it was almost frozen, and picking at the cold, chewy pizza in bed, Sharif explained, 'I think the funny thing about my parents breaking up is that I always thought of them as one person. Like lying here in bed, we're two people, Candida and Sharif, who are choosing to share the same space. But with my parents, it was like one person, one creature in the bed, an Amma-Abbu-Amma beast, so you couldn't tell where one began and the other ended, like they were physically joined together. When we were little, Omar and I would come into bed with them some mornings, and I swear you couldn't get between them, they were so moulded together in their sleep. We always had to go on either side.'

'I think that's so sweet,' said Candida. 'They must have been very much in love. Don't forget they had you when they were very young.'

'The thing is, I don't think they were in love for so very long,' said Sharif. 'But they were still joined together in this thing called a marriage – joined isn't even a strong enough word, it's like they were conjoined, like Siamese twins; they were still tightly wound together in the mornings when they slept, like they didn't have a choice. Like that thing in Dr Dolittle, a push-me-pull-you, the same creature but with two heads that wanted to pull in different directions. I could see that they were falling apart, I saw it more and more, but I didn't think they'd ever break up, because they were just . . . stuck together.'

'Marriage is like that,' said Candida wisely. 'It provides an odd kind of glue that sticks you together when you should have split up ages ago. My daddy was married once before he met Mummy, an arranged marriage. He never talks about it much, but he said that once you're stuck in an arrangement like that, you feel bound to it; even though it never had anything to do with love.'

'Why don't you ever talk about love?' Sharif asked curiously.

'What do you mean?' Candida asked, widening her eyes.

'I guess I mean, why don't you ever say that you . . .'

He paused with embarrassment. 'Oh, you know, don't make me say it . . .'

'Say what?' asked Candida, looking at him in genuine confusion.

Sharif took a deep breath, and tried to think of a way he didn't have to say the words; it would be way too humiliating to have to ask outright. 'Do you remember that Indian pop song that I told you we used to dance to when we were children in the flat above the restaurant?' he asked.

'Yes,' Candida nodded. '*Ilu, Ilu!* means I love . . .'

Sharif interrupted her. 'That. Why don't you ever say that. *Ilu,* I mean. You know how I feel about you.'

'Oh, is that all you meant? Well, you know how I feel about you, too,' Candida said, smiling warmly. 'It just seems such a big word, and we're maybe too young to use words like that unless we're really sure we know what they mean, and besides, it wouldn't be fair, to you, I mean. How could I talk about things like that, when I still can't even tell my family about us, until I'm sure that Daddy is better.'

'He might never get better,' Sharif said petulantly. 'He's getting on a bit, isn't he? I think my old grandad could give him a run for his money.'

Candida leaned over to his furrowed brow and kissed him between his eyebrows where the flesh had gathered in a frown. 'You look so cute when you do that,' she said, getting out of bed and stretching her arms.

After Candida had left, Sharif threw away the pizza box and beer cans with a flourish; he took a lazy man's satisfaction in that the only washing up he had to show for his romantic lunch was Candida's wine glass, and the knife and fork she had insisted on using. He left these on the draining board, in the hope that one of his flatmates might wash them up for him. Micky had moved in after he had finished his A levels, and had proved to be surprisingly well house-trained.

Sharif decided to pop by the Tooting house on a whim. He knew his mother was moving some of her stuff out that afternoon with his grandad, who was helping her move to his barely used Clapham flat. Omar was still in Spain, and she had deliberately not asked Sharif to help, as she didn't want it to look like she was asking him to take sides against his dad. As he got to the front door, he heard raised voices. Perhaps Dad had come back, and they were having an argument. But then his parents never really had arguments. When they were angry at each other, there were just lots of long, painful silences, punctuated by unnecessarily loud clattering in the kitchen or bathroom. He went to walk away, but then curiosity got the better of him, and he quietly let himself in the back door, and went into the kitchen.

He heard his mum speaking crossly upstairs, and realized with a shock that she wasn't arguing with his father at all, she was arguing with Nana, his grandad. He'd have thought that she would be a bit gentler with him, given his dicky ticker.

'How dare you speak about my boys that way,' Shona seethed with uncontrolled fury. 'They have absolutely bloody nothing to do with you, or Amma, for that matter. You know, as far as I'm concerned, you're not even related to them. It was me, I made them, I made them happen without any help from either of you.'

'As far as you're concerned? Shona, you're speaking like a madwoman. They're my grandchildren, whether you like it or not. Just because you've had this insane need to confess to the world and break up your marriage for the sake of some Irish teacher you've just met, you can't expect us all to accept these things. I love Omar, but he's not gay, he's just a perfectly normal boy who needs help. Maybe we could send him to a psychiatrist, to get him over this funny phase. And Sharif, how could you ever have let him date Candida? Were you mad? Didn't you think about the consequences?'

'I wanted to meet her,' Shona admitted, a little stubbornly, 'and I knew you would never introduce me, but at least Sharif did. I know now that I was very wrong not to tell Sharif about her. But I really didn't see the harm in them dating for a bit. It was only for a little while, anyway.' Sharif's ears had pricked up. How did his grandad know about Candida? Perhaps he knew her dad? Sharif suddenly realized the reason for Candida's father's irrational hatred of him – it all became clear. His grandad must have told Candida's father that his grandson was disreputable, and caused the whole bizarre vendetta. To think that his own Nana was the back-stabbing old dog that had caused him so much heartache. Sharif went to march up the stairs to have it out with him, when his Nana's next words stopped him in his tracks.

'I don't believe I'm hearing this! Didn't see the harm!

Shona, you really are mad. She's my daughter, for God's sake. They're not children any more. What if they had slept together, or, God forbid, he had got her pregnant? It's illegal, I'm sure it is. She's his aunt!'

Sharif's heart felt like it had actually stopped beating, and just begun to swell and swell until it filled his whole chest. He walked out of the kitchen, out through the garden, and out to the street in a daze, where he had barely managed to round the corner onto Tooting High Street before he retched violently into the gutter, throwing up everything he'd had for lunch, and kept retching until nothing but painful hot gas and sour drips of stomach acid came up. Straightening up, and wiping his mouth on his jacket sleeve, oblivious to the outraged looks about him, he didn't stop walking until he reached his flat, where he practically ran up the steps and shut the door behind him. He went to the kitchen to get some water for his dry and burnt mouth, and on seeing Candida's wine glass and cutlery in the kitchen sink, he did something he hadn't done since he was a small child. He burst into tears. He picked up Candida's wine glass, cradled it against his face, and sank to the floor, sobbing against the grubby yellow-painted wall.

Won't Let Us Have a Breakdown

CANDIDA HADN'T HEARD from Sharif for over two weeks; not since he'd given her cold pizza for lunch. He didn't reply to her flirtatious text messages, or return her phone calls. For the first few days, she thought he'd decided to be cross over her stubbornness for refusing to say 'I love you', and didn't think too much of it. For the next few days, she thought that he really must care to be so stubborn about not calling back, and felt a sneaking admiration for his tenacity. She began to wonder what harm there might be in giving him the three little words he wanted; they were just words after all, just spoken puffs of air. '*Ilu, Ilu!* means I love you,' she hummed to herself at home, testing out the words with the pop song that Sharif had told her he used to sing along to when he was little.

By the second week she stopped thinking that it was about their not-quite-tiff about *Ilu, Ilu!* but something much more serious. Perhaps he was ill, perhaps he was so cross with her he'd run off to join Omar in Ibiza. But if he was ill, he'd let her know, wouldn't he? Unless he was in hospital with something terrible. But then Omar would tell her if something had happened; he was the only member of Sharif's family who knew that they were still together. She decided to text Omar, and was appalled and embarrassed by his delicate, walking-on-eggshells reply. Sharif was definitely still in London, Omar texted back, and was definitely fine. He was working on some new material for the band, for some big concert in the autumn. The subtext to the text was unmistakable: Omar obviously thought she'd been dumped, probably in the same abrupt way as Sharif's legion of previous girlfriends, and that she was too vain, or not quite bright enough, to have worked it out yet. Candida couldn't believe it. Sharif loved her, didn't he? She began to doubt herself – perhaps she was too vain, and had tested his patience too much by keeping their relationship a secret for so long. She decided, like her father before her some four decades previously, that the only way out of this sea of troubles was to take arms against it, and confidently stride in.

She went to Sharif's flat the next morning, arriving early to avoid the chance that he might not be in. Sharif never got up, much less left the house, before ten a.m. if he could possibly help it. Confident that she was looking her fragrant, glowing best, her newly washed hair shining lustrously in the morning sunshine, Candida pressed the bell. Micky from the band answered, his voice crackling on the ancient intercom. 'Who is it?' he asked suspiciously.

Candida, who almost never lied about anything, paused for a moment, before saying, 'Postman.'

She heard some muttered expletives, before he said, 'OK, I'll come down. Is it a package or something?'

'Mmm-hmm,' she assented, feeling a bit foolish.

When Micky opened the door to see Candida, looking both radiant and nervous, the only words he could spontaneously muster were, 'Focking hell.'

Candida walked past him and up the stairs, ignoring him as he ran up behind her, whispering urgently, 'Candida, he doesn't want to see you. He'll be furious that I let you in.'

'Well, I want to see him,' she said resolutely, her lips very tight to avoid them trembling. She got to the door of the flat, and pushed it wide open before Micky could get to it, or any other fellow conspirators hiding in the flat could shut it in her face. She stood in the narrow hallway. 'Sharif?' she called.

Sharif came loping out of his bedroom, unshaven, hair sticking up, wearing nothing but a pair of fashionably baggy sports shorts. His stomach looked very concave, and the muscles on his torso sharper and stringier, like he hadn't eaten properly in days. His eyes widened slightly at seeing her, but otherwise he gave away nothing. 'Hello, Candida, you're looking well,' he said with infuriating calm.

'Well, you're not. You look awful. What's going on?' she said shortly. She wanted to run up to him and comfort away whatever it was that had made him avoid her, but his indifferent demeanour made the few feet between them too great a distance to negotiate.

'Mate, I'm so sorry, she tricked me, she told me she was the postman,' Micky started to explain. Sharif's lip twitched, almost as though he was trying to suppress a smile. 'Yes, I can see how you thought she might be the postman,' he said drily.

'Please go away, Micky, Sharif and I need to talk,' Candida said firmly. Micky was younger than her, and she found that he tended to listen to her deferentially as a result.

'Please go away, Candida. Micky and I need to work,' Sharif said, imitating her. 'We're working on some material for the band, you're interrupting us.'

Micky looked indecisively between the two of them, Candida pale with concern, and Sharif pale with what might prove to be unexploded fury. He decided he'd rather not be alone with Sharif after he had just expressly disobeyed his orders to keep Candida out of his way; Sharif had a filthy temper when provoked. 'I need to pop out to get . . . something, anyways,' he said weakly, and walked out of the door and back down the stairs.

Candida looked back to Sharif. 'What's going on, Sharif?' she asked softly, entreatingly, her lower lip now trembling just slightly despite herself.

Sharif looked at her, an angel in his hallway, her hair shining like a halo around her face, and her summer dress of pure sky blue. He faltered for a moment, before recovering himself. 'I'm . . . going back to bed, Candida. I'm working. You can make yourself a cup of tea if you want, before you go. You know your way around the kitchen, don't you?' He wandered back into his room, and Candida stood still and stunned, until she heard the taunting sound of chords being strummed casually from his guitar. Furious, she strode into his room. 'This isn't funny, Sharif. Is this your sick way of telling me that we're over, just like that?'

'Funny ha ha or funny peculiar?' said Sharif, without

humour. 'You know, you're right, I am a little bit sick,' he added. 'And yes, we are over, just like that.'

'Sharif!' Candida exploded. 'What the bloody hell are you talking about! Why are you doing this? I deserve to know why!'

Sharif looked at her sadly from his bed, and started strumming a melancholy tune. He loved Candida too much to tell her that they'd been having an incestuous relationship for months; he didn't want to destroy her as he'd been destroyed. She didn't deserve to be hurt that way.

'No, sweetheart, you don't deserve to know why,' he said softly, regretfully, dropping his bravado for a moment.

Calmed slightly by his change of tone, Candida sat down next to him on his bed, and reached out to touch his stubbly cheek. 'Sharif, darling,' she entreated gently, 'I do not accept this. I do not accept this break-up. I simply won't, and that's all there is to it. I'm going to stay here all day until you speak to me about what's happened, so you may as well start speaking to me now.'

Sharif stopped strumming, then started picking out the thread of a haunting melody. 'I guess I wouldn't accept it either, if I were you. But that's all there is to it. You kept telling me that it takes two to make a relationship work. Well, I know that it only takes one to break it up. So it doesn't really matter whether you accept it or not. That's just the way it is.'

Candida looked at him blankly for a minute, and then her smooth, lovely face crumpled into a wet, soggy mess of angry sobbing. 'You bastard!' she spat through her tears. 'Why are you trying to hurt me so much? You promised that you would never hurt me, never leave me, never let me go. That's what you said. You promised!'

Sharif watched her break down, with her head in her hands, and tears started running down his face, too. 'I know I promised,' he said miserably. 'I'm sorry. Candida, please stop crying. I can't do anything about it. I really can't.'

'Is this because I didn't say "I love you?"' Candida said suddenly, seizing at the cheap, forlorn hope that all their hurt could be whisked away with the three puffs of inconsequential air that she had so far withheld from him. 'Because I do, you know I do. I love you, Sharif. I love you.' She held her breath after saying the three little words, as though she really believed that they might have made everything better, as if by magic.

'I know you do,' Sharif said, shaking his head. The long-awaited words made no difference at all now. If anything, they probably made everything worse. Candida started sobbing again, with deep, guttural, choking tears, and Sharif just sat there, watching her, powerless to do anything about it. He had just broken the heart of the woman he loved and he couldn't even tell her why; he couldn't even let her know that his heart had been broken first.

When Candida started to quieten down, Sharif leaned over and handed her a piece of paper with musical notation – a song was written on it. 'I wrote this for you, I guess to say goodbye. I was going to send it to you, but you're here now. You can take it with you, if you want.'

Candida looked at the scrawled notation and scribbles. So this was it, then. This was all the explanation that she was going to get for the end of their relationship, some unintelligible code that she was expected to decipher. 'You know I can't read music,' she said, not bothering to add that he also knew she had never been able to read his chaotic handwriting. She held the song back out to him, and when he didn't take it she put it down on the bed between them. 'You'd better play it to me.'

Sharif hesitated. 'I don't think so; I don't think I can . . .'

'Sharif, please!' Candida insisted. 'It's the least you can do. You can't just give me something you know I can't understand and expect me to trot off happily with it.'

Sharif sighed, and nodded. 'If I play it to you, will you just leave?'

Candida nodded, crossing her toes in her sandals while she wiped the tears from her red and swollen eyes.

Sharif started playing the same set of melancholy chords that he had picked out just a few moments before, and began to sing very softly, deliberately looking down at the neck of his guitar, and not anywhere near Candida at all.

'Dark clouds of depression, they leak from every pore
Our loved ones' lies and repression, can't protect us
   any more
I promised to stay with you
And to keep away the pain
But we didn't know what we were doing
And so we hurt ourselves again.'

Sharif glanced up at Candida briefly, to see her staring at her feet, and biting her lip furiously. He looked down swiftly before she could catch him and began to sing the chorus:

> 'There were dark clouds of desire, when we lay so
>   close in bed
> Now the dark clouds of depression, have left our
>   memories for dead
> And when we breathed,
> We infected the air,
> And I could cry,
> We didn't know enough to care
> I knew you loved me, though it wasn't what you said,
> But I won't let us have a breakdown
> I'll let it have me instead
> I'll let it have me instead.'

Sharif was going to begin the second verse, when Candida spoke. 'Stop,' she said, 'please stop.'

'There's another verse,' Sharif mumbled, both disappointed and relieved that she didn't want him to finish. He picked up the piece of paper to hand it to her. He didn't know what reaction he'd expected from her, when she didn't even know what the song meant. He had sort of hoped that despite everything, she'd somehow understand without him having to tell her. That the song would be enough to absolve him from responsibility, to ease the pain of what he knew he had to do.

'Sharif, darling,' Candida said, suddenly very calm and purposeful. 'It's a beautiful song, but it's not about us. It's about you. I've understood it all now, and I'm sorry that I didn't before. You're not breaking us up because there's something wrong with us, you're breaking us up because you're depressed. You're talking about us having done some terrible thing, and we haven't, we really haven't. Irrational guilt is a classic sign of depression.'

Sharif sighed. 'I'm not breaking us up because I'm depressed, I'm depressed because I'm breaking us up. Look, you promised to go.'

'Don't preach to me about promises,' Candida said sharply, before reaching out for his hand appeasingly. 'Sharif, don't you understand? Depression is an illness. It's a disease. We can go to the doctor's and get counselling, get a prescription. We can cure it. I'll help you; I promise I'll be here for you, I won't make us hide any more.' Her eyes shone with hope.

Sharif shook off her hand. 'You were right to make us hide. Get out Candida, please. Don't make me force you.'

'I'm staying right here,' she said stubbornly.

Sharif couldn't take it any more. He'd sung his swansong, and he had no emotional energy left. He couldn't be calm, or nonchalant, or kind, or rational any more. He simply snapped. 'Fuck off!' he screamed at her. 'Just fuck off! You shouldn't be here. We should never have been together. I wish I'd never fucking met you.'

Candida backed off as though she'd been hit, and all her composed demeanour evaporated, as she couldn't stop herself crying again. 'You don't mean it,' she said through her tears. 'You're ill.'

'Get out! I said get the fuck out!' Sharif screamed and, grabbing her arms, he dragged her out of his room and out of the hallway, pushing her brutally out of the door. He slammed it behind her, and heard Candida slump to the floor on the other side. Petrified by his bewildering, unbidden violence, she got up and raced down the stairs and out into the street, to sob in the safety of her car.

Sharif watched her leave from the window. So that was it. He had not only broken the heart of the woman he loved, he had made her hate him, too. He had made her afraid of him. He reflected that she was the lucky one; she would never miss him now, the way that he would miss her. She would never long for him the way he longed for her. He would become a footnote in her life, the boyfriend who went crazy and violent and dumped her for no reason, who she was well rid of. He wished she could become a footnote in his life, like Ali, and the girl after Ali, and the many girls before. But he knew that nothing but utter oblivion could take away the pain he felt in the deep pit of his stomach, in the throbbing chambers of his heart which was thumping so loudly he thought the treacherous organ might explode out of his chest and fly after Candida, falling in a bloody, irresolute heap at her terrified feet.

Oblivion. Sharif knew exactly where he could find it. He went to the kitchen cupboard, and pulled out the bottle of vodka that he had asked Micky to buy the other day. He poured it down his throat like medicine, letting it splash over his face in his haste. Sitting back on his bed, with a third of the bottle drained, he quickly realized that alcohol alone wouldn't work. He went to the bathroom cabinet, and pulled out every bitter pill it contained, both medicinal and recreational. Popping them out of their foil containers, he thought how pretty they looked, like sweets. As he downed them with vodka, he started singing the counting nursery rhyme that Shona had taught him and Omar as children, to the tune of the Inch Worm song; 'Two and two are four, four and four are eight . . .' he sang to himself, swallowing the pills as he went along, 'eight and eight are sixteen, sixteen and sixteen are thirty-two . . .' Having taken all the pills, he walked unsteadily back to his bedroom, finishing off the vodka with deep swigs that made him almost spit it back up again. 'Two and two are four . . .' he continued. 'I knew you loved me, though it wasn't what you said. But I won't let us have a breakdown, I'll let it have me instead . . .' He felt nothing any more. In fact, he felt much better. He slumped on the bed, and as he passed out his stomach and guts spasmed involuntarily, so he lay comatose in a blissful stupor, in a puddle of his own vomit.

Micky came back to the flat. 'Sharif, is the coast clear, mate?' he called out, letting himself back in. He went to Sharif's bedroom, and took in the scene from the door. 'Aww, mate,' he said helplessly. He would later remember, with no little shame, that he stood there in shock for a full minute before he ran to the phone to call an ambulance.

Confessions Across a Hospital Bed

PARVEZ AND SHONA faced each other across Sharif's bed in St George's hospital. His stomach had been pumped, and he looked bruised and horrible, with a drip trailing out of him. 'He's so still. Why is he so still, if they say he's not in a coma?' Shona asked, holding her son's hand carefully, so as not to displace the needle which was taped into his veins.

'He's just passed out, they said he'll come round soon,' Parvez said soothingly. He added, 'It will probably hurt too much for him not to come round. The anaesthetic will wear off soon.'

'We were so lucky he threw up some of it first, we were so lucky that Micky was there,' Shona said. 'I can't believe I let this happen, it's all my fault.'

'This isn't your fault, Shona,' Parvez said wearily.

'You're a saint not to blame me, but I still blame myself. Sharif will blame me when he wakes up, and he'll be right to. I should have told him the truth.'

'It wasn't your secret to tell,' Parvez said simply. They sat in silence for a few minutes, with nothing but the flimsy pale curtains hanging around the bed of their frail, pale son to separate them from the rest of the bustling hospital ward. Parvez broke the silence. 'How's the flat? Rashid's flat in Clapham, I mean. Are you quite comfortable there?'

Shona sighed at this polite attempt at small talk. 'Yes, thank you. It's quite comfortable. How's the house?'

Parvez shrugged. 'Quiet. Big. I'm rattling around in there. At least I've got the dog, although she's become a bit quiet recently, too. I guess she misses you.'

Shona nodded. 'I miss her too, but it wouldn't be fair to take her to the flat, she needs a garden to run around in.'

'Is that all you miss?' Parvez asked curiously, without bitterness. 'Just the dog?' He cleared his throat, and then spoke quickly. 'Shona, I want to say something. I know this isn't the right time or place, but I really don't know when the right time or place would be. Do you remember how I said that I didn't want you leaving, and that I'd forgive you, and we should stay together and try and work it out . . .'

'Parvez, please . . .' Shona started.

'No, please let me finish,' Parvez said. 'That's what I said a few weeks ago. But I just want you to know that now I think there was one thing you were right about. We weren't happy. We hadn't been happy for a long time. I do forgive you, and I do miss you, of course I miss you, but I don't miss being unhappy. There. That's all. I've said it.'

Shona looked at him with surprise. She hadn't expected this accord, this capitulation from him so soon. How ironic, that the first thing they had managed to agree on in years, was the merits of their separation. 'You're not in love with me any more,' she said with comprehension. 'I'm glad.'

Parvez shook his head, with a rueful half smile. 'Goldie, you don't understand. I will probably love you until the day I die. I always have loved you, not for your degrees or cleverness, and not for your perfectionism or your criticism, and definitely not for your cooking. I loved you despite all those things. I loved you for your heart, your good, kind heart.' He reached over and touched her lightly on her chest, the flat of his palm resting gently above her left breast, without passion, but with tenderness. 'The thing is, Goldie, the way I see it, I've been a very lucky man. For over twenty years I got to live with the woman I loved, the woman who sacrificed everything she had to be with me.' He paused, and withdrew his hand from her with a touch of embarrassment at his emotion. 'But I think I deserve to spend the next twenty years with someone who loves me, with someone who doesn't feel that being with me is a sacrifice.'

'You're letting me off,' Shona said, her eyes bright with tears at his generosity. 'You deserved so much better than me.'

'Maybe I am letting you off. But you must know that I didn't want better than you,' Parvez said. 'And you gave me our beautiful boys.' He stroked Sharif's hair gently back from his face. 'As I'm in the confessing mood, can I tell you a secret? Deep down, I always thought that the boys weren't really mine. I thought about all those secretive clinic visits you went on, where you didn't want or need me to go at all, and then the boys came, and they were so pale, practically white, just like your father's family, and they were so much their Amma's boys, and not like me at all. I thought that the clinic had given you another man's sperm to conceive.' Parvez shook his head ruefully again, 'I thought that for years, and kept it hidden so far down that nobody would ever guess. Who would ever guess that I doubted my own children? And then Omar suddenly claimed to be gay, and I was so bloody furious at him, and more than anything, terrified for him, for what the future might hold for him if he didn't snap out of it. And then I got the call that Sharif was in hospital, and I felt like the ground had been taken away from under my feet . . . and I realized how much I care about them, and I knew that they were my sons after all. That they always were and always will be. Whatever happened all those years ago, they're my sons.' He looked questioningly at Shona, and held his breath. He had told her his secret, now he was waiting to see if she had one, too.

'Of course they're your sons,' Shona said, in answer to his unspoken question, her voice trembling with emotion. 'Did you really not see that Sharif had his daddy's eyes, right from when he was a baby?' She paused, and then continued falteringly, 'But you're right about one thing, I have kept something from you, all these years.' Parvez looked up quickly, and held Sharif's unconscious hand for support, awaiting the verdict he'd been dreading. 'The truth is . . . the truth is, that the boys are yours, but they weren't mine. Genetically, I mean. I didn't produce enough eggs when I went to the clinic. I signed up for a scheme where we got eggs from a donor; it was a Caucasian donor, there weren't any Asian donors in the scheme. That's why the boys were so pale.' Shona stumbled over the words, unwilling to stop. Here, at Sharif's hospital bed, she too felt the need to confess, to unburden herself from a deceit that she had held so long it had become part of her, a parasite woven into her body. 'You spent years worrying about whether they were yours, and I spent years worrying that they'd realize they weren't mine. My boys, I went through hell to conceive them, and grew them out my own flesh and blood, and yet they weren't my flesh and blood, not like they were yours. I didn't want them to ever find out that I wasn't their mother.'

Parvez took a deep breath and leaned back in his chair, rubbing his face with his hands in disbelief. 'My God, Goldie, how could you have kept that secret? For all this time. Of course you're their mother – nothing could ever change that.' He looked at Sharif's still, pale face, and said with confusion, 'So does that mean that Sharif and Candida aren't related at all? That's why you didn't stop them dating?'

Shona nodded. 'You see, it really is all my fault. I almost killed my own son for the sake of keeping my own selfish secret, like some stupid Greek tragic heroine. Candida's not his aunt; the boys have got nothing to do with my Amma or papa.' She stopped herself running on in self-loathing, as both Parvez and she became aware of their son shifting, and his lips beginning to move.

'Mum?' said Sharif, through dry, rasping lips. 'What did you say?'

'Darling!' Shona cried, and pulled his hand to her lips.

'Oh, thank God. Candida's not related to you, darling. Your Nana didn't realize. He's coming over now, he's bringing Candida. I'll explain it all to them, I'll explain to everyone. Just get better, darling, and it'll all be all right. I promise.'

Sharif could hear his mother talking, but it sounded like she was underwater; he could see her and his father's relieved faces, overhanging him like twin moons swimming over the clouds of his sheets. Amma-Abbu-Amma; the push-me-pull-you of his childhood, but this time they were facing the same direction. This time, for the first time, he was lying in the bed between them. He heard a soft pattering, the step of someone running so lightly it was like dancing. The white curtains around his bed were pushed back with a decisive gesture, and there, standing at the foot of his bed, was an angel in a sky-blue dress, a radiant halo of lustrous hair around her head, and a hand stretched out to him, in forgiveness, and understanding. 'You saw the girl who'd make your dreams come true,' he thought, his own weak hand stretching out to meet hers.

The Mother and Child Reunion

IN THE EARLY hours of the morning, the phone began ringing in Shona's Clapham flat. She swore to herself, and put her head under her pillow to drown out the din. 'Shona, are you there?' the familiar, insistent voice of her mother called out. '*Arré*, so pick up!' She began the sing-song chant that grated on Shona more than nails across an old-fashioned blackboard: 'Pick up, pick up, pick up... Pick up! pick up!!' Shona groaned, and reaching across to the bedside table, obeyed.

'Ouf, Amma, please stop calling at this time. You know it's three in the morning here. Why can't you wait like a normal person?'

'Tch, always so slow, Shona,' her mother said, before adding coyly, and rather bitchily, 'Why so slow? Do you have *company*?'

'Why are you calling, Amma?'

'Why do you think I'm calling, you stupid girl. It's your uncle's wedding next week. When are you bringing your father back to Dhaka?'

'I didn't know the wedding was next week,' said Shona, surprised. 'I guess I haven't been invited.'

Henna sighed. Why was she cursed with a daughter as slow as her father? 'Of course you haven't been invited, dear. I don't want to offend you, but adulterous little harlots who leave their Pakistani husbands and then shout about it to the world don't get invited to respectable people's weddings. If you had half a brain in your head, you'd have done whatever you wanted, but just kept quiet about it. People don't mind other people misbehaving, they just prefer not to know about it. Do you remember, when you were little, Shona? For New Year's Eve we always went to the respectable parties that didn't serve alcohol, but that didn't mean we didn't drink, we just brought our own in secretly and spiked our punch.' Henna giggled slyly at the memory of tiny little whisky bottles tied to the underside of her arms beneath her voluminous long-sleeved shalwars.

'Well, I don't care if I haven't been invited. Uncle Aziz is an old hypocrite, anyway. And I'm not bringing Papa back to Dhaka; I told you already, he's not going back. He's going to spend his retirement here, with Verity, if she forgives him. If he goes back at all, it'll be to finalize your separation. You'll finally be a free woman,' she added, hoping her mother might have come round to this idea as being a good thing. 'You'll get your own settlement, your own income, you could do whatever you want, go travelling, anything . . .'

Henna exploded at Shona. 'You *shorer bacha kuttar bacha harami*,' she shrieked, the expletives falling freely from her lips. 'I ask you to do one thing for me in your sorry little life, and you refuse! You've ruined your life, and now you want to ruin mine. You ran out on your husband for some Irish tramp you met last week, and you've raised a faggot and an overdosing drug-abuser. You were a bad wife, a bad mother, and now you're a bad daughter, too. I disown you Shona! I have no family any more!'

'You haven't had a family for years,' Shona screamed back. 'Don't you DARE tell me what it is to be a bad mother. You never even knew I was there. You just used me like some commodity, some bauble to brandish, someone to boast about to your friends. You were never there for me, you were never there for my boys. I had twin sons in a foreign country and I had no one to turn to for help, but you didn't care. You didn't even come to see them until they were at school. They love you, you know – they think you're bloody fantastic. But you don't even know the first thing about them – you don't know their first names, do you? Or their birthday, do you? Do you, Amma?' She paused for air, breathing heavily. 'So, you're disowning me? That's a bloody joke – you disowned us all years ago, long, long before I married Parvez and Papa came to England. And you know what? You can't have us back now. Enjoy what you've got, Mamma, it's all you'll get.' Shona hung up, slamming the phone down violently. She pulled up her knees and held them tight, rocking on the bed and shaking with fury.

Dermot, who had gone to the kitchen when the phone rang, came back through, and put his arms around her, holding her warmly against him. 'It's OK, sweetheart,' he soothed comfortingly, and although he had no idea what

Shona had said, as she had spoken in Bangla, he added, 'Bravo for standing up to her.' The phone began to ring again, and he felt Shona's heart thumping faster and faster, anticipating her mother's shrieking rebuttal on the answering machine. He got up, and eased the phone cord out of the socket gently. 'Give yourself a break, eh? We don't want you getting upset, not in your condition. I'll make you some camomile tea, and then we'll try and get back to sleep. What do you think?'

Shona nodded dumbly. She wondered when she was going to summon up the courage to tell her mother that on top of all her other sins, this adulterous harlot, this bad wife and bad mother who had raised a faggot and an overdosing drug-abuser, had also managed, miraculously, after years of sterility, to get pregnant.

Shona still didn't quite believe it herself. Her periods were never completely reliable, and after three months without one, her natural thought had been that she was prematurely menopausal. When the doctor suggested a pregnancy test, she had almost refused out of sheer embarrassment, and was shocked to see an incontrovertibly positive result. She had told Dermot straight away, unsure of his reaction, and his excitement had worried her even more. Shona was sure it was a false alarm but she was sent for a dating scan immediately, as the doctors thought she might already be quite far along. They were right; she was fourteen weeks pregnant.

She saw the baby moving in the ultrasound picture,

whilst Dermot held her hand tightly, and she still didn't quite believe it. All the dedicated preparation she'd done for her twins – the special diets, the folic acid, the not-drinking, the exercise, the medication – it had taken years of work to conceive. And yet now, with no preparation or warning at all, this child had come from nowhere. It was tempting to romanticize and say that the child had come from love alone. She was forty-three, and she was having a baby. She had to look at the scan picture every once in a while, just to prove to herself that it wasn't some phantom daydream.

It was in the rosy glow of her unexpected achievement that Shona finally managed to succeed in that other test she had expected to fail. Despite what seemed an appalling drive on her long-awaited driving test, her examiner had passed her, chiding her indulgently to check her mirrors more often while he wrote out her certificate.

A week later Shona was preparing for her first day of school for the autumn term. There would be no students there for the first two days; she was more worried about the reactions from her colleagues about the changed state of her relationship. Most of them would know by now that she had left Parvez, but few would realize that she had taken up with Dermot. No one knew that she was precariously carrying his child. She was putting all her administration in order when the bell rang insistently. She wasn't expecting anyone; Omar had taken a summer job in the local adult education college above Sainsbury's, to pay for his Ibiza holiday; Sharif – who had stopped pretending to work at the restaurant – was working flat out for a big concert that his band had been booked for at the end of September; and Dermot was at the school already, attending a meeting for all department heads. Perhaps it was Papa – maybe things were not going well with Verity, after she had finally found out the truth, and he needed his flat back. She went downstairs to open the door, and stopped short in shock. Standing on the steps, resplendent with her enormous Gucci sunglasses and a small mountain of matching leather luggage, was her mother, while a black cab with a ticking meter waited patiently behind her.

'This is my daughter that I was telling you about,' Henna said indulgently to the cab driver, in her still heavily accented English. 'She's a teacher, you know.' She leaned over to Shona to peck her on her astounded cheek, whispering in her ear, 'Shona moni, you had better pay the cab. I forgot to change my travellers' cheques at the airport. And give him a tip so he can carry my things upstairs.'

Sitting decorously on the sofa, with a cup of tea in hand, and chewing on some shortbread she'd bought herself at the airport, Henna chatted amiably to Shona, as though their last conversation hadn't happened, and as though her visit was completely expected.

'It's not a bad apartment, this,' she said, looking around. 'Your father always kept it very well. Too small, though. Much smaller than the place in Paddington that his company paid for. This used to be Verity's flat, you know.'

'No, I didn't know,' Shona said warily, sitting on the chair opposite her mother, waiting for Henna to explode at her. She decided to get it over with: 'So, how . . . was the wedding?'

'How is the wedding, you mean – it's happening today. I'm sure it's all very dull and tedious, and that the guests have just turned up for the food. They're having the reception in a hotel. No imagination, those two. I left them a card, though; I said I hoped that Aziz would be very happy with his pointy-nosed elderly, ugly bride, and that she'd be very happy with her baldy-headed elderly, ugly groom.' Henna smiled smugly with pride at her parting gesture, and looked to her daughter for approval. 'I only said the truth, that's what you're so fond of these days, isn't it? I thought it would take lots of practice, like learning English, but I found it very easy. Wonderfully easy. And quite refreshing, I don't know why I don't do it more often.' She stretched out her arms in a cat-like, satisfied gesture.

'Why are you here, Amma?' Shona asked quietly.

'Well, I'm doing what you said, dear. I'm giving tired old Dhaka a break, and I thought I'd travel. Spend some time in the UK, with my daughter and my grandsons. Get to know my new son-in-law; I hope I like him more than the first one. And I thought I'd give you a hand, what with you being a working woman now,' she added disingenuously, as though Shona hadn't been a working woman for years already.

'A hand with what?' Shona asked. Her mother was hardly equipped for helping with housework or cooking, or anything else, for that matter. Her skills lay solely in acting, singing and dancing.

Henna looked at her indulgently. 'With the baby, of course. You're not a young woman any more. I was already a grandmother when I was your age. You'll need help with the baby. Omar told me all about it, although he thought I already knew; he and I are becoming great pals on email.'

Shona said nothing, looking very hard at her mother in shock, and then she threw herself into her mother's arms, squeezing her fiercely and knocking the breath out of both of them. 'Oh Mamma, thank you,' she said, trying hard not to cry, not quite sure what exactly it was that she was so grateful for.

Embarrassed at such a display of extraordinary affection, Henna patted Shona's back tentatively. 'Tch, you'll injure yourself diving around like that,' she said. 'Jau, Shona, go make your old mother some more tea.' When Shona went to the kitchen, Henna took out her compact and checked that her daughter's embrace hadn't shifted her exquisitely applied maquillage. Motherhood wasn't really a role she had willingly chosen, she acknowledged to herself, satisfied that her lipstick was in place and her eyeshadow remained smoky and elegant; she had only been a starry-eyed teenager when Shona was born, barely more than a child herself. Motherhood had been expedient, that was all; it was her get-out-of-school-free card. But perhaps now she had reached her sixties, now she was almost a grown-up, perhaps she could choose to be a mother, and a glamorous grandmother, too. After all, Omar and Sharif were adults now, and quite interesting young men, too; they didn't bore her like Shona had when she was a teenager. Maybe she might even like the baby when it came along – the benefit of being a grandmother was that you could coo and spoil but not have any of the tiresome responsibility that went with parenting, and when you'd had enough, you could just hand the baby back.

Shona popped her head back around the kitchen door, and caught her mother patting her powder back into place. 'Mamma, you told everyone in Dhaka that you were coming to the UK to join your husband, didn't you? You told them that you'd agreed to join him in his retirement here, rather than have him join you in Dhaka. You covered up why he wasn't going back.'

Henna winked at her conspiratorially. 'I might have . . . given that impression, Shona moni. Truth-telling is all very well, but it doesn't do to tell everyone everything, you know. One messy public separation in the family is quite enough to be getting on with for a while.'

Party in the Park

THE END OF September didn't seem like the ideal time for an outdoor concert, Parvez thought; it was bright, but it just wasn't warm enough any more to hang around outside for hours. And Victoria Park in Hackney didn't seem like the most prestigious location – miles from anywhere, and not even near a tube line. He didn't think there'd be much of a turnout. So he was surprised, when he approached the park with Omar, at how busy it was. There were flyers promoting the concert all over the gates and trees and lamp posts, and there were fast food vans and drinks stalls – an almost carnival atmosphere. He heard the music thudding in the distance. 'They haven't started already, have they?' he asked, checking his watch. He'd treated himself to a satisfyingly chunky Rolex for his birthday. It was in steel and gold, and reminded him of the substantial gold money clip he'd had melted down all those years before. He'd wanted the watch for years, but he had never dared get one before as Shona had disapproved of extravagance.

'I'd keep that hidden if I were you, Abbu,' Omar said.

'No, Sharif's set was due to start in twenty minutes, but he's texted me: they're already running a bit late. Balti Ballads is just one of the bands on the playlist; they've got an early shift.'

As they approached the enormous stage, Parvez looked at it in disbelief. The figure on the stage was a skinny, dark speck, but screens all around showed him to be a dissolute-looking youth droning into a mike. There were hundreds of people around, maybe even over a thousand. He hadn't realized what a big thing this was; he had been persuaded by Omar to come along to see Sharif play in a show of support, but he had thought it wouldn't be very different from when Sharif used to play in his school concerts, or down the local pub.

Omar saw his father's surprise, and grinned. 'They've done brilliantly to get this gig. They're one of just two unsigned bands who were asked to play – everyone else has a deal already. There'll be scouts here from the music labels, and most of the fan club too, hopefully.'

Parvez nodded authoritatively, as though he knew what this jargon of unsigned, deals and scouts meant. Had Omar really said that Sharif's little school band had a fan club? 'Do you want a drink?' he asked his son. He could do with one himself.

In the same part of the park, but closer to the stage, Ricky laid out a blanket for Verity and Candida. 'Thank you, darling,' Verity said, unpacking a little picnic basket. She pulled out a couple of large thermos flasks, looking apologetically at Candida. 'I know you prefer white wine, darling, but I thought it might be a bit too nippy for that. I've done us some coffee and hot chocolate.'

'That's lovely, Mummy, thank you,' said Candida distractedly, looking at her phone. 'Sharif says they're a bit delayed. I'm going to go and see if I can go backstage to wish them luck.' She did up the laces on her tennis shoes, and ran down towards the stage.

Verity and Ricky were left alone on the blanket. 'When are we meeting the others?' she asked Ricky.

'They should all be here now, but we'd never find them. Omar gave me directions to some pub on the edge of the park, we're to meet there after Sharif's band have played their piece,' Ricky said, pouring out two cups of coffee and crumbling brown sugar into them.

'I'm really looking forward to seeing Shona again; she's such a lovely woman. Such a credit to you,' Verity said, a little hesitantly.

Ricky looked at her in wonder and, taking her hand, reverently kissed it and then turned it over to kiss the palm. 'What did I ever do to deserve you?' he said humbly. 'All that time I wasted away from you, running back for weekends in Bangladesh, just to keep up a stupid pretence.'

'It's all in the past, Ricky,' Verity said, 'and it didn't matter that you went to Bangladesh occasionally; you did have to see your mum, after all. What mattered most, is that you came back.'

'That girl at the drinks stall liked you, son,' said Parvez with some of his old bonhomie, sipping his not quite cold beer. 'I could tell.'

'Abbu, please stop doing this,' said Omar, embarrassed, before riposting shrewdly, 'besides, I think it was you she liked – she must have a thing for stylish older men.' He was only half joking; his father looked rather dashing that day, in his dark jeans and expensive blue sweater. Omar suspected that his Abbu was unconsciously reverting to the dandy he'd been before he'd married his mother.

'OK, enough,' winced Parvez with discomfort at the compliment, marring his good looks with a frown. 'I'll stop going on. But you know I only do it because I worry about you; you've chosen a hard path. You were already an ethnic minority, now you're a sexual minority in an ethnic minority.'

'Abbu, I didn't choose anything. It's just what I am. And there's nothing so hard or difficult about it any more – it's not like it was when you came to England.'

Parvez sat for a moment, remembering when he had got off the plane with woefully insufficient funds, still in his wedding suit, with no plans beyond getting to his cousin's sweet shop in Tooting. Back then, he had been dismayed into silence by a cab driver's reaction to his accent. And yet here they were, Omar in college, and Sharif at this big event, a thousand people waiting to hear him play. Perhaps things were different. 'Did you want me to give you a lift to college next week, son?'

Omar smiled gratefully. 'That would be great, Abbu. I'll take you out for tea or something. My treat.' Omar hesitated for a moment, before adding lightly, 'Maybe you could stay and meet some of my . . . friends.'

Parvez understood what he meant, and shook his head. 'I'm trying, Omar. I promise I'll keep trying. But I'm not ready for that, not yet.'

Omar smiled to hide his disappointment. 'It's OK, Abbu. I understand.'

Shona and Dermot were sitting a little way away from the stage, where they had a good view of the screens. 'He should have been on by now,' she said impatiently.

'He'll be on soon enough,' Dermot said soothingly, 'Stop fretting, it'll be fine.'

'They've just never done anything like this before, this could be their big break . . .' she said, and then paused as Dermot raised an eyebrow at her. 'OK, I'll stop fretting about the concert, and start fretting about afterwards, when we have to meet everyone in the pub.'

'That'll be fine, too,' Dermot said. 'Parvez has never been anything but civil to me; maybe he knows how puny and pale I feel standing next to him. And don't forget that I practically saved your dad's life, so he won't be demanding pistols at dawn for breaching your honour.' He pulled Shona towards him for a hug. 'So how's the baby bump?' he said, patting her tummy.

'Still barely bump,' said Shona. 'There's nothing there at all. If I hadn't had the scan I still wouldn't have believed it. I was enormous with the boys at this stage. And with the boys, I was really sick, not just in the morning, almost all the time. But with this one I haven't felt even the slightest bit ill,' she complained.

'Isn't not being ill meant to be a good thing?' said Dermot affectionately. 'I think they're coming on.'

Shona watched as Sharif and the band loped onto the stage and her handsome son's face appeared in close-up on the big screen. He looked so much like his father. They erupted into one of their most popular songs, to tumultuous cheers and screaming from the front. Young kids, who had sat down while the dirgeful youth was on stage, jumped up and began to dance in the cool September air. During the first chorus, an insatiably catchy, jingly Indian riff came up, and then Shona saw her.

Henna made her entrance, resplendent in a flowing silk dancer's outfit, with loose trousers and sleeves and a glittering embroidered bodice, bracelets at her ankles and wrists, and her hair elegantly swept up. She led a trio of Bangladeshi dancers who stamped and swayed to the music. Shona watched her mother on one of the screens; she looked beautiful, she looked twenty years younger, her face transported with happiness as she performed to hundreds of admiring strangers in the park, her life's ambition fulfilled. It had been Henna's idea to create a dance to go with this song, and although Sharif had his doubts initially, it worked wonderfully. Shona was bursting with pride for both of them, and almost wept at the sight.

Dermot was watching her curiously. 'You're glad, aren't you, Shona, that you told them all the truth?'

Shona smiled and nodded reassuringly at him, her eyes shining with tears. She knew that she was still learning how to tell the truth, or rather unlearning how to deceive; gradually unspinning the silken webs she had woven into her conscious and unconscious life, that had become so much a part of her they were like something innate. It was just like learning to speak a new language, Shona thought to herself: the more she practised, the more fluent she would become.

Acknowledgements

The following people helped me enormously with this novel, which was written in a succession of rented apartments during a French winter, while I was pregnant and we were renovating our ruined farmhouse. My husband, Phil Richards, gave me tireless, unselfish support and a room of my own. My mother, Niluffer Farooki, told me inspirational stories and cooked untold delicacies whenever I returned to visit her in London. My sisters, Preeti Farooki and Kiron Farooki, gave me confidence whenever I had a dark night of the soul, with their cheerful and unfounded assumption that I could write. And my beautiful niece, Raman Newton, helped me to remember what it was like to be a little girl.

I'd also like to thank Geeta Nargund of St George's Hospital in Tooting, for her advice on fertility treatment, and not least for the treatment she gave my husband and me, which enabled us to have our wonderful little boy, Jaan.

And finally, I must thank my editor, Sarah Turner, for her infectious enthusiasm in championing my work; the team at Pan Macmillan for the tender care with which they have treated my manuscript; and my agent, Ayesha Karim at Gillon Aitken, for her support and advice.